Also By the Author

The Menmenet Series
The Jackal of Inpu
The Lion of Bastet
The Bull of Mentju
The Menmenet Series Box Set

The Founding Fathers Mysteries
Murder at Mount Vernon

The Pirates of Khonoë
Hyperkill

The Blockchain Killing

DEATH OF A GOLDEN STATE

A Military Thriller

Robert J. Muller

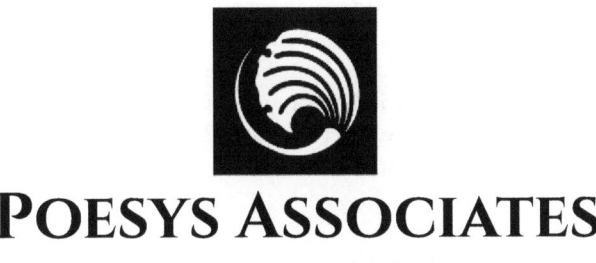

POESYS ASSOCIATES
San Francisco

Copyright © 2024 Robert J. Muller

All rights reserved. Published in the United States of America
by Poesys Associates, San Francisco.

www.poesys.com

ISBN: 978-1-939386-16-8 (print)
ISBN: 978-1-939386-15-1 (ebook)

Library of Congress Control Number: 2024916802

Library of Congress Subject Headings:
Political fiction, American—California.
Suspense fiction, American—California.
Women in combat—California.
Women soldiers—United States—California
Coup d'état—United States—California.
Political corruption—California
Misconduct in office—California.
Post-traumatic stress disorder.

This is a work of fiction. Names, characters, businesses, places, events, locales, and incidents are either the products of the author's imagination or used in a fictitious manner. Any resemblance to actual persons, living or dead, or actual events is purely coincidental.

Cover Design by Brandi Doane McCann,
https://www.ebook-coverdesigns.com

Manufactured in the United States of America
Published December 1, 2024
First Edition

To my sister,
Colonel Grace E. Edinboro, CAANG (Ret).

"...anyone who thinks fomenting coups is a good idea just doesn't get out enough."
   MILTON BEARDEN, A FORMER CIA STATION CHIEF, WASHINGTON POST, 7/13/2022

To be able to say how much you love is to love but little.
   PETRARCH, IL CANZONIERE

When the dogs begin to smell her
Will she smell alone?
   STONE TEMPLE PILOTS, "PLUSH," CORE, 1992

I do solemnly swear (or affirm) that I will support and defend the Constitution of the United States against all enemies, foreign and domestic; that I will bear true faith and allegiance to the same; that I take this obligation freely, without any mental reservation or purpose of evasion; and that I will well and faithfully discharge the duties of the office on which I am about to enter. So help me God.
   TITLE 5 U.S. CODE 3331

CHAPTER ONE
Twelve Missing Tanks

"God damn HETs," growled Sergeant Leroy Briscoe, fuming at the wheel of his Humvee troop carrier behind one of the named massive vehicles. He gripped the steering wheel with white knuckles. First, it was pitch dark at 0100 hours. For their purposes, that was excellent. One disadvantage was the potential damage to his vehicle if he hit the thing. The California Army National Guard would take it out of his pay. And the orders were no lights until they entered the freeway. Didn't want anyone seeing much activity at the base. Well, God damn it, he couldn't see anything either. Shoulda requisitioned night-vision gear.

Then the looming trip up the freeway. What an adventure, running up 101 from Camp Roberts to Sacramento behind these slugs. He envied the other dudes that took the LA, Frisco, and San Diego assignments. Long experience had taught him how things worked in the Guard. He understood this exercise wouldn't leave much time for partying.

What worried him most was the lack of infantry support for his tanks. Colonel Brickhouse had patted him on the shoulder and said there weren't enough troops available for a combined force. "Don't worry, soldier, there's no way you'll face anything dramatic. Nobody's going to be ambushing you or firing RPGs up your ass. Take my word. They're commuters, not insurgents." Briscoe had enough terrible memories from Afghanistan to miss having the guys around the tank for insurance. The sluggish pace only increased his feelings of vulnerability. A drop of sweat formed on his temple, tracing a path down the side of his face. But the Colonel knew his business. Briscoe cleared his throat and put his mind back on driving.

The three heavy transports trundled past Gate 4 at Camp Roberts, carrying their brown Abrams M-1 tanks. At 0100 hours on a Sunday morning, no cars moved on the freeway. But the HETs moved like huge tortoises even with no traffic. Briscoe, exasperated, tapped his boot against the floor, creating a reverberating thumping in the confines of the crawling carrier. The crew behind him muttered, so he stopped. To get his mind off his troubles, he went over Colonel Brickhouse's plan. This was not an exercise. Live ammo. Get the tanks positioned and await orders before moving the tanks onto the Sacramento freeways. That's when the fun would begin.

The Dream again. Two nights in a row. As Colonel Chazz Silver peeled herself out of bed, the heaviness seemed to seep into her bones, leaving her limbs sluggish and uncooperative. Tuesday, and the rest of the week still to come. Not good. She needed some hope for the week.

In her bathroom, the mirror reported the bad news. Her normally lively eyes were now clouded with worry, dark circles etched beneath them. It was as if the Dream left an indelible mark upon her, a lingering presence that she couldn't shake off.

Monday had been a series of minor crises at Joint Force Headquarters, the headquarters of the California Army National Guard. Most were the normal crises that the Chief of Staff had to handle, and she'd handled them as usual. None of them seemed serious enough to bring on the Dream again. So, why? Hoping that the Tuesday issues would be easier and would let her recover her usual dynamism, she prepared for work. Yet, deep down, Chazz couldn't help but acknowledge the ominous significance of needing hope on a Tuesday. It was a bad omen, a sign that navigating the week ahead would need more discipline than she had. A premonition. But Chazz knew from long experience that, despite the dread that lingered within her, she had the strength to navigate this. She'd done it for twenty years.

The monotonous task of clearing the petty administrative business of the day engrossed Chazz at JFHQ until Captain Serrano tapped lightly on her office door frame. His expression reminded her of the uneasy feelings she had about the day.

"Colonel Silver, we've got a curious thing happening at Camp Roberts." Carlos Serrano had become the person she most relied on as Chief of Staff. She'd grown to appreciate his diligence and intelligence over the first six months of her appointment. If he saw a problem, it was a problem. Roberts?

Camp Roberts had been blessedly quiet since the last procurement scandal. Chazz took a moment to check her email, hoping for some respite. No notifications of anything wrong. No paperwork filed that would bring Roberts to her attention. Serrano didn't have any paper in his hands. Nothing dire so far.

"All right. What's up, Captain? Is this official?" she asked, her voice laced with curiosity and apprehension in equal amounts.

Serrano hesitated, then responded with carefully chosen words. "Unofficial, ma'am. A friend in the logistics section there contacted me with, well, a rumor. No SIR yet."

That told Chazz two things. Whatever Serrano had, it was significant enough for a Serious Incident Report. Since there was no SIR, command at Roberts was unaware of the problem.

"Have a seat, Carlos," she said. She moved to the small conference table that took up most of her office. Once they'd settled themselves, she fixed her eyes on Serrano intently and said, "OK, fill me in."

"Tanks. Twelve of them. Yesterday, they're neatly lined up in the parking area. Today, they're gone." Chazz suspected a joke, but Serrano's voice held uncertainty, not humor.

"Training exercise?"

Serrano dismissed her hope for a reasonable explanation. "Nothing scheduled, according to my friend. And moving twelve tanks is major. It would take at least forty-eight troops. That's not a training exercise on the firing range. Plus, he says there were no orders."

Well, that left only a supernatural explanation. She kept her sarcastic response light, asking, "Did they just roll away on their own?"

"Tank carriers are gone too. And three troop transports, along with three fuel carriers."

Chazz had doubts. "How reliable is this 'friend' of yours, Captain?"

"Well, whenever we get together for a drink, he always sticks to Coke, ma'am."

"Huh. And no signs of hallucinations?"

Serrano chuckled. "Nope. He's saner than I am."

"Why no SIR?"

"He says he mentioned it to his boss in logistics and got shut down with no explanation. That's when he reached out to me."

"I see. Well." She looked at her wall clock. "Nothing we can do without an SIR, and that goes to TAG, the Adjutant General. Let's goose them a bit, see if we can get things moving. Schedule a Teams meeting with somebody in command at Roberts, say for 1030."

"Yes, ma'am." Serrano got up and left. Chazz's unease deepened as she acquired a new sense of urgency. She'd done what she could by scheduling the meeting, but twelve missing tanks? Just like that, her hope for a smooth day, if not week, vanished in the blink of an eye.

The Teams meeting began promptly at 1030. A large wall monitor adorned the spacious conference room. Chazz sat at the table, armed with a legal pad and pen, Serrano next to her. As the video feed flickered to life, the bewildered countenance of a portly colonel greeted the participants. The caption at the bottom of the video feed read "Brickhouse." Colonel Brickhouse had a broad and jowly face, accentuated by his closely cropped hair, which gave his head a square-like appearance. Another video feed materialized, showcasing Lieutenant Flattery, a slender individual sporting black horn-rimmed glasses and a discontented expression.

Chazz introduced herself, breaking the silence. "Colonel Silver from JFHQ, Colonel Brickhouse. And this is Captain Serrano, who serves under my command. You seem to be minus some tanks."

"Tanks? What tanks?" The man's brow furrowed.

"Twelve M-1s, older model. Long-term storage." She checked the short writeup Serrano had placed in front of her just before the meeting. Her unease from the early morning returned. Twelve tanks missing, and the commander of the base has no clue.

"What?" Brickhouse turned his head, eyebrows rising. "Flattery, have you seen anything about missing tanks?"

Flattery's head turned. "No, sir."

"You're supposed to have twelve tanks for training exercises, Colonel," said Chazz.

"Well, sure. Of course. I'm confident they're right where they should be. I didn't mean—"

"Fine. Check. I'll wait. You got a phone? Call logistics." Her voice was steely. There was no plausible explanation for twelve tanks vanishing. This was a significant breach in security, and it was her responsibility to resolve it.

"Ah, sure. Sure." Brickhouse's eyes shifted down, a tell of embarrassment. "Flattery, you have that number? Call 'em."

"Yes, sir." The lieutenant muted himself and turned off his video. Chazz heard his voice from Brickhouse's audio feed but couldn't make out the words. After a minute, Flattery's face appeared once more. Flattery appeared uneasy, his eyes darting back and forth as if searching for escape.

"They're gone, sir," he reported.

Brickhouse pursed his lips. "Maybe they're out on exercises."

Chazz smiled again. She wasn't smiling inside. She made her reply crisp and to the point. "Colonel, I'd know if there was an exercise big enough for twelve tanks. So would you. There isn't."

Brickhouse grinned. "Don't worry, Colonel. I'll track 'em down. I'm sure there's a reason for them being out."

Every word spoken amplified the gravity of the situation. The silence that followed Flattery's revelation and Brickhouse's optimism hung heavy, filling the space with a sense of urgency and the need for swift action.

Chazz responded firmly, her voice cutting through the air like a sharp blade. "Well, perhaps. But let's make sure we're using those tanks, not joyriders or terrorists or whatever. It would be a real good idea to find 'em. Soon. And if you can't find them, TAG will need an SIR." She felt the pressing weight of the situation .

"Look, Colonel," said Brickhouse, trying for camaraderie. "Let's not escalate this to command until I've checked into it, OK? Please. And I'll owe you a drink if you ever get to Paso Robles."

You bet you will, you incompetent—Chazz shut down her judge and switched on her diplomat. She could taste the bitter words she wanted to say. Instead, she said, "All right, Colonel. But don't take too long, OK? Twelve tanks, that's a hefty chunk of change, and my boss won't be happy about it if we can't find 'em. Tomorrow at noon. Right?"

"Right. Will do, ma'am." Brickhouse's voice had lost the camaraderie and gained a note of determination. The two images disappeared from the monitor.

Chazz dismissed Serrano and walked back to her office, her steps echoing on the linoleum. The air smelled of bureaucracy, filled with all the red tape she'd need to spin if Brickhouse filed an SIR. Not precisely a crisis. Old tanks were old tanks. But she'd need to rework her plans for the next week or two. Still hope for the day.

Plans. Oh, shit. Lunch with Tom.

CHAPTER TWO
The Blind Pig

"9TH AND J, 9TH AND J," muttered Chazz to herself, taking a sharp left with her hands sliding around the wheel. She'd never been to this restaurant, but Tom wanted to try it. Anyway. 9th and J. One way, damn, around the block. And a parking place! The day was looking up.

As Chazz exited her car, the heat of the day hit her like a hammer. Sweat pearled on her forehead as she walked down the block to the restaurant. The Blind Pig Grill was in an oldish office building, shiny windows reflecting the low buildings and crap architecture of most of the Sacramento downtown. Chazz tugged open the door and a blast of artificially cooled air struck her face. The sweat dried away swiftly as she waited for the hostess to return. A tall blonde, pleasant smile, eyebrows raised. At her OCPs? Downtown Sacramento was not used to military uniforms, putting her outside its comfort zones. The crowd here was suit-and-tie, expensive coiffures, and shiny shoes. Her boots were shiny enough, but otherwise? Well, tough.

"Hi. I'm meeting a friend, Tom Peña," she said. A friend. Was she in love with Tom? Great sex, and he and she hit it off, but…. Why was there always a "but" with her? Like with Tony. Distinct personality from Tom's, unique attractions for her. Tony Ridger was a Marine. They had a lot in common. They'd had an affair in Iraq. His marriage claimed him when he redeployed back to the States—ships in the night, OK. Then, after the pandemic in 2020, he called her out of the blue in San Diego. Stationed at Pendleton now, no encumbrances. They were together six months before she pulled the plug on it because of his behavior. She didn't want to second-guess herself. And yet, here she was doing just that.

Now, she was getting close to Tom. He didn't have Tony's jerk qualities, but his new job gave her pause. She felt her muscles tense, thinking about it. Why? It was the way he was reacting to it. But the spark was there between them, just like with Tony. Friends, or lovers, or something more? Or another "but." And did she need to confront this now, or could she wait until her "but" emerged spontaneously? Did she want this new chapter in her life to end? If so, why? Chazz thought of herself as a reasonably liberated modern woman, but she didn't like to pry open the shell she'd created around herself. The result was the "but" approach to her love life. All this ran through her overactive mind in a second. Then she jerked her attention back to the restaurant rather than descend any farther into the dangerous areas within her mind.

The hostess did a quick check on her seating screen. "Yes, I have the reservation. Mr. Peña hasn't arrived. We can seat you, or you can wait over there if you like." The hostess glanced at the comfortable bar chairs around low tables near the bar. Half the chairs held women in stiletto heels and slinky silk or men in Armani suits and large watches. Laughing over whatever they considered interesting in their lives, into which she had little insight. Or interest.

"You can seat me, thanks," she said, smiling a meaningless smile.

The hostess led her to a two-person table looking out on 9th street. Her military-issue boots sounded very loud to her on the polished wood floor, but nobody seemed concerned. She sat and looked out the window at a depressing reality. Boarded-up windows, empty stores, and a few derelicts scattered around. The mirror image of the restaurant interior. But Chazz's mind had moved from Tom and stiletto heels back to tanks. After all, the missing tanks were far more important than her stressed relationships or how she fit into American society. She was in the Guard with all the responsibility she could handle. But sometimes the stress got the better of her. How the hell do twelve tanks go missing and the guy in charge isn't aware of it? Incompetence only goes so far to explain—

"Hi, beautiful."

Tom leaned over her and kissed her cheek. Her mind flashed to her earlier unease. Then she relaxed, and her military obsessions drained away. Friends? Let's see. She reached and drew him down to give him one on the lips. More than friends, yes. The touch of his hand and lips warmed her, overriding even the tanks. And the unease. The "but" receded in her mind as her good-looking more-than-friend sat across from her, his grin expressing his pleasure at her flirting.

"So," she said, smiling, "this is the place you chose for a celebration?" She nodded at the window.

Tom looked out the window, grin in place. "Yeah, dumpy neighborhood, ain't it?"

"Why here?"

"It's a short walk from the Capitol. Guy in the office said they have great cocktails and a fucking smasher of a grilled pork loin," replied Tom. "I'll brave the gates of hell for a grilled pork loin. And they have a Mexican chef. Adobo."

"What has adobe got to do with it?"

"Adobo, my dear, is a seasoning. Cumin, coriander, dried chiles, epazote. The chef rubs it over the tenderloin and grills it. Out of this world."

"If you say so."

"I do say so. Try it, you'll love it. Cocktail?"

"No, I'm driving. And working."

"Come on, live a little. I'm celebrating."

The server handed them handwritten menus on thick paper and said, "We have a special on the Tequila Sunrise. Clase Azul."

"We'll have two."

"No, Tom." Chazz waved the server away. "What's the blind pig deal?" she asked Tom.

"Who the fuck cares? I'm here to celebrate." Tom's large personality seemed even bigger than usual to Chazz. Not a bad thing, but it could be overwhelming. Tom continued, "Just think, Latinos in charge in California for the first time since the Gold Rush."

"That's a good thing," Chazz said, stretching the truth. Her unease returned. Tom was now the Deputy Chief of Staff for Strategy for the newish governor, Chip Sanchez. She'd met Tomás Peña when he was a political consultant for State Senator Menendez. The senator headed the Military and Veterans Affairs Committee, which dealt with veteran's benefits for Guard reservists. They'd sat next to each other during a hearing and one thing led to another. The spark had quickly flared into flame between her and Tom, and the last six months had seen some of the best action in the bedroom in Chazz's experience. Now, here he was, a Big Deal working for a man who had barely squeaked into the governorship in a recall election. Hence the unease. Chazz was apolitical, particularly about California politics. Her job was to protect the state, organize and advocate for her troops, and do her duty, not to think about the nonsense most politicians thought about. And Tom was becoming a politician. Working for a failed actor playing a politician, even worse. Would his politics leak into their relationship and force her to make a choice?

Tom grinned. "Damn right it's a good thing. It's our turn. Goddamn Anglos have broken this state. No offense," he said.

"None taken," she replied amiably. "How's our semi-elected governor working out for us?"

Tom grimaced and shook his head. "He's got to live that recall election down, doesn't he? OK. He only got 17% of the recall vote, but it was more than the other 73 candidates. Fucking weird state."

Sudden laughter from a nearby table startled Chazz, but it was nothing to do with their conversation. Just a couple of suits on their third Sunrise. The lunch crowd had filled the restaurant, which was now bustling and filled with the noise of unimportant conversations. She smiled and asked, "What's your strategy for that?"

"It's a secret." The tell: his eyes dropped away from looking into hers.

She grinned. "You got nothing, do you?"

"Not yet," he grinned back. "But we will. We're working on big changes."

Time to be direct, indirect wasn't cutting it. "Tom, you're worth way more than working for that jerk. Why are you doing this? Selling out?" Surely he could see that the governor was out of his depth.

The grin disappeared. "No, no, Chazz. This is a great job. I'll have an immense impact on the state. Who knows, maybe it will lead to political office for me."

"Sure." She shook her head in wonder. "Sure it will." Passion and enthusiasm were a fine thing, but in her opinion, Tom overestimated his chances of success with Sanchez. Time would tell.

The server returned with an orange-and-red cocktail. "Tequila Sunrise special. Chef says it's on the house, Mr. Peña."

Tom laughed. "See? I'm a player now."

"Oh, please. A Tequila Sunrise does not make you a player, Tom. Not even in Sacramento."

The server interrupted with a smile. "May I take your orders?"

"Two adobo pork loins," said Tom, handing him the menus.

"And for the lady?" The server smiled at Chazz.

Tom laughed out loud. "Good one."

"What if I don't like pork?" asked Chazz, a little nettled. She liked pork fine, but she didn't like taking orders out of the chain of command. Tom was not a superior officer, after all. He was her lover.

"Try it! Best in the world," replied Tom. "Made from blind pigs."

Chazz's choices were to eat pork or get up and leave. Her body sent signals that told her she didn't want to leave. Was a lunch order gone wrong enough to make her toss a relationship with a man she knew she could love, a man who made her feel with every inch of her body? He was just being a man who knows what's best for his girlfriend. She shook her head and smiled and forgave his overstepping. But she needed to tell him, however mildly, that he was out of line.

She said, "All right. But the next lunch? I get to order for *you*."

***

The adobo pork proved scorching, even while its aroma promised a wonderful meal. Chazz, not a fan of fine dining, had never experienced the intense impact of ground chile pepper, at least not to the extent she now faced.

"See?" said Tom. "Told you it would be great."

"Great. Yeah. And hot." She sipped her cool water to douse the flames consuming her tongue. That organ gave up the battle and went numb after the third slice of pork.

"Hot is great. You're gonna get used to Mexican hot."

Chazz, benumbed, felt this was too much innuendo for lunch. She gulped some more water and said, "Tom. You're pushing it."

"Not yet."

What was the border between innuendo and outright dirty talking? Was there a point of no return, a Rubicon to cross between them? Chazz considered their last passionate encounter. No, the die was cast there. Her body grew a little hot, and it wasn't from the chile peppers.

Tom saw her flush. "You're thinking about tomorrow night, aren't you?" Tom grinned in anticipation. "So am I. I've been obsessing about it since last weekend."

Tom's assurance raised doubts in Chazz. This rapid progression of intimacy made her uncomfortable, even as her body responded to it. Sex led to intimacy, intimacy led to sharing, and sharing meant talking about things like the Dream and why she kept having it. She wasn't ready for that with Tom, not yet. And she was sure he wasn't ready to hear it. She hadn't talked about it with Tony when they were together in San Diego for just that reason. And Tom now seemed even worse about boundaries than Tony had been. She said anxiously, "Maybe we're moving too fast, Tom. We need to slow down. Maybe—"

"You were the one proposing dinner at my place, lover. As I recall."

This was too much for Chazz. "I can damn well un-propose it if you don't shape up. What the hell's wrong with you?"

A flash of anger passed over Tom's face as she gave him her command look. But it dissolved quickly into a sheepish grin.

"You're right, you always are. Why I love you. I just get so high when I'm with you, Chazz. It's been a while since I felt this way. Irrational exuberance."

"That's money, not sex."

"You're saying sex is rational? Or do you object to exuberance?" He said this with such obvious relish that Chazz knew he was debating, not arguing. Pulling her chain. But it wasn't a joke.

On the defensive, she said, "I'm not objecting to anything, Tom. I just feel a little pressure. The last time I felt this pressured, I killed a bunch of Iraqis who were trying to kill me. This…it worries me, to feel this strongly. And I won't get a medal at the end of it all."

The seriousness of this confession stopped Tom cold. He surveyed his empty plate and rearranged the knife and fork on it while he considered what to say. A busboy reached for the plate, startling him. He smiled and raised his hands out of the way, giving him the appearance of someone refusing a request to jump off a cliff.

"I'm out of practice, Chazz," Tom confessed. Chazz interpreted his expression as vulnerable and didn't believe it for a minute.

"At what?" she riposted.

"Relationships." He grimaced. "Got burned as a kid. Figured I'd be better off not getting too close."

She smiled at the picture he presented, which his general air of exuberance and assertiveness belied. She pushed back. "Aww. So you're getting cold feet?"

He backpedaled, realizing she wasn't buying it. "No, no, Chazz! The reverse!"

"Hot feet."

He laughed, reassured. "Yeah. Exactly. Hot feet. When I'm around you, it sizzles, and I dance. I'll admit I got no idea where this is going, but I want to explore, OK? Is that OK?"

"I think so. A little more space to breathe, though, Tom."

He reached across the table, and she again put her hand in his. He rubbed it with the other hand. "I'll give you all the space you need, Chastity. All you need. Just say when you need it." He looked into her eyes. "Should we cancel tomorrow night?"

She smiled. "No. I'll give it a shot. I...it sizzles for me, too. But...."

"Just say."

"Don't call me Chastity, ever again. I am *not* chaste." She squeezed his hand and let go. His willingness to consider her needs had her forgiving him, and his touch reminded her of her desire for him.

"Would you be interested in dessert?" The smiling server was back, small menus in hand.

Chazz looked at her watch. "I'm late, Tom. Got tanks to find." She arose, placing her napkin on the table along with two $20 bills. "I'll be at your place at seven tomorrow."

She looked back as she approached the restaurant door. He was staring out the window at Sacramento, lips pursed, apparently ignoring the server. She smiled and opened the door to the heat of the Sacramento midday sun.

CHAPTER THREE
The Governor's Office

"Colonel Brickhouse from Camp Roberts is on the line for you, sir."

With a gentle touch, Sally Reed, the governor's assistant, pressed the polished button to transfer the call to the governor. Her voice masked her underlying anxiety, hiding it behind a facade of professional composure. The day had gone super well, but she'd reluctantly stayed late at her boss's request.

"Just this once, sir," she had said, her voice tinged with unease. "You know my husband doesn't like it."

"Yeah, yeah, Sally. Be a good sport, just this once, OK?" Chip Sanchez had smiled his best actor's smile.

But as the day progressed, Sally couldn't shake off her worry. Her mind kept wandering back to the previous night, replaying the intimate moments with Ted. A mix of conflicting emotions churned within her. Despite the amazing sex, restful sleep, and delicious breakfast, Sally needed some space. She craved solitude to regain her sense of individuality. Ted had done nothing wrong. It was just an overwhelming desire for some time to herself.

Sally's anxiety grew as the clock continued to tick. By the time she transferred the call to the governor, Sally was mentally drained. The worry took its toll, leaving her feeling emotionally raw. She was clueless how to handle the situation with Ted, so she resorted to leaving for work every day and coming home refreshed.

The job had proven more than reasonable after two months, with only a few late nights. She loved working for this man, Chip Sanchez, even with his mood swings. Sally had signed up with him after Ted dragged her to one of his rallies in Sacramento for the 2028 recall election in June. She'd grown tired of the lecherous state senator she'd served for five years. For Christ's sake, she was fifty years old. It was time for some fun. So she'd quit when Chip asked her to come on board.

Chip sure made life interesting. Maybe he'd take her with him back to Hollywood when this governor gig wrapped up. The only snag: Ted hated everything about Hollywood, making an exception only for Chip. Ted thought it was full of libs, but Sally didn't care that much. In her daydreams, she saw herself at parties with actors and actresses and big-money producers. And if Ted didn't like that, he could go screw.

As Sally gazed at the blinking light on the phone, her cheeks dimpled. The soft murmur of Chip's voice came to her through the closed office door, muffled by the thick carpet. She'd bet that Chip had concocted something extraordinary with the Guard, and it sent a shiver down her spine. Lost in her thoughts, Sally's mind wandered to the image of National Guard troops lined up in perfect formation in a Sacramento review. Her admiration for the governor's leadership grew as she imagined him commanding respect with his authoritative presence.

And Chip spent so much time with General Dupont. The mere mention of his name evoked a time when politeness and formality were virtues. Sally adored General Dupont's perfectly tailored uniform, every crease and button meticulous, symbolizing the discipline and dedication Ted admired. Spit and polish, Ted called it.

Chip would lead the state with compassion and effectiveness. The possibility of people giving Chip a fair chance through his strong leadership ignited a fire in Sally's heart, fueling her unwavering support for his governorship. Sure, the poll numbers stank right now, but he'd show them. He would.

But she was now eager to get home. She didn't want Ted ordering in pizza and drinking too much. Or accusing her of anything. That would send her anxiety through the roof.

Alone in his office with the door shut tight, Chip Sanchez, the recently elected governor of California, picked up his phone. "Colonel Brickhouse? Good news, I hope."

"Yes, sir. You requested me to inform you once things were in motion. The tanks left Camp Roberts at 0100 hours this morning en route to Sacramento, San Francisco, Los Angeles, and San Diego. All units are in position and ready for action."

"Excellent, my friend. Great work." Work that General Dupont had told him couldn't be done. He'd done it with two calls, one to get the right man's name at Roberts, and the call to Brickhouse. The tanks' presence eliminated Myron Dupont's excuses for delaying the state takeover. Proving Myron wrong sent him over the moon.

"What else do you need, sir?" asked the colonel.

"Not a damn thing, Colonel, now that I've got my tanks." Chip gripped the phone tightly, a warm flush spreading over his face. "Thanks. And I'll put you down for something big in the new government, OK? I'll need friends, friends who can get things done."

"Thank you, sir. I appreciate your confidence in me."

Chip leaned back in his office chair, basking in the moment's euphoria. His mind raced with visions of himself at the helm of a new government, surrounded by capable individuals like Brickhouse. Endless possibilities and the exhilaration of power filled his mind. Once this surge had died down, he remembered his faithful assistant and went out to the outer office to release her.

"OK, Sally, you're free now. Give Ted my love."

"Yes, sir." His assistant had her coat on and her things ready to go on her desk. She smiled, picked up her bag, and left without further ado. Chip grinned. Sally was the perfect fit for the job. She got things done in spades, and she was loyal to a fault. Ted was a lucky man. He'd have to meet him sometime. Chip himself wasn't ready for marriage. He had the liberty to do as he pleased with women. Angélica, for instance. And wouldn't the changes in the state surprise her! He looked forward to their next bed date with anticipation.

Chip rubbed his hands and headed back to his office with its liquor cabinet. Time to celebrate. Wait until Myron found out he'd handled the tank thing himself. He'd sensed a certain distance in Myron as they'd talked about creating a new government after the coup. This would prove that he was presidential material. Getting things done, that was the point. Executive action. He splashed a double tequila into a glass and toasted his reflection in the dark window of the California State Capitol. His first swallow released the weight of the world. He was ready to forge his path as the president of California, with loyal friends who got things done.

CHAPTER FOUR

Tanks in the Streets

THREE DAYS IN A ROW. The Dream.

It was Wednesday, and the weight of her workload loomed heavily upon Chazz. She didn't need this unwelcome visitor to dominate her work week. She sat on the side of her bed, massaging her forehead and glaring at the carpet. The dream-rape itself woke her this time. Self-defense: her brain wasn't up to living through that ordeal again.

The world outside was coming alive, suburb-quiet at five in the morning, still dark outside. She got up, turned on the light, and found her slippers, the nice cozy ones that kept her feet warm but did nothing for her PTSD.

Post-traumatic stress, PTSD. Self-diagnosed, since she'd never reported it. She'd just packaged it away with the other PTSD-inducing events of 2005 in Iraq. Didn't matter to anyone except her, and only on bad days. She could cope, as long as she didn't have too many bad days. It was September 2028. She should have moved on after the horror two decades old. The firefight, the aftermath, the rape. But she hadn't. On a bad day, every movement required an extra effort, as though she dragged the full weight of her past behind her.

Chazz flinched as the blaring sound of her phone's alarm clock pierced through the silence, causing her heart to race. Chazz grabbed the phone from her night table. She punched the stop button with a finger so hard she dropped the phone, which bounced on the carpet and went under the bed. She swore and got down on hands and knees to retrieve it. Her hands shook so much she nearly dropped it again. Her head throbbed with a dull ache. She dumped the phone on the nightstand, swore again, and headed for the bathroom.

The cold water shocked her as she splashed it onto her face, hoping to wash away the Dream and the dread it evoked in her. She studied the bleary-eyed hag facing her in the mirror, water sprinkles dotting the front of the T shirt she wore in bed. Somewhere in there was the confident, well-groomed, efficient colonel she needed to be for her working day. That colonel would find her during the hour-long drive from her house in the suburbs to East Sacramento. That colonel wouldn't let the PTSD define her. She would cope with the daily operations of the Guard. And the missing tanks. And Tom. But right now, the face in the mirror just sneered.

Late in the afternoon, Chazz spotted Captain Serrano in the kitchen area, talking with another officer. When she approached him, he walked her back to her office. Chazz picked up the frustration in his voice as he updated her on the situation at Roberts. "I called twice, ma'am. Got Flattery both times. Brickhouse was in meetings, or so Flattery claimed." Serrano grimaced, clearly nettled. "Not sure I believed him."

Chazz repressed the impulse to swear, facing the weight of an unproductive six hours. What was up with the tanks? Tomorrow would tell the tale.

"OK, Carlos. I'm heading home. Long day. Check in again with them first thing in the morning, right? Keep pushing. If we hear nothing positive by lunchtime, I'll call and get the SIR moving."

"Yes, ma'am."

Chazz looked forward to a relaxing run in the cool of the early evening, followed by a nice, hot shower and a leisurely meal from the microwave. Exhausted by three dreadful days, she would hit the sack early to recuperate. She maneuvered her car onto the freeway to become part of the lengthy procession of cars crawling westward.

She moved onto the I-5 connector and looked down to see them: two M-1s resting on the city street under the freeway overpass. Chazz's eyes widened in disbelief as she inched forward, unable to do anything. The shoulder of the overpass was too narrow to navigate, so she was stuck. The noxious fumes from the diesel truck in front of her, combined with the urgency of the tanks, made her want to puke.

There was one thing she *could* do. She hit the call button on her steering wheel and said, "Call 911."

"Police emergency, how can I help you?" said a tinny male voice out of her car speakers.

"Hello. This is Colonel Silver of the National Guard Joint Force Headquarters. I've spotted some stolen tanks. Under the bypass to I-5 from I-80."

Dead silence from the phone.

"Hello? Anyone there?" she said.

"It's a criminal offense to make crank calls to 911, lady," said the voice. "We have your number, and we prosecute."

"Well, check it out, dumbass, and you'll find I'm Chief of Staff of the California Army National Guard. This is not a crank call. My God."

"Please hold."

"Fuck." She waited, drumming her fingers on the steering wheel, watching the tanks pass by underneath her as she rose over them at a crawl. Where was the next exit? Crap, a mile down the road. Inch by inch, her car crept over the road.

"Colonel Silver?" Somebody new, male voice. She gripped the steering wheel tightly.

"Who am I speaking with?" she asked.

"Lieutenant McCullough, California Highway Patrol. They transferred your call to me."

"Lieutenant, I need some backup to deal with this."

"The dispatcher said something about tanks. What kind of tanks?"

"M-1 Abrams."

A pregnant silence developed as McCullough absorbed the situation. He said, "I...I'll need a bit more information, Colonel. Bear with me, please. This is unusual."

Chazz suppressed her impulse to scream. She took a deep breath. "OK, Lieutenant. It's simple. I got a tip yesterday that twelve tanks, M-1 Abrams, have gone missing from our armory at Camp Roberts near Paso Robles. I'm heading home for the day on I-80, when I stumble on two tanks under the I-5 overpass. Just sitting there. I need backup."

"Let's see, I-80, I-5, let me find it here. I'm in Yuba City, not that familiar with the Sacramento area..."

Yuba City. Why Yuba City? Yuba.... She toned down the frustration in her voice to urge politely, "Can you transfer me to someone in the central city office? Right now?"

"Here it is...Oh my God. There must be twenty overpasses there. Colonel, where exactly...we have a camera near there, let me...."

"Fuck fuck fuck." Chazz banged on the steering wheel with her hands. "I need officers here right now! I'm in traffic, stuck, can't move to the exit. Get them dispatched." She punched the navigation system up on her dashboard and swept it around to find the street names under the overpass. "Third and W, Lieutenant. I'll get there. Dispatch backup now!"

"I can't get a visual underneath the overpass, Colonel, too many obstructions. That's the one heading to North 5, or...which one of the three there? If I turn the camera...."

About to scream at him, movement ahead of her yanked her head back to the freeway. Cars were speeding up ahead. Chazz's car moved down the overpass as the cars in front of her speeded up. The shoulder widened as she entered the on-ramp to I-5. She swung the car onto the shoulder and accelerated past the slow-moving commuters to the next exit. She said as calmly as she could, "I've reached the exit. Have the officers meet me under the overpass."

"Colonel, don't you think—"

"Just get them here, Lieutenant! Now! Third and W, damn it!" She ended the call.

She took two wrong turns before finding the streets back under the freeway. As she pulled up to the tanks, coming to a screeching halt, a Highway Patrol SUV pulled up behind her with its light bar flashing. She got out of her car.

"Colonel Silver?" asked the patrolman who climbed out of the police vehicle.

"That's right," Chazz replied, thankful that she was wearing OCPs and boots.

"Can I see some ID?"

"Sure thing." She proffered her Army ID and California driver's license. "And who am I speaking with?"

"Officer Shanley, ma'am." He handed her ID back to her. "Now, what about these guys?"

No one was visible near the tanks.

"They didn't get here by themselves, officer."

Shanley looked a little helplessly at the imposing vehicles. "Do we just go up and knock?"

Seeing the humor in the situation, Chazz smiled. "Guess not. Let's try your loudspeaker and see what happens."

"Are these guys armed and dangerous?"

She told Shanley, "I don't know, officer. But I can tell you that your Kevlar doors won't cut it if they are."

Shanley and Chazz contemplated the tanks. No sign of life. No threatening behavior. Other than being tanks on the streets of Sacramento, that is. Chazz shivered. Before, her concern had been solely about the tanks being missing. But here they were, on public streets. Doing what? And why? Well, first things first. You couldn't scramble an egg without breaking the shell.

Shanley squared up and nodded. "OK, Colonel. You should pull back."

"Just do it, officer. I'm fine."

The officer took the hint, getting back into his SUV and grabbing a microphone.

"Anyone in the tanks, please step out of the vehicles, showing your hands."

At least he wasn't requesting license and registration. Chazz looked up at the tank hatches. Nothing. Shanley repeated his broadcast.

The driver's hatch on one tank creaked open, and a helmeted head with very sharp eyes emerged. The eyes saw her and called, "What's up, ma'am?"

Chazz walked to the tanks and looked up at the emerging soldier. National Guard insignia, sergeant. Combat uniform, glasses, black skin shining in the sun. He waved at the CHP officer, showing both hands were empty.

"Colonel Silver, JFHQ, sergeant. What the hell are you doing here with these tanks?" Shanley stepped up beside her, posture resolute.

The sergeant directed his eyes over her shoulder. She turned. A second CHP SUV parked behind the first one, and two officers emerged from the vehicle, hands on their guns.

"Ma'am, I'll have to ask you to step back from the, er, the vehicle," said Shanley.

"Sure. Go to it." She let the officers approach the tank and stepped back a few paces. The driver's hatch on the other tank opened a crack, and eyes studied the situation from inside.

"Sergeant?" asked Shanley. "Can you tell us why you have two tanks parked here?"

"Orders, officer." The sergeant smiled. "It's an exercise."

"Are these tanks from Roberts?" shouted Chazz from behind them. The CHP officers reflexively ducked, startled by her outburst. Shanley turned and glared at her.

"Would you mind butting out, Colonel? We'll handle this."

"So handle it. I want my tanks back," retorted Chazz.

The sergeant said, "My orders are to hold position here until tomorrow morning. HETs will come to pick us up. Can't tell you more than that, officers. Orders." The sergeant smiled. "The Colonel is not in our chain of command. They just haven't put her in the picture. Check with my command at Camp Roberts. Tell them it's Sergeant Briscoe. Ask for Colonel Brickhouse."

Officer Shanley strode back to his SUV and picked up his mike and spoke into it. The cops and Chazz all waited until a crackling reply came from the car's radio. Shanley acknowledged the response and replaced his mike. He rejoined the group.

"Base confirms the exercise from Camp Roberts, Colonel. I'm afraid there's nothing we can do for you."

"Damn it, there's no such exercise! I'd know." The frustrated Chazz turned to look at her largest problems.

Shanley grimaced. "We can't do anything more here, Colonel. You'll have to handle this with your people. No crime here."

The three CHP officers exchanged nods. They returned to their vehicles and drove away.

Chazz swore an unladylike oath. The sergeant smiled, saluted, and dropped through the hatch and closed it. The other tank's hatch closed as well. She was too mad to return the salute.

Time to kick the problem up to higher authority. She couldn't let it wait until tomorrow. Chazz took out her phone and called her boss's mobile. He'd be heading home after work, just as she had been.

"Dupont here. Colonel Silver?"

"Yes, sir. Do you know about the missing tanks?"

Silence. Then the general responded, "No. What missing tanks?"

She explained the Roberts situation and her current status. The tanks slumbered on, lit by the setting sun, as she held her phone tightly to her ear, leaning against the treads of Briscoe's tank.

"And these tanks are just sitting there? Under the freeway?" Dupont asked.

"That's right, sir."

"I've heard about a proposed exercise, didn't know it had gone ahead, though. Well, Colonel, I'll take it from here. You go on home. I'll follow up once I get out of my car, all right? But I'm sure it's fine. Who the hell would steal tanks in Paso Robles and park them under a freeway in Sacramento? It must be poor communication."

"But sir—"

"No, really, Chazz. Go home. I'll handle it. That's an order."

"Yes, sir." She punched the hangup icon on her phone and shook her head. Then she kicked the tread of the tank next to her and walked back to her car, muttering under her breath, "Bastards. I swear I'll court-martial every single one of you fuckers when I find out what's going on."

General Myron Dupont put on an earbud and tried the governor's private phone three times. Each time, he listened to the governor's not-very-funny voicemail message and the beep. Myron impatiently called the public number of the governor's office and got Sally, who said she'd check if the governor was available.

Parked on a quiet side street, Myron tapped his fingers restlessly on the steering wheel. The seconds dragged on in eternal silence. Chip was taking his sweet time. Myron understood why. Chip didn't want to face the consequences of his foolishness.

The governor's assistant's voice crackled in the silence. "He's tied up on a phone call right now, General. Can he call you back?"

Myron suppressed a growl. Myron had a basic principle of common sense in mind. Never upset an assistant unless you're about to fire them or it's life and death. Yours, not theirs. "Sally, I'll need to interrupt him. This is important and can't wait."

"He won't like it, General," advised Sally, caution edging the words.

"I don't—" Myron bit his tongue to stop what was coming out of his mouth. "Sally. It's important."

Sally sighed. "I'll tell him. Please hold, General."

More waiting. He distracted himself by holding the steering wheel and imagining driving up I-80 to the Tahoe condo, his happy place.

"Myron!" Myron winced as his earbud exploded with sound. The governor's robust voice was what you'd expect from an action-movie actor. It also brimmed with annoyance. "What's so damn important? I was talking to my girlfriend in LA. Now she's all hot at me for hanging up, I'll bet. *Las Latinas, comprende?*"

"Listen up, Chip. The cat is out of the bag."

"What the hell does that mean?"

"My command knows about the tanks. Moving them into place was a mistake. Did I not explain that so you understood?"

"Sure, but—"

"Chip." Myron looked around uneasily. The only visible person was a vagrant poking at a city garbage can. The caution was reflexive; nobody could overhear him in the car. A sense of isolation swept over him as he stated, "We'll have to move things up."

"That's fine, Myron. We're ready. We are. It's time."

Myron shook his head. The bastard was his usual overly optimistic self. Optimism didn't win wars. "We're not ready, but we'll need to move, regardless." He heard the resignation in his own voice and regretted it.

"So tell me, Myron, why you don't have control over your 'command,' whatever that means."

"I do, but not for this. I've got sharp people in top positions, Chip. We need them on board or sidelined while the operation proceeds. Tanks aren't just tanks, Chip. They need infantry squads to protect them and supply operations to refuel and repair them. They need operations teams to direct tasks and locations. I need more time. Now I don't have it."

Now his voice held anger, and he regretted that too, just not as much as the resignation.

"Just trying to help, Myron. My God, when you told me it would take weeks to get those tanks into place, I couldn't believe it. Two days! That Brickhouse proved super helpful."

"I'm sure." Myron tasted bile when he contemplated the commander of Camp Roberts. Brickhouse was always helpful when he thought it would put money in his pocket. Myron knew that, after the dust settled, the Guard would be minus at least one colonel. "Now we've got unsupported tanks sitting under freeways, making people nervous."

Chip, unmoved, asked, "Who's the cat unbagger, Myron?"

"My Chief of Staff, Colonel Silver."

"Oh. Her." The Governor paused, "She'd be hot if she didn't wear fatigues all the time, Myron."

Myron Dupont wasn't very woke, especially on feminism, but this was excessive. "Listen: 'hot' isn't a relevant word for a senior colonel in the National Guard. Not ever. Colonel Silver got a Silver Star in Iraq for killing a bunch of insurgents, taking an RPG up the tailpipe of her chopper. And nobody calls 'em fatigues anymore, Chip. OCPs. And they're standard working uniform for us. I've got 'em on right now."

"Yeah, sure. But, Myron. You're not hot with or without 'em." The Governor's horsey laugh rang out from the car speakers.

This from the leader of the independent California Republic. Just fine.

The governor responded to his silence. "OK, OK. Just a joke. Look, can't you send her on a trip or something? Keep her out of the way until we're in power. You can do that."

"I'll *have* to do that, Chip. Because of the tanks."

"Bitch, bitch, bitch. Myron, I got things need doing. Laws to sign. Not to mention my irate girlfriend. Gotta go, Myron."

Myron Dupont sat in his car for a minute, breathing deeply and thinking things through. Sanchez posed a problem and needed containment. Myron would work with Tom Peña to keep the governor from going rogue in the future. Colonel Silver would take some finessing to allay her suspicions until he could organize getting her out of the way. The dashboard clock told him he would be late for dinner with his wife and kids, sure to precipitate more tearful reproaches from his much younger wife.

He shook his head as he started up his car. Life was full of curve balls, particularly when you worked with a certain kind of player. You don't have control of the game, and all you can do is give it your best shot. But you don't win ball games that way. Or wars.

* * *

"Got a minute, General?" Chazz stood in the door of her boss's office. The early morning sunlight streamed through his window. She hadn't slept much, the tanks consuming her mind. But not sleeping was better than dreaming.

"Sure, Colonel. Come on in. Is this about the tanks?"

"Yes, sir."

Chazz settled herself in the chair across from her commanding officer and smiled. "This all sounds ridiculous, sir, but—"

He interrupted, showing her a palm. "No, no, Chazz. You're right to be disturbed. This is a breakdown of communication. I've checked with Roberts, and the commander is sorry for the trouble." His chair squeaked as he leaned back.

Chazz said with asperity, "Brickhouse claimed to know nothing about the tanks when we met with him yesterday."

"He wasn't in the loop. Look, Colonel, you know damn well Roberts is not—well, they still haven't recovered from last time." Even talking about the arms thefts exposed last year at Camp Roberts embarrassed him, Chazz realized. Dupont was an excellent commander, and she had suffered zero problems working for him, but this was new.

"I understand, sir. But it's my job to keep the Guard ready to respond. Poor communication suggests that the command at Roberts isn't doing its job. Here's what I'd like to propose, sir."

Chazz handed the General the one-pager she'd composed first thing when she got in. The sleepless night crystallized her thinking, and three cups of coffee had made her sufficiently energetic to put it all in succinct, if not elegant, prose. The situation, now that she'd seen the tanks, required direct action rather than waiting for Brickhouse.

General Dupont took the memo, handling it like it was fresh out of the oven. He put it on his desk and read. Then he read it again. Chazz leaned back in her chair, waiting, eyes wandering around the General's rather spare office. Pictures of his young wife and kids. A small row of books between ornate bookends, the most prominent and bulky a recent biography of General U. S. Grant. Chazz had minimal experience with

General Dupont's personal life, and his office revealed little information about the man behind the uniform.

"Colonel, it's an admirable plan, but it's too much."

"But, sir, it's very simple—"

He raised a hand to stop her. He explained. "We're over budget, Colonel. The Governor and the Legislature want us to rein in spending where we can. An investigation like the one you propose will pull soldiers away from their regular duties. It'll generate expenses and paperwork far beyond normal. You must remember what happened with the last extensive investigation."

She did. It had been a large-scale fraud uncovered in the procurement offices. The fraud had gone on for months, consuming the Chief of Staff (her penultimate predecessor) for a year. The investigation generated a trail of tears for the civilian contractors and officers involved, both the fraudsters and the investigators. But the Guard was better for it, however much it had cost.

"Yes, sir. Of course, sir. But this level of miscommunication shows a serious problem with command. And tanks—is this 'exercise' needed? Tanks in the streets? What is it preparing for, a major armed insurrection?"

The General winced. "Colonel, let me handle this. Just a quiet disciplinary talk with the command at Roberts, maybe a little housecleaning. That will take care of the problem. There's no real wrong-doing here, just…a failure to communicate."

"But, sir, communication is essential." This was getting near Chazz's obsession. Everything bad that had happened in her career was because of poor communication. Like the Iraq thing. It didn't have to happen. Intelligence picked up the ambush, but some dopey analyst played drone games or whatever those guys did rather than warning troops in the area about insurgents accumulating weapons. Then the ammunition supply trucks made their scheduled run, and bam. An ambush and a huge firefight. If she hadn't flown by, more soldiers would be dead now. And if the convoy hadn't been there at all, her gunner would still be alive instead of burning to death in the chopper crash. Poor communication?

She said, "Sir, we have to take action. The Guard has to be ready to respond to whatever, wildfires, insurrection, invasion. If we can't communicate properly, we're not ready." She didn't want to contradict her boss, but this truth needed saying.

"I get your point, Colonel," said General Dupont. "I get it. But this—" He put his hand on her memo. "It's an overreaction. I understand you're just doing your job. But this level of response isn't necessary. Let me take it on. I'll make sure those responsible understand what they need to do, OK?"

Chazz had spent enough time with General Dupont to hear what he was really saying—stand down. The General liked to persuade rather than order. She'd seen others push past his persuasion, only to fall afoul of his underlying determination and his unwavering certainty that he knew best. And the chain of command was everything to her.

"Yes, sir." She stood up. "I understand, sir. I'll leave it with you."

The General stood and dismissed her with a smile. No blame, no shame. As long as she complied. Her face muscles relaxed from their forced cheerfulness as she beat a tactical retreat to her office.

CHAPTER FIVE
The Dark Forest

THE LONG THURSDAY WORKDAY FINALLY struggled to a close. Chazz found the bureaucratic daily process even more tedious than usual, punctuated by tank-filled thoughts and distractions. Dinner with Tom that night would help with that. But she needed to transform herself and let go of the day's cares. Burdening Tom with all this nonsense wouldn't help their relationship.

Chazz changed her clothes in the minimalist office ladies' room with its faint aroma of air freshener. OCPs and a tight bun at lunch downtown wouldn't work for a dinner in a man's apartment. No. She went so far as a daring silk blouse unbuttoned to show some cleavage, but no dress or skirt. Soft, loose pants. First, a complete change of underwear style to support all this. And after all that, heels. She brushed out her dark brunette hair in the mirror, untangling the knots from the bun. Adding only a touch of makeup and a subtle lip gloss finished the transformation.

She stepped back and looked at the woman that had emerged from the colonel's uniform. She shivered slightly and smiled as she saw a powerful and vulnerable woman showing curves in all the right places. Her features needed little makeup, a fact usually obscured by her military dress and demeanor. This woman emerged all too rarely these days, and Chazz was delighted to see her again. A sense of liberation took over.

Two wobbly steps in the high heels convinced her to go back to her military issue boots, at least until she got to Tom's. She emerged from the ladies' room and made it to the front in full view of her command and everyone else in the place. She sensed their eyes on her. No blame, no shame. Let them think what they thought. Their problem, not hers. And so on, all the way to her car. The eyes faded, and her mind stretched ahead with anticipation for the evening with Tom.

Tom's small condo apartment was in a "good" part of Sacramento, the Midtown neighborhood near the river. His windows overlooked a sprawling park. A serene residence conveniently close to his workplace. Chazz changed back into heels and navigated through the silent walkways of the condo complex. Tom answered his door with a glass of something in his hand. He handed it to her along with the cheek kiss and an arm wrapped around her waist, closing the door with his foot. The peck moved onto her lips, and she struggled to hold the glass upright while balancing on the heels and responding warmly to his overtures.

Tom nuzzled her neck, holding her close. "Good to see you, Chazz. God, it's good," he whispered. He moved his hand to caress her neck, sending a shiver down her spine. Amidst this pleasure, her mind abruptly filled with images of a dark forest, the fear overtaking the pleasure of the kiss. She tensed up, focusing on balance, keeping the glass steady, keeping her flighty mind on a leash. The fear touched her childhood subconscious, according to the therapist she'd seen for a time. After she returned from Iraq and quit the Army. The forest had lain silent for the past couple of years. But tanks in the streets, she hadn't seen those since Iraq. And she'd had The Dream again. How much pain lingered below the surface? But she had this, she could control it. A little wine spilled from her glass, and her stomach clenched, but that was it. Wasn't it?

"You're tense, Chazz," Tom said with a soothing voice. He gently massaged her shoulders.

Chazz cleared her throat and said with a strained voice, "Bad day at the office." She sipped the chilled white wine. Control, control. She had this. Why could she be so cool under enemy fire, but a simple kiss sent her into a dissociative fit? The delicious wine cooled her fear to a lingering unease. She encouraged it by asking, "So, what's for dinner?"

"Let's go look," he said. She smiled as they turned toward the small kitchen, her stomach slowly loosening. Strong and enticing aromas filled her senses. Tom's exuberance gave her the confidence she needed to get back to normal. And the food would help. Maybe the stomach thing was just hunger. Chazz was famished, and she told him so. She sniffed the air. She couldn't identify the tantalizing aromas, but they promised a delicious meal, another way to get back to normal.

Tom approached the kitchen with a determined look. "Appetizers first, then—"

"You do realize that this is a major role reversal, right?" Chazz joked. "I should be cooking for you."

He smiled a crooked smile and said affectionately, "Chazz, you are many things, wonderful things. But a cook isn't one of them."

She grinned. "I'm happy to let you humor my lack of relevant skills, Tom." She turned toward the dining area as Tom put things together in the kitchen. He had set the small dining table informally, without candles or other silly romantic things. Tom was all about the food, not the formality of fake romance. And she was exactly where she needed to be.

Tom approached the table balancing two steaming bowls. "First, a little soup, *pozole rojo*, with dried corn and pork and chiles, the best!" The fragrant scent filled the room.

No question, the wonderful smells from the kitchen came from this soup. It tasted truly savory and delicious as it went down. The tender, plump kernels of white corn and the shredded pork provided the heft while the thick, red, savory liquid provided the flavor. A dinner by itself. But this was only a small bowl. Accompanied by a light salad with lime dressing, counterpoint to the heavy ranch-style dressings she was used to. The warmth of the soup further calmed the storm within her, rejuvenating the earlier feelings of power and liberation.

"Bad day, huh? Want to unload?" asked Tom, returning to her earlier tension.

She shook her head. "Not really. Nothing secret, only poor management and my boss nixing a plan." She'd learned long ago to keep things light, never to burden lovers with her deeper struggles. Tony had been the exception. But she wasn't there yet with Tom. It would come with time.

"That would be General Dupont?" he asked.

"Have you met him?" The general spoke with the governor regularly, so it was likely Tom had encountered him.

"We've had dealings. Nice guy. By the book." Tom concentrated on his soup. "He and the governor are pretty close."

"Politically, you mean?"

"Yeah, and they share some history."

Chazz frowned in thought, making a stab at reconciling the disparate images she held of the two men. "Isn't the governor on the radical side? An activist?"

Tom put down his soup spoon and grinned with amusement. "The governor follows the votes, my dear. Right now, it's a delicate dance between left and right, woke and not-woke."

She replied, "You're a pragmatist, Tom. Do you have any strong political commitments?"

"Can't afford to, Chazz." His smile broadened, eyes crinkling. He picked up his spoon and sipped soup. "Anyhow, the governor and I see eye-to-eye on the Latino situation in the state. *La Raza* is part of our blood, literally. Just not everything the activists push, that's all."

"So he's a political con man?" How far could she push Tom? Politicians, particularly those of the con man persuasion, always seemed to create more problems than they solved. She couldn't resist teasing Tom as her skepticism grew. It was in her nature.

But Tom took it in stride and answered genially, "There you go again, all judgy. Give him a chance. With me doing strategy, you'll see things happening that are brand new. He's got guts and balls and is going to use them."

"I didn't need that vision at dinner, thanks." She finished up her soup and munched some lime-dressed salad, savoring the contrasting flavors. "General Dupont, though—he's Quebecois-American, not Latino. Not a lot in common with Governor Sanchez, I'd have thought."

Tom shrugged. "Sure, different backgrounds, but they share views on many issues, Chazz. Dupont has a lot of practical experience with things that matter to California, and Sanchez values his expertise. Besides, the Guard benefits from its being close to the governor, right?"

She sipped some wine. "We stay out of politics in the military. Non-military politics, at least. Bad for discipline."

"Dupont understands that. But his advice is practical, actionable, and effective." Tom pursed his lips. "What did he turn down? Your plan for what?"

"I can't talk about that, Tom," she said with a smile to soften her refusal.

"Military secrets. God, I love military secrets. They're like sex toys for the brain."

She rolled her eyes. "I didn't need that vision, either. My God."

But he persisted. "Yesterday, you said something about tanks. Is that what he rejected, some plan for tanks?"

"I shouldn't have said that. Forget it." The image of the insubordinate sergeant smirking at her from the tank hatch flashed through her mind. And Dupont's refusal to do anything about it, leaving her no choice but to walk away from the problem. And Tom's persistence surprised her, disturbing the calm waters within her.

"What?" Tom caught the irritation. "What's up, angel?"

Increasingly uncomfortable with the conversation's direction, Chazz simplified her response to the essential point. "His indirect way of doing things frustrates me. He's not weak, but he's not direct. I like direct."

"That's the truest thing you've ever said. Direct. Yes." Tom drank some wine and smiled again. "Direct. I don't think I've ever known anyone as direct as you."

Suddenly, she felt uneasy. Had she pushed things too far? As her words hung in the air, uncertainty settled between them. "Too direct?" she asked, her eyes locked with his as she searched for signs of trouble.

Tom reassured her, "Never, Chazz. Nothing like that. You keep that quality. It's what I love most about you." He reached across the table, and Chazz put her hand in his. Warm and gentle, the human contact did more to reassure her than his words. Tom held the moment just long enough to restore her calm, then stood and cleared the table.

From the kitchen, Tom called, "Now for the main course. *Mole rojo.*"

He emerged with bigger bowls this time, filled with a thick, dark red, steaming stew. More spices, ones she couldn't place.

"What's in this stuff?" she asked, inhaling the wonderful aromas and enjoying the dark red mysteries in front of her.

"Puréed chiles, tomatoes, tomatillos, chicken, lots of spices, and chocolate."

"Chocolate? You're kidding." She looked at him doubtfully, eyebrows rising.

"Not sweet American chocolate. Mexican chocolate, the savory kind. The kind the Aztecs ate."

She filled a spoon. Good. Not too spicy, just right for her. She ate some chicken and enjoyed the chocolate in the aftertaste.

"Different. Really different, Tom. But good."

"Glad you like it. My mother's recipe, with a little less heat. When we're married, she'll teach you how to make it for me. With more heat, of course!"

"Um..." Her brow crinkled. "How did we end up discussing mothers-in-law? Let's hold off on that, Tom."

He laughed, keeping things warm between them despite her prickles. "Sorry, fantasizing. Having someone make a *mole* for you is even better than sex."

She shook her head. "Rain check on that one, too." A wonderful dinner was a notch below a wonderful fuck for her, but the relationship was still young. Too much, too fast. She changed the subject back to his life, wanting to learn more about the governor. "Tell me more about Governor Sanchez. What's he like to work for?"

"Crude and rude, but solid behind the tough guy act."

Since that described 90% of the military guys she'd worked with over the years, Chazz asked, "He's not ex-military, is he?"

"Not that I know of. But he likes to talk military."

"In what way?" She savored a piece of chicken, tender and sweet in the dark red sauce.

"Oh, like send in the troops, law and order, protect the nation."

"Sounds more right-wing than left-wing."

"It's all the same, Chazz. Wings are for chickens." Tom grinned and munched on a piece of the said bird. "The essence of politics is telling people what they want to hear. It's about telling other politicians what you want them to do, then making them do it."

She laughed. Curious now about his role, she asked, "Where does 'strategy' come into it?"

"That's the part about making them do it," he replied with a sardonic grin.

"And what does our Governor have in mind? What does he want other politicians to do?"

Tom got serious. "He's fed up with all the time-wasting federal regulations and strictures. All those caveats on highway funding? And the loopy Federal agencies screwing up the environment, resource extraction, and corporate malfeasance. And now the immigration crap, shutting down our farmers for no reason. He's fed up with the feds these days. You must have heard that he and the president have had words. When the *New*

York Times and the *Washington Post* report your dinner conversation verbatim, it's not a good thing."

At least the governor was direct. Too direct? Only the president could decide that. She didn't care, even though they were both in her chain of command.

"He's stuck with that," she replied, slurping more *mole*. "Since California voted 95% for the president's opponent in the last election. The Department of Defense even pulled military units and ships out of California in retaliation for that vote." She spoke with some feeling. The feds had made her job harder as morale in the state troops washed away like the coastline in Big Sur.

Tom clenched his jaw and stared out the window, thoughts elsewhere. Then he leaned forward, his eyes taking on the intense look she'd only occasionally seen. "I wouldn't be too sure about his being stuck. California's rich enough to stand on its own, you know. We could easily walk away from the feds' actions without hesitation. Like the new law forcing us to open the offshore oil fields to the Texas oilmen. Christ, what a balls up. Santa Barbara will be awash in black gold, literally. Sure thing."

"The federal government would sue."

He waved a hand, leaning back in his chair, and sneered. "Let 'em. We can handle it."

She eyed him, eyebrows rising again. "You're serious, aren't you?"

He leaned forward again, and the words spilled out, fast and furious. "Yeah. We have to do something. It's like we're being pushed into the ocean one executive order at a time. Gotta put a stop to it somehow. That's the strategy part. How to get the feds to stop their nonsense and get real." Tom heard his own intensity and modulated. He grinned and sipped his wine. He injected a little glee and said, "Gonna show those bastards what's what, I'll tell you. Wait and see."

Chazz smiled at Tom's contagious enthusiasm, even though she didn't share his passion for politics. But she knew that passion was his middle name. All kinds of passion. Redirecting that impulse toward softer things would get her what she wanted.

She said, "I love your passion, Tom. You rate politics higher than sex." She toasted him with her wineglass and added, "I hope you don't get so wrapped up in your boss's political plans that you won't go on vacation." She sipped her wine and smiled. "With me."

Happy with the new theme of the conversation, his face lit up as he said, "I'll go anywhere with you, beautiful. Anywhere at all."

"A nice, quiet, romantic beach somewhere, no politics, no people, and no distractions."

Tom grinned. "How about Antigua? 365 beaches, one for every day of the year. Cancun. Playa de Carmen. La Paz. Cabo. So many beaches in the Caribe and the Golfo. And *México!*" He pronounced it the Spanish way, making it all sound exotic and warm and inviting. And passionately romantic. The romance stayed with them for the rest of the dinner.

Afterwards, the two of them relaxed on the comfortable couch, drinking an aged tequila that Tom recommended as a cure for insupportable workdays and reticent bosses. As the warmth filled her, she leaned against him, his arm around her shoulders, the warmth of his body against her side. They talked about this and that, swapping stories from their pasts. She stayed away from Iraq and the shadows of dark forests, and he stayed away from LA and the ghosts of his childhood.

She sighed gratefully as she kicked off the hideous high heels. Tom lifted her legs up and across his lap. He looked down at her with hungry desire. Their lips met in passion, and their hands explored each other in increasing urgency.

Chazz murmured, "Not the couch, Tom. Let's—"

He stood, lifting her in his arms and carrying her into the bedroom. The late summer evening light dimmed around them as they made love and slept. As she drifted off, the tastes of spiced chocolate and fiery passion lingered in her mind. Her love deepened for this man as he whisked her away from dark forests to a world filled with heat and passion. Those feelings filled her sleep with peace, and she did not dream.

CHAPTER SIX

The Whistleblower

Chazz greeted Captain Serrano with a cheery smile when he knocked on her office door at JFHQ on Friday morning. Serrano had the intense expression he got when something he did went sideways. Not the usual worried brow, shifting eyes, or nervous hands most officers wore under those circumstances. More like bracing himself for incoming.

Chazz shifted in her chair to make herself comfortable, smiled as warmly as she could, and said, "Good morning, Carlos. Thank God it's Friday. What's up? And don't worry, whatever it is, we'll deal with it together."

Serrano's face reflected his relief at her support and said, "My friend at Roberts called me this morning, ma'am. Early."

"How early?" She looked at the wall clock: it was 0815.

"0300, ma'am. He was worried."

"Worried. About what, the tanks?"

"Yes. No. More. There's a shitstorm at the base. At Roberts. The leak made command hit the roof."

"Why? They've told us it was a planned exercise."

"That's why my friend is worried. It's bullshit. There's no exercise."

"How does your friend know this?"

"He works in Colonel Brickhouse's office, ma'am. He'd have seen the orders for any exercise or for moving tanks off the base. No orders, ma'am. No secret memos or classified material. Only tanks moving. There were no orders for the troops involved, either. Tanks, HETs. Even the fuel trucks are gone."

"Who made this happen?"

"The base commander, ma'am, Colonel Brickhouse. And…" The Captain hesitated. "My friend overheard him complaining to Lieutenant Flattery about the leak after the Teams meeting with us. But, ma'am…." Serrano hesitated, unsure about what he would say. The bracing look returned.

"Go on, Carlos. What else?" Chazz braced for impact herself. Whatever Serrano was about to say, she was aware she wouldn't like it.

"Governor Sanchez, ma'am." Chazz at first thought she'd misheard, then her heart sank. This must be why he had feared her reaction. Calm response required.

"The governor? What about the governor?" She kept her tone to asking a question, not demanding a justification.

Serrano cleared his throat and said, "The governor contacted Colonel Brickhouse the day prior to the tanks vanishing. My friend heard nothing more about the call, ma'am. But it wasn't a social call."

Chazz took this in. The clock on the wall ticked in the silence. She slowly said, "You're saying the tanks deployed on Governor Sanchez's orders? Is that what you're saying, Carlos?"

"My friend thinks so, ma'am. That's why he called me so early. He's worried something is wrong." Serrano locked eyes with Chazz. "And he's afraid that if anyone finds out he's the leaker, he'll be court-martialed. I didn't have a clue what to tell him, ma'am."

Chain of command. A knot formed in Chazz's stomach. This was serious. "Who is this officer, Carlos?"

Serrano licked his lips and frowned. "Lieutenant Sellars, ma'am. Joseph Sellars. We call him Joey." Serrano's voice conveyed a familiarity beyond military camaraderie.

"We?"

"Friend of the family, ma'am. We grew up together."

"He's got something to worry about, Captain. The chain of command. Sellars is leaking information about his commanding officer. To you, not through an official whistleblower complaint." She shook her head with regret. "A formal complaint wouldn't change much. If Brickhouse finds out Joey's the leaker, he'll read him the riot act. Joey is about to get a taste of the military's unwritten rules."

"Can you help him somehow, ma'am?"

She said reluctantly, "I'll think about it, Carlos." Her interference would just make it worse for Sellars.

"He's really worried, ma'am. Not just about himself, about the tanks and the lies."

Chazz was not worried something was wrong. No, she was *sure* something was wrong. She knew exactly who to call to find out what it was. Sellars's problems paled in comparison to hers. The governor? The knot in her stomach tied itself a little tighter.

Chazz closed her door, the soft click punctuating her need for secrecy. She kept her voice low when her lover answered.

"Chazz? Hey, gorgeous. Couldn't wait to hear my voice after last night? Chazz. I can't remember a better time for me. You—"

"Shut up a minute, Tom. This isn't about last night."

"OK, Colonel Direct."

Great. She'd offended him, right off the bat. She hunched over her phone. The knot in her stomach was still tight with tension. It leaked into her voice. "And don't take offense. This is serious." Chazz shifted in her chair and wished this wasn't happening. "Are you ready to listen?"

"OK, OK. Go ahead."

"Tom, something's come up that bothers me. About your boss."

"What about him?"

"He's ordered the Guard to take up positions around Sacramento. In tanks. No announcements, no press releases. He may plan to take some kind of illegal action."

Tom, taken aback, responded, "Whoa there, cowboy. What makes you think that?"

"I've seen the tanks. I have information that they're deploying on his orders. There's nothing written. You told me last night he's fed up with, well, the Feds. Is he planning to use military force against protestors or anyone else who gets in his way?" She had a hard time believing what she was saying. How would Tom react?

Silence on the line. A few seconds passed and Tom said, "Chazz, if you see something wrong, you need to talk to *your* boss. But honestly, I can't see anything good coming out of this. You're not—you wouldn't tell him I told you about this stuff, are you? Dupont, I mean?"

"No, Tom." She squeezed her eyes shut, then opened them. This wasn't the "Oh, gee, you're right, Chazz!" response she'd expected. The walls of her office suddenly seemed to close in on her. She swallowed and said, "I'll deal with it here without naming you."

"Thanks, Chazz." The relief in his voice made her wince. Just how involved in the governor's plans was he?

Too much tension. She said reassuringly, "Everything will be fine, Tom. And…I love you." She hoped that would diffuse the strain between them and bring back a sense of normalcy. It fell flat.

With no joy, Tom said, "Yeah, me too. Look, gotta go."

Chazz hung up and stared at the wall clock. 9 a.m. and the day was already heading south.

Military whistleblowing history was not pretty, especially if the hero was a woman.

Chazz's military career had ingrained in her the chain of command. She had never gone outside her chain of command. Not once. Even for the rape. Easier to bury the pain and maintain the status quo. The chain of command to her meant discipline, responsibility, support, and certainty. It was the backbone of her job.

Deep down, she dreaded confronting General Dupont, evident in her hesitance to blow the whistle. After all, he had brushed off her concerns and disregarded her proposals for addressing the discipline issues at Roberts. But, she reminded herself, the chain of command. He was her commanding officer.

She had to give him a chance to respond. The phone wasn't right for something like this. Three things required in-person confrontation: breaking up with someone, firing someone, and telling someone something they didn't want to hear. She arose, determined, and briskly walked down the hall to General Dupont's office, her footsteps echoing on the linoleum floor. Her rap on the door echoed in the corridor.

"General? Can we talk?"

"Sure, Colonel. Have a seat."

She sensed no anxiety in the man. But her boss was never anxious. She sat and considered how to proceed. The silence grew uncomfortable.

"All right, Colonel. What's the problem?"

"The governor, sir."

General Dupont blinked and sat back in his chair. "The who, now?"

"Governor Sanchez, sir. He's ordered those tanks into the streets. Outside the chain of command, sir. He's planning to do something drastic."

"Camp Roberts has assured me—"

"I have new intelligence, sir, from people at Roberts." Chazz spoke with more urgency that she normally used. "There was no exercise, that's just a story somebody invented. It's a coverup. The governor is central to it all."

"Colonel, that's quite an accusation. How good is your information?" His skeptical eyes regarded her.

"It's good intelligence, sir. I've seen the tanks with my own eyes. I trust the people who informed me and have no reason to doubt them. Say 75% sure." Chazz leaned forward, eyes locked on her boss's. "Let me investigate, sir, as I proposed yesterday. I can nail this down. Just me, no others involved, no serious cost to the Guard. It's too important to ignore, sir."

"Chazz…." The General was shaking his head.

"What can I do to persuade you, sir? Let's visit the tanks, sir. Confront them yourself. They won't be able to ignore you. You're their ultimate commander. Sir, you—"

"Colonel, stop. Just stop." The General sat and looked at her in silence for a minute. "I'll take this to TAG, Colonel. No other choice. He won't like it. I don't like it. The governor sure as hell won't like it. You're going to persist with this?"

Chazz realized she'd reached a point from which there was no coming back. The chain of command stretched tight, her commanding officer's exasperation clear. But her oath gave her little choice. She burned the bridge. "I'll take it to the feds, sir, unless you do something. DoD, DoJ. I'll have to. It's my oath."

Dupont's face softened into resignation, but he had conditions. "Fine. I understand. All right, Colonel. I'll take it up with TAG, and we'll investigate. And, Colonel, now that you've passed on the responsibility, stand down. Back to your job. Keep your distance until we understand the situation. That, Colonel, is a direct order. Do you understand?"

"Yes, sir."

The chain of command had survived intact. As she walked back to her office, Chazz wondered why she was not relieved to have passed on the responsibility. A fine thing: your commander might order you to stand down, but you couldn't order your own brain to do that. Only the exceptionally lucky had a brain that adhered to a chain of command. At the least, she knew she could handle an excessively active brain while she did her job. She'd done that for years.

CHAPTER SEVEN
Marching Orders

Tom Peña frowned after General Dupont's call. The general had been blunt: Tom needed to control Chip's exuberance if their operation was to stand any chance at success. Trouble was, he was clueless about how to do that. Suggesting strategic plans was one thing, but Chip didn't respond well to restraint. To Dupont, this was crucial, and he wouldn't tolerate it for long. He was too by-the-book. Time was running out. Tom stared out of his ground-floor window at the enormous park, and the trees told him nothing at all.

His desk phone rang, jolting him from his thoughts. He picked up the receiver, and a familiar voice said, "Sally here, Tom. He wants to see you."

"OK, be right there." Whatever the governor wanted, this was Tom's opportunity to rein him in.

He slipped his mobile phone into his jacket pocket, loosened his tie to show he was working hard, and took the elevator up to the governor's office.

Sally Reed, the governor's private secretary, greeted him with a warm smile, eyes crinkling. A graying brunette in her early fifties, Sally exuded confidence, friendliness, and competence. Tom speculated again on why she had hitched her star to a loser like Sanchez. Oh, right—the people of the great state of California had elected him governor. But she was not aware of The Plan. He smiled.

"Go right in, Tom," she said, waving at the door to the inner sanctum.

Chip told Tom to sit and closed the door. Tom settled into the comfortable chair, while the governor walked over to the big window and stared out, hands in his pockets. Tom recognized his deal-with-a-problem stance. Chip said, "Tom, Myron's got his knickers in a twist about the tanks."

"I heard, sir." Tom nodded.

The governor turned and cocked his head. Here came the deal-with-it part. "He says we need to move things up. Any problems with that?"

"Are you asking me or telling me?" Tom smiled.

The horsey laugh rang out. "Telling. But we got a serious problem. Besides Myron and the tanks, I mean."

"What's that, sir?"

"This lady colonel who works for Myron. She saw the tanks and raised a stink. Let's find a way to handle her, too."

"Uh. Sir."

Chip's face lengthened as he perceived the consternation in Tom's voice. The governor wasn't impervious to body language or tone of voice. But money and votes were the only things he cared about. Or roadblocks. Was Chazz going to be a roadblock?

"What?" Chip asked, raising his eyebrows.

"I'm seeing her."

Chip stared at him, perplexed. "Who?"

"Colonel Silver. She's my, well, my girlfriend." This wouldn't help with Chip's exuberance.

"Oh, Jesus Christ." Chip shook his head in disbelief. He took a few steps toward Tom and threw up his hands. "Why the hell date *her*, Tom? Why her? Good God, aren't there enough gorgeous young Latinas running around for you to fuck?"

"We clicked." Tom kept his voice even. No point in escalating this conversation, which was already heading downhill fast. He crossed his legs and leaned back in the chair.

"Well, goddamn it, un-click. Dump her." Sanchez shook his head again. "No, wait. What did she tell you?"

"About…?"

"The tanks. Or what she thinks. About us."

"She doesn't want to talk about tanks. Despite my glowing recommendation, she thinks you're an idiot. She thinks the world of Dupont but wishes he'd be more direct when he tells her things."

"Right about that last one, anyway. The guy's a shuffler. OK, Tom. Don't dump her yet. We can use her." Now the governor paced back and forth in front of the window. "You just have to distract her. You can do that, right, Tom? I bet you've been doing it for a while. What's she like in bed?"

"None of your business. Sir."

The horsey laugh rang out again, echoing off the walls of the room. "Damn right it's not. I have my own problems. Angélica is *so* damn pissed off at me." He paced. "Anyway, distract the hell out of her, Tom. She could ruin this whole thing. Set us back months. Distract her."

"I can do that, sir." But could he? And how? Chazz was not a person you could easily distract. She'd only support the coup if it succeeded, and maybe not even then. Duty was everything to her.

Chip grinned. "And while you're distracting her, try some pillow talk. Get her perspective on what's up with Dupont. I don't trust him."

Tom uncrossed his legs. This had gone far enough. "She's not in a position to know anything about Dupont's worries about the coup."

"I bet she knows things just from working for Dupont, even if she doesn't understand what it all means. Find out, Tom. Get her in a position to know, then tell me all about it. OK?" Chip's eyes sparkled with suggestive humor. Despite himself, Tom's mind went to the passionate night he'd just spent with Chazz. This was no good. Tom sighed.

Chip was in a decisive mood. Time to let it go. "All right, sir," Tom said.

"Now, we gotta move things up. I'll need your plan for how to set up the Emergency Broadcast thingy right away. And the speech announcing independence. It's gonna be tricky, Tom."

Tom shifted into strategy-building mode. "Yes, sir. The trick to a coup is to appear clear and decisive, no waffling. Once you declare the state independent, it's a matter of asserting it and making that fact as real as possible."

Chip smiled happily. "Oh, it'll be real. Everyone hates the feds now, Tom. They'll be celebrating in the streets once we're the California Republic. Even those racist Valley bastards will do the dance."

"How is General Dupont's part of the plan going?" Tom knew perfectly well, having spoken to the man a few minutes earlier. But he wanted to learn what parts of the truth had made it into his boss's limited understanding of reality.

Chip walked back to the window and said, "He's pissed off about the changes, but he's got everything lined up. He tells me he's got enough troops on board to handle things. He'll stand down the rest or sideline them with busy work."

"What about the federal troops?"

Chip walked over and sat on the couch facing Tom. He folded his hands around a knee and started his lecture. "Dupont tells me that our dynamic president is pulling troops and ships out of California as fast as he can. The son of a bitch hates our guts and wants to screw us in every way possible. He's even telling the military that's still here to ignore everything we do. So they will, and then it will be too late." A chuckle. "We make 'em all an offer they can't refuse, double their salaries and deport the ones who turn it down, or just shoot 'em. Take the ships and planes and stuff. The president wouldn't dare start a war against us, given the widespread support for the new country. And like you suggested, we'll offer to hand over the nukes. Like Ukraine did, back in the day, the stupid bastards. Then renege, of course. That'll put the president on the right track. No boots on the ground. He won't be able to do anything about it in time. Great idea, Tom."

"I hope you're right, sir."

The governor leaned forward and jabbed a finger at Tom. "Tom, you know I'm right, and I want plans in place to *make* me right. Got it?"

"Yes, sir. Got it." Top of the list: distract Chazz. He knew exactly what to do.

Chazz had arrived at work early. Since she was coming from Tom's condo, her usual hour-long commute had shortened to a few minutes. As a result, she had parked near the JFHQ building instead of the usual faraway parking slot.

At 1100 came the red roses, twelve of them, in a glass vase. The delivery guy walked through the whole damn department office to deliver them. Chazz was certain her face was the same shade as the roses. But Tom's effort was heartfelt, and she gave him credit for it. It *had* been a magical night.

After a hard morning of ignoring thoughts of tanks and now roses, she was more than ready for a solitary lunch out. She strode out of the building to find the parking lot baking in the scorching midday sun. She had unwittingly parked her car in a spot that allowed the sun to assault her driver's seat and steering wheel, unshaded.

She stood, summoning the will to sit and fry her butt, when a voice sounded behind her.

"Chazz, can we talk?"

Her lover's voice and the memory of the night before brought a smile to her face. A tight embrace and a passionate kiss followed.

Breaking free from the embrace, Chazz said with a smile, "What brings you here?"

"Chazz, I've been thinking." His face was serious. Her smile faded.

"This can't be good," she said, forcing out the humor. "You thinking. Are we breaking up?"

"No, Colonel Direct, we're not breaking up. I want to marry you."

She blinked and waited a few beats for the punch line. It never came. He just stood there with a silly smile on his lips and a look in his eyes she'd never seen before.

"OK, you're serious. That was it? The proposal?"

"Yeah. Didn't have time to get a ring. Stupid custom anyway. We're too old for that shit."

The heat from the car warmed her as she stood with the door open, his words settling more deeply into her consciousness. He abruptly stretched his arms toward her to gather her in, and she went back into her dark forest. She regained control, but too late. He was standing back, looking wounded, his left hand rubbing the spot on his jaw where she'd slapped him.

"Oh, Tom, I'm so sorry! I just—"

"What the hell, Chazz. All you had to do was say 'yes' or 'no.'"

"How about maybe? But not now. Not now, Tom."

"Can I ask why, or will you shoot me?"

"I can't…" She shook her head in dismay. "Tom, you're moving so fast. I can't process it, standing here. Give me some space. I asked you, before. Remember? Space."

"Take all the space you need, Colonel." He stopped rubbing his jaw and smiled, visibly shedding his involuntary angry reaction. "Take it, Chazz. I'm sorry it was so sudden. I just, well, I had marching orders. The right thing at the right time. Or so I assumed. I'm sorry I did it so badly."

"We need to talk about this." She considered her busy afternoon schedule and said, "We could have lunch. Not," she said, "The Blind Pig. Some casual, neutral place. You pick."

"How about that diner around the corner? That's neutral enough." He made his voice cheerful, but his eyes told the story of his disappointment.

"Yes, Tom. Great," she said with forced enthusiasm. "I'll meet you there." The words hung for a moment in the air between them. Then she turned toward her car, dismissing him. No more passionate embraces today. Her hand resting on top of the open door, she watched him drive away. Marriage. How was she going to explain it to him? Explain the slap? She'd have to tell him everything. Every little detail. Everything she never wanted to even think about ever again.

She got into her car and yelped as the hot seat fried her ass.

* * *

The Wolfe's Door diner's proximity to JFHQ and its name both came from the retired Guard sergeant major who ran it. Sergeant Wolfe assumed that loyalty and rank would get him all the lunch business from JFHQ, but it didn't. Most of his customers came from nearby government offices, Corrections bureaucrats with a few Sewer District people scattered among them. The few Guard soldiers who patronized the diner were all old buddies of Sergeant Wolfe. None were officers.

Except Chazz. This was Tom's choice of neutral ground. Chazz knew the sergeant major by sight but had never spoken to him. He had retired to his diner the year before Chazz became chief of staff. Dressed in OCPs, she stood out in the small diner. Sergeant Wolfe nodded at her, but the man had a stone face. His diner smelled of ancient grease and old coffee, and the diner itself appeared to predate the sergeant major by many years.

Tom waved at her from a booth at the very back of the diner. She assumed that was his notion of a private place where they could hash out anything from a prenup to a restraining order. Privacy seemed a distant dream in the Wolfe's Door. But she didn't care about privacy. She just had to resolve the situation with Tom.

His face lit up when he saw her. She couldn't help but smile back, even though she was about to break his heart. Her biggest problem at this point was her behavior in the parking lot, when he had surprised her. The Slap. He would want an explanation. She could apologize and move on, but would he accept that? She wouldn't, in his place.

Chazz slid into the booth on the other side of the table. She felt the rough edge of the cracked red vinyl as she slid into the middle of the bench. Tom reached out; she took his hand, and he brought it up to his mouth and kissed it. She smiled and pulled away gently. Despite everything, it was going well.

Wearing a white apron spotted with unidentifiable stains, the sergeant major set glasses of water in front of them. He pointed to the menus in a small holder on the table with a thick finger. She obeyed orders and pulled the thing out and looked at it. The usual sandwiches, bacon cheeseburgers, and a few gourmet items like meatloaf. Bet the sergeant major made a mean meatloaf. She looked up at the man.

"I'll have a turkey sandwich, no onions," she said. She imagined freshly baked bread with butter-roasted turkey breast, hand-made mayonnaise, and Dijon mustard. Might as well get her fantasies out of the way.

"We don't put onions on anything here," the sergeant major replied helpfully.

"No problemo," said Chazz. "And a Coke, please." She looked at Tom.

"Same for me, but no Coke. And no onions." Tom grinned.

"I just said—"

"Sorry, bad joke. It's fine." A snicker came from the next booth. Privacy, indeed.

The sergeant let out a low growl and walked away.

"Racist bastard," Tom muttered.

"Tom! Be nice."

"I'll always be nice to you, Chazz." He held out his hand again, but this time she didn't take it.

She said, "I need to explain the slap, Tom."

"No, no, no. You don't, Chazz. You do not have to explain anything. It was me. I'm sorry."

"But it wasn't you. And I—"

"Let's start over, beautiful. Did you get the flowers?"

"Yes. Yes, I did, Tom. They're lovely, but…." She had no words. A senior colonel sitting at her desk wondering and fearing what everyone else in the office thought about the huge floral arrangement deposited on that desk after passing through all the cubes.

"Too much? You love roses. I wanted to prove I loved you. After last night."

"You don't have to prove anything, Tom."

"I'll prove it again tonight if you'll come over to my place."

"Tom," she remonstrated, smiling.

"Here's your Coke," said the sergeant, setting down a can.

"Thanks," said Chazz, and the sergeant abandoned them. "Tom, we need to talk about…your proposal."

Tom's voice was low and steady. "Only if you want to, Chazz. It stands. I love you. I want you to be my wife. Forever."

She parried, "You don't know me."

"I know you, Chazz. I learned all about you the first time we made love."

"You don't know me, Tom," she repeated. The pressure was building again. She could feel it in her stomach. The trees were growing there. She couldn't afford to go dissociative on him right now. This had to be gentle and firm and normal. Normal. She cracked the Coke can and drank. It was warm, the carbon dioxide exploding in her throat. She coughed, but the distraction relieved the pressure.

Tom said, "Tell me, Chazz. Tell me what more I need to learn. I can handle it."

"Tom, why do you want to get married? Why now, all of a sudden? We're going along just fine."

His eyes fell to the table, and he took a sip of water. He looked up at her and said, "I've wanted to marry you since the first time we made love, Chazz. I just haven't had the guts—"

"Here you go," the sergeant said, pushing a plate in front of Chazz, then another in front of Tom. They stared down at the white bread and flaccid white turkey peeking out from under a leaf of greenish-white iceberg lettuce. Tom opened and closed his mouth in silence.

Chazz carefully removed the little white plastic spear that held the thing together, picked it up, and took a bite. No onions, and nothing much else besides the lettuce and a tiny amount of mayo and a slice of processed lunch meat. Utterly tasteless.

"Wow." Tom, restored to fluency by her bold move on the food, examined his own sandwich carefully.

The sergeant asked, "Anything else, folks?"

"No. No thanks, we're set," Chazz said around the gummy mouthful she'd taken.

"Enjoy," said the smiling sergeant as he walked away.

"You were speaking of guts, Tom."

"Yeah. Well. OK. Look, Chazz. Why I want to marry you? You're you, that's why. I want to be with you for the rest of my life, to sleep with you every night. I want to have children with you."

"Tom, that ship has sailed." She bit off some more sandwich.

"OK, sorry, got carried away."

"You do not appear to be thinking clearly right now. Eat your turkey."

"I can't eat this."

"Have some hot sauce," Chazz said, handing him the bottle of Tabasco from the small wire rack at the side of the table. "That will help."

He grimaced and took the bottle, unscrewed the cap, and shook drops of Tabasco onto his sandwich.

"Tom, you put it in the sandwich, not on the bread."

"What the hell does it matter where I put it?" She wasn't quite sure if he was scorning her interrupting his romantic advances or laughing at her practical approach to life. Which, of course, was her best effort to derail the conversation so she could gather her resources.

She bit the bullet. "I can't marry you. At least, not now."

He leaned back against the booth. "Is that final?"

"For now, yes."

"You're being awfully solemn about it."

"Just…direct, Tom. Like you said. I just can't. It's not in me to marry anyone right now." And suddenly she knew with certainty that she could not, would not, explain why. Not to Tom. She couldn't do it.

"Is it the Guard? Your job? What if you quit? I have lots of money, Chazz, a great job, a great future, I can support you, or you can find a less stressful—"

She swallowed the gummy blob that had prevented her from interrupting.

"Tom, stop. Stop right there. Yeah, sure, it's the Guard. That's my life, Tom. That's who I am. Maybe I'll retire soon, and then I can think about marriage. Not yet. So, just stop. OK?"

"Do you love me?"

"Yes, I love you."

"Do you, though? And can we go on making love and being lovers and loving each other? Without marriage?" His hand had formed a tight fist on the table, squeezing the bottle of Tabasco.

"Probably."

"Probably? How do you feel, Chazz?"

She smiled. "You're pushing too hard, Tom. Let's just go with it and see what happens, OK? Is that enough for you?"

"For now, I guess. As long as you love me." He looked at his watch. "Jeez, I got to get back. Look, Chazz, let's get together tomorrow at my place. Would that be good for you?"

"I guess so."

"OK. I'll call you."

"Fine. But no more flowers. OK?"

Tom carefully screwed the cap back on the Tabasco bottle, placed it in the rack, and slid out of the booth. He leaned down and kissed her on the lips, holding the back of her head under her bun. He put a ten on the table and moved fast to the diner door and out.

"Everything OK here?" the sergeant asked, coming over with a coffee pot.

"Sure."

"He didn't like his sandwich? What's that red stuff?"

"Blood."

"What?"

"Joke. Tabasco. I don't think he was hungry." She finished the last of her sandwich and washed it down with the last of her warm Coke. Mission accomplished. "Check, please."

"Is he in, Sally?" Tom said.

"I'll check to see if he's available, Tom," Sally replied, smiling at the big man. She pressed a button and murmured into her headset. She looked up at him and grinned. "Go on in, Tom. He's in a good mood today."

"Yeah, I'll bet."

"You two are hatching something, aren't you?" She grinned. "Some legislative coup?"

Tom looked at her, startled, then realized she was using the word as a metaphor. "Yeah, Sally, we got something good cooking that will fix those bastards in the Legislature."

"Now, Tom, you're talking like Chip."

"Must be catching," he smiled.

"Where the hell is he?" The roar came through the closed door.

Tom walked past the grinning Sally into the inner chamber. There was his boss, putting on the silly little green rug with the cup at the end. The ball rolled into the cup.

"How the hell can you stand that game, boss?"

"Gotta deal with *los gringos,* Tom. They don't know how to play *pitz,* and they think this idiot game is a great way to talk business without being overheard. So I'm practicing."

Pitz was the Mayan word for the ancient hip-ball game played in the courts of the Aztecs and Mayans. Full of war symbolism and bloody gods. Tom smiled. Chip was definitely in a good mood.

"Reporting back, sir. I proposed."

"Proposed what?" The governor rolled another ball in place with his foot and adjusted his putter.

"Marriage."

"Oh, for Christ's sake." The governor looked at him, exasperated. He had avoided marriage so far in his career, saying that most of his predecessors had divorced and he wanted to short-circuit that tangle. Instead, he played around with several girlfriends, which the media loved.

"You said distract her," challenged Tom.

"Yeah, but marriage?" He got a pensive look in his eye, which was both rare and not a good sign. "You think Angélica would go for that? Is she that dumb?" He shook his head and addressed himself to his ball. He putted.

Tom played his losing card. "But she turned me down."

"Damn. Lucky son-of-a-bitch!" Sanchez smirked. "OK, so that ploy failed. What's your next move? We gotta do something about this woman." He cocked his head at Tom, lips quirked. "*Now,* Tom. Before she does something really unreasonable, and we have to deal with her the hard way." He rolled another ball into place and looked over at Tom again. "And if we do that, Tom, you're history. Out of a job. And minus a girlfriend."

Tom gritted his teeth. "Chip. Are you threatening to kill my girlfriend?"

Startled, the governor straightened up from his putting stance. "No, no, of course not, Tom. Just to fire her, transfer her to the Mojave, or something like that. End her career."

"Be careful, Chip. This is my future wife you're screwing around with." Tom at once wished this metaphor unsaid, given the governor's propensity for bad sex jokes. But this time, the man restrained himself.

"OK, Tom, OK, get a grip. Everything will be fine. You only need to do your part."

"I'll keep her busy, like you said. She loves me."

"Sure she does. Who wouldn't?"

Tom rethought his options and decided on a new approach. Direct action.

"Sir, I need a vacation."

"What the hell?"

"Say a week. That ought to do it. You don't need me here during the operation. And you sure as hell don't need Chazz here."

"Vacation where?"

"A little beach in México. North of Manzanillo on the Costalegre. With no cell service or Internet. Right?"

"*Excelente,* my boy, *excelente.* Yeah, a week ought to do it. She's hot. A week on a beach in the sun, she'll even be hot enough to marry you." He resumed his practice, again putting the ball into the cup.

"We were planning to start the coup two weeks from now. It's Friday today. I can get all the planning done by tomorrow, and I can keep her busy for a week in the sun. You and Dupont can surely get the business going by Monday. Can you call Dupont and get him to give her the time off?"

Sanchez walked over to his desk, leaned the putter against it, and made the call.

CHAPTER EIGHT
The Vacation

As Chazz crept up the I-5 connector on her way home, her eyes took in the tanks still positioned under the freeway. So no conclusion to the phantom exercise. Between that discovery, the heat of the day, and a pileup on I-5, she was stewing by the time she got home. She turned on the air conditioning and poured herself a glass of chilled water. She went out to the patio and rested on a shaded lawn chair, waiting for the house to cool down, but the simmering discontent persisted.

Ten minutes later, still angry, she heard her phone ringing on the kitchen counter where she'd left it. She went into the house and picked up the phone. Tom.

"Hello, Tom. I didn't expect you to call until tomorrow."

"Yeah, I couldn't wait. I have an idea, Chazz. Why don't we both take a break and go on a beach vacation like we talked about the other day? I'm ready for a great time on a quiet beach."

"I don't know, Tom...." With the marriage proposal still fresh in her mind, she was reluctant to commit herself to a week away with him. Too awkward right now. With the tanks still squatting under the freeway.

"Chazz, there's this beach. It's on the Costalegre, north of Manzanillo, on the Pacific coast. It's near where my family's from, Chazz, and I still have relatives down there. They have this cute little cabin that's all by itself on the beach. Imagine this picture. Beautiful sand, warm ocean. No sharks, no cell phones, no Internet, no people, and endless sky and ocean. And if you want people, meet some of my family. They'll welcome you with open arms. You can see more of who I am. A week on the Costalegre and you'll lose all your stress. Take my word."

"Tom, I've got things going on at work, urgent things. I can't just drop everything and go to the beach for a week."

"Sure you can. You must have some good people working for you who can pick up the slack. You need a break, Chazz, and you deserve one. So do I. You need to feel the sun's warmth on your face and the ocean breezes. And we need to get to know each other better, to understand where we're going. Think of it as a meditation retreat."

"Sure, Tom. Meditation. Right."

"OK, so there'll be some loving involved. Or not. Totally up to you."

Chazz sighed. "It sounds heavenly, Tom, but I just can't—"

"Please think about it, Chazz. Overnight. Ask Dupont for time off. I'm sure he'll give it to you."

The last beach she'd spent much time on was a fake beach next to a fake lake on an estate built for one of Sadaam's dead sons. She had not enjoyed it. Too many ghosts and a stifling 105 degrees among a crowd of rowdy Army buddies.

She vacillated. "I'll think about it, Tom. Overnight. I'll call you tomorrow, all right?"

By the time she'd put the phone back on the counter, she knew she wasn't going to the beach. The house was cool enough now to inhabit, so she put a mac-and-cheese dinner in the microwave, zapped it up, and devoured it. Then she sat on her couch and tried to read, but all she could think about was a white beach, a sun-kissed body, and infinite sea and sky. Damn the man.

Chazz's decision held firm when she got to work Monday morning. But Captain Serrano stood at her locked office door, waiting patiently. She unlocked her door, waved Serrano to a seat, and said, "I need coffee. You want some?" Serrano shook his head. Chazz wasted no time getting back to her office from the coffee machine. She closed the door, shutting out the morning office chatter, then scalded her tongue on the hot coffee.

"Well, Carlos?" she asked, pushing the coffee away to cool. Serrano did not appear to have good news for her.

"No, ma'am. Not well."

"Another 3 a.m. call?"

"2 a.m., ma'am. He's frantic. Something terrible is going on, and he can't get any information about it. They're keeping him out of the loop. He says the base commander keeps sending him off to check on distant storage facilities so he's out of the way. They must suspect he's the leak, ma'am."

"What the hell are they hiding?"

"My friend says more troops have left the base without orders. In armored vehicles, too. Bradleys. My friend tried to ask casually about what was going on, and that's when they started sidelining him. Ma'am, is there anything you can do for him? He might be in danger down there." Serrano's voice had taken on a note of urgency.

"In danger at a Guard camp." She sighed. "Sure, Carlos. I'll have him detached from Roberts for a special assignment in my office. You draw up the orders and we'll have them executed and transmitted right away."

"Thanks, ma'am." Captain Serrano headed off to his task.

Chazz picked up the desk phone and called Camp Roberts. Colonel Brickhouse was unavailable. Lieutenant Flattery was with him. They were in meetings all day, important ones that wouldn't allow a callback before next week. Unless she had a critical problem?

Since the critical problem was her own lack of knowledge about what was going on, she couldn't get past those roadblocks. But she knew someone who could. Up the chain of command.

General Dupont, the next link in Chazz's chain of command, raised a restraining hand. "Before you say anything, Colonel, Roberts has satisfied me those tanks will move by Monday."

"Yes sir," Chazz acknowledged. "Have you briefed TAG on the situation, sir?"

"Not yet. I only spoke to Roberts command an hour ago."

"Sir, there's more going on now."

"What now, Chazz?" The general sounded weary and looked at her with a glum expression.

"Troops are leaving Camp Roberts in Bradley fighting vehicles, sir. Without formal orders. No one is answering the phone, either. They're 'in meetings' or some such bullshit."

"Let's keep this civil, Colonel. These are Guard officers you're disparaging," the General said.

"Yes, sir, sorry, sir. But—"

"You say Bradleys? How many troops?"

"I can't get any information on that. Sir, we need boots on the ground down there. I can be there in three hours, or an hour, if you give me a chopper from Mather. I can fly it myself. All I need is the orders to investigate, sir."

"I don't see the emergency, Colonel. You're blowing this thing all out of proportion. Roberts command assures me—"

"They're lying, sir. They're deploying the tanks and troops without orders. I don't know what the governor's up to—"

"The governor again?" Dupont was skeptical.

"The governor, sir. My source is certain all of this—the tanks, the troops, the Bradleys—is all based on verbal orders from the governor. And other sources think—"

"Who is giving you this information, Colonel?"

"Captain Serrano, on my staff, is talking to a friend in the commander's office at Roberts, sir. He sees all the orders going out. There are no exercises or other orders for any of this."

"Have you talked to this informant?"

Chazz felt the thin ice under her crackle. "No sir, I didn't, but Captain Serrano—"

"But you didn't talk to his friend. Who, I may say, does not seem very reliable as a trusted officer." The General paused, then asked, "He is an officer?"

"I...I'd prefer not to reveal his rank, sir."

"Not good enough, Colonel," said General Dupont. "I would have expected more from you."

The General leaned back in his chair and cocked his head. He continued, "Is everything OK at home, Chazz?"

"Sir?"

"No family problems or other stresses? Does all this come from the ordinary things you do in your job?"

"No, sir." Now she was getting hot. Next thing he'd be talking about PMS, and she'd probably be looking for a gun. She tried to calm her response. "No, sir, it's not. This is real, sir, not just some little girl's fantasy I'm making up for the fun of it." Despite her best efforts, her voice trembled a little.

"Well, from an impartial, outside observer's perspective, Colonel, you don't make much sense. Do you have anyone you can talk to about things?"

"You, sir. That's what I'm doing right now, right here, talking—"

"I mean emotional things, Chazz. How you're feeling, your personal stresses. You could talk to the Command Chaplain."

"Sir, I do not need counseling. I need to investigate missing tanks. And I need to do it now, because there's something—"

The general cut her off. "Look, Colonel. I've done everything I can on this. Let's say something is going on. You're too involved now to be objective about it. I can hear the emotion in your voice. Let's compromise. I'll call the FBI in Los Angeles, tell them your concerns, let them investigate, hear what they have to say. They're in charge of criminal investigations at Roberts. We can go from there. All right? You'll have to give them your sources."

"I think it's too urgent to delay, sir."

"That's all I can offer, Colonel. Work with me on this."

This was going nowhere. Why was the man so stubborn? But it was clear he wasn't going to budge, so she had to take action on her own. She said, "Sir, may I request a leave, say for a week? A friend has suggested a nice beach in Mexico. I'd rather be here, doing my job, but if the best you can do is the FBI, then so be it. Captain Serrano can help with the FBI's investigation. But I have to get away for a while. I've accrued at least 45 days, sir."

"Granted, Colonel. Take two weeks. I'll put in the authorization right away. Start your leave tomorrow. Dismissed."

Chazz stood and marched out of her boss's office without looking back.

Chazz stiffly entered her office and closed the door. She picked her cell phone up and called Tom.

"Chazz, it's great to talk to you! Are we on for that awesome beach?" He was in a jovial mood now. Too bad.

"No, Tom, I can't do it." Her face was grim as she delivered the bad news. "There's something very wrong here, and I have to figure it out. I'll do it on my own, talk to some people, pin things down, and put a stop to it."

"Chazz. Have you lost your mind? Did Dupont approve this?"

"No, he's beetle blind. He refuses to see what's right in front of him. He's turning it over to the FBI. I've got to go down there, to Roberts, to investigate it myself." Against direct orders and way outside the chain of command. She shook her head at her own obstinacy.

Tom agreed. "Chazz! Honest to God, you're—"

She raised her voice a little. "Tom, I don't need to hear this. I don't. I can't go sit on my butt for a week, as much as I'd like to be with you. Can't do it. This is not happening on my watch."

"What, exactly? What do you think is going to happen?" The intensity in Tom's voice reminded her that Governor Sanchez was his boss.

"The governor plans to use Guard troops to solve some problem he's facing." She grimaced to herself, then said, "Troops and equipment moving without formal orders. That's not what the Guard is for, Tom." She left unsaid her logical conclusion that, if the governor had such a strategy, Tom knew about it. Maybe it was his idea. If so, he was lying to her.

"He's doing nothing of the sort," Tom retorted with some heat.

"What about the tanks? What about the troops?" she demanded.

"Troops?"

"From Camp Roberts, he's brought in more troops in Bradley fighting vehicles."

"Chazz, you're imagining all of this."

She replied coldly, "No, Tom, I'm not. And this conversation is over." Not just lying, but gaslighting.

"Wait, wait, please don't hang up, Chazz. Look, I'm sorry, I didn't mean to upset you. We need to talk about all this, not on the phone. My place, for dinner? I'll make something simple. We can have a glass of wine and talk it all out. Tonight?"

"Not a chance, Tom." A feeble attempt to smooth things over. But she smiled at the thought of a nice glass of wine and not going home to a stifling house. No, no, no. Not with a liar.

He tried again. "OK, how about we meet up at the Tequila Museum, have a drink and talk? Seven o'clock?"

The Tequila Museum was a popular, vibrant bar a block from the Capitol, definitely not neutral ground. But at least it was public. She could use the opportunity to pump Tom for information. Looking closely at her motives, she realized she wanted to use her lie detection skills. She found she couldn't just leave things where they were with Tom. Was he a liar or not?

"All right, Tom. Seven, at the Tequila Museum. We'll talk. And, Tom— I don't imagine things."

CHAPTER NINE
A Military Exercise

General Myron Dupont maneuvered his 2013 Toyota Corolla down 10th Street past the Capitol and into the Capitol Garage. He grimaced as he always did at the Planned Parenthood health center next to the garage entrance. His own stance on abortion came from a longtime faith in a church that condemned the practice. So far, he had made no headway in convincing Chip to ban abortions once they completed their takeover. But not a deal killer. California wasn't there yet, and Chip's politics were always in line with what the voters wanted. But every goddamn time he parked here, there it was. In his face.

He walked back down 10th and up to the side door of the Capitol, went in, and identified himself to the guard. He got to the governor's office just as Tom Peña came out in a rush, almost knocking him down.

"Whoa, whoa, Tom," Myron said with a smile. "We old folks move kinda slow."

"Sorry, General," Tom said. "In a rush. Got a date."

Myron lost his smile. "Are we having a meeting or not? To map things out?"

"Yeah, no, not with me. The Governor's expecting you, of course. Drinks with Chazz. I have to talk her down."

"Jesus Christ, that woman. I thought if I gave her two weeks off, she'd be out of our hair. What's she doing, Tom?"

"You gave her two weeks off?"

"I did. Earlier today. Kinda told her to take it, if you follow me."

"She didn't tell me that. What's she up to?"

"Well." Myron raised his most sardonic smile. "If I don't know, and you don't know, Tom, I'd say we were in a lot of trouble. So is this 'date' an all-night affair, or will you be back?"

"Christ, General, whatever it takes!"

Myron shook his head in resignation. "OK, then get on with it. But I'll need your support for whatever Chip fucks up, OK? Tomorrow. In the cold light of day. Right?"

Tom grinned. "Right, General. You text me the details, and I'll be there tomorrow morning, no matter what. OK?"

"Sure, Tom."

"Oh, and General, he's already into the tequila." Tom grinned again and patted him on the back. Myron winced and sighed as he watched the big man disappear down the hall. Damn civilians. He shook his head disconsolately and went into the governor's office.

"Chip, we've talked about this before. If we're going to plan this thing properly, we have to do it sober."

"I'm sober, Myron. One goddamn shot of tequila ain't enough to get me high."

Myron had his doubts about the truth of this assertion, but given the governor's exuberant personality, he couldn't argue with it. The man always acted like a happy drunk.

"I was talking with Tom outside, in the hall. I'd rather he be here, but he's got more important things to do, I guess."

"*Qué macho!*" the governor chortled.

Myron cleared his throat. "Right. Shall we get on with it?"

He walked over to the table and unrolled the map of Sacramento, weighing it down with the four otherwise unused law books from the shelves. Then he unrolled a smaller map of California next to the Sacramento map. He'd considered getting some toy tanks and a can of those toy soldiers so the governor would have a visual aid to his understanding. But in the end, the tone had to be serious, serious enough to get Chip to focus on the reality of it all. Toy tanks wouldn't help.

Chip joined him, shot of tequila in hand. "OK, Myron, what have you got for me?"

"First, let's be clear about what's really important, Chip. Troops, tanks, all the trappings of power are not important. What's important is that we make everyone think we're running an independent country. We need everybody to wake up the next morning as citizens of the California Republic, not the United States. Right?"

"Why is that the most important thing? I like tanks, Myron."

"I know you do, Chip. See, most folks—military or civilian—are do-nothings. They take it in and roll with it. Faced with people in charge and running things, everyone will fall in line. If we make the new country seem inevitable, it will be."

"OK, but what about the tanks, Myron?"

Myron sighed. "I've stationed the tanks where they'll do the most good, at choke points on the freeways and main roads. Once they're positioned to stop traffic, everything will come to a complete stop. The traffic jams will act as barricades."

"Show me."

"Here, here, here, then the rest scattered across the main roads over there," he pointed toward East Sacramento.

"And the troops?"

"They should arrive sometime tomorrow. I've got them stationed at a construction site at the old Mather Air Force Base and at a closed facility down in Riverside. No one will notice them there."

"How many men?"

"About 100 in each location."

"Jesus Christ, is that all? What the hell are we going to do with 200 soldiers?"

"Whatever we need to, Chip. Look, we're not going to fight a big battle. We need to deal with some speed bumps. Make the new country inevitable. We need a few squads to control things here and there, you know? That's why I wanted this meeting, to identify the 'things.' We haven't really talked about the people."

"You mean the people we need to lock up?"

"Yes, Chip, I mean the people we need to lock up."

"So I should make a list of all my political opponents?"

"No. You should make a list of the people who would be effective at causing us trouble. That's not the list of your political opponents."

"Right. Bunch of wimps." This from a man who got seventeen percent of the vote. He did get more of the vote than his sixty-nine opponents in the recall election. And the recalled governor got eighty percent—to recall him. That guy is not going to give us any trouble.

"So who do you think we should intern, Chip?"

"Highway Patrol leadership, they hate me. 'Cause I slashed their budget. They all have guns. And the Attorney General. She's an attack dog, and you know how tight she is with the homies in LA. And she wants to be president bad." He grinned. "We could send her to Washington to explore her future."

"We should round up all the FBI agents and deport them, too. What about the locals around the state?"

"Mayors. Let's see. Oh. San Diego, what's his name?"

"Garrido."

"Yeah, that's the guy. He supported me but he's been trying to undermine me for months 'cause I wouldn't give him a job."

"He's pretty popular down there. And that's where most of the federal military is right now. OK, add him to the list. And the LA mayor. She's got that town's politics locked up, so let's lock her down."

"Yeah. Funny how these guys are Latinos but don't know what they need to do, huh?"

"Anyone else?"

"Let's see." Chip scanned the map of California. "Frisco is a complete mess. We oughta send troops down there just to clean up the streets for 'em. And the rest of the state is totally feeble."

"Legislature?"

Chip smiled. "We'll cut power to the rooms downstairs. They won't know what to do. They'll spend the whole coup looking for the circuit breakers. Oughta post a squad down there, too, so they don't accidentally get in the way."

"Remind me why we think the California Republic will work as a country, Chip." Myron was testing the governor now. Because if he didn't understand what really made California work, he wasn't fit to lead it.

"Money, Myron. Corporations and finance and tech and resource extraction and agriculture. All we have to do is provide water and maintain the grid, and Californians will go on their merry way. If we get rid of the feds, we can do what we need to do instead of bowing and scraping to the regulatory agencies in Washington. And once we open the borders to our Latino brethren, we'll have all the workers we need to make it all happen. Hey—that's the inevitable part, isn't it?"

Myron smiled. "You bet. How is the bank coming?"

"Fuck knows. Tom's handling that. He keeps muttering about digital currency, and I know he's had some pretty expensive lunches with that banker in Frisco who's gonna be the new central bank president. What about your people, Myron? The Guard."

"I've identified the officers and men who are likely to actively support us, Chip. Unfortunately, my boss, TAG, is not one of them, and we'll have to intern him. There are some gung-ho types in the infantry and military police regiments who might mobilize against us, and that's on my plate. I'll distract them, and if I can't, we'll intern them. I only wish I had two weeks to do it."

"Does that include your Chieftess of Staff?"

"Yes, like *Colonel* Silver." Myron emphasized the rank to counter the governor's obvious disdain for female officers. "She goes on leave tomorrow."

"Are we going to stage battles with loyalist Guard troops?"

Myron smiled. "Chip, the National Guard is mostly paper. We call people up and tell them to come in when we need them. And really, only you and the Adjutant General can do that, with the Joint Operations Center at Mather. We're interning TAG, and I've already sounded out the director of the joint staff. JOC will help us coordinate the operation. In fact, I'll oversee things from there. So..."

"So, not a problem, Myron. That's the locals done. What about the feds? What's preventing the U.S. Army from kicking our asses when they find out what's going on?"

"Well, two things. One, what army? And two, why do you think they're going to find out?"

"OK, explain, Myron."

"One." Myron held up a finger. "The U.S. military has closed just about every base in California in the last thirty years. Not needed in our brave new post-Vietnam world. Right?"

"Right."

"And the current president has moved troops out of the remaining bases, taken ships away from the naval bases, and moved or not replaced aircraft. Right?"

"Right, because he hates us and wants to destroy us. He's cutting funding for infrastructure and social services left and right. Not to mention his taking away our entire labor force by his crappy immigration policies. That son of a bitch is the one big reason to go independent."

"Exactly. OK, two. Who's left? A bunch of careerist hacks in charge of a few disorganized troops. And the hacks report to a political Department of Defense that has told them to ignore everything we do. But, just to be sure, I've 'coordinated' with that department to let them know we're going to conduct a major security exercise. They'll have no idea what's really going on. I'll just push it up to next week. Oh, and I've sent word around that we're going to conduct a major test of the Emergency Broadcast System throughout the state."

The governor smiled. "OK. First thing next Monday morning, then. Move your troops to their targets, position the tanks, and we'll be ready for the EBS announcement of our new government." He finished his tequila and poured another. "Have a drink, Myron! You deserve it."

"Thanks, but I've got dinner with the kids waiting for me. I'll see you bright and early Monday morning, Chip." Myron stood and shook hands with the next president of the California Republic. He hoped like hell that Chip would be sober by Monday.

Chip Sanchez, seated in his comfortable office chair, half-way through his third double tequila, needed to talk. He'd talked himself stupid with Myron, but he couldn't say what he really wanted to say about how good he felt.

Chip picked up his mobile phone and pressed on the contact with the naked picture of his girlfriend, Angélica. Every time he made a call, he got a hard on.

"Hi, Angel! It's me."

"Who's calling, please?"

Which was bullshit because she had caller id like everybody else. Still pissed off 'cause he'd hung up on her.

"Don't be like that, Angel. You know I love every little bit of you from the tip of your nose to your—"

"Don't say it, Chepe. I told you last time."

"You love it when I talk dirty." And she'd called him by his real name. The one he'd replaced with Chip, an Anglo name. He'd never have survived his white-boy private high school as Chepe.

"Yeah, and I so love it when you don't talk at all. What I don't love is you hanging up on me."

"Sorry about that, Angel. I really am. But I'm governor now, and sometimes business—"

"Is business more important than me? Because, if so, fuck you."

"Yeah, about that."

"Not until we get things straight between us, you jerk."

"The only thing straight between us you need is my—"

"Don't say it, Chepe. I don't want to talk dirty." He heard her light a cigarette and exhale. "Exactly how many have you had, Chepe? To make you this horny?"

"Don't get on my case, Angel. I've just made a big—"

"Fuck's sake, Chepe. I don't give a shit. Who is she?"

"What?"

"Who the fuck is she? The one you're fucking up there in Sad-Sac town. Or is it more than one?"

"I don't know—"

"Fuck you don't, Chepe. You think I'm stupid? You think I can't smell the whore on your breath even through this phone?"

"Angel, Angel—"

"Don't Angel me, you conceited piece of dirt. First, you apologize for fucking around. Then you apologize for hanging up on me. Then you buy me an engagement ring and set the date. Then, and only then, I may decide to let you fuck me." Another exhale. "And if I don't see that ring soon, there's gonna be some really happy *editores de periódicos* all over the state, and México too. Get me?"

Chip downed the rest of his tequila and made another executive decision. Angélica was on the list of people to lock up. The sooner the better. "Gotta go, Angel. Let's talk, Tuesday, about that ring. OK? Bye."

CHAPTER TEN
Ending the Affair

Chazz waited outside the Tequila Museum and did a slow burn. 1945 hours. Tom was late, and their need to get things straight was urgent. Dire. It was a warm evening, and the noise inside combined with her anxiety to push her out onto the sidewalk to wait. Stylishly dressed men and women came and went, sneaking looks at her OCPs. No heels tonight.

"Sorry, sorry," Tom's voice said behind her. He opened his arms for a hug and kiss, but she dodged and gave him the stink eye.

"You're late. You knew this was important, Tom."

"Yeah. The Governor went on and on. I finally had to walk out on him. Say, you didn't tell me Dupont gave you two weeks of vacation. What—"

"I'm not going to the beach, Tom. I have things to do. And how did you find out about that? Did you talk to General Dupont?"

"Saw him in the hall as I was leaving. He mentioned it."

What was the General doing with the Governor?

Chazz said, "Let's skip the drinks and just talk. Here."

"Chazz. Let's go in, have a drink, get comfortable—"

"This won't be a comfortable conversation, Tom. I don't need a drink, either."

Tom looked at the people drinking and eating at the outdoor tables around them. "We need some privacy for this, Chazz."

Chazz pointed to a bench further down the street, and the two of them moved there, out of range of the bar traffic. They sat and stared at each other.

Finally, Tom said, "I was serious about marriage, Chazz. I love you."

"Of course you were serious, Tom. So was I. I can't do it, not right now. But that's not—"

"Please, Chazz, think about it. We'd make such a great team."

"Tom. Shut the fuck up and listen."

Tom pressed his lips together as if to stop himself from saying something he'd regret. He relaxed and said, "OK, talk to me. What's wrong?"

"Every damn thing, Tom. I told you about the tanks and the troops."

"The Governor isn't planning anything like what you think, Chazz."

"No? And how are you so certain?"

"I work with him every day, practically all day, on strategy. I'd know."

"Exactly. And that's my problem, Tom."

"What, exactly?"

"You *would* know. And you're lying to me."

The tell again. His eyes dropped to his lap. Then he looked up at her and said, eyes limpid and pleading in the light from the bar, "Don't do this, Chazz."

"Do what, Tom?"

"Make me choose."

"I'd say you just chose, Tom." She stood up.

He scrambled up and put his hands on her shoulders. "Sit down, Chazz, we need to talk about this."

"What's the Governor doing, Tom?"

"I can't tell you."

"Is General Dupont involved?" How could he not be, with all the Guard activity? And he'd been talking to the Roberts thugs. Her mind closed on the implications. What was going on?

Tom didn't help, saying again, "I can't tell you."

"What the fuck?" She stepped back from him and glared. The people sitting at the sidewalk tables down the street looked at them nervously, seeing potential conflict.

Tom just shook his head. "Marry me, Chazz. Marry me."

She faced her lover with new eyes. Was she such a poor judge of character? How big was the lie? Was he trying to get her out of the way? Her Tom was still there, but something dark had obscured him. She could spend time figuring out what it was. But what was the point if he wouldn't tell her the truth?

"Let's talk tomorrow, Tom. Early. I have some thinking to do. Alone."

The evening heat oppressed her as she walked to the garage where she'd parked.

Chazz lay awake, mind buzzing. She looked at her phone: 0312 hours. No sleep and none likely. She got up, went to her kitchen, and made some coffee from a jar of instant. She sat and drank the warm coffee-like liquid, indifferent to its taste but needing the stimulation.

She was not a multi-tasking person. She liked to think things through in straight lines, from top to bottom, making sure she understood everything before deciding. Tonight, her brain was all over the place. Tom, Dupont, Roberts, Serrano and his friend, tanks, Bradleys, troops.

Tom. Her heart ached with longing for him, but her head ached with other emotions. He'd gone from lying to her to the more truthful but even less helpful act of denying her the information she needed. He knew, but he wouldn't tell her. How was that not a complete betrayal of everything she believed in? How could she go on with him, given this barrier between them?

Why wouldn't he tell her? Because she was in charge of tanks and troops and many other military things in the state. She could do something about it. About what? What was the semi-elected governor trying to do, stare down some imaginary opponent by appearing rough and tough?

The only problem the state had right now, besides drought, wildfires, energy, and crime, was that the federal government was doing everything it could to make the problems worse. Crisis after crisis, and she had to deal with it as part of her job. General Dupont moaned about it every single day.

Tomorrow morning—today—she'd give Tom one last chance to come clean. One last chance to save their relationship. But all that paled in comparison to the real problem: her duty.

Why wouldn't Tom tell her? Because she would *have* to do something about it. Her duty was to intervene and stop any illegal action of the Guard. Which had to do with Dupont giving her two weeks off. Dupont must be involved as well. What would happen while she was away? Tanks and troops. If this were Venezuela or Myanmar or Iraq, she'd be pretty sure it was a coup.

But this was Sacramento, California, the United States of America.

Tuesday morning, early, she called Tom.

"Tom, I'll ask again. What is the Governor doing?"

"I can't tell you, Chazz."

She felt silly asking it, but she had to. "Is he working with General Dupont to stage a coup? To take total power in the state?"

The phone was silent for a long time. She heard Tom sigh. "I can't tell you, Chazz."

"God damn it, Tom! If the Governor is abusing the Guard, I have to stop it. Tell me."

"I can't, Chazz."

"We're done, Tom."

"I know, Chazz. I'm sorry."

"So am I. You'll be sorrier, soon."

"Christ, Chazz. Chazz, you—"

"Goodbye, Tom."

He sighed. She hung up.

CHAPTER ELEVEN
Dissension

Myron shushed his wife's son and daughter, who were giving each other hell at the breakfast table. Tom's name on the ringing cell phone screen forced him to answer the call. The kids continued to ignore him, and his wife remained silent, off in her own world. Myron considered taking disciplinary action, but he had to deal with Tom first. He pursed his lips, frowned at his wife, and walked into his office to take the call.

"Tom. How did it go?" Myron asked.

"Not well, General. We…she broke up with me." Tom's voice on the phone sounded a little shaky to Myron. How shaky? Was Tom going to be a problem?

"I'm sorry to hear that, Tom." Nice response; anodyne, supportive, but not mushy. Keep the guy on track.

"Yeah." Tom cleared his throat. "General, I'm sorry to interrupt your breakfast and all that. But Chazz…well, she asked me if you and Governor Sanchez were planning a coup. She knows you're working closely with Chip."

"Well. That's not good." Disastrous. Myron knew Chazz's style. No nonsense, just the facts, ram the charge home and fire. Definitely not the desired state of affairs.

"And I can't find a way to change her mind."

"So you call me." Son of a….

"Sorry."

Damn it. He wanted his hand-picked Chief of Staff on board with the coup, not doing everything she could to stop it. She'd be an invaluable asset. But that was Chazz. Irreplaceable as an asset, terrifying as an enemy. Have to lock her up. No way around it. Myron shifted his phone to his other hand, pursing his lips. Unless....

Tom asked in a stronger voice, "What are you going to do, General? With her, I mean?"

Myron cleared his throat, then did it again. He firmed his voice and said, "We'll intern her with TAG. Before Monday."

Tom took a sharp breath. "Can't you persuade her to think about being a part—"

"Not Colonel Silver. No. She's all about duty and honor. She'll bite like a bulldog and tear our arms off."

"Come on, General. Throwing her in jail won't help us in the long run." Pleading now. Us. The man thought he had a chance to repair this with Chazz. He wasn't so much concerned with us as with himself.

Myron smiled sardonically in the morning light streaming into his office. Time for honesty. "Tom. Get over it. She'll come around with time, or she won't. Either way—"

"General, I'm asking it as a personal favor. Please."

Myron sighed. "I can find a place to send her to keep her occupied. I'll have to divert her suspicions from me somehow. She won't get her two weeks leave, because there's a huge scandal brewing somewhere in the far reaches of the state that requires her immediate intervention. Something to do with the governor's manipulating the guard. She can't ignore a direct order. That will render her unable to stop things. And I'm going to call Chip and tell him we're delaying things until the end of next week. How does that sound?"

Tom smiled and said, "Perfect." But Myron caught the tone he'd heard in briefings throughout his career, officers agreeing insincerely with their chain of command even though they knew it would lead to disaster.

He said, "You don't sound like you agree."

"No, it's OK. At least you won't throw Chazz into a dungeon. I just wish this weren't happening."

"You and me both. But it's happening, Tom. Are you still on board? Because—"

"Yeah, sure. Now more than ever, since I have nothing to do at night." Tom hung up.

If he could joke, he'd be fine. But Tom's record in Myron's mind now had a little question mark. If Colonel Silver knows…it's because Tom told her. Or hinted enough to let her guess. Loose lips….

Myron thought about his beautiful young wife, their wonderful family, their quiet home life, and how much he wanted to make the state safe for them. He thought about what would happen to them if the coup failed. If he failed. He wished for the thousandth time he had the personality to generate the support needed to make California independent. He knew he could count on himself, on his own actions and plans. But he needed Chip Sanchez and Tom Peña for their charisma and political acumen.

"I can't do this alone," he said to his empty office. He stared out the window at his manicured backyard.

Myron opened his office door and heard the kids screaming, so he closed it and paced, considering his options. Finally, he picked up his cell phone and called Chip Sanchez.

"Hey, Myron. Are you calling to give me an update?" Chip's voice lacked its usual boisterous quality. Myron suspected a terrible hangover. That didn't make his job any easier. Better just come out with it.

"Yes, I am, Chip. We'll postpone the action until the end of next week." Myron made a mental note to send a message to the tank crews. The delay would certainly upset them. Brickhouse had strung these men along with the need to act to save California. Sitting in a tank for over a week waiting for action might dampen their zeal.

"Huh. Why?" Chip asked, the suspicion clear in his voice.

"Tom called. He told me Colonel Silver showed him the door, and she has suspicions about what's going on. I'll need time to deal with it."

Which was as good an excuse as any to delay things until Myron was sure everything was ready. Chip didn't want to hear that, he knew. Injecting Chazz into Chip's thinking might slow him down, make him consider things more carefully. A vain hope. Chip Sanchez was not a deep thinker.

"What?" The governor was not pleased. "Damn it, I thought you had things under control, Myron. You're stalling. Lock her up. Before Monday. The day the coup happens."

"I have a way to sideline her. It's solid. But Tom doesn't want her in jail, and—"

"Who the hell cares what Tom wants? Myron, I swear to God—"

"Chip, calm down. What's wrong with you? We can't lock up everyone in the state."

"Wanna bet?" Chip yelled.

"Don't shout, Chip. I can hear you."

"Yeah? Well, listen to this. *Lock her up.*"

The governor hung up. Myron grimaced and dialed again. Ring followed by voicemail. He dialed twice more, and on the third try, the governor picked up.

"Myron, *madre de dios,* you're a pain in the ass!"

"Chip, we need Tom. He's the strategy expert. I can do the military part, but he's the key to the politics. He's got the contacts. He's got the feel for it. You're going to need him on board. Fully on board, Chip. And Colonel Silver is a part of that calculation, whether you like it or not. Even if she's shown him the door."

"I'll talk to him. It's fucking ridiculous!"

"Keep him on board, Chip." Myron knew that, without Tom, he'd have to deal with an unrestrained Sanchez. Myron and Tom working together could influence the governor. An unchained Sanchez would be intolerable. A leader with his eyes on the sky, not on the cliff in front of him.

* * *

Chip Sanchez badly wanted to tear something apart. But the governor's office was no place for destructive tantrums.

His head was exploding with pain. OK, too much tequila last night. But Myron had not one clue. Everything just poked along. Delay, delay, delay.

Worse, Angélica wasn't answering her phone. He'd called her three times in the last hour, and the bitch refused to pick up. She wanted to teach him a lesson; he was sure of it. Well, he'd sure as hell teach her a lesson. Put her in jail for life.

Christ, his head hurt.

Chip picked up his desk phone and asked Sally to get Tom Peña to his office as soon as he arrived and to find him some damn ibuprofen. He tried to putt on his office green but gave up after two misses made him want to blast the ball through the window. He yearned for the bar but understood that a drink wouldn't help. Out of ideas, he stood at the window, gazing at the messy hedges and lawns below. God damn, couldn't even generate the budget for a decent force of gardeners for his Capitol grounds. That would change. So many things would change.

At 8:15, his phone buzzed, and he strode to his desk and answered.

It was Sally. "Tom's here, sir," she said.

"Send the bastard in," Chip growled. He tacked on a belated "Thanks."

The door opened and Tom walked in. He was clearly in a more somber mood than usual, which suited Chip just fine. Tom handed Chip a bottle of ibuprofen.

"Here, Sally said to give this to you."

Chip struggled to remove the cap, eventually succeeded, and took four pills. Without water.

"What the hell are you doing, Tom?" he demanded, slamming the plastic bottle down on his desk. The cap flew off and several pills scattered.

Tom raised his head a little at the tone and said, "You're talking about Chazz."

"Damn right."

"I tried, Chip, but she wouldn't listen to reason."

"That's not what I mean."

"Then what?"

"You had the balls to tell Myron not to lock the bitch up?"

Tom's face closed. "She's not a bitch. Sir. I don't want you calling her that."

"Or what? You'll quit?" Chip laughed. "You're in too deep, Tom. But, OK. Colonel Silver." He performed a sardonic quarter bow and spread his hands. "There. Respectful enough? I told Myron to lock her up right now. But he says you don't want that. So he'll play some long game by sending her off to investigate a mirage. No extreme measures, just getting her out of the way." He shook his head.

"Which is perfectly reasonable, Chip."

Chip took a step forward and looked Tom hard in the eye. He punched out the words. "But it means postponing the coup, Tom. Until next Friday. I want this to happen now! Each day passes with nothing happening."

Tom, not intimidated, smiled. "You're too impatient, Chip. Good planning and getting the details right are critical to the plan. Myron must have told you that."

"You're both snails! You crawl along in the hedges of life." Chip felt this bit of improvised poetry was one of his best efforts. But Tom seemed unimpressed.

"What do you want from me, Chip?" Tom demanded.

"A goddamn coup! Power! All the stuff we've been talking about for weeks! No, months! And I want it now!"

"I understand your impatience, Chip, I really do. But Myron and I know the system better than you. How it works. What it takes to clear the hurdles. You don't want to just crash around knocking things over. Have a strategy and a plan."

"Yeah, yeah. OK. You're right. But we're getting off topic. Which is Colonel Silver. That..." Chip swallowed what he was about to say. "Contain her, Tom. Locking her up is the easiest way to make sure she won't act against us. Lock her up!"

"No. And if you do it, I'm gone. To the feds." Tom crossed his arms and looked steadily into Chip's eyes.

"God, my head hurts," said Chip, rubbing his forehead. "And this ain't making it any better."

"A week, Chip. That's not too much to ask."

"Nine days! A week from Friday! Get out of my office, Tom. And tell Sally to cancel my remaining appointments for today."

"Sure thing, Chip. Happy to oblige." Tom walked out and gently closed the office door. Chip returned to his station by the window and waited for the ibuprofen to kick in, watching the hedges. Fucking snails.

"Sally, is Tom in there yet?" Myron asked. It was 1000 hours. He had arrived at the governor's office after calling for an emergency meeting to resolve the situation. He and Tom had to get Chip under control, and they had to do it today.

Sally replied, "No, General Dupont. He went out for some air, he said. I called him and told him about the emergency meeting. He should be here soon."

"Good. I'll wait here until he arrives." Myron pursed his lips. "Sally, what's his mood?"

"The governor?" The executive assistant smiled. "He's not at his best right now. I gave him some ibuprofen, but you know how it is."

"Sure. I know how it should be, too." Myron frowned, displeased.

Sally defended her boss. "He's entitled to the occasional bender, General. Nobody's perfect."

"Not when—" But Myron caught himself. Sally had no knowledge of the coup. She wouldn't understand. He shook his head.

"What's the emergency, General?"

"Can't tell you, Sally. Too sensitive."

Sally grinned. "How exciting. This is the first super-secret thing I've seen since I started this job. Well, you guys will handle it, whatever it is."

Tom Peña entered the office. His displeasure with the world showed in his clenched jaw and frown.

Myron held out a hand, and Tom took it and shook. "Hello, Tom. Your call surprised me, but we can put things right if we talk to Chip together," he said. His eyes darted to Sally, and Tom nodded slightly to show he understood.

"Shall we?" said Myron. He nodded to Sally, who touched a button and spoke into her headset.

"Go right in, gentlemen," she said.

Myron held the door open for Tom, stepped into the lion's den behind him, and closed the door.

"Ganging up on me now?" asked Chip, forcing a smile.

"Someone has to," Myron said. He tried to calm the governor down. "Look, Chip, we all have to be on the same page. A team. For the duration. Otherwise, this just won't work."

"OK. Have a seat," the governor said, waving his hand at the sofa and chairs surrounding the gold coffee table, a garish addition to the blue-and-gold-themed room.

All three men crossed their legs. No one spoke.

Myron finally bit the bullet. "We have to work this out, gentlemen. We can't afford any dissension between us at this stage of the game."

"You told me earlier that I was in too deep to quit, Chip," Tom said. "I'd like to point out that you're way deep too. We all are."

"Yeah, yeah. I get that, I really do. But I won't be a roadie for you guys. When we go independent, I'm the leader. I'm the front man, the lead singer. You got that?"

Myron spoke quietly. "Yes, Chip, we understand. Nobody wants you to be a roadie. But you won't get the chance to sing if the band breaks up. Right? The coup will fail."

"Sure, I understand that. But we won't fail."

Myron said, "I'll take care of Colonel Silver, Chip. Right away. My solution will keep her away throughout the operation. It's the best way, Chip. Let us do our jobs."

"Oh, all right." Chip shook his head, then stopped as if it hurt too much. "I understand this means a lot to Tom. I'll go along. But no more delays, right?"

Tom, looking more like his usual self, nodded.

Myron, taking a risk, said, "And stay off the tequila, Chip. All right? It's doing us no good. Just for a week or two."

"Myron, when I need advice about my drinking, I will ask you."

Myron shook his head in exasperation. Dealing with his team's misbehavior was just as challenging as handling his kids. Or his Chief of Staff.

The governor's door opened, and Tom and General Dupont came out. Sally judged from their expressions that the meeting hadn't gone very well for them. Should she say something to cheer them up? She opened her mouth, caught a glare from Tom, and closed it again. What was wrong with everybody today? First Chip, now Tom. Even the general didn't look like his usual unflappable self.

The two men left without closing the governor's door behind them. Sally got up to close it, but Chip yelled at her to leave it open to clear the air.

She sat back down and stared at her desk. Should she complain about the shouting? The senator she'd worked for had yelled every single day, and she'd complained, and he'd laughed at her. It was one of the reasons she had quit. Sally liked this job and didn't want to lose it, or quit because it had gotten ugly. A little patience. That was what Chip needed. A little patience.

"God damn it, Sally. This shit doesn't do a damn thing!" shouted Chip from the open doorway. He shook the ibuprofen bottle at her. The cap flew off and pills scattered over the floor. "Jesus. Get me something stronger. Now!" He turned away.

Stronger. Like what, oxycodone? The governor was drunk. She checked her watch. It was 10:30 in the morning, and the governor was drunk. This was the worst she'd seen since she'd been on the job.

She pursed her lips in determination, she got up and walked to the door, dodging the pills on the floor. She said, "Sir, there really isn't anything stronger."

But he was already self-medicating over at his little bar.

"It's all right, Sally. Those guys make me mad. I didn't mean to take it out on you."

"Tom was pretty upset, sir."

"I would be too if my girlfriend—" The governor shut his mouth tight and shook his head. "Never mind, you don't want to know. Anyway, forget it, I'm fine." He continued to pour tequila into his glass. A triple, by the look of it. Sally shook her head.

"Sir, you really—"

"Hey, Sally. Why don't you take the rest of the day off? You deserve it. There's nothing urgent going on. Go on home, make a good dinner for Ted, enjoy yourself. Tomorrow will be better."

Nothing urgent. Just six appointments, a lunch with two senators, and two afternoon meetings. She'd convinced Chip not to cancel all these important meetings. But she knew better than to protest when a boss got this down.

"All right, sir. The calendar's on the computer, OK? You take care."

Nothing urgent happening. Something sure *was* happening, and Sally had no idea what it was. She used a piece of paper to push the pills over to the side of the room. The janitors would take care of them. Tom's girlfriend? Colonel Silver? So nice, and so good-looking too, even in uniform. Sally had liked her immediately when Tom had brought her by to meet Chip. She hoped nothing was wrong there. Did the governor have a girlfriend? Sally sighed, put her phone and the book she was reading into her bag, and left for home.

CHAPTER TWELVE
Military Deception

AT 0600 ON WEDNESDAY MORNING, Chazz had brewed a pot of coffee to stimulate her thinking. Now, an hour later, she sat sipping it and contemplating her next move. She absentmindedly looked around the sparsely furnished kitchen, not really seeing anything. If her suspicions were correct, she wouldn't get any help from the Guard. She was on her own. That made it difficult. Usually, she would call in the Criminal Investigation Division and get them to chase after the rats. Without Dupont's support and approval, she had no standing with the FBI. Without the resources of the Guard, she had to turn to the active-duty U.S. military for help. Someone in California who could mobilize forces to deal with the governor.

The useful people she knew in the military lived out of state. They'd either moved on with their careers or retired to civilian jobs. When she'd resigned from the Army and joined the Army National Guard, she'd lost touch with most of them.

Ridger? Tony Ridger. They'd had an affair in Iraq. Funny how she hung out with Marines instead of Army officers. He'd sworn undying love. But he'd gone back to his wife in the States when Chazz explained that dying in Iraq precluded such love, and she had to focus. They'd reunited with an affair in San Diego when the Guard stationed her there and he was at Camp Pendleton after his divorce. But Tony had issues with her career.

His being such a jerk made her give up on him as a lover. But he was still a friend.

What about Kat Taylor, the Marine pilot who'd hung out with her in Iraq? The last she'd heard, Kat had wangled her way into a gig at the USMC Mountain Warfare Training Center. But the MWTC stood utterly isolated up in the mountains over the Sonora Pass. Kat was amazing, but she wouldn't be of much help way out there. And Chazz hadn't reconnected with her in several years. Kat sometimes asked too much of her. For her own good, of course. Still…she picked up her phone.

The phone in her hand rang. Dupont. What the hell did he want?

"Yes, sir?" she answered.

"Sorry to spring this on you, Colonel. I have to cancel the leave we talked about yesterday."

What now? Was Dupont planning some trick to get her back under his thumb?

Dupont continued, "I apologize for doubting you, Colonel. You were quite right. The governor is definitely up to something."

Chazz sat up straight. Finally he understood. "Yes, sir. As I explained—"

"Things are in motion, Colonel. Now, I think it's best if we keep this between us. The situation at Camp Roberts is bad, but there are….other, more important things going on."

"What have you learned, sir?"

"Air support. It's not just the tanks. The governor has apparently alerted the air logistics people at Channel Islands ANG Station that he'll need transport and air support within the week."

"I see. What—"

"I want you to check it out, Colonel. Get down there. Look, you're going to need an excuse to be there, and we've got one. An officer accused a lieutenant colonel on the base of assault. The commander investigated and cleared him, but the officer objected, so it found its way to the Air Guard commander. He's short on personnel right now, so he asked if I had anyone that could take this on. When I talked to the air base commander, I learned about the governor's request. Now, the situation requires a higher-ranking officer to conduct the investigation of the lieutenant colonel. That officer is you. You have extensive aviation experience. There are problems with chopper maintenance records that led to a confrontation. You're perfect for the job. It's a great cover for you."

"I understand, sir." But a small, nagging doubt crept to the forefront of her mind. It seemed…pat. The chain of command from the air guard base command down to her was a little convoluted. But orders are orders.

She asked, "Any word from the FBI on the Camp Roberts situation, sir?"

"Just that they've sent a couple of agents up to Paso Robles to investigate. No word yet on whether they've found anything, but I'm sure they will. But, Chazz, I want you to focus all your attention on Channel Islands. Forget Roberts."

Not likely, not at all. Those tanks were real; that airbase thing was just a rumor. But orders were orders. "Yes, sir. The air station—that's the 146th, right? Near Oxnard?"

"Yes. The commander is Colonel Delfina Ortiz, Air National Guard. Do you know her?"

"No, sir," Chazz replied. On her watch, Channel Islands had never raised an issue that required her to give the place any attention.

"You need to find out if she's working with the governor. She could just be a pawn." The general paused, and Chazz imagined his usual calm smile. "And find out what happened with the assault case. I'm sure you can resolve that quickly. I'll give you a week, Chazz. We can't afford any more time than that."

"Yes sir. I'll leave shortly. I'll take a flight from SMF to LAX and rent a car, if that's OK."

The general paused before answering. "Just keep the expenses down, Chazz. You understand the situation we're in with the governor. He controls our budget, and he's the target of your investigation. If there's nothing to it…don't do anything crazy. Any questions?"

"No, sir."

"Then good luck." The general disconnected.

Chazz stepped over to her patio window and looked out at the artificial grass. If she did something, it wouldn't be crazy. Oxnard. Not so far from Paso Robles. It was 175 miles to Camp Roberts, a three-hour drive. She'd spend enough time at Channel Islands to cage the wild geese he was sending her to chase then drive up to where the action was. She'd call Tony or Kat when she'd found out more. But she had one ally she could use right now. She returned to the kitchen and picked up her cell phone.

"Captain Serrano, this is Colonel Silver. Have you heard from your friend at Roberts? Has he reported for duty at headquarters yet?"

"No, ma'am, he hasn't shown up. I sent the orders you signed yesterday. But I'm a little worried. He said he'd report for duty this afternoon. I've called, but no answer."

The nagging doubt in Chazz's mind grew larger. She said, "I'll be at Roberts in two days. What's his name and phone?"

"Lieutenant Joey Sellars, ma'am." He gave her the number.

"And check on those tanks. See if you can find any more in Sacramento. Or any other major cities. Use the satellites if you can get access. If they move, call me. We need to nail this down, Carlos. We need to know exactly where things happen. And when."

"Yes, ma'am, I understand."

"Carlos, General Dupont has ordered me down to Channel Islands to handle an investigation of a lieutenant colonel there." Chazz hesitated. Did Serrano need to know there was more conspiracy involved? Dupont had been explicit about keeping it between them. "You're in charge. Any trouble, I want to know it right away, so call me."

Chazz retrieved her duffel bag from the back of her closet. She stuffed in some necessary changes of clothes and packed her laptop, then packed her sidearm in its travel case. By 1100, she was at the Sacramento airport buying a ticket to LAX and checking in the travel case.

CHAPTER THIRTEEN
Channel Islands

Arriving at LAX, Chazz had searched the Internet for cheap motels near the Channel Islands Air National Guard Station. There were no motels at all. Broadening her search, she found a nice little place five miles away from the station in a tiny town called Port Hueneme, which she couldn't even begin to pronounce. When she looked up the town, it turned out to be a Chumash phrase meaning "Resting Place." Taking this as a great omen, she booked a room.

Upon arrival at the motel, the desk clerk helpfully informed her they pronounced it "Why-nee-me," which also seemed prophetic in its own way. She also discovered that, aside from the deep-water port and a huge Seabee naval station, the main retail business in town was a series of recreational cannabis stores. The desk clerk told her they were starting up a cannabis farmers' market, but with little success. Terrific. And she'd just missed the annual Banana Festival. Three billion bananas came through the port each year, easily funding a huge celebration. Chazz expressed regret at having missed the big do and got her room key.

The room was clean and brightly lit by new LED lights. Years of abuse had scarred the desk, but the bed was comfy. Propping herself up with a pillow, she dialed the number for the station and got Colonel Ortiz. They agreed on Chazz showing up at 0900 hours on Thursday, and Ortiz told her how to find her office. She sounded rather abrupt. Ortiz might hate the outside interference in an internal dispute. But she might just have secrets. Tomorrow would tell the tale about that.

But tomorrow was a long evening away. She walked to the beach, where she found a small seafood place. It was closing, so she got takeout and ate it on a table by the beach, listening to the wind rustle the palm trees. She walked out along a long fishing pier and leaned against the railing, breathing in the salty Pacific air and taking in the glorious sunset. She wondered what the hell she was doing here. Would Colonel Ortiz prove to be a villain or just a bent-out-of-shape commander? Would she find anything at Camp Roberts? Where the hell was Sellars? Nothing but obstruction from beginning to end.

To clear her thoughts, she envisioned a beach on the Costalegre, watching the sunset sitting next to a man she loved, the same ocean but a different mental space entirely. But Tom's pressure, his proposal, and his insistence on having his own way in everything replaced her fantasy. She'd made the right decision to end their affair.

A seagull landed on a piling nearby. The bird eyed her but remained silent. Her mind returned to her duty: investigating the governor's actions. And Tom worked for him. Tom must know all about the governor's actions and motives. Whatever her frustrations, she had to honor her sworn oath to the country. There was nothing more important than that. Again, the right decision on Tom. But it still hurt.

The seagull, tired of waiting, flew away, as there were no pickings to be had. The sun had moved below the horizon, the sunset turning gray. She sighed and began the walk back to her motel in the gathering darkness.

Chazz walked into Colonel Ortiz's office at 0859 on Thursday morning. The drive from Port Hueneme had been a straight line for five miles, right to the gate of the Air Station.

Colonel Ortiz rose from her desk to acknowledge Chazz. She was a strong-looking woman a bit shorter than Chazz, about fifty, with a medium brown Latina face unused to smiling. Her hair showed hints of white. The two colonels shook hands briefly, and Ortiz motioned to a straight-backed metal chair near her desk.

"Have a seat, Colonel Silver."

Chazz sat down. "I appreciate you taking the time to see me this morning, Colonel Ortiz."

"Sure." The commander sat and regarded Chazz with a grim expression. "Not that I had a choice."

"So I understand. General Dupont said that you investigated and found no basis to charge anyone. I'm here because the officer involved took it up the chain. Is that right?"

"Yes, Colonel, he did. Over my objections." Ortiz's stiff posture and narrowed eyes suggested she was indeed bent out of shape about the whole thing. It might make Chazz's job more difficult, but she wouldn't let it stop her.

"Tell me about the situation," she suggested, "and we'll go from there."

"Colonel, how long have you served in the military?"

"Enlisted in 2001, so about twenty years. Is that relevant?"

"I think so. What about in the Guard?"

"Back from Iraq in 2006 and mustered out, then joined the California Army Guard."

"So you know how things work."

"Pretty much. I've held several positions in the Guard. That includes some work with the 40th Combat Aviation Brigade in Fresno. I'm the COS of the Army Guard. I'd better understand how things work. What are you getting at, Colonel?"

"Going up the chain of command is out of line."

"I understand your perspective," Chazz said. Noncommittal was best at this point in the investigation. But she was up against a seriously bent-out-of-shape officer. And it *was* out of line.

Ortiz grimaced. "I'm glad, because this is all crap."

"OK. That's what I'm here to find out." Chazz smiled. "Why don't you summarize what happened?"

"Nothing happened, Colonel."

Hard going. Try again. "Could you summarize what Lieutenant Colonel Calvo thinks happened?"

"Better not. Let him tell you himself. He's suspended with pay. If you want him, call him. Here's his cell phone number. Have at it."

Chazz said, "I need coffee, Colonel. The motel in Port Hueneme lacked amenities."

Colonel Ortiz smiled. It definitely wasn't natural for her.

"Sure thing, Colonel."

"And a desk? And a wireless password? I have my laptop right here," she said, lifting her laptop bag.

The colonel grumbled, stood up, and exited the office without waiting for Chazz. Tough going.

Ortiz showed her to a battered metal desk in a large room with several such desks. She provided the wireless password and the location on the network of the relevant documents. She showed Chazz the coffee machine and gave her a Costco paper cup, on which she wrote "Silver" with a sharpie. The clear implication: don't take up any more space than necessary, including using more than one coffee cup. And don't waste any of the commander's time on this nonsense.

Chazz put the cup on her desk and unloaded her laptop. As she opened it, she advanced a pawn as a casual question. "General Dupont tells me you're getting ready for an op for the governor. Pretty unusual, isn't it?"

"Yeah, but we're ready, if that's what you're asking." Ortiz, her arms folded, gave Chazz a defiant stare.

"Just curious. What's it all about?" She typed in the wireless password, and the little icon lit up. Success.

"Don't know. The governor hasn't sent a detailed request yet. Just, 'be ready.' I've called in my troops."

"I haven't seen any exercise or op cross my desk."

"Poor you. Colonel, this ain't your business. You're not Air Guard." Her face showing impatience, Colonel Ortiz continued, "I'll leave you to it, Colonel Silver. Got real work to do. I don't think you'll find anything I haven't already, but you're welcome to try." Her tone was sardonic, as was the smile that deepened the marionette lines around her mouth, giving her a grim look. After she left, Chazz grabbed her cup and checked on the coffee machine. Coffee cold, machine off. Chazz turned the machine on and sighed. Ortiz would not help her with her secret investigation into the governor's actions. Chazz wasn't sure if the colonel was even telling the truth about it. Returning to her desk and laptop, she searched for what truth there was.

By 1030 hours, Chazz had drunk two cups of the warmed-up coffee. She'd found nothing at all about the governor's request. She had familiarized herself with the complaint, the documented evidence, and the aftermath. What a mess. It was all about an alleged coverup of negligent chopper maintenance. Lt. Col. Calvo claimed that the lieutenant in charge of ensuring effective maintenance, Michael Hines, had falsified records to cover up his negligence. The evidence was negative: Calvo could not identify a mechanic who had performed the work. The work itself was not verifiable—inspection and replacement of parts, and all the parts were there, but who knew whether the maintenance was done properly?

Better get the rest from Calvo. There was a he-said/he-said exchange that Calvo apparently took amiss. But Calvo didn't clearly spell out what the assault was about. Let's hear his thoughts. There was no phone anywhere for Hines. She should ask Calvo for that. She entered the digits for Calvo's number.

"Yes?" A male voice, gruff, lower registers.

"Lieutenant Colonel Calvo?"

"Speaking. Who is this?"

"Colonel Silver, Chief of Staff from JFHQ in Sacramento. I'm at the Air Station and just spoke with Colonel Ortiz. I'm looking into the incident you reported. Can you come to the station today to talk about it?"

"Sure. Shoots my golf game, but what the hell. Half an hour?"

"Fine. See you then, Colonel."

* * *

Chazz fantasized about a nice pastrami on fresh rye bread, one of her favorites. Calvo was late.

At 1230 hours, an officer walked up to her desk and asked, "Colonel Silver?"

Calvo wore OCPs and had a buzz cut, a square Latino face with thin lips, a big nose, and a widow's peak. Two narrowed brown eyes met hers.

"Colonel Calvo?" she asked.

"You must be the big deal from JFHQ." He looked at her insignia. "Army Guard? What the hell?"

"Orders, Colonel. No one else available. Check with TAG or your commander if you want." She paused and waited, staring at him. He was a big man, broad-shouldered and thick-necked. A bear.

"Ma'am. Good to know someone's finally paying attention."

"Let's get on with it, Colonel. We could go to lunch."

"Not here, not today. I already ate. Let's go to my office, more private."

Chazz's stomach growled as she followed the man down the hall to a small office.

"Is there a spare chair somewhere?" she asked.

"No, ma'am. I can sit on the desk if you—"

Chazz looked at the metal desk, bare except for a magazine. The magazine cover featured a man dressed in civvy camos with a hunting rifle and a flap-eared cap. There was an inset of a snarling bear. She read the upside-down title on the cover: *Hunt & Shoot California.* Terrific.

She said, "Let's go find a conference room."

"Yes, ma'am. Next building over."

"Wow. Luxury conditions on this station."

"Yeah, it's pretty minimal. We spend most of our time working on the machines or in the air." Chazz inferred from his tone that sitting at a desk reading a magazine or talking to a desk-jockey colonel from Sacramento was a low priority for Lieutenant Colonel Calvo. He wanted to slow down this process and make it harder to uncover the station's secrets, if there were any. Time to control the narrative.

She said briskly, "OK, let's skip the meeting and get to it. Why don't we spend some time looking at the choppers you mentioned in your report?"

"Yes, ma'am. I'll have to explain a little on the way. About choppers and maintenance and so on." His eyes measured her and found her lacking, and the twist of his lips suggested an attitude dangerously close to insubordination. Was mansplaining against regulations? It was.

"Looking forward to it, Colonel," Chazz lied.

Chazz and Colonel Calvo emerged from the headquarters building into the bright sunlight of a Southern California day.

"We can walk over to the facility, ma'am," Calvo said, pointing to the large hangar building across the road. "One of the aircraft is still in the hangar."

"One?"

"Yes, ma'am. The others are out on a large readiness exercise right now."

"Is that part of the governor's request?"

Calvo's mouth opened and closed, then he said, "No idea what you're talking about, ma'am."

"OK, never mind." Interesting contradiction between Calvo and his boss. Something to look into later. How far out of the command loop was Calvo these days?

Calvo led them across the road, explaining the maintenance process as if to a child. As they entered the hangar, Chazz saw a single Black Hawk chopper sitting forlornly off in a darkish corner.

"Why is this one here all alone?"

"Anomalous rotor coupling in the aft rotor, ma'am. The mechs should have it fixed by tomorrow."

"Is that the problem you found?"

"No, ma'am."

"Maybe you should explain a little bit about what happened." Chazz knew the Lieutenant Colonel would be more than happy to explain everything. In detail. As to a child.

"Yes, ma'am." Calvo stopped and looked around. "Four UH-60M Black Hawks here, ma'am, including this one, for routine major maintenance. With the big exercise coming up, the maintenance crew was under a lot of pressure to get things done. I supervised the whole thing. A young lieutenant, a woman named Hines, brought me the maintenance paperwork. I noticed a discrepancy in some of the sheets and asked her about it. She got real defensive, ma'am, and I didn't like her body language, so I took her to the chopper and had her show me what the crew had done. I checked the supposedly replaced parts, and they sure didn't look new to me. So I called the lieutenant out on it. She got real disrespectful, ma'am. Real disrespectful. Said there was no damn point in replacing perfectly good parts. The work would take too long and command would ding the whole crew for the delay. So I reported her."

The lieutenant was a woman. First name Michael. You never knew these days. But it explained a lot, given Calvo's behavior so far.

She said, "The incident report said assault."

Calvo grinned. "Yeah. She got in my face."

"In your face?"

"Yeah. Right up close and screaming. That's why I added assault, 'cause she sure assaulted my ears."

"Uh huh. And Colonel Ortiz looked into it?"

"She says she did, ma'am. But she cleared the choppers for the mission and told me the incident was closed." Calvo's lips thinned as he remembered his displeasure with that action.

"And then...?"

Calvo smiled a grim smile. "I wasn't ready to let it go, ma'am." He pressed his already thin lips into a single line. "It was the disrespect. If the Colonel wanted to risk the part failing, OK, that was on her. But the lieutenant's disrespect, that was on me. Can't let that go, ma'am. Not and maintain discipline. And Colonel Ortiz, well, she was just showing support."

"Support."

"Yeah, like, for another woman."

"Sure thing, Colonel. Did you express your concern to Colonel Ortiz?"

"I did. She told me to bottle it."

"In those terms?"

"Well, no, ma'am." Calvo smiled. "Something along the lines of, 'Let it go, Paul, it's not a big deal.' But it was, ma'am. The colonel wasn't standing there in my shoes. She couldn't."

"I see. Then you went up the chain."

"Yes, ma'am. Couldn't help it."

"And Colonel Ortiz took it badly."

"I guess. Ma'am."

"OK, let's see the chopper."

They walked over to the Black Hawk. Chazz noticed an airman working inside the chopper. Calvo ignored him and opened a couple of maintenance hatches. He pointed out parts he thought the maintenance crew ought to have replaced. The parts looked new to Chazz, and she said so.

"Yeah, well, the lieutenant got the crew to replace the parts after I left. She was that kind…" Calvo didn't finish, thinking better of his language.

"And you didn't take any pictures?"

"No, ma'am. It was no big deal. I figured we'd resolve it right away. Didn't happen, but it was too late after that."

"There's no evidence at all to support your account, Colonel."

"No, ma'am, I realize that. But it's all true."

"Did you question the crew later about the fixes? Did anyone witness Lieutenant Hines's conversation with you? And the 'assault'?" She could barely get the word out.

"No, ma'am, we were alone. And the crew supported the lieutenant." Calvo's jaw clenched, and he said, "They lied. They were afraid they'd get in trouble for the poor maintenance. Or maybe they were being overly loyal to the lieutenant."

"Hmm. Well, I suppose the next step is to speak with Lieutenant Hines. Where can I find her?"

"Um. The Colonel approved an emergency leave for the lieutenant, sick kid or something. She'll be back by Monday, though."

"Today's Thursday." Chazz shook her head. "I can't stay that long. I'll have to come back. Do you have her phone number?"

"No, ma'am."

"Honestly, Colonel Calvo, with so little actual evidence, there's not much of a case for me to investigate."

"I realize that, ma'am, but—" Calvo's tone progressed from lazy to urgent.

Chazz raised a hand. "I'll talk to Colonel Ortiz again, OK, Colonel? But for now, just relax and work on your golf game. I'll let you know what happens, or Colonel Ortiz will follow up."

"Yes, ma'am," said Calvo, lips tight, not happy with being kicked to the curb.

They walked back to the base headquarters building in blessed silence, and Chazz left Calvo to his hunting magazine.

What about lunch? Then Camp Roberts.

Myron Dupont looked over the San Diego logistics plan spreadsheet for the tenth time. There was a problem with the numbers, but he couldn't find it. He rubbed his eyes, itchy and tired from lack of sleep and too much computer time.

His desk phone rang. He picked it up and said, "Dupont."

"General, this is Colonel Silver, calling from Channel Islands."

"Oh, yes. What have you found out, Chazz?"

"Not much, sir. The complainant, Lt. Col. Calvo, has nothing to prove he's being mistreated. May I speak freely, sir?"

Myron sighed. When had she not? "Surely, Colonel."

"Calvo is a misogynist who doesn't like the woman he claims attacked him. He hates working for Colonel Ortiz, a woman. I think that's why he went outside the chain of command. I've found nothing to support his claims."

Myron smiled to himself. Ortiz and Calvo, what a pair. He'd never met Calvo, but Ortiz had said he was the perfect foil for Colonel Silver. He'd keep Silver busy out of spite, she'd said. But Chazz was wrong about their relationship. Calvo and Ortiz worked well together. Excellent team players in the operation.

He asked, "Anything on the governor?"

Silver hesitated, then said, "Not really. Ortiz says she's ready, whatever that means, and Calvo knows nothing about it."

They both knew everything about it. Myron's plan was working. Silver believed he was on her side.

He opened his mouth to reply, but Chazz continued. "I should talk to Lieutenant Hines, but she's not available until Monday. I'll do it by phone from Sacramento."

"No, no, just stay down there, Chazz. I'm sure you'll get more information from her in person. And you need to get more on the governor's ask. Take a three-day weekend off and enjoy yourself." In Oxnard. Just finding something to do would keep the Colonel busy until Monday. Better nail it down, though. He said cheerfully, "That's an order, Chazz. Have a good time."

"But sir—"

"No, Chazz. We have to finish this, and it's best to do it in person. Have you talked to Colonel Ortiz about your conclusions?"

"No, she's gone home for the day."

"Well, that's another reason to stay. No objections, Colonel. It's an order. Follow up on Monday."

"Yes, sir."

Myron hung up the phone and sat back in his chair. He'd heard a note of satisfaction in his subordinate's voice that set off a faint alarm.

Myron picked up the phone and called the lieutenant at the Mather command center who was coordinating intelligence for the operation. He asked the lieutenant to locate Colonel Silver's cell phone.

Five minutes later, the lieutenant called back. "En route on 101, sir. Crossing the Santa Clara River bridge into Ventura."

Ventura. Damn it. The woman was surely on her way to Camp Roberts. He had no choice, now. Tom wouldn't like it, but locking up Silver would make Chip ecstatic. The operation will speed up, and Tom will have to accept the inevitable. He picked up the phone again.

"Brickhouse here."

"Colonel Brickhouse, this is Myron Dupont. Listen, Charlie, we got a problem."

"Yes, sir?"

"Colonel Silver is on her way to your base. From Channel Islands. She'll need three hours to get to you, and she won't like what she finds. You need to deal with her."

"Yes, sir. No problem, sir."

"You have my authority to arrest her for insubordination and intern her."

"Yes, sir."

"Good luck, Charlie." Myron hung up and smiled. One less problem on his plate.

CHAPTER FOURTEEN
Camp Roberts

CHAZZ MERGED ONTO 101 IN Ventura, dreading the three-hour drive ahead. With a full stomach and one eye on the traffic and the other on the phone in its holder, she cranked up her long-tedious-drive playlist and settled in.

Somewhere around Pismo Beach, the phone interrupted "Plush" by the Stone Temple Pilots. Cursing, she looked at the caller ID: Tom. How appropriate for the song. But she wasn't in the mood to talk to the man.

She touched the answer button on her steering wheel and said, "What do *you* want?"

"Huh. And hello to you, too. I didn't have time to talk to you before you went down south. Chazz, there are things I have to say. I'd rather do it in person, but since I can't, I called."

"I'm working. Even if I weren't working, I'm not interested. There could come a time when I want to listen to you. Right now, I don't. Goodbye."

"Chazz—"

She hung up on him. The song resumed. The passing scenery flowed by without Chazz consciously seeing anything. Their breakup was too recent for her to have lost all her feelings for him. Her daydream on the beach at Port Hueneme told her that. But the stubbornness and the controlling behavior—it was getting close to restraining-order territory.

And how did he find out she'd gone south? Dupont. Or—a disturbing possibility—he planned the whole thing with his boss the governor and the general. The general, who had just ordered her to stay put in Port Hueneme for no good reason. They were stalling her, that's what they were doing. And Tom was adding his own method to the effort.

If she needed confirmation of her conclusion that she was on her own, Tom had just provided it.

Chazz stopped at the main gate of Camp Roberts to show her ID. The guard checked over her car and waved her through. In the rearview mirror, she could see the guard on the kiosk's phone. They knew she was here.

The last time Chazz had visited Roberts was with General Dupont, for a conference. That had been six months ago, right after her appointment as COS. Driving down the same road, she felt like an outsider, a spy. She resisted looking over her shoulder. Best act like the officer in charge of Guard operations. She had every right to be here.

The base headquarters building was just as she remembered it, and she entered as though she owned the place. She marched down the center hall and found the commander's office she'd visited before. The outer office was empty. Only to be expected; Guard funding for assistants was nonexistent these days. She thought of Dupont's complaint about the governor's attitude towards the Guard budget and smiled. If the governor was collaborating with Dupont, Guard budgets would be more intriguing. There might be drawbacks, though. For everyone else.

Chazz poked her head into the commander's office. Also empty. So she went hunting. Finally, she came across a sergeant carrying a bundle of folders.

"COS Silver, Sergeant Blake." She read the name off his name tag. "I'm looking for the commander, Colonel Brickhouse."

"He's been out on the CACTF all day, ma'am," Blake replied. "Inspection. With Lieutenant Flattery. It's 1800, so he may have gone home for the day."

"The CACTF?"

"Combined Arms Collective Training Facility," he reeled off. "Bunch of fake town buildings used for urban warfare training, ma'am."

"How do I get there?" Chazz had a vague memory of visiting the facility.

"Past the Historical Museum, turn right on the main road, head past the Range Control, left at the junction, and down half a mile. You can't miss it."

"Thanks. Oh, and I want to talk to the FBI agents. Are they still around?"

"FBI?" The sergeant raised his eyebrows. "What would they be doing here?"

"No one like that around, Sergeant?"

"No, ma'am, not to my knowledge."

"OK, thanks. I must have heard wrong."

"Yes, ma'am."

"How about Lieutenant Sellars?"

"He's transferred out, ma'am. Left two days ago."

"I'm out of luck today, Sergeant. Well, thanks."

Chazz found the CACTF without too much trouble, just one wrong turn. A concrete road surrounded the facility. There were several buildings scattered about: a church, a few houses, and several walled compounds. She remembered the facility from her visit. It was showing its age now, after ten years of the military treating it as an urban killing field. The place made her itch. The desert scrub and the walled compounds reminded her too much of Iraq. You go into places like this with rifles and every sense on full alert.

No one was around and nothing moved, but a black SUV sat next to one of the walled compounds. She parked next to it. She waited in her car, silent, for five full minutes, window down, all senses attuned. Nothing stirred. The car roasted in the relentless sun overhead.

Chazz honked the horn, emitting the anemic sound that Asian cars make. The noise echoed off the buildings around her but dissipated into the desert landscape that surrounded the ghost town. Another minute; nothing moved.

She got out of the car and peered through the SUV windows. Empty. The whole situation made her skin crawl. She walked over to her car, popped the trunk, and got her Sig Sauer sidearm and holster from its travel case. She hooked the holster to her belt and strapped it to her leg after checking the magazine and the safety.

"Is anyone here?" she called. The words echoed off the concrete buildings surrounding her. No response.

She walked through the compound wall gate to the nearest building and pushed open the entry door. The afternoon shadows from the compound wall obscured the interior as she looked around.

The doorjamb next to her exploded as the bullet hit it, sending a shower of wood and plaster in her face. She threw herself to the floor and rolled inside the room, coming up into a crouch with her sidearm in her hand. The bullet had come from outside the compound. She looked around the room. Stairs up to a second level, a door to another room, a short hallway to what looked like a bathroom—dead ends. Not enough choices.

Then she noticed the trapdoor on the floor. A tunnel. There were tunnels all over these buildings, she remembered. They connected all the buildings. She'd seen tunnels like that in Iraq and never liked them, and as a chopper pilot, never entered one. She could fight the killer outside or flank him through the tunnels. Surprise would be better.

She raised the trap and lowered herself into the tunnel, closing the trap above her. Dark as pitch. Chazz fumbled for the phone in her pocket and found the flashlight icon.

She saw a foot. The foot, toe down, around a corner in the tunnel, didn't move. She inched forward, pistol ready, crouching. Foot, leg, body. Man in OCPs. No sidearm. With a massive, bloody exit wound in his back, he wasn't going anywhere. She touched the man's neck. Ice cold and rigid. Dead for a day or two. She turned him over and aimed the flashlight at his chest. Name tag right next to the entry wound: Sellars. Yep. One mystery solved. They'd plugged their leak by taking him out. These guys didn't take prisoners.

She played the light across the floor. No pools of blood. Killed somewhere else and dumped here later. Excellent temporary hiding place. She kneeled down over the body to search it for anything useful.

Sounds behind her. Trap door. Fuck.

Chazz scrambled up, holstered the gun, and headed down the tunnel. She brought up the compass app on her phone and oriented herself. She worked her way north-northwest, toward the building across from the compound. As she advanced silently through the tunnel, she considered the possibilities. Brickhouse as the shooter? Both of them, Flattery and Brickhouse? One of them was in the tunnels, and she had to be careful. The other one could be anywhere. She pondered the idea of a squad of hunters, but it appeared improbable. No transports. The facility was quiet and deserted except for the SUV.

She turned a corner and faced a choice. Some bright boy had thought troops needed a crawl tunnel for authenticity. Excellent training, no doubt, just not today. Yet, that was the direction she had to go. She crawled, elbows and knees scraping along the tunnel floor, coming out into an open area with a dirt floor and concrete bracing. And there was the trap door.

Chazz switched off the flash and raised the trap slightly. All was quiet, no enemy in sight. She pushed up the trap and pulled herself out. It took her a few seconds to catch her breath and regain her balance, then she peeked out a window. There was her car and the SUV, baking in the afternoon sun. There was the compound. No one stirred. She heard a scrape behind her and dropped to the floor, gun in hand. Another scrape. It came from the second floor. Chazz eased to her feet and tiptoed to the stairs. One step, another. She reached the level where she peered into the hallway above. No one. Another scrape from the room up front. The door to the room was ajar. Chazz crept past it and saw a man crouching at a window.

"Freeze! Hands up!" she yelled. The man jumped and raised his gun. Chazz fired three shots as the gun came up. The man fell backwards. Chazz stepped forward, the gun held out, looking for another target. Silence fell. She holstered the gun and looked down at Lieutenant Flattery's face. Another problem solved. Flattery could have fired the earlier shot. But he might just be covering the compound while Brickhouse attacked.

Chazz left Flattery's body where it was and ran downstairs. No sign of life outside, despite the gunfire. Time to go. She opened the door to the building. She pulled out her car fob and unlocked her car, the lights flashing their acceptance of the signal. Wait wait wait. No movement. Brickhouse was still in the tunnels.

Chazz ran to her car, gun in hand, crouched low to present a lesser target. She ran in between the SUV and her car. She reached to open her door, but stopped and looked at the SUV. She raised her gun and shot out the two tires she could see on the left side of the SUV. That should stop any pursuit.

She threw open her door, got in, and floored the accelerator, careening onto the concrete road. Two loud reports and a sudden shattering of her back window as a bullet found its target. Brickhouse had come out of the tunnel. She saw him run to the SUV in the rearview mirror. The SUV swung around, but Brickhouse quickly found out about the damaged tires, and the SUV fell behind.

Chazz turned onto the dirt access road at high speed, kicking up a cloud of dust. She maintained high speed through the base's main gate, hitting the freeway on ramp doing seventy-five. After a moment of indecision, she merged onto the southbound lanes and headed back to Port Hueneme. She had some unfinished business and an opportunity. She'd learned what she needed to know about Camp Roberts. Now she needed new transportation, what with the shattered back window and all. That Black Hawk in the air station hangar would suffice.

***

It took twenty minutes for Chazz's overactive brain to wrestle down all the issues confronting her. As Paso Robles flowed by, she came up with a plan. The "Purple Heart Trail" sign flashed by. She didn't want another one of those medals. She needed to throw the bloodhounds off her scent. She pulled off the highway and parked in a gas station parking lot to make some phone calls.

Chazz called General Dupont on his mobile number. She steeled herself to sound the right note of false bravado to his questions. But he didn't pick up, and the phone went to voicemail: perfect.

"General, Colonel Silver here. I'm heading back to Sacramento to talk with you about problems with the assignment. I'll fly up and meet you tomorrow morning. There shouldn't be any problem getting back to Channel Islands by Monday."

When Dupont got that voicemail, he'd already know about the incident at Roberts. He would presume she'd gone north to confront him and would search for her there, on the road, or at her house. She'd be at the Air Station getting that Black Hawk in the air.

And now it was time to break the chain of command. She found TAG's office number in her contacts and called. His assistant answered.

"I'm sorry, Colonel Silver, TAG is away on leave and unavailable. Can I help you?" he said.

Chazz considered leaving a message about the assassination attempt and the coup she knew was in the works. She knew that the assistant would think she was crazy. Maybe she was.

"No, I'll call back on Monday. Just tell him I called, please, and that it's a serious problem with General Dupont." The assistant promised to deliver the message. Chazz put the phone in her lap and stared blankly at a family gassing up their huge SUV and its accompanying motorboat, taking up three gas pumps in the process. Normal folks. Nothing was normal anymore. Time to lay down a smokescreen. She dialed Tom and got him.

She said, "Sorry I was so abrupt, Tom. Bad day. We need to talk in person, I get that. I'm heading back to LAX now in my rental car. Can we meet? Can you come to my house early tomorrow? 7 a.m.? I'll be meeting with General Dupont later in the morning, so it needs to be early. I want to talk it all out. Can you do that?"

"Of course. I'll see you then."

"All right, Tom." To better cement the deal, she added, "I love you, and I'll give you a second chance. Goodbye." She hung up. A second chance to prove he's a son of a bitch. But that would convince Dupont when Tom told him she expected to meet with him tomorrow.

But tomorrow she'd be flying out of Channel Islands. And getting together with some old friends.

CHAPTER FIFTEEN
Escape from Channel Islands

Chazz parked in front of her motel room and sat back in the car seat, exhausted. She had to eat and sleep. Tomorrow, when she'd recovered, she would deal with that chopper. She pulled herself out of the car, locked it, and fumbled for her room key while juggling the bag of Chick-Fil-A junk food she'd bought in Ventura. The small light above the door barely broke the surrounding darkness. A car door opened, and she looked back toward the sound. A huge Black man got out of a small Korean sedan. He stared at her as he walked toward her in the dark. His bald head shone, reflecting the lights of the motel sign. He had a broken nose, and the line of his mouth had a determined expression.

Her autonomic defense mechanism differed from most people's, something to do with Iraq and the Silver Star on her dresser at home. She didn't freeze, and she didn't run. She dropped the bag and the key to the ground to free her hands for action. Too bad she'd locked her Sig in the trunk. She'd thought Chick-Fil-A was pretty safe without it.

As the guy approached, the car's second door opened and a small Black woman emerged looking alarmed.

"Ollie!" she said in a loud voice. "Introduce yourself! You're scaring her."

The man stopped and grinned, then stood to attention and saluted.

"Colonel Silver? Tech Sergeant Oliver Jones. From the Air Station."

Chazz unclenched her fists and returned the salute. "Sergeant. You startled me."

"Sorry, ma'am. I get too on-task sometimes."

The woman came up beside Sergeant Jones. He glanced at her and then at Chazz.

"Uh, ma'am, my wife, Shirelle Jones. Definitely my better half."

"Shirelle," Chazz acknowledged. "Pleased to meet you."

"Yeah," said Shirelle. "Likewise, but get on with it, Ollie."

"Can I see some ID, Sergeant? You're not in uniform." The man was wearing jeans and a t-shirt that showed off his large biceps and huge forearms.

"Yes, ma'am. Off duty right now." Jones pulled out his wallet and extracted his Air Force ID. "Here you go."

She held the ID up to the dim light. Everything looked right, so Chazz returned the ID and asked, "How did you find me, Sergeant?"

"Ain't all that many motels around here, ma'am. And a lucky guess: this is the closest one to the station."

So she was hiding in plain sight. Have to do something about that.

Shirelle said, "Ollie," and made moving motions with her hands.

"May we come in, ma'am?" asked Sergeant Jones. "It's kinda private."

Chazz picked up her bag and her key and opened the door to her room. She placed the bag on the scarred desk, then arranged the seating: Shirelle on the desk chair, Ollie on the bed, and herself in the armchair. Chazz grabbed a towel from the bathroom and spread it over the armchair, as her OCPs weren't exactly pristine from her tunnel crawling. Sergeant Jones grinned while his wife inspected Chazz's attire with a skeptical look. Neither of them asked about it.

Over the next half hour, Chazz confirmed her suspicions. Sergeant Jones had overheard Calvo's story while working on the Black Hawk chopper in the hangar. Everything in the story was false, including Lieutenant Hines. No such person existed. Jones knew Ortiz and Calvo were playing a game with Chazz, but he didn't understand why. It just didn't feel right. So he told Shirelle, and she insisted he find Chazz and tell her the story.

Chazz gently probed if Jones knew anything about General Dupont's sending her down, but he didn't. Ortiz and Calvo couldn't have done this alone, she was certain. Dupont's sending her to Channel Islands had been a sham from start to finish, except it wasn't really finished yet. Her original suspicions about his collaboration with the governor returned with a vengeance. And had Dupont somehow orchestrated the assassination attempt at Camp Roberts as well? What had she gotten herself into?

She said, "Sergeant, thank you for all of this. Look, things are getting interesting in Sacramento. I can't disclose anything further. Can you meet me at the hangar tomorrow at 0900? I want to see that Black Hawk."

"The Black Hawk? Why?"

"Come on, Ollie. You said your piece, we're done. Let's go home," Shirelle said. "Colonel, you got all we got to give. Up to you, now." She got out of the chair. Sergeant Jones scrambled to his feet. "And we ain't never been here. Bye now."

"Wait. Please, hold on a second." A brief debate in her mind, and she voted for trust. "Sergeant, how would you react if I told you the governor plans to secede? Take the state out of the Union?"

"I'd say you were kinda crazy, ma'am." Ollie smiled. "No offense."

"Where do I work?"

"JFHQ, ma'am."

"Who do I work for?"

"General Dupont, ma'am."

"Imagine I told you the general was part of the coup plot. What would you think then?"

Ollie's mouth opened and closed. Shirelle's eyes narrowed sharply.

Chazz leaned forward. "He is. That's why I'm here. To get me out of the way. Other conspirators ambushed me at Camp Roberts. I dodged a bullet." And killed a man. But Ollie didn't need to know that.

"Ollie," Shirelle said in a caustic tone. "You can't—"

"Shirelle, be quiet now. The Colonel sounds like she knows what she's talking about."

"What I'm afraid of, Ollie." Shirelle gave Chazz an unyielding stare, lips tight. "No way. No way."

"Just meet me, Sergeant. I need that chopper. That's all. You were repairing it, you said. Is it working?"

"Close to it, ma'am. I can have it shipshape by 0900, no problem."

"Will you do that? There won't be any medals in it for you. I don't want to order you to do it. It's a funny situation."

"Yes, ma'am, you called that one right."

"*Ollie,*" Shirelle said.

"No, Shirelle, I got to do this. I signed up for the Guard. I been workin' for the Guard for fifteen years. And I took that oath. And I meant it."

Shirelle shook her head. "Pig-headed, Ollie. That's what you are." Shirelle looked at Chazz. "You take care of my husband, Colonel. Or you'll answer to me."

"Yes, ma'am," Chazz said. "See you tomorrow, Sergeant."

The sergeant held the door open for his wife and closed it gently behind him. Chazz heard their car start up and drive away. She had at least one person on her side now. A random thought occurred to her: Shirelle Jones definitely had command potential. Overcautious, but very strong. She grinned. Shirelle was on her side, too, just not willing to admit it.

Chazz went to her car and took her sidearm out of its travel case. Others could find her if Jones could. She should be ready for them.

Chazz woke up in the motel room at 0300, drenched in sweat. She lay on the bed and stared at the ceiling, recovering from Jones and her dreams and thinking hard about the past. Iraq. A writer had claimed that the past is not even past, and she couldn't deny it. Considering running to Tony, even as a friend, brought back some memories that she'd rather have avoided. Now, in the dark, she dropped her barriers.

It was a simple air support mission in 2005. A squad encountered a group of Anti-Iraqi Forces and needed air support to suppress their fire. Her gunner fired the Apache's chain gun with precision into the group of attacking AIFs, who scattered—those that were left alive.

The release of tension after the mission made her think about Tony. About what she'd said to him in response to his declaration of love. Had she been too harsh? But you couldn't be in love in Iraq. It wasn't possible. At least, not for her. It took all her emotions to deal with the fighting and the killing. She had feelings for him, of course. But so did his wife. At least, according to him, which she found pretty cold.

But then came the toughest part. The part that had her sweating at 3 a.m. A bunch of AIFs ambushed a convoy of Army trucks moving supplies to a forward operating base. The convoy radioed for help as she was passing by, and she responded, circling the Apache around as she got oriented, all thoughts of Tony banished. Her gunner, Lieutenant Ripley, spotted the AIF trenches and asked for a strafing run. The chopper fired its chain gun and a Hellfire missile at the first trench, but the enemy didn't retreat. They fought back.

Chazz gently turned the stick for a second run, but an RPG came out of nowhere and destroyed the chopper's tail. It was like being caught in a hurricane as the chopper spun around, out of control. The machine hit the ground at an angle that sheared off the front of the chopper, killing Ripley but leaving her hanging halfway out of the cockpit.

Stunned and disoriented by the impact, Chazz took a few deep breaths to clear her head. She unbuckled her belt, took off her helmet, grabbed her M4 rifle from its sling, and climbed down from the fallen chopper. One look at the chopper made it clear she had to get far away. She was on the other side of the downed chopper from the AIFs, and her choice was either to find a way to get to the convoy around the trenches or to run away as fast as she could. Then the icy fear took over, the fear that drives you into the fray. For her, the coldness meant she could act.

She checked out the M4, then scouted the action on the road. The AIFs had resumed their fire on the convoy from the two trenches. Her pass had hit the front trench hard, but there were still fighters there, and the rear trench fighters were unharmed. As she approached the trench, she watched the AIFs fire on the convoy. Behind her, the chopper exploded in a ball of flame, and a fighter holding a rocket launcher glanced up and spotted her. The fear intensified.

Before the man could do anything, she raised the M4 and fired several rounds into him. Then, as her body responded to the force of the weapon, she coldly sprayed the heavy fire into the trench, which erupted in chaos. Forcing her feet forward, jumped into the trench, and advanced along it, taking out everything she saw in her path with the M4, burst after burst. Despite the return fire, she kept shooting until there were no more fighters left to kill.

An AIF jumped up from the front trench and started firing his AK-47 at her. She ducked behind a corpse and felt the bullets hitting the lifeless body like blows from a furious boxer. Then fire from the convoy riddled the attacker, driving him forward into the trench. She emptied the M4 into him to neutralize any threat. Out of the corner of her eye, she saw one of the dead men in the trench raise his rifle. She swung her weapon around and hit the rifle away from him, then slammed her boot into his head.

By the time she'd made sure the AIF was dead, the convoy soldiers had laid down a barrage of fire, allowing her to kneel and reload the M4. No time for checking other bodies. Fear drove her into the front trench, rolling under the covering fire. Again she cleared what was left of it, her stomach aching with fear and now with fatigue, an utter tiredness that slowed her actions. A few AIFs climbed out to escape, but the convoy troops shot them down.

Suddenly, everything went silent. Funny how the silence was the clearest part of the memory. The rest was a blur of fire, dirt, and fear. She couldn't remember anything but silence as the convoy troops put her in a transport and headed for base.

* * *

Chazz didn't remember much about the trip back to base, except that she had fallen, exhausted, into Tony's arms. Lying in her motel bed twenty-three years later, she still remembered the warmth and comfort and safety of those arms. She remembered the soothing sounds. But she remembered none of the words. It had all been wordless. A wordless scream as the chopper went down, the wordless fear as she cleared the trenches, and a wordless exhaustion as the convoy soldiers helped her to their vehicle. No words, only images. The images stayed real, even after all this time, lying in bed sweating.

And the next morning, in bed with Tony, the silence evaporated.

"I tried," he'd said. "I tried, Chazz. To make you see how I feel when I'm with you."

A married man arguing about love with another woman lacked conviction. She looked at the man who'd held her, comforted her, for hours. He seemed distant, pulling away, even as he professed his love. He was half dressed, slowly fastening his uniform belt, looking down and not at her. Her stomach tightened, but this time not with icy fear. She knew. It was over. But it died a lingering death, and that hurt all the more. And it had led to the twisty threads and paths of the dark forest in her inner heart.

They agreed to take it day by day, but he secretly requested a transfer home. And then he was gone. Leaving her with a Silver Star and a drinking problem, along with a keepsake, his Iraq challenge coin. The self-pity didn't last long. All it took was several grave errors of judgment.

She and Kat had had a few drinks at a party thrown by some Army guys. First mistake: going to the party. Second one: more than a few drinks. And third one: flirting with a colonel she'd met at the air base. When he saw that she was a wee bit under the influence, and Kat had temporarily disappeared to the ladies' room, he said he'd take her back to her quarters. He didn't. He got her into a bedroom somewhere, she wasn't even sure where anymore. She fought it, but the alcohol had won the battle for him before he even started. He brought her back to the party just in time to find Kat looking for her. She kept her mouth shut then, and since. Then she had Kat's friendship to make her whole again. She thought. Until the Dream started.

Something had to give. Leaving the Army, she joined the California Guard, stepping back from wars.

Then, fifteen years later, getting together with Tony again in San Diego, and this time it was she who left. She gave him back his challenge coin. Quits. Until now. Maybe.

And here we are. She got up, washed her face, took a drink of cold water from the motel bathroom faucet, and fell back into bed. Tomorrow —today—was another day.

Tom eased his Porsche Taycan EV into the cul-de-sac where Chazz lived. He was a little early, 6:45, but he had wanted to make sure he got there on time, and he'd never been to the house before. The cul-de-sac was quiet on a Saturday morning, not a soul in sight in any of the houses.

He parked and turned off the engine, then sat back and thought about why. Why he'd never been here. Chazz had always come to him. It wasn't that she hadn't offered, she had. He remembered thinking that it was too far out of town, that it was the suburbs, that it was easier for him to cook in his own kitchen.

It came down to self-centeredness. He'd made every excuse in the book, but it was all about him. And she'd accepted that, without complaint. Or had he missed it? That lunch at the Blind Pig. He'd come on too strong, and she'd pulled back a little. He'd kept going, sure of himself. Too sure. And that stupid proposal. Me, me, me. Was he a narcissist? Should he see a shrink, get a second opinion?

Well, right now, he needed to be on his best behavior. This meeting was about Chazz, not him. He needed to listen, not talk. Hear, not tell. Then he had to do whatever Chazz needed him to do. He loved her and needed her and their relationship. Whatever it took.

"Shit," he said to himself. Stupid again. A woman like Chazz was not interested in a doormat. Placating her was exactly the wrong way to approach a woman like her. She'd just throw him out.

The clock on his dashboard ticked over to 7:00. He got out of the Taycan and walked up the concrete path to Chazz's door, checking the address to make sure he wouldn't disturb any neighbors by ringing the wrong doorbell at this ungodly hour. He rang the bell and waited.

And waited.

Rang the bell again. Nothing.

He glanced around to check on the neighbors, then walked over to the large picture window in the front of the house. The shades were almost closed, but he could see inside. No lights, no movement. He walked around the side of the house by the fence and found the kitchen window. Nothing.

He went back to the front. Sure enough, there was a neighbor, in slippers, holding a folded up newspaper and looking at him suspiciously. Tom smiled and said, "I'm looking for Colonel Silver. We're supposed to have a meeting."

"Huh. Chazz hasn't been around for a few days. Her car isn't here. She always parks in the driveway. Sure you didn't misunderstand?"

"I must have. Well, thank you."

She stood him up. The god damn woman stood him up. Anger surged.

He covered his anger with a smile and regrouped. She could have had an accident. Or something. He pulled out his phone and dialed. Voicemail.

"Chazz, it's Tom. I'm outside your house, and you don't appear to be there. Give me a call and we can reschedule, OK? I really need to talk to you."

The neighbor smiled. Tom smiled back, not meaning it, then got into the Taycan and drove back to Sacramento, not sure what had just happened but very sure he didn't like it.

Chazz ate a snack bar for breakfast, ignored a call from Tom at 0710, reached the Air Station at 0850, and entered the hangar. It was a Friday, but the place was a ghost town. She tried three doors before finding an unlocked one. The old Black Hawk sat in the back of the hangar. Sergeant

Jones was on top of the chopper, deep in the rotor repair. He climbed down and faced her, wiping his hands on an oily rag.

"You're early, ma'am. I'm about done. I need a replacement part for the assembly. Once I install it, this bird will be happy to take you wherever you need to go." He paused. "You need armament, ma'am? Hellfires? Won't be easy or quick, but I know a guy—"

"No, just the chopper." She examined the lovely lady that would let her fulfill her duty. Sudden warmth filled her stomach. It had been too long.

"OK, ma'am. And they ain't no machine gun. Training chopper, see? I'll just walk over to supply for the assembly part. Back in five minutes." Jones headed for the door.

Chazz paced around the chopper, inspecting it. It had been a while since she'd flown a Black Hawk, though she'd done the required simulations and training over the years to keep her qualifications up to date. This chopper looked older than she was, so she shouldn't have any problems, at least if Jones knew what he was doing. Still, a sense of unease lingered in her stomach. It wouldn't hurt to check out the controls.

She climbed up into the open cockpit. Both the pilots' seats were empty. Chazz smiled when she saw a pilot's helmet on the co-pilot's seat, courtesy of Sgt. Jones. She put the helmet on and sat in the pilot's seat.

Being back at the controls felt good. The bird was old, though, and it showed. By the looks of it, retrofitted with new tech. She looked up through the top windshield at the big rotor blades. Home. Of a sort.

"What the hell are you doing here?" yelled Lieutenant Colonel Calvo, his furious head poking in through the open canopy door. He reached out with both hands and grabbed her clothes and pulled. She grabbed the collective stick and stopped him from pulling her out, and swung with one hand. He dodged, then leaned back in. Her mind clouded as she went again to her dark forest. She flailed to evade Calvo's grasp, but he gripped her uniform sleeves and pulled, hard. Momentum sent them both tumbling down to the hangar floor.

Chazz scrambled to her feet. The fall cleared her mind. She pulled her sidearm from its holster, but Calvo kicked it out of her hand. He had no gun, but he was dangerous. She faced him. He took a fast, low hook at her stomach. She deflected, and he landed a hard, straight left jab to her nose, knocking her back. She evaded his followup kick and collided with the chopper's side. He moved in and threw another punch. She ducked under it and landed two punches to his side, spraying blood from her nose onto his clothes. He grunted again and swept a foot around, tripping her and sending her to the ground. He straddled her and used both hands to pull off the pilot's helmet. Chazz used her knee to good effect on his balls. He screamed his outrage and fell off to the side.

Chazz scrambled to her feet, as did Calvo. Another quick left jab to her nose, this time with an audible crunch. She caught him under the chin with a powerful uppercut, and he recoiled, shaking his head. A large arm wrapped around his neck and put him in a chokehold. He grabbed at the arm and pulled, but Sergeant Jones was too strong. Calvo kicked and struggled but gradually gave way and collapsed, out of air.

"That's enough, Jones, don't kill him," Chazz said, gasping for air herself. Jones let Calvo fall to the ground.

"Ma'am, that's some serious blood you got there," he said. He looked around and picked up an oily rag from the hangar floor. He offered it to her, and she wadded it up and held it to her nose.

"Broken nose," she said.

"What?"

"Bro. Ken. Nose." She enunciated the words more clearly.

"Well, shoot. Ain't no medics around today, ma'am. And what are we gonna do with the Colonel here?"

"Call 911 when I'm gone."

"Yeah, ma'am." Jones hesitated. "About that," he began. Bad news was clearly coming. "Supply doesn't have the part. Got to order it. This bird ain't flying today, after all. Sorry, ma'am, I truly am."

Chazz pulled the rag off her nose. It was still bleeding. She put the rag back and held it. She walked over to the Black Hawk, picked up her sidearm, and holstered it.

"Got to go, Sergeant. Take care, and say hello to Shirelle from me." Chazz grimaced and headed for her car.

CHAPTER SIXTEEN
Manzanar

THE NURSE AT THE PORT Hueneme urgent care clinic let out a startled gasp when Chazz walked in. Was it the sight of blood, the smelly, oily rag, or the bloody stains on her OCPs? The nurse remained silent. The other six patients avoided looking at her, and the room filled with an uneasy silence. Chazz didn't take it personally. They had their own problems, and hers would only delay resolving theirs.

She explained to the nurse that she'd been in an accident at the air base, and the bleeding wouldn't stop. The nurse sat her firmly in a chair and said, "The doctor has several urgent appointments today. You'll have to wait. Please fill out these forms, and we'll schedule you in." The nurse handed Chazz a clipboard full of forms. Insurance and medical history forms. A drop of crimson blood hit the top form. She pressed the oily rag tighter against her nose.

"I'll have to pay up front with a credit card and get reimbursed," she said. Her HMO insurance company liked its patients to come to its facility, but the nearest one was in Ventura or LA. The VA clinic was also in Ventura. Was there a special insurance program for Silver Star heroes? If so, she knew nothing about it.

"Oh." The nurse smiled but realized that was an inappropriate reaction to a bleeding soldier. Her voice took on the standard professionalism. "All right. Just fill out the contact information and the medical section. List any medications you're taking. It might be several hundred dollars." Her critical gaze fixed on the rag. "Maybe more. If your bank declines your card, we won't treat you. And I'll need a photo ID."

"It should be fine. Here." She handed the nurse her credit card and driver's license. "Thanks so much for your help. Do you have a clean cloth and an ice pack? The swelling is pretty bad." She took the rag away from her nose. Blood dripped onto her OCPs, and the nurse winced.

"I...think we do, please, er..." She motioned to suggest that Chazz put the rag back on her nose, which she did. The nurse left and returned with paper towels and a freezer ice pack.

"Put the ice pack in some towels. Only twenty minutes at a time," she said, handing the supplies to Chazz. Chazz offered her the rag, but the nurse shook her head and raised her hands in refusal. Chazz dropped it on the floor and focused on the towels and ice pack. The coolness took some of the heat away from her nose. The nurse left and returned with a bin labeled "Hazardous Waste" and a medical instrument resembling oversized tweezers. Using the tweezers, she gripped the rag and dropped it in the bin, then swiftly cleared everything away. In a few minutes, she returned with Chazz's credit card and identification.

She said, still calmly professional, "We've put a $2,000 charge on the card, Colonel Silver. After we treat you, we'll update the charge to the correct total bill." She handed Chazz the card with a tight-lipped smile and left her to it.

Just then, her phone rang. The caller ID said "Tom." He'd gone to her house for the 0700 meetup and she hadn't shown up. She ignored the call. Voicemail beeped. The phone rang again, and she ignored it again. When the phone rang again, she opened her contacts and blocked Tom's number. She deleted the voicemail as well. Things were bad enough without Tom. The practical details of getting treatment for her injury kept her busy. She didn't need the stress of rehashing everything with Tom. One thing at a time.

The woman near Chazz shifted to a chair on the other side of the room. Chazz leaned back in her chair and held the ice pack to her throbbing nose. She could handle a broken nose, no problem. But the rest? She'd need military help.

Tom's mind was full of Chazz after he got back to Sacramento. She'd stood him up. He was distracted as he walked through the door of the governor's office. Sally Reed grinned and said, "Go right in, Tom. The governor is all excited about something." Sally looked up at him from her chair. "Whatever you guys are planning sure has Chip worked up."

Tom reconsidered his usual sardonic response and limited himself to praise. "You're a gem, Sally. Thanks!"

Tom knocked and entered the governor's office. Chip stood by the window looking out over the grounds with a big smile on his face. In a great mood, but that smile meant a Big Idea. Not good.

"*Hola,* Tomás. I just had a tremendous idea!" And there it was.

"And what would that be?" replied Tom, forcing a grin.

The governor strode over to his desk and picked up a piece of paper. He waved the paper around. Tom took it and glanced at it. Names of people—government and bureaucracy officials. All neatly typed up in two columns to fit on the page.

"What is this, Chip?"

"Everyone Myron and I suspected could get in our way. I had Sally type it up."

"Jesus Christ, Chip! We've kept Sally out of things. What were you thinking?"

"Yeah, yeah. I told her this was a working session I was putting together."

"And that's the big idea?"

"Hell, no." Chip rubbed his hands together. "When we talked about this, Myron told me he had troops in different places ready to arrest these guys. And girls. Right?"

"I guess. And?"

"So, where do we put them?"

Tom looked at the governor blankly and said, "OK, I'll bite. Where?"

"Manzanar."

"Um. What?"

"Jesus Christ, Tom, didn't you learn anything about California history in high school?"

"I know what Manzanar was, Chip. What's that got to do with—" It hit him. A concentration camp. "You're not suggesting we put all these people in a concentration camp?" Manzanar was the most notorious of the World War II relocation camps for Japanese Americans. Over 100,000 of them at its height. Tom had visited the site as a kid. Bleak didn't describe it.

Chip protested, "Why not? The place is ideal for our purpose."

"Oh my God."

"What's wrong with it?"

Tom looked down the list. The attorney general. Mayors. Police chiefs. FBI agents. National Guard officers. Specifically, Chazz. Right there, number thirty-four on the list. Right next to the adjutant general of the Guard. And she had stood him up for the 7 a.m. appointment at her house. He'd called, but she wasn't picking up. But this idea—he'd better nip it in the bud.

"I don't think we want to be in the business of running concentration camps, sir." Tom struggled to remember the full amount of reparations the U.S. had paid to the internees of Manzanar and the other camps. Millions. No, a billion. A billion and a half dollars. This was crazy.

"Just for a while, Tom. Say a month or two. Or three. Until we can block the obstructionists politically."

"Jesus, Chip—"

"We've got to put them somewhere and control them, and we don't have an endless supply of jailers to do that. It's the whole point of a concentration camp."

"Yeah, but—"

Chip returned to his stance by the window. His voice took on a critical tone, and he demanded, "Tom. You're the brains of the operation. What's wrong with it?"

"It's infamous! Manzanar is a stain on the state's history. The media, no, everyone will—"

"No one will know, Tom. Only you and Myron. And the guards, of course." The governor smiled sardonically. He shrugged and raised his hands palms up. He raised his voice to make his point. "And anyway, no one really cared, did they? The same will happen here. These are enemies of the state! The voters will understand that. Whenever we decide to have an election."

Tom desperately searched for something he could use to convince the governor to drop his idea. Chazz in a scorching concentration camp. Billions of dollars in reparations, after the war crimes trial. Aware of Chip's tendency to dismiss abstractions like reparations and war crimes, he crafted a feeble yet practical argument. "It's, it's a federal National Historic Site. With a ranger. The feds will overrun it."

"Come on—remember those crazies from Nevada who took over that wildlife refuge? The feds just stood around for weeks, then the idiot president pardoned the jerks. And the place only has one ranger? We'll just add him to the list. Or pay him to be a guard. Why not?" The governor grinned. "After all, it's ours now, not theirs."

Tom called General Dupont from his car as he drove toward the old Mather AFB.

"Myron, we've got to talk."

"OK, what now?"

"Not on the phone. Meet me in front of your command center and we'll drive and talk. No ears. I'll be there in five minutes."

He found Myron waiting outside the Guard command center at Mather. The general climbed into the passenger's seat.

"What's so important, Tom? I've got a lot of things to do to get this thing going. All these interruptions—"

"Yeah. Well, listen. Chip wants to put everyone in a concentration camp."

"You mean the internee list?"

"Yeah. He says Manzanar."

"What about Manzanar?"

"He wants to use it as the camp."

Myron cocked his head. "Well, he's had worse ideas. Suitable location. Way the hell out there."

"My God, Myron. The *optics*." Tom grimaced. "Running a concentration camp. I didn't sign up for this."

"We can make it so no one knows where they are. To prevent rescue attempts and crowds of reporters moaning about the victims."

"But after that, Myron. When the media gets hold of it. How the hell are we going to justify ourselves? We had this nice little concentration camp, so we moved a bunch of important people there in cattle cars?"

"We'll use transports, Tom. I've been working on the logistics."

"Fuck the logistics, Myron! You're going to tell your kids all about how daddy set up the concentration camps?" And how would he explain it to Chazz? If she ever spoke to him again. Tom felt the waters close over his head.

Myron sighed and looked ahead as Tom drove in circles through the streets of East Sacramento. "Tom, it's all about logistics. My kids will be fine. We've got to intern these people. They're dangerous to the operation. We can't put them in the local jails. We don't have enough troops for several camps. Let's see, about 100 people. Manzanar has a couple of blockhouses, replicas, but they'll do. We're going to need some trailers. We can requisition some of those FEMA trailers, sure we can. I bet FEMA will even deliver them for us if I can make up a plausible excuse."

Tom groaned. "Not FEMA, Myron. First, they're federal. Second, they're bureaucratic. Third, they're incompetent, especially at delivering things. You gotta find another way. Manzanar is too hard. Find another way."

"Tents. Bivouac tents. We'll need to harden the facility. The rangers wouldn't need much security. I'll assign a company of MPs to it. They'll set up tents until we can figure out the logistics for more permanent facilities on site."

Tom asked, despite himself, "How many soldiers is that?"

"One company? Four platoons, thirty men each, lieutenants and a captain to command, plus a group at the MP battalion headquarters to manage the operation." Myron pursed his lips. "They'll bivouac for a few days until we get the tents over there."

"Are these soldiers involved in the coup?"

"No, just the officers, some sergeants. Soldiers are good at following orders. They're used to their chain of command, so no one will question it." Myron smiled. "I've already got a great story, a covert operation to contain a terrorist infiltration in the state government. The troops will love it."

"This is nuts, Myron."

"It just takes the right perspective, Tom. It's really all about the logistics."

After dropping Myron at the Guard command center, Tom drove home, ideas for saving Chazz flooding his brain. None seemed more workable than simply telling her what she needed to know. A shot of tequila from his home wet bar helped strengthen his resolve. Christ, he was getting as bad as Chip. He picked up his phone to call her. He got voicemail and left a message asking her to call, making it urgent. Tom tried a few more times before giving up and placing his phone on the kitchen counter with a frown. The first three calls had rung and rung, then gone to voicemail. The fourth got no ring at all. Chazz had blocked him.

She'd blocked him.

God damn it. He wanted to save her, not stalk her.

But now she'd blocked him! Well, desperate times make desperate men. He picked up the phone and called Myron.

"Yes, Tom? What now? Did Chip have another idea?" asked Myron.

"Yeah." Tom modulated his voice to a casual tone to sell the lie. "A good one. He wants me to take Chazz myself. I told him I didn't like the idea of soldiers grabbing her, and he suggested I do it."

"She said she was coming in to talk with me today, but she hasn't shown up," said Myron. Tom sensed trouble. Myron's words were easy, but his tone was ominous.

Tom confirmed the problem. "Yeah, she asked me to go to her place early for a talk, but she wasn't there."

"Tom." Myron's voice took on a controlled urgency. "She's on to us. I just got a deranged call from Brickhouse at Camp Roberts. She showed up there against my orders to stay at Channel Islands. Brickhouse, that stupid bastard, ambushed her and tried to shoot her. She ended up killing Flattery and getting away. I'm getting the CHP down there to arrest her as an armed and dangerous killer." He paused. "I don't want you involved in this, Tom. I didn't want to tell you, given your feelings for her. But—"

Tom was beside himself. "What were those bastards thinking? God damn it, Myron, this is out of control. We can't be assassinating people." Especially Chazz. Fucking *hell*.

"Not without orders, anyway," Myron said. "But yeah, we're losing discipline. We have to move, Tom. Now. Today. I'll send out all the arrest orders tomorrow, then we'll move on Monday."

"I'll take Chazz, Myron. Don't set the CHP on her, not yet. She'll come along with me. I'll get her someplace safe, for her and for us. This is not negotiable, Myron. No police, no Chippies. Where will you keep the Southern California internees until the camp is ready?"

"L. A. County Jail. The Pitchess South Detention Center in Castaic. We've got deputies there that have signed on to our operation. They'll hold up to fifty prisoners for a week, telling no one. Then Manzanar. Once we have the tents set up."

"OK, give me their contact information. You call them and tell them I'm coming with a prisoner. I'll find Chazz and take her there and make sure she's OK. I'm doing this, Myron. No arguments."

Myron gave him the information and some fatherly advice. "You're going to regret spending so much time on her, Tom. Colonel Silver isn't marriage material. Much too independent."

"That's your opinion, Myron. I have to help her. I owe it to what we had between us."

"You're not thinking clearly. But all right. I'll call the communications center, get a triangulation on her cell phone, and call you back. You owe me for this." He hung up.

"God *damn* it!" Tom threw some clothes into a carryon suitcase and headed out. By the time he reached LAX and rented a car, Myron should have Chazz's location.

"Hi, Angel, it's me," Chip said, leaning back in his office chair, his feet up on the desk. After Tom left, he'd told Sally to go home so he could call Angélica without revealing anything. Sally was an efficient assistant, too efficient not to notice Chip calling his girlfriend to lure her into a concentration camp. Detention facility. Whatever.

"It's so good to hear your voice, Chepe," his girlfriend replied sarcastically. "You got something else to say? Or just more bullshit to pile on?"

"Angel, Angel, don't be mad. I'm sorry I hung up on you, OK? Sorry, sorry, sorry. I apologize. I apologize profusely."

"Oh my God, Chepe. Those words, coming out of your mouth. Are you on your knees? On your knees, you bastard!"

Chip smiled and shifted a little in his chair to make himself more comfortable. "I'm on them, Angel. I am."

"Take a picture and send it to me. After you take your pants off."

How much humiliation can a man take? He said, "OK, that's enough. When do you want to see the ring I bought you?"

Angélica was silent. Then, in a completely different tone of voice, she said, "*¡Híjole!* A ring?"

"Marry me, Angel. We are made for each other." Tom was right. They'd believe anything you said if it had the word "marry" in it. Stupid.

But there was a catch. Angel came right back with it, her voice taking on a barrio quality. "I told my brother Juan what you did, and he don't want me to marry you."

Chip took his feet off his desk and sat up. Juan Arguello? Oh, shit. Now he had the worst *jefe* in Tijuana pissed at him. That only confirmed his decision.

"Look, Angel, we can make it up to Juan. Let's meet up tomorrow and talk about it. I'll bring the ring down and we can work it out. In bed."

"Chepe, show me the ring first."

"Of course. Hey, I'm coming down to Glendale tomorrow for a CHP ceremony. Come, let's have lunch at a great little restaurant I know, and we'll talk."

"Glendale? What the hell's in Glendale?"

Chip laughed. "The CHP, for one. Trust me, Angel. This place is great. *Muy romantico*. Meet me in front of the building at ten, OK? North Central Avenue, can't miss it."

"Bring the ring, Chepe. Or I'll tell Juan to have you killed." He heard her lighting a cigarette.

Chip hung up and laughed. She wouldn't get the chance. This was too easy, easy as beans.

Chip called his friend Jim Kane, the commandant of the CHP Southern Division, and laid out the plan. He sat back in his chair and put his feet up again. The whole Manzanar thing had been a great idea, and putting Angel in a cage there was an even better one.

CHAPTER SEVENTEEN
The Beach

CHAZZ CONSIDERED HER OPTIONS WHILE waiting for the doctor. There was plenty of time. She had arrived at the clinic at 1000 hours, and the doctor saw her at 1415. "Urgent" care, of course it was. By 1445, the doctor had anesthetized, packed, straightened, and bandaged her nose. The ice pack the nurse had provided had long since melted into jelly, but they gave her another one. Or rather, they sold her one, along with a week's supply of oxycodone, which carried warnings about overdose and addiction. They scheduled a follow-up appointment in two days to check on her nose's healing and to remove the packing if possible. Great. She left, poorer by $5,275.67, with no intention of keeping that appointment.

The situation was dire. Ortiz and Calvo would look for her. Damn sure Dupont would, once Ortiz told him what had happened. And there was the Flattery killing, too. By now, Brickhouse must have returned to his base headquarters and reported the disaster at Camp Roberts. She had to find federal troops to deal with the situation.

Chazz left the clinic and crossed the parking lot to her car. She opened the trunk and strapped on her sidearm. She heard a car door open behind her. Not again. She turned and did a double take. Tom Peña. Her cheeks flushed with adrenaline. Tom got out of his nondescript Mazda rental car and stepped toward her. She suppressed her flight response and stood her ground.

"What are you doing here, Tom?" she asked in her newly muddled voice.

He stared at her, his mouth open. "Chazz…"

"Yeah. Ran into a fist. Is that why you're here, Tom?" she demanded. "To finish the job?"

"It's, no, I…. Oh, Chazz." He reached for her, but she stepped back, avoiding his embrace.

"Just stop, Tom. Why are you here? And how did you find me?"

"Let's go find somewhere to talk, Chazz, where you can get comfortable. It's…very private. I'll answer all your questions."

"No."

"Chazz, please. You're—"

She reconsidered. Despite her mixed feelings, Tom could provide the information she needed. Public would be better than private, though.

She closed her trunk and said, "Let's go down to the beach and talk." She led the way down the street and onto the beach. He caught up and walked beside her.

"Chazz, I flew down here because you blocked my calls. You didn't show up at your house this morning to talk."

She nodded to herself. Stalking her. She turned slightly away from him and unsnapped the restraint on her holster.

Tom reassured her. "Chazz. I have things to tell you. You're in danger."

She found that snorting was no longer a practical option, so she grunted and said, "No shit."

"Was that someone from the Air Station?" He indicated her nose with his head.

She nodded. "Guy named Calvo. I left him unconscious." She tried to put some menace into the last words, but it's hard to sound menacing with a bandaged broken nose.

"Jesus Christ. This shit ain't hitting the fan. It's exploding all over the place." They reached the edge of the beach, and Chazz pointed to the long fishing pier. They walked out along it. A few screaming seagulls flew in and out of the heavy surf. The pier was empty of people.

Tom said, "I can't say everything I want to. You're not stupid, Chazz. Just the opposite. You must have figured out there's some heavy shit coming down."

"Yeah, Tom, I've figured that out. The bullets at Camp Roberts, they were pretty heavy. You know all about that, right?"

"You're on a list. A list of people…" Tom hesitated, avoiding eye contact.

"To be killed?" Tom had known about Brickhouse's plan to kill her at Roberts. He was part of it. He was here to rectify the mistake. She backed away, hand on her gun.

His eyes snapped back to her face. "Oh, God, no, Chazz. We wouldn't—the assholes at Roberts did that on their own. No orders, Dupont didn't know, and I sure as hell didn't. Dupont wants to arrest what he calls dangerous people, and you're on that list. And Dupont wants to arrest you now, before things happen. He knows you're here, not back in Sacramento. He says you killed someone." Tom cleared his throat. "I insisted on bringing you in myself." He walked over to the railing and stared out at the sunlit Pacific Ocean. He said, hesitating, "To Pitchess. And then…to Manzanar. I'm so sorry, Chazz. I want you to be safe."

"Jail. And a concentration camp. Safe?" That was worse than thinking he wanted her dead. "And the charade at the Air Station?" she asked. "Ortiz and Calvo? Was that your idea?"

"No, but I knew about it. They wanted to distract you until next week."

"Why? No, let me guess. You're on a tight schedule and the tanks are getting too hot to hold, so when does it start? Wednesday? Thursday? I'll bet the schedule's moving up now. Monday?" Her mind jumped to another clue. "That Mexican beach. And the wedding? That too? All a charade." She kept her hand on the gun.

Tom shook his head impatiently, then ignored most of her questions. "Look, Chazz, I meant what—"

"Why should I listen to you? I should call the cops right now." She took her phone out of her pocket for emphasis. She shook it in his face.

Tom gritted his teeth. He grabbed the phone from her and threw it overhand into the ocean. The sun flashed off the device as it flew. Not a thought passed through her mind as her body reacted on its own. She didn't even draw her gun. She lunged at the man she had loved, arms outstretched, and pushed him over the wooden railing into the crashing surf below. Then she ran.

CHAPTER EIGHTEEN
So It Goes

TOM FLAILED IN THE WATER, not knowing which way was up, blind. He'd hit the water with a huge belly flop that knocked the air out of him. He struggled to breathe but found only water. Salt water. He flashed back to age 11, when he'd slipped in his father's fishing boat and fallen into the bay. He'd learned to swim since then, but the panic twisted his mind away from the skills he needed to survive.

But he was a survivor. He fought down the panic, swallowed the salt, calmed his limbs, and floated. That oriented him in the water, and he rose upward. He thought about kicking off his shoes, but he suddenly broke the surface. Sun low in the sky, shore to the left, pier looming above him. The surf pushed him toward the beach. He pulled with his hands to speed up. It wasn't long before his foot scraped the sand.

He staggered out of the surf with a light but cool offshore breeze at his back, his clothes soaked and his eyes stinging from the salt water. His shoes squelched as he trudged up the wet sand to the drier part of the beach above the surf line. He made for the palm trees rustling in the wind and the path beyond them. His right foot hit a rock, invisible in the sand, and he lost his balance and fell sideways. He tasted ash. His face rested in a beach fire ring full of ashes. After rolling off the rocks, he lay on the sand in a downward spiral of hopelessness. Chazz's white-bandaged face, teeth bared, ferocity leaking out of her eyes, arms outstretched and rigid filled his mind. Not the image he wanted to remember.

He climbed to his feet and, more carefully now, trudged up the rest of the beach to the parking lot. Orienting himself, he walked across the lot to the road, then on up the sidewalks to the clinic where he'd parked. No sign of Chazz's car anywhere. She was long gone, if she had any sense, and he knew she had more sense than anyone he'd ever known.

He'd put off calling Myron with the good news. It was time. He leaned against his car and pulled his phone out of his soaking jacket pocket. Well, guess what? Waterlogged and inoperable.

The urgency grew inside Tom. Chazz's escape did not absolve him of his duties. He was all in on the new California Republic.

He'd passed a small motel on his way to the clinic. Returning there, he walked into the office, but no one was behind the counter. Tom reached for the desk bell and brought down his hand. Someone moved in the back room. A young woman, blonde hair, T-shirt and jeans, came out from the back. When she saw what awaited her, she froze.

"Ohmygaw...." She turned to escape from the nightmare of a soaked, soot-stained, sand-frosted six-foot-tall monster that would attack her, extract her liver, and eat it while she watched. Tom imagined this scenario based on his limited knowledge of young blondes from the southern part of the state.

"Wait...please. I need help." He said this with quiet urgency.

The woman froze again and pivoted back, her hands covering her lower face. Her eyes grew wide.

"I'm...I fell into the ocean. I'm not as dangerous as I look. Can I use your phone?" Tom smiled to put energy into his ask. He was clueless about how she saw him. How far would the sheer force of his personality move her to accept him?

It was enough. The woman dropped her hands from her face, pursed her lips, and approached the counter. "Really?" she asked. "You fell in?"

"Off the pier. An accident. I don't want to talk about it. Phone?"

"Oh. My. God. You're sure you don't need an ambulance? I can call 911." She grimaced. "But I'm not supposed to let guests use the office phone."

"No. I'm fine. Just wet. And cold. Can I have a room? With a phone? And a shower?"

"I guess." The woman tapped on her keyboard. She looked up. "Any luggage?"

"In my car." He turned and pointed to the rental car sitting peacefully in the parking lot.

"I'm not supposed to give a room to someone without luggage."

"I can go get it. If I collapse on the way, you can call 911, OK?" Another smile. He pulled out his wallet and handed her his credit card.

The woman smiled despite herself. "Oh, all right. I'll give you a room on the first floor. Do you promise not to drip on the carpet?"

"I'll undress right at the room's door. How's that?"

The clerk looked alarmed but quickly resumed typing with determination. She picked up the credit card and grimaced. She used a tissue from a box on the counter to dry the card. After swiping the card, she retrieved an old-fashioned room key from a drawer. She slapped it down with his credit card, a pen, and the credit slip. Tom scratched his signature on the slip and moved it toward her. She gingerly took it and put it in a drawer.

"Checkout's at 11 a.m. Extra towels in the closet. Call if you need—" She stopped short, unwilling to encourage further contact. The woman kept her eyes on her computer as she reeled off this standard spiel. Tom theorized she was reluctant to look at the mistake she was sure she was making.

"Sure thing. Thanks."

Myron sat in his home office after finishing dinner with his family, doing nothing other than trying not to call Chip. His teeth tightly clenched, he kept stopping himself from picking up the phone from his desk. This was worse than dieting. He worried about what Chip might do next that would force overly hasty action. Action that Myron knew would only cause more trouble down the road. He'd counted on Tom to keep the man in check, and now Tom had disappeared on a knight's quest to rescue his damsel in distress. This picture of Colonel Silver made him smile. She had equal chances of saving Tom, and as for being a damsel...he smiled again. His hand crept toward his phone.

The phone suddenly rang, making him jump. Relaxing his shoulders, he breathed and picked up the phone. The caller ID said The Governor. Answering Chip's call was much better than calling him. It allowed Myron to keep his facade of imperturbability.

"Yes?" he asked in a calm voice.

"Myron, where the hell is Tom? I can't get him on his phone."

"I have heard nothing from him since he left for LA."

"Well, shit. He left hours ago to pick up that...woman."

"I know, Chip. He hasn't called or texted."

"We got to move, Myron." The governor loudly hammered out the words.

"Not on a Friday night. Nobody's ready."

"Hell. Tomorrow morning, then. But we gotta do it *now*. Start things rolling. If Tom doesn't take her out, she'll go to the feds. Myron. Is Tom still with us? I mean, on our side? Has she got him by the balls?"

"She's a very persuasive person who gets things done. That's why I wanted her on our side. But Tom? He's solid." Solid enough. But Chip had a point. Myron realized he had little choice in the matter with Silver running around blowing things up.

Chip doubled down. "I sure as hell hope so, Myron. Because if he's not, we're in deep shit. Let's roll the tanks first thing. Shut everything down. Then set up the Emergency Alert Network takeover so we can shut down the media and make our announcement. How quickly can you jail the individuals on the list?"

"I've already sent the list to my field teams. They've started arresting the politicians, and the purge of the Highway Patrol is underway. The schedule calls for the coordinated arrests of everyone on the list by Tuesday morning's announcement."

Mollified, the governor grunted his approval. "I want Tom at the announcement. And Myron—no more goddamn delays. Got it?"

Myron pursed his lips, then said, "We'll all do our best, Chip. Remember, the trick to winning wars is to be ready to change your plans when things change on the ground." Rear-guard action at best. Covering his butt at worst.

Chip dismissed the possibility. "Yeah, yeah. Myron, I want to hear that fat lady singing by Tuesday morning, and I don't care how she arranges the music." The governor hung up.

Myron gently placed the phone on his desk, walked to his office door, and called out, "Honey, can you make me a pot of coffee? I have a long night ahead."

"Oh, Myron," his wife's voice complained from the kitchen. But he heard the sounds of the coffee maker filling.

Friday night at six was the worst time to take I-5 through LA. Heavy traffic, stopping and not going. Chazz kept the sound system on full blast to keep herself awake. Her nose throbbed with pain. Couldn't stop for pain pills. Couldn't drive with them, either. The throbbing would keep her awake. Downtown. Long Beach. She headed for Santa Ana. The traffic picked up speed.

Disney Way. Chazz felt an irrational wish to stop and lose herself in the theme park. She couldn't get the damn Mad Hatter teacups out of her head. Why the teacups? Her father. It had been her sole positive experience with her father. Before....

Stop it. She had enough on her plate without bringing up all the old family trauma. Chazz closed her eyes briefly, then opened them to find it wasn't so brief.

She was falling asleep at the wheel.

Dreaming. She forced herself not to think about Tom. Had she killed him?

Keep driving.

The Orange Crush interchange.

Irvine. Irvine? Irvine.

That's it. Must stop, or she'll die by car instead of by bullet. Or kill some citizen.

She turned onto CA-55. There was a nice motel nearby that she knew. Off the beaten path. No one would look for her in Irvine. Would they? And it had a garage. Get the car off the street. Security of sorts.

Gun case in the duffel. And...better change the bloody OCPs. They wouldn't cut it for the motel staff. The bandage would be bad enough. She looked around. Nobody in the garage. She dug her spare uniform out of the duffel. Five minutes later, mission accomplished.

Within an hour, with her gun under her pillow, Chazz was fast asleep, letting a dose of oxy do its work.

Tom sat on the motel room bed, towel wrapped around his waist. A brief shower had restored circulation in his limbs and rational thought to his brain. He picked up the room phone and called Myron.

"Where the hell are you?" asked Myron.

"Port Hueneme."

"Why aren't you *here?*"

"I had an unfortunate accident when I tried to take Chazz."

"Do I want to know the details?"

"Just that she's somewhere else now in her rental car, and she knows we want her in jail. And that stupid bastard Calvo roughed her up before she cold-cocked him. Broke her nose. It's all bandaged."

"Jesus, Tom. I'll get the Highway Patrol after her. Son of a bitch. She's got to be heading for the feds. Maybe Pendleton."

"Yeah. OK. I'm done. Put her where she can't do more damage. Oh—and my phone is kaput. So is hers." He read off the phone number of the motel room.

Myron said, "We're moving. We can't wait, with Silver out there rolling around like a loose cannon."

"I figured you would. You've started arresting the internees?"

"Yes. Orders out to all the mechanized units and troops. How soon can you get here?"

"Tomorrow morning."

"This is important, Tom."

"I'm done. I need a good night's sleep, Myron. When is the EAN announcement? Chip's got my speech already."

"We've told the Office of Emergency Services the exercise will start at 11 a.m Tuesday at the Warning Center at Mather. We'll cut the connection to the Virginia federal center, and Chip will deliver his declaration. That barely gives us time to position the tanks here and in LA." The general paused and asked, "Are you in good enough shape to be at the announcement? Chip wants you there, and I want you there—to keep him on track."

"I'll be there," Tom said, feeling ancient. "I'll fly back from LAX tomorrow."

"Tom."

"Yes, Myron?"

"Please don't screw this up. Between Chip and organizing this thing, I don't need more problems."

The general hung up, and Tom put the phone back in its charging station. He fell back on the bed and stared at the ceiling. The day's events played over and over in his mind, offering no comfort for Chazz's rejection. Then, in the space between obsession and sleep, he indulged his memory of their love.

Myron looked up the new Highway Patrol chief's personal number. The arrest of the entire CHP leadership had put them all in the holding cells he'd prepared at Sacramento County Main Jail, leaving Ed Woodford in charge.

"Ed? Myron here. Listen, I know you're busy getting things in order over there, but I need to ask a favor."

"Is it related, Myron? Jesus, I'm up to my balls in alligators, and they're snapping. This is all happening too fast."

"One of my officers has gone rogue, Ed. My chief of staff, Colonel Silver. She's somewhere between Santa Barbara and San Diego, and she's going to cause a lot of trouble if we don't stop her."

"Have your people pick her up. LA is a mess right now, and I'm short on resources." Woodford snorted. "Do you know how much land there is between Santa Barbara and San Diego? It's a third of the state, Myron. How in hell can we find her?"

"I'm sure you'll find a way," Myron said, appeasing the man. "But Silver killed one of our officers at Camp Roberts and fled the scene. She's armed and dangerous, and she'll come after us if she gets the chance. I can't take that chance."

"Fine. Why not use your personnel for this?"

Myron got direct. "I want every CHP officer you can muster down there looking for her. She was in Port Hueneme. Who knows where she's heading? Pendleton?"

"Myron—"

"Ed, if your job is too hard, let me know, OK? I'd be happy to find a replacement."

"OK, OK. Send me her profile, DNA fingerprint, and transportation details. We'll set up an image scanner check for all the cameras in the area. And the patrol vehicles. Cell phone? Anything special to look for?"

"You need to talk to Hertz at LAX about her rental car details. I'll send the Guard profile. Name is Colonel Chastity Silver. She's 5'11", dark brown hair, no body fat at all, blue eyes, Caucasian. She'll be wearing standard Army dress. No cell phone anymore. Oh, and she has a broken nose, bandaged. She's armed. And very dangerous." Myron pursed his lips. Why not be explicit? This was the new Highway Patrol. "Ed, give the order to shoot to kill."

"Wow. I'd love to meet this wonder woman, but that ain't gonna happen. OK, I'll have my team work on LA and Orange County. Is that all, Myron?"

"Yes, that's all, Ed. For now. Thank you very much."

Myron leaned back in his chair. It really was too bad about Colonel Silver. She was an outstanding officer and the Guard's best COS in a while. He'd miss her, but he'd rather see her dead.

Now, time to get those tanks moving.

CHAPTER NINETEEN
Baghdad by the Bay

"Sergeant Briscoe?" His phone's caller ID read "Brickhouse."

"Sir," Sergeant Leroy Briscoe acknowledged. He was more than ready for the call. The tank crews had gathered around a small campfire they'd built under the I-5 overpass. Might as well be fucking homeless. They couldn't even see the stars. The freeway above was blocking them all out, for chrissakes. They'd chopped down one of the ornamental trees nearby for firewood. The stuff was too green and smoked like hell. Living rough sucks, even for soldiers.

"I've received the order to move, Sergeant. Sorry about the delay. Politics up the line. Orders are to position your tanks on the freeway at 0800 hours Saturday morning. You have the position coordinates?"

"Yes, sir."

"If you encounter any resistance, make it clear that you are in charge, and you aren't going anywhere."

"Force authorization, sir?"

"Do whatever you have to, Sergeant. No rules of engagement. I want those freeways shut down by 0815 Tuesday."

"Yes, sir! But, sir—we need an infantry squad. We can't—"

"No time, Sergeant, and no troops available. Get it done."

"Yes, sir."

Briscoe put down his phone and said to his crew, "Rock and roll time, guys! 0800 hours tomorrow."

He made sure each soldier understood his instructions. Tonight they would do the pre-action prayer circle, catch a few ZZZs, then suit up and get it done. Briscoe stretched his hands out toward the fire. This was one for the history books. And Briscoe knew they'd spell his name right. He'd make sure of it.

The Alemany Farmers' Market at the foot of Bernal Heights in San Francisco was abuzz with activity. Early food shoppers, prepared for their weekly bonanza of organics and local specialties, stood outside the market wondering what the hell was going on. The traffic jam of farmers' trucks and cars didn't help.

Instead of the usual food stalls, there were twenty military transports lined up across the market. Three tanks blocked the Alemany Boulevard entrance. At the back of the market were three HETs—tank transport flatbeds—and a fuel tanker. Three soldiers with MP armbands stood in front of the tanks, trying to persuade the farmers and shoppers to go home. No one moved.

The frustrated MPs retreated behind the tanks after a farmer threw an organic lettuce, followed by an organic tomato from another farmer shouting expletives. This was about money, big money. Saturdays at the Farmer's Market kept many farmers solvent. They'd paid their fees for their stalls, and they weren't about to back down for a bunch of military idiots.

One by one, the tanks cranked their big cannons down to aim directly at the farmers' trucks. Heads popped out of turret hatches and manned machine guns pointed at the crowd of shoppers.

Silence fell. Ten minutes later, on a bright September morning in San Francisco, the streets had cleared.

San Francisco mayor Roger Whitelaw was enjoying his first Saturday off in weeks. Crisis after crisis had required his presence at City Hall virtually every weekend during the summer. That the Board of Supervisors had created each crisis through their incredibly stupid behavior didn't reduce the impact on the City. And what the supervisors didn't screw up, the new governor in Sacramento was happy to screw up for them. A failed actor running the state, just what Roger needed.

What with the ongoing sewer replacement program that had destroyed three homes with a block-wide sinkhole on Green Street in Pacific Heights and the carfentanil crisis among the homeless population, he'd barely had time to take a walk, much less his favorite bike ride across the Golden Gate Bridge. Carfentanil. What idiot had come up with that one? Used to tranquilize elephants, it was the perfect drug to clear out the homeless population one overdose at a time.

Roger pondered these and other civic puzzles as he powered his bike across the bridge from his trip up the Marin Headlands. It was easier now that they'd opened up the west sidewalk on Saturdays. You didn't have to compete with tourists gawking at Alcatraz, the jewel of the Golden Gate National Recreation Area. The island ought to bring in millions to the City but instead was part of the U.S. federal government's mismanagement program. That's what he liked to call it: mismanagement. Outright theft. He could house 20,000 homeless people in the Presidio alone if not for the recalcitrant feds and their GGNRA scam.

He slowed to a crawl as a gaggle of bikers stopped in front of him. Military uniforms. Must be some kind of excursion. But they shouldn't block the bridge sidewalk. He'd have a gentle word. He stopped and raised his hand in greeting.

"Hey," said one man with the insignia of a lieutenant. "You're the mayor, right?"

"Yes, that's right. You—"

"You're under arrest."

"Um." Roger blinked. "What?"

A large military vehicle came to a stop in the nearest bridge lane, right next to Roger. The military men dropped their bikes on the sidewalk, grabbed his arms, threw his $13,899.36 carbon fiber bike over the edge of the bridge, and hustled him into the vehicle.

"What the hell's going on!" he shouted. "My bike—" He pulled at the hands holding him, to no avail.

"Hood him," said the lieutenant, and a soldier pulled a black hood over Roger's head while another zip-tied his hands behind his back.

"Go go go!" a voice said, and Roger felt the vehicle accelerate.

What now? At least the suicide net would catch the bike. The mayor, for once, was speechless.

CHAPTER TWENTY
The Highway Patrol

Chazz opened her eyes and wondered for a bleary minute where the hell she was. She lay sideways on a bed, fully dressed in her OCPs, her mouth parched and her face hurting like hell. The Dream again? Couldn't remember. And the pain was worse. Why?

Then memory returned. She groaned, rolled over, and got off the bed. Her feet took her across the motel room to the small bathroom. She turned on the light and examined her face. Yep; she still looked like a war casualty. No obvious sign of bleeding. The urgent care doctor sure knew what she was doing. She'd have to see about getting the packing removed soon.

Chazz reached under the pillow and pulled out her Sig, carefully placing it in the gun case and returning the case to the duffel bag. She pulled out her toothbrush and hairbrush and managed to apply the right brush to the right task. The coffeemaker in the room burbled to produce a paper cup full of coffee. She sat on the bed and sipped. She still felt like crap. But she was awake now.

When she checked out, the desk clerk stared at her nose bandage. A fall, she told him. He sympathized. As she folded up the receipt, she asked, "Is there a big-box electronics store near here? I need some things."

"Yes, ma'am. Go two blocks, then turn left and go two more blocks to reach the mall."

She easily found the mall and bought a prepaid smartphone. Her next step: tell it to the Marines. It was time to get help. She found that her subconscious had chosen the helper for her. She was halfway to Pendleton. She sat in her car in the parking lot and tried to remember Tony Ridger's cell phone number. It finally came to her, and she dialed.

"Hello?" The voice was Tony's, but his tone was questioning. "Who is this?"

"It's Chazz, Tony," she said.

"Doesn't sound like Chazz's voice," he replied doubtfully. "And this isn't Chazz's number."

"Yeah. I lost my cell phone. And I've got a giant bandage over my broken nose and a bunch of packing in it. Use your imagination, Tony."

"Last time we talked, you said I didn't have any."

She laughed. "True. Sorry about that. I was mad at you, I remember."

"Yeah. I think we've both gotten over it. What has it been, three years?"

"About that."

"It's good to hear from you, Chazz. We should get together. Are you in San Diego?"

"No, Irvine. And I'm not looking for a date, Tony. I need help, fast."

"What kind of help?"

"The military kind. The Marine kind."

"Um...what?" Tony asked. She imagined that surprised look he was so good at.

"Tony, I can't talk about this over the phone. Can I drive down to Pendleton so we can talk?"

"Sure, I guess. Give me a hint?"

"National security, that's all I'll say. I need to talk to the commanding general. Get me onto the base, Tony, and we'll take it from there."

"OK. Irvine? Turn into the San Onofre gate. I'll meet you there. I assume you're still with the Guard?"

"Chief of Staff, senior Colonel now, Army Guard."

"Jeez. I guess I was wrong about your career. OK, getting onto the base shouldn't be a problem."

"See you in two hours."

She rethought her tactics, got out of her car, unlocked the trunk, and put on her sidearm and holster. Better sorry and safe than just sorry.

As she drove through San Clemente, Chazz reexamined her relationships with Tony. Iraq, and the wild times she'd had there. Three years ago, when he'd wormed his way into her bed after his divorce, just as she was moving up in the Guard. Those affairs didn't last long. His marriage and her war focus clashed in Iraq. In San Diego, his being a jerk about her career broke them up. And now? She knew he was a friend. A friend with the connections she needed.

San Onofre Beach coming up, time to turn off to Pendleton. The exit—

A siren wailed behind her and she looked in the rear-view mirror. Highway Patrol. She looked at her speedometer. Sixty-five. She'd set the cruise control once the morning commute traffic had cleared. Chazz eased her gun out of its holster, making no movement with her shoulders, and put it on her lap.

She slowed. The CHP car came right up behind her, overheads flashing. They sounded their siren again. Chazz pulled onto the shoulder. She left the car's systems on. The Chippie was on his radio. He looked at her and opened his door. He crouched down behind it, and the loudspeaker said, "Step out of the car with your hands visible. You're under arrest."

When she hesitated, the CHP officer repeated his instructions with more emphasis. "IF YOU DO NOT GET OUT OF THE CAR WITH YOUR HANDS VISIBLE, WE HAVE ORDERS TO SHOOT." Very loud. Unnecessarily loud. Chazz got the message. She had to be quick and accurate. And she'd have to act before his backup showed.

She raised her left hand and waved, then cracked her door, appearing to comply.

She turned, clasped her hands around the gun handle, aimed, and fired four quick shots through the missing rear window at the patrol car. The hits on the radiator spurted, minor explosions of fluid. A bullet narrowly missed her and shattered the windshield. Great. She turned, floored the accelerator, and set the gun on the passenger seat, leaning down to make a smaller target. The car dinged a warning, door was still open. She stretched and closed it. She heard a thud and knew another bullet had lodged somewhere. At least it wasn't in her. Shooting into moving cars was unprofessional. And wouldn't the damage please the rental car company? Her insurance wouldn't cover any of this.

In two minutes, she'd reached the Basilone Road/San Onofre exit. Once on the base, she'd be out of the CHP's jurisdiction. Ignoring the stop sign, she made a sharp left turn with screeching tires. She slowed the car as she approached the concrete barricades at the San Onofre Gate and stopped at the kiosk. Her mind was already busy coming up with a story about the two missing windows as she fumbled for her Guard ID.

CHAPTER TWENTY-ONE
Tony

THE MARINE MANNING THE KIOSK saluted and took Chazz's identification. He examined both sides, then glanced at the car wreckage and her injured nose. At least the uniform was fresh. He handed the card back to her without comment.

A red Mustang Mach-E GT zoomed up and made a sweeping U-turn by the side of the road. The door opened and Tony stepped out, smiling. He walked over to the kiosk. The Marine saluted, and Tony returned it. He leaned into her side window. "Nice car, Colonel Silver. Will it make the thirty miles to my place?"

"Oh, ha. Yes, it will, Lieutenant Colonel Ridger," she said with a smile. She'd noticed the oak leaf insignia on his OCPs. They'd promoted him. "Tony, it's so good to see you."

"You'll have to move along, sir," the Marine said, smiling. "Traffic, you know?"

"Aye aye, corporal," the colonel said, straightening up. "Follow my car, Chazz. I'll drive slow."

Chazz pulled forward and followed Tony's Mustang down Basilone Road at a sedate 60 miles per hour. The turns into the base bewildered her. After what seemed like an eternity, they pulled into Tony's driveway in front of his quarters. She parked behind the Mustang. Tony got out and opened her door, and she stepped out and hugged him.

"You've grown up," Chazz said, after the brief hug and peck kiss. Her friend appeared more purposeful and serious than before. Maybe his promotion had played a role. Or maybe it was the responsibility of his new job, whatever it was.

"And you haven't changed at all," he said untruthfully.

"You're a terrible liar," she said.

"Well, the nose thing is certainly different. And the car isn't really your style." He walked around it, inspecting the broken windows. "Goes with the nose, though, doesn't it?"

"Tony, can we go inside and talk? It's…I'm in trouble. The state is in trouble."

"OK, Chazz, sure. Can I carry anything?"

To answer, she opened her trunk and pulled out the duffel, then retrieved her gun from the passenger seat and holstered it. Tony cocked his head and half-smiled but said nothing.

It was a small, one-bedroom house with a living room, kitchen, and dinette. Pretty standard officer housing for Pendleton, she imagined.

"Drink?" he asked.

"Just water, thanks. I have to stay sober to talk to the base commander."

"So it's serious, huh?" He grinned. "Figured as soon as I saw the Sig. You might as well have that drink. I checked with MCIWEST HQ. General Simmonds is away. He'll be back Monday."

Chazz's heart sank. "What about the XO?"

"If this is important, wait for Simmonds. The XO is, well, let's call him indecisive. Simmonds likes to be in charge. He picks his subordinates to make sure he is."

"Damn!" She slapped the kitchen counter in frustration.

"Chazz. Have a beer. Sit and tell me all about it." He led her into the small living room. Anxiety tightened her stomach. Would Tony believe her? Chazz wasn't sure if she would believe her story if she were in Tony's position. But she had to try.

***

"I fired four rounds into the CHP's radiator to disable the car. So I made the San Onofre exit without pursuit, and here I am," Chazz said, finishing up her sad story and her beer.

"Another?" asked Tony, raising his empty beer can. He hadn't said anything, no expression on his face, even when she'd described the attack at Camp Roberts. She decided not to mention the Flattery killing just yet. Too much information, even for Tony. And she wasn't sure how he'd react to it.

"No, empty stomach. I couldn't stop for lunch."

"Let's get some pizza delivered. Domino's is open."

"Your tastes haven't changed."

"I disagree. I've opened up to gourmet offerings. Ham and pineapple."

Chazz shook her head. Far from pozole and molé with Tom. But to her, food was about the person you were eating with. No pineapple on pizza, though. She had standards. Spinach, in a pinch, but no fruit.

"Let's get cheese," she suggested.

"I'll get pepperoni, too. I'm a Marine."

While they waited for the pizza, Chazz asked for Tony's thoughts about her problem.

He sighed. "Jeez, Chazz. This all sounds pretty damn paranoid. I mean, you got the bullet holes to prove it, but—a coup in California? Tanks in the streets? The Army Guard taking over? The governor? Guard officers in assassination plots? Killing?" Seeing her face, he apologized. "Sorry, Chazz. I believe you, of course I do. But it's hard to imagine. I mean, the U.S. won't just stand by and let this happen. There are 36,000 Marines on this base that will stop it, if nothing else."

"I'm not so sure, Tony. They won't lift a finger without pressure. I put a lot of miles on the road thinking about it. The president hates California and is doing everything he can to cut off resources. Offshore drilling back on? Colorado River water rights taken away? The farm worker immigration shutdown? And you know what he's done to the military here with base closings and troop transfers."

"Am I ever. That's why I'm a lieutenant colonel."

"What do you mean?"

"I've been moving around and climbing up the ladder since Iraq. I joined the First Raiders before we reconnected in 2022."

"Special Ops?"

"Communications, and if I tell you any more, I'll have to kill you. That's why I didn't tell you. Secret."

"Uh, huh? That and you didn't approve of my career change to the Guard." Then she remembered. "Didn't they move—"

"Yeah, part of our wonderful Defense Department's pulling out of California. They moved to Camp Lejeune. It took several years and finished up in '22." He pursed his lips. "That's when I looked you up and we…" He cocked his head and smiled. "I wanted stability. You wanted a different career."

"You're still here after six years. That's pretty stable."

"I like California, and I'm too old to learn to like North Carolina."

"Then you must have transferred into a different group?"

"MCTSSA I2SD."

"Um."

"Yeah. If they added two more letters, I wouldn't remember it all. Marine Corps Tactical Systems Support Activity Infrastructure and Information Services Division."

Chazz parsed this gem. "You work on computers."

"I manage people who work on computers."

"A step down from Iraq."

"Look who's talking."

The doorbell rang. Pizza delivery. Chazz gritted her teeth in frustration. First Tony's career, now pizza, and she still didn't know whether Tony would help. Tony laid the boxes out on the kitchen counter and they shared out the food. But all this history and pizza didn't distract Chazz. She needed action, not talk.

"Worst pizza ever," Chazz remarked, savoring the burnt garlic.

"Worse than Iraq?"

"You mean the stuff they served in the mess hall they called pizza? That doesn't count. It wasn't pizza."

"But you just ate most of yours."

"As I watched you finish yours ten minutes ago."

"What can I say? I was hungry."

"Sure, Tony." She grinned. "This is your second lunch, right?" She knew the bottomless pit this man represented.

"Well, yeah. I ate right before you got here."

Chazz shook her head. Men. And he did what men do when they want to avoid talking about things.

She said, "Nice job."

"What do you mean?"

"Deflecting the coup discussion into a Tony discussion."

"Damn. Busted."

"This is real, Tony. I'm here to fix this."

"You need Simmonds, and he's not here. And I can see it's upsetting you."

"Upsetting..." She gaped. "Tony. Let me lay it out for you. My commanding general, my commander-in-chief, and my boyfriend are conspiring to commit seditious treason by seceding from the United States. This coup violates God knows how many federal laws, the Constitution, and most importantly, the oath we took as soldiers."

"OK, Chazz, I get it. I do. Simmonds will handle this. Calm down and pull yourself together. You've been through a lot these past few days. You need to be at your best when you talk to the general." His eyes narrowed. "Wait a minute. Boyfriend? Is that the Peña guy? The governor's chief strategist you talked about?"

"Yeah. Sorry that slipped out. You're deflecting again."

"Ulterior motives. We can sit around all day and argue or tell stories, whatever you want. One thing, though. Your car situation. We need to deal with that."

She walked Tony out to the cars. Her wreck, sitting next to his shiny new Mustang, had him shaking his head now that he knew how it had got that way. She showed him the bullet hole in the passenger seat.

He said, "God was your co-pilot, Chazz." He stuck a finger in the hole and grimaced.

"I've run out of luck, Tony," she replied. "God has ejected to save himself."

He rubbed a hand across his chin. "You need to get rid of this car, Chazz. Too identifiable."

"You got a chopper I can borrow?" She walked around the wreck. "Or maybe an Osprey? How do I explain this to the rental car company?'"

"Tell them someone stole it. You have insurance, right? And someone will."

"What do you mean?"

"Steal it! We've got to get rid of the car. Too easy for the CHP to spot once you're off base." He walked around the car, looking at it and thinking. "OK, here's the deal. There's a storage shed in the north part of the base that's no longer in use. Stored front-end loaders or something for a construction project. Lots of these abandoned sheds scattered around the base. No one ever cleans up after their projects. I looked at this one out of curiosity. Nothing but spiders and dust. Let's put your car there. If anyone finds it, it will be just another abandoned stolen car." He grinned. "Then a drive through the outback. Like we did in Iraq, remember?"

She did. His theory had been that if they stayed off the highway and went to random places with no people, there would be no IEDs. She had been just enough in love to buy that. They quit after the third hair-raising adventure. She eyed the Mustang.

"Huh. What can I do for a ride? If you can't get me an Osprey, how about your car? It's a Mach-E GT, right? It only needs Hellfire missiles to be as good as an attack chopper."

He got into the Mustang EV, and she got into her wreck, and he drove through a series of dirt roads to the shed. Isolated and ignored, perfect for a place to dump a wrecked car.

* * *

After closing the shed door on her wreck, she settled into the passenger seat of the Mustang. Tony grinned and proposed, "Care for a test drive? Show you what this lady can do? There's a remote part of the base…like Iraq, only cooler." Chazz glanced at the Mustang's temperature gauge—83°F. But then, Iraq's temperature could hit 125.

She shut Iraq out of her mind and asked, "It's a lady?"

"All ships are female, Chazz. At least to Marines."

"Does she have a name?"

He smiled. "Yes."

She waited. He kept smiling but said nothing.

Her lips curved. Marines.

Tony drove them out about twenty miles to a flat, brown plain in the northern part of the base. No cars or people in sight.

"An old firing range," he said. "Base fast-car fans use it for weekend testing, drag racing and such."

"Bleak."

"Yeah, but fun. The only downside is that you have to wash your car after every session. The dust gets really thick. Better than the salt flats, though. That stuff corrodes everything," he said as he lined up the car. He got out, opened the back hatch, and extracted two helmets.

"Here, put this on. Better safe than sorry."

She looked at this ridiculous man. "Does this thing have airbags?"

"I don't know. Never had to find out." He pointed at the embossed lettering announcing all sorts of airbags all over the car.

"Now. The acceleration and speed test. See that tree?"

The tree seemed implausibly far away. And suddenly it wasn't. When she caught her breath from the G-forces, she said, "That's some acceleration."

"Yeah. Fifteen seconds to 145 m.p.h. I've hacked the software. Ford limits the accel to protect the battery. Wimps. Can't do it too often. Burns up the engine, too."

"I'll bet."

Tony showed her what his red lady could do with a practiced series of test-drive moves, cornering and braking and so on. Then he gave her the con, and she gingerly put the car through its paces, taking her time, feeling the acceleration and the balance of the car under stress. Tony advised her the whole time, urging her to go faster and to bring the car to the very edge of control. It was very much like the sex she remembered with Tony, powerful and deeply satisfying. She executed a racing change at 120, much to Tony's delight. Was she a Mustang kind of woman? Maybe now she was. She'd decide. After Simmonds.

CHAPTER TWENTY-TWO
A Panic Attack

"God damn it, Myron, I thought you were taking care of her!" shouted Chip.

"Don't shout, Chip, I can hear you," said Myron. It was 1300 hours on Monday, and Myron had been working nonstop since Sunday night, coordinating arrests and getting troops to Manzanar. Now Chip had called him at Mather Command Center for a serious confrontation about Silver. "Colonel Silver is not easily 'taken care of,' Chip."

Chip complained, "Brickhouse told me he would—"

"Colonel Brickhouse ambushed her on his own initiative, without orders from me. The man is unbelievably stupid. And he missed. So he's also useless."

"Why didn't you tell me about her escape before?"

"Because I suspected you'd do exactly what you're doing, Chip. Taking your eye off the ball. You need to concentrate on your speech, not on minor details."

"She's not a minor detail, Myron."

"I mobilized the Highway Patrol to go after her. Last night. I just got the text message about her escape ten minutes ago."

"Wait. She's escaped *again?* If she takes this to the feds, they'll sure as hell send in the troops."

"No, they won't."

"How can you be so sure?"

"I'm in the military. I know how the people involved think. Nobody in California will lift a finger, and Washington will ignore the whole thing." And of course, I have some special relationships that will help.

"God damn it. Tom went down there alone yesterday. You said he called you. What happened? When will he be here?"

"Tomorrow. He'll be there at the Warning Center at Mather."

"Why isn't he already here?"

"Colonel Silver knocked him into the ocean and got away. He's recovering in a motel down there."

This revelation silenced Chip for once. Then he asked, "Three escapes. *Three*, Myron. You're sounding like Wile E. Coyote. Where is she? Where did the Highway Patrol corner her?"

Myron balanced the possibility of further stupidity with the need to reassure the man.

"They found her on Interstate 5 near San Clemente. She shot up their patrol car and got away."

Chip made a gurgling sound and asked, "Where's she going? Mexico?"

"My guess would be Pendleton, Camp Pendleton, the Marine base. It's right there. The CHP has found no trace of her south of San Clemente on I-5 or the surrounding highways. When they get shot up, they get real diligent. They couldn't get on the base or even check with the base MPs. I refused permission for them to do that. Too risky, with the announcement happening tomorrow."

"The Marines! Great." Chip glared some more. "How many Marines are stationed there?"

"Chip, concentrate on your speech. It doesn't matter. Ignore the Marines." Myron smiled and relented. "About 36,000, after the latest brigade withdrawals."

"Jesus Christ. You'd better hope it doesn't matter, Myron. You'd better just hope it doesn't. Or my office will look like Iwo fucking Jima."

* * *

After the governor hung up, Myron considered what to do about his concerns. The operation was fully engaged, no reason to keep allies in the dark. He called his old friend, Marine Brigadier General Martin Simmonds, the commanding general of MCI-West at Camp Pendleton.

"Marty, how are you? Long time no see."

"Yeah, good to hear from you, Myron. You guys need to use our bombing range or something?" He cleared his throat and added, "I'm in San Diego, meeting with the Navy. But I can—"

"No, I just wanted to give you a heads up, Marty. One of our officers has gone rogue and killed a fellow officer. She was last seen near San Onofre, so she might head your way. CHP encountered her. There were shots fired."

"She?"

"Yes, it's my Chief of Staff, Colonel Chastity Silver. You met her—"

"Oh, yeah, no way I'd forget Chazz. Killed a man, you say?"

"An altercation at Camp Roberts, they told me."

"Hell of a fight. Anything to do with your 'little project,' Myron?" smirked the brigadier.

Myron smiled and lied. "No, not really. But I don't need the complications, *comprende?* Not right now."

"When is it all coming down, Myron?"

Myron smiled. "No wisdom like silence, old buddy. Pay attention to the news on Tuesday."

Simmonds seemed pleased. "I feel good about this, Myron. Real good."

Myron wished he could say the same. "Marty, please check things out at the base. Just in case Colonel Silver tries to hide in the wide-open spaces. OK? If you find her, lock her up and throw away the key. And let me know."

"Yeah, OK. If she's on the base, she'll have signed in somewhere. I'll get the MPs on it first thing Monday when I get back."

"Thanks."

"*De nada,* Myron. Give 'em hell!"

CHAPTER TWENTY-THREE
The Brig

"Are you hungry?" asked Tony when they'd returned to his quarters.

"Not really. The late pizza lunch was enough."

Tony stepped toward her. "Why not…get reacquainted? You have until Monday. That gives us two nights to ourselves. Maybe more, after."

A pass? Of course it was a pass. He might have grown up a bit, but he was still Tony.

"Tony, I'm not the best company right now." She patted the couch. "I'll sleep here."

"Hell you will, Chazz. No, listen. I love you. In Iraq. In San Diego. And now. I screwed up. I won't again."

The hell of it was, she felt the pull. The old tug that Tony created in her gut. And she needed him on her side. But not *at* her side?

"Tony, I don't…I can't—"

"This Tom Peña you told me about. He's it? The big man in your life?"

"Was. Not anymore." Was she lying? Yes, and no. Despite everything, Tom still held a place in her heart, quietly simmering away. And of course Tony picked up her ambivalence.

"Bullshit. The way you talk about him? You're conflicted." He smiled his special Tony smile to show her it was OK, but she didn't buy it for a second. She shook her head, ridding it of the remnants of her love for Tom, at least for now.

She told him, "He stalked and assaulted me, Tony. He's an abuser. I can't get past that."

"Sure you can. You will. Women always do."

OK, so he hadn't quite grown up. She slapped him gently with one hand to show her disapproval of his piggishness. And she had to break him out of his amorous bubble.

"Tony, there's more at stake. Simmonds—"

He interrupted, showing her his palm. "OK, yeah, sure. But if you're over Peña, why not me? At least for a little while? Even just one night?" He wore that familiar boyishly charming look. And he *was* boyishly charming. Whatever part of her heart belonged to Tom, a part belonged to Tony. Her analytical mind considered the idea that maybe she was running to abusers for some dark reason. Her emotional mind told her she needed human contact. A lot. And it told her to ignore her analytical mind.

"Don't worry, Chazz. We'll figure this out. I'll help you all I can with Simmonds. No strings." He reached for her hand. She let him take it. Then she moved closer and kissed him. His reaction triggered other things. Then they moved from the too-small couch to his bedroom.

She stripped off his uniform piece by piece, exploring, remembering all the good times. He was in pretty good shape for an aging computer guy.

"You don't sit around much, do you?"

"Work out. Twice a day. This counts as one for today."

"I'll make sure you get a good workout," she said, gripping and massaging. He growled and picked her up and carried her to the bed, then took off her uniform. She pushed him back and got on top, and things got active. When they were done, she lay on top of him, gasping along with him.

Tony said, "You—"

"Don't, don't say I needed it. I wanted it, Tony. There's so much wrong. I wanted something right. And this was so right."

They slept on and off, alternating dozes with sex until Chazz collapsed, her body satiated and her mind empty. All the crap receded into the distance of their physical pleasure and activity. Tony found the places on her body that made her tremble inside. And she remembered what he liked. And found new things. Finally, toward morning, they slept deeply. And she did not dream.

Chazz opened one eye. Her hand moved of its own accord under her pillow to grab her Sig. Thoughts took shape, and she relinquished the weapon and sat up. Light came through the window, and she could see the slumbering form of Tony Ridger beside her.

Army and Marine were supposed to be the ones fighting in a bar, not sleeping together. But Tony was still Tony, even after twenty years. After two nights with him she felt safe, and she needed—what? Sex? Sure, but more than that. Love? Maybe, although her periodic total exasperation with the man argued against it.

Without waking him, she silently slipped out of bed, retrieved her Sig from under the pillow, and headed to the bathroom for a shower.

Tony sat naked on the bed as she emerged from the bathroom wrapped in a towel. He grinned.

"That was all right, Chazz."

She smiled. "Yeah. But I don't want a habit, Tony. I have things to do."

"What do you want to do first?" He stared with guileless eyes.

She walked over to the bed and knelt on it. "Fucking Marines," she said. The towel dropped as she slid the Sig back under the pillow.

At 0900 hours, Tony and Chazz emerged from his quarters into the bright sunlight of a Pendleton Monday morning. Chazz focused her entire being on telling General Simmonds about the coup. Tony drove her in the Mustang, and Chazz watched the unfamiliar little town that was Pendleton pass by as they wound their way to the garrison headquarters. The building buzzed with activity.

Tony talked them through several layers of guards and administrators until they reached the commanding general's office, where the assistant asked them to wait a few minutes. The assistant disappeared into the inner office.

After a few minutes, Chazz got the feeling in her stomach that preceded major combat operations, an anticipatory queasiness.

"Tony, I don't like this," she muttered through clenched teeth. Silence had fallen. The earlier activity had faded away.

Tony turned to her, surprised.

"Chazz, you went through hell. I thought you wanted this."

She stood up. "Tony, we have to—"

"Freeze! Hands where we can see them!"

Suddenly, from two separate entrances to the office, there were ten Marine MPs in full camo battle gear, all pointing pistols at them. Chazz never even imagined going for her sidearm. When they have the drop on you like that, you either surrender or die, and she wasn't ready to die.

Tony, less intimidated than Chazz on his home turf, stood with his hands half raised and said, "Hey, guys, we're just waiting—"

"Shut up and put your hands up. Now!" The lead MP signaled to his cohorts, who fanned out and surrounded the pair. Tony had raised his hands to match Chazz's actions. The MPs took Chazz's gun, handcuffed her and Tony, and told them to sit down. They did. The lead MP knocked on the general's door.

"All clear, sir. Both suspects are in custody."

The door opened, and General Simmonds appeared. Back in the day, he'd have been chomping on a cigar. He had the Marine look that Army soldiers responded badly to in bars. They'd met at a no-host bar in San Diego during a conference. A bad memory, but better than the current one.

"Well, well. Colonel Silver. Good to see you again. Nice of you to drop by instead of forcing me to pick you up." He gave the lopsided half-smile that his face naturally fell into.

She said, "Sir, I want—"

"I don't give a rat's ass what you want, Colonel. Just be quiet until we're done here." He looked at Tony. "Colonel Ridger. Explain this. What is this fugitive doing on my base?"

Tony's face was noncommittal, though Chazz thought he must be shitting bricks. She would have been, under the circumstances. "Sir, she's a full Colonel and the COS of the Army Guard in Sacramento. She's an old friend. She has a Silver Star."

"Were you aware she's on the run from a murder?"

Tony's mouth dropped open. He caught himself and blurted out, "No, sir, I was not! That's crazy."

Chazz just shook her head, tired of the nonsense. "It was self-defense, sir." Tony gaped at her, then pursed his lips and glared at his commanding officer. Chazz continued with her main point, the coup. "But I have to tell you—"

"Sure it was, Colonel. Save it for your court martial." He spoke to Tony. "Lieutenant Colonel Ridger, you're under preliminary restriction at your quarters until the court martial. Check in every two hours."

Tony asked, "What will happen to—"

"Not your concern, Colonel. I suggest you keep your mouth shut until you are told otherwise." He addressed the MPs. "Escort Colonel Silver to the brig. Escort Lieutenant Colonel Ridger to his quarters."

"Aye-aye, sir," said the senior MP. "Come on, ma'am," he said as he grabbed Chazz's arm and pulled. "Corporal, escort Colonel Ridger."

CHAPTER TWENTY-FOUR
Martial Law

Tom caught up with Myron and Chip outside the Office of Emergency Services Warning Center at Mather. En route, he turned on the radio and tuned in to the traffic updates. Everything was about the impassable freeways. Myron must have positioned the tanks. Nothing but confusion about the traffic jams. No actual reporting about tanks blocking things. Typical news coverage.

Chip was wearing a military-style jacket with an open-necked shirt, the de rigueur attire for emergency announcements these days. He'd replaced his usual governor's seal patch with the new rampant bear symbol he'd chosen for the seal. The surrounding text now read SEAL of the PRESIDENT of the CALIFORNIA REPUBLIC. Tom smiled, reflecting on an extinct animal as the symbol for the newly born country. But Chip had made his choice.

"Glad you could make it, Tom," Chip said, the sarcasm heavy in his voice.

Tom ignored the barb and asked, "Are you ready for the speech, sir?"

"Damn right I am. And so is California."

The trio marched into the buzzing situation room. The subdued lighting accentuated the monitors and screens glowing with video and graphics showing the current state of affairs. Two Army Guard soldiers stood at the door. Myron whispered to them, and they walked over to the floor supervisor standing by the main communications console. They took his arms and handcuffed him and led him out of the room, which fell silent.

A podium stood in one corner of the large room, with the American and State of California flags behind it flush against a neutral backdrop. A video camera sat in front of it. Tom saw the press secretary and his assistant carrying a box over to the podium. They pulled down the American flag and put up another California flag. Tom and Chip had decided to just keep the California Republic flag as it was. Why not? Saves some money for the new government. The assistant press secretary put up a Velcro seal on the podium to match the one on Chip's jacket. Fast work, getting all that together. The assistant then approached the video cam and fiddled with it, while the press secretary set up the lighting.

Myron walked to the communications console. A technician looked up at him. Myron said something, and the technician flipped a switch.

"OK, General," he said. "The Virginia feed is down. I've disconnected the California network from the feds." He flipped another switch. "Governor, you're live when you press the button on the podium. Your speech will be on the teleprompter and also sent as wireless alerts. Watch the monitor while the emergency alert announcement plays, then go ahead."

"It's 'President,' son," said Chip with a smile. "Don't forget it."

"No, sir, yes, sir," said the young man sheepishly.

Myron said, "Thank you, Kevin. Great job."

"OK, let's do this," Chip said.

The big digital clock on the wall ticked up to 11 a.m. Chip pressed the button and watched as the emergency bulletin played, replacing all the broadcasts in California. Then he fixed his eyes on the green dot on the video cam and spoke.

"My fellow Californians, I speak to you from the seat of government in Sacramento. I must express our concern and anger at the recent actions of the federal government in our state. Allowing oil drilling off our coast.

Federal interference with our border disrupting our farms. Refusal to honor prior financial commitments to the state. One blow does not call for a response, but after absorbing many attacks from the illegitimate government in Washington, D.C., we must act because the situation is dire.

"I therefore terminate the Treaty of Guadalupe Hidalgo and declare the California Statehood Act of 1850 nullified. The United States of America no longer controls the territory of California, which now resumes its status as the independent California Republic founded in 1846. In the coming days, the California Republic will form a new republican government. It will seek recognition from other nations of the world, and it will hold free and fair elections. Until then, I declare California to be under martial law. I have assumed the role of President and Commander-in-Chief of the Republic until next year's election. I appoint General Myron Dupont of the California Army National Guard as military governor of the Republic until the end of the state of emergency.

"Please stay calm, go about your daily business, and help make the transition as seamless as possible. Thank you for your attention, and for your continued support of your democratically elected officials. God bless the California Republic." Chip paused and held his pose while Kevin switched back to the emergency bulletin.

Myron commanded, "OK, Kevin, play the emergency preemption broadcast music until further notice."

Tom spoke up. "Did you get the right music, Kevin? Not that old crap, 'I Love You California,' but 'California Dreamin', right?"

"Yes, sir, you bet!" Kevin said. "Terrific speech, Mr. President!"

Tom, who had written that speech, smiled. One task down, thousands to go. The image of Chazz at Manzanar flashed through his mind but faded as he focused on what came next for his country, the California Republic.

* * *

The crowd of protesters in front of Sergeant Briscoe's tank made him uneasy. The president's announcement had brought people out of their stalled cars, and more and more had gathered, voicing their disquiet.

An unholy noise came from above. Briscoe looked up. A chopper, commercial. As it twisted and turned over the freeway, he picked out the logo of a local news station. Shit. Me and OJ.

"Hey, you!" came a call from below. Briscoe turned his attention down to the young man standing in front of his tank. The man yelled, "This is stupid! This is the United States, not some banana republic! Get the hell out of our way."

"Please get back in your car, sir," said Briscoe, forcing himself to stay calm. "Go about your business. Like the president said." Briscoe cursed to himself. With infantry support, this guy would be on the ground instead of screaming profanities. Still, this hero had nothing but his bare hands and his mouth behind him. Got to do every damn thing myself.

The man yelled, "President hell! What kind of fascist bullshit are you guys pulling?" He began to scale the tank.

Briscoe dropped through the hatch and closed it. He said to his gunner, "See that Lexus EV pulled over on the shoulder?"

"Yeah, I see it," said the soldier.

"Put a shell through it."

"But—"

"Just do it. They're getting rough. That will take care of it. Nobody in the car. I checked."

"OK, Sergeant."

The Lexus took a direct hit and blew all to hell, taking along an enormous chunk of the concrete guard barrier on the side of the elevated freeway. Parts of the car and the concrete rained down on the street below.

Briscoe swiveled the turret around to point directly at the cars on the freeway. He watched through the viewport as people ran away from the tank. The young man dropped off the tank and ran for it. Briscoe aimed the 50-cal at one of the empty cars, a Toyota Prius, and blew it to pieces with a burst of 50-caliber rounds. The hybrid's gas tank exploded with a beautiful burst of flame. The young man began to zig-zag as he ran between the stopped cars. Not that it would have done him much good. Not with the 50-cal. Briscoe let him run.

"That should do it," said Briscoe. Then the news helicopter flew right over his tank. He gave the go-ahead, and the gunner blew the chopper out of the sky.

"Fake news," Briscoe snarked to himself.

Roy and Steve huddled together under the 280 flyover to 101 in the center of San Francisco. Roy had been homeless on and off since Iraq, Steve since the first Gulf War. Couldn't shake their habits, or not for long. They'd found each other last year when Steve wandered out of Golden Gate Park one day and fell over unconscious at Roy's feet. Roy worked for a nonprofit that helped the homeless get off the streets. They liked to employ ex-homeless people that had gone through their program as ambassadors who their targets would trust. In just one week of employment, Roy discovered each homeless acquisition amounted to $5,245 per day for the nonprofit. That paid his salary and that of the nonprofit executives. A nice little scam.

But they didn't like it when you started using again. And just about everyone did. He'd helped Steve get to SF General, and when they discharged him, they moved in together in Steve's brand-new tent. No gay stuff. Two junkies worked better for personal security than one.

They'd been in the tent on Folsom Street listening to golden oldies on a local radio station when the governor gave his speech.

Now, Roy liked to think of himself as reasonably pragmatic. He hadn't voted in years. Not even for Obama. Needed a mail box. It wasn't worth the stress, even if he could have gotten an exemption or a P.O. box. But he paid attention. He had a phone during the Trump years to monitor the daily chaos in Washington. Pandemic hit, funding dried up, phone stolen, not replaced. Same old story.

But Steve had this little radio, solar, dynamo crank. Nice.

Until they found out they were living in, what? A third world country with a fascist dictator. Sure was what it sounded like, with martial law and all. Then it flashed through the local homies, tanks on the freeway, stopping traffic. One at the bridge, another near Bernal, by the farmer's market.

Well, shit. Time to go check it out. Better than lying there listening to the Mamas & the Papas on loop.

So they huddled under the flyover. Tank it was, Abrams M-1. Parked across the off-ramp, controlling traffic on both 101 and 280. Cars parked for miles. Nothing moving, not since the 50-cal had shot up a couple of heroes on a motorcycle making an end run down 101. Every once in a while the turret dude would put a bullet in a car just to hear the noise.

Steve smiled that goofy smile he got from time to time.

"What's up, Steve?"

"Got a secret, bro."

"You ain't got nothing, Steve."

"No, no. See, I got these friends. In the Haight." Steve hacked a heavy smoker's cough.

"Yeah? On the street?"

"Nah, sharing a house."

"Why aren't you sharing it with them?"

"Fucked stuff up one too many times."

"So, great friends. Don't sound like they got anything we need."

"Wrong. They got TNT."

Roy sat up straight. "Like, the real thing? What are they, Taliban? Daesh?"

"Fuck no. Ex-something-or-other. Stuff is left over from the good old days."

"And you found out about this how?"

"Smelled it. Opened a box, there it was. That's when they kicked me out."

"How much of it?"

"Enough for some sticky bombs."

"Fuck yeah!"

Two hours and some bus rides and shoplifting got them back under the flyover with everything they needed. Roy decided they didn't need new socks, they'd use some of the old ones they had. They'd stopped on Folsom, stuffed the TNT into four socks, and did them up with wicks. Steve used an old Target bag to carry the socks and a bottle of paraffin lamp oil they'd hooked from a nice little shop in the Haight.

Silently, they crept up the bank of the flyover and shimmied under the tank. Roy could smell the jet fuel. He'd breathed it a lot in Iraq.

Steve doused his socks with the paraffin. He passed the bottle to Roy, who did the same. They each stuck two socks on the treads of the tank.

Roy watched as Steve pulled the boosted butane lighter out of the Target bag.

"You want to do the honors, bro?" whispered Steve. "My hands shake too much."

"Thanks." Roy took the lighter. "Get out of here."

Steve crawled out from under the tank, stood up, and ran like hell. The 50-cal cut him down with a short burst.

"Shee-it," Roy said, and clicked the lighter. When all four socks were lit, he slipped back down the flyover bank unobserved to take cover before the bombs did their work.

CHAPTER TWENTY-FIVE
A Problem Solved

"Hey, Sally," Chip Sanchez said as he walked through his outer office, a grin on his face. Sally Reed looked ill to Tom's unbiased eye, but she smiled and stood up.

"Mr. President."

"Heard the news, huh?"

"My husband called and told me to check the stream, sir." She looked at her monitor, which showed a streaming video of a waving California Republic flag that played "California Dreamin'" over and over.

"Well, just fine. Now that you're special assistant to the president, I'm doubling your salary." Sally smiled a pained smile. A little shaky. As Chip walked into his inner office with Myron, Tom stepped over to Sally and tried to calm her down.

"Everything is going according to plan, Sally. It's a big surprise, but it's all for the best. Are you all right?"

"Sure, Tom, sure. It's just. Well. Ted says it's the best thing that's happened to the state since Reagan. I'm overwhelmed. I'll be fine."

"Who's Ted?"

"Oh. My husband. Big supporter of the gov—the president." Another shaky grin. "Got me the job." She looked down at the keyboard on her desk. "Job."

Despite Sally's inability to concentrate, Tom had faith in her eventual recovery. Chip should give her some time off to process and recuperate. He patted the special assistant on the back. He followed Myron and Chip into the president's inner office, leaving Sally to process her promotion.

Myron was talking. He stopped and smiled at Tom. "Tom, listen to this. I got a call from my friend Marty at Pendleton right before the announcement. Colonel Silver is in custody at the base, charged with murder. Marty says we need to arrange for her transfer to a local jail as soon as possible, since she's being held at a U. S. federal facility. I'll work out the details of the prisoner transfer to Pitchess."

Tom swallowed. At least Chazz was alive. "That's great, Myron," he said. Then he processed the big fact: the Marines would not intervene in the coup. That was big news. But thoughts of Chazz in a concentration camp consumed his mind.

Chip obsessed about Chazz too, but in reverse. "Take her to Manzanar, Myron," he said. "Out of the way."

"Of course. It can wait a day or two. Don't worry, she's out of commission."

"If you say so," Chip grumbled. Then he grinned and changed the subject. "Tom, great anthem choice!" The anthem played from Sally's computer came through the open door to her office.

Tom tore his mind off Chazz in Manzanar and back to his job. "Myron, the Marines. Are they—"

Myron didn't want to talk about the Marines. "Later, Tom. We have work to do."

Time to lighten the mood. Tom joked, "The anthem focus group considered 'Hotel California' and 'Californication,' but nothing beats the Mamas and the Papas." People loved that old-timey sixties hippie schmalz.

Myron cleared his throat, clearly not interested in the Mamas or the Papas. He got down to serious business. "Now, let's talk about the next steps in the plan. Tom, what about the central bank? Is the new currency ready, or do we stick with the dollar for a while? Are the banks falling in line? What about the agricultural cooperatives?"

Tom settled into a chair and told them about the central bank he'd created down in San Francisco and the logistics of the new California dollar. There was much to discuss before lunch.

Tom and Chip returned to the Capitol at 1:30, after their celebratory lunch with Myron, who returned to his command center. Chip took Tom's advice and gave Sally time off until she recovered. She said she'd be back the next morning but thanked Chip for his consideration.

Chip broke out the tequila bottle as soon as Sally was gone.

"A drink to celebrate, Tom." He poured two double shots of the agave juice and offered a toast to the new republic. Tom sipped, aware that now was the time to keep his wits about him. Chip could be unpredictable after a big win like this, especially liquored up.

"I want to talk about México, Tomás," Chip said.

"What about it?"

"The first country we should approach for diplomatic relations, no? Gonna be questions about territorial integrity and so forth, since we just tore up Guadalupe Hidalgo. How should we approach it? Who should be the special envoy?"

The two discussed diplomatic relations for half an hour. To his credit, Chip held back on the tequila; being president seemed to have somehow magnified him. He was sharper, more focused than before. Tom's anxiety about the future of the country under Chip eased as they talked.

After they agreed on a special envoy, Chip asked Tom what had happened down south. Tom, tasting the salt water in his memory, cleared his palate with a swig of aged tequila.

"I don't want to talk about it."

"Come on, Tomás. Give."

Tom hemmed and hawed a bit, then gave Chip an abbreviated version of the sad story.

"Goddamn Wonder Woman," said Chip.

"Good analogy," Tom said with a smile. "No golden lasso, though."

"Lucky for you. It's the only reason you're alive." The horsey laugh grated on Tom's ears, but the fact was that he was right. Tom had seen Chazz's hand resting on her gun. She'd truly thought he was going to kill her.

Chip reacted to his expression. "Look, Tom. I understand your attachment to her, but we have to get rid of her. She's killed one man and incapacitated another. Two, including you. We can't afford to have her running around loose."

"Chip, she'll buy into it once she sees we're in control."

"I called Brickhouse right before we went to lunch. He's pissed about Flattery."

"So what?"

"So, he wants to do something about it. I told him to take charge of getting her off the Marine base. He's going down there."

Tom drew in his breath in a sharp hiss. Brickhouse? But he was the one—

Chip grinned. "And then she's gone. No problem for us anymore." He took a swig of tequila and waved the glass. "*Se fue con Dios,* you know?" He laughed.

The morning after the president's announcement, Lieutenant Colonel Alfredo Calvo paced in front of the Channel Islands Air National Guard Station headquarters building. Brickhouse was late. He looked at his watch. 0845. OK, Brickhouse wasn't late, Calvo was early. He couldn't help himself. Brickhouse's call turned his life around. Things hadn't gone so well recently.

Calvo fancied himself a pretty good lothario. The sporadic affair he had with Ortiz, as an example. Delfina was a hard-case air force officer, but she fell right over for him. She kicked him out when she discovered his two other lovers. She'd taken him back twice and kicked him out again twice. But she never proposed transferring him out of Channel Islands, not once. He'd be in her bed again before the month was out.

But he utterly misjudged the colonel from Sacramento. The masculine bear hunter bit usually worked, and he'd just assumed she would like it. She proved to be a harder case than Del.

Where the hell was Brickhouse? If they wanted to arrive early enough at Pendleton, they should leave now. Sooner this got done, the better.

He wondered where that bastard Jones had gone to. After Calvo regained consciousness, the local cops found no other individuals present and inquired about the identity of the 911 caller. He put two and two together. Jones had been the only man on duty that day. Bastard. The cops followed up, and it turned out Jones and his wife and kid had vacated their apartment in Oxnard. AWOL. He'd got Del to report Jones. After she'd finished laughing. He'd show Jones what pain was.

Nobody would be laughing then.

Calvo cracked his knuckles as a black SUV pulled up in front of him.

"Get in," said Colonel Brickhouse. "We're late."

CHAPTER TWENTY-SIX
The End of the Line

CHAZZ SAT ON THE BENCH in her brig cell, leaning against the concrete wall after a poor night's sleep. The MPs brought her breakfast on a tray. She'd asked to see a lawyer, and she'd told them the governor was planning a coup. The MPs ignored her requests and exchanged smiles when she mentioned the coup.

Around noon, she heard the guards talking with someone and overheard her name, Silver. She got up from her bunk and walked over to the bars. She was not happy to see Colonel Brickhouse, accompanied by Lieutenant Colonel Calvo and two Marine MPs. The group walked up to her cell.

"Time to go, Colonel," an MP said. "These gentlemen have a transfer order countersigned by General Simmonds. You're to go with them to a Guard facility for further processing through to a secure detention facility. Am I understood?"

"These guys will kill me."

"Am I understood, ma'am?" the MP repeated, ignoring her.

"Fuck you," Chazz said. She walked back to the bunk and sat down.

"Sergeant, get her out," Brickhouse ordered. "I want her in full transport restraints."

The MP spoke into his radio and waited. Two more MPs appeared carrying a bundle of thin chains. The lead MP unlocked her cell door and approached.

"We can make this easy or hard, ma'am, whichever you prefer."

"They're going to kill me, Sergeant. I will not comply." She stood, preparing herself.

The MP motioned to the other three. They approached Chazz, and when she judged them close enough, she engaged them with hand-to-hand. After taking some punches and kicks, an MP grabbed one of her arms. She twisted and slammed his jaw with the heel of her hand, but the distraction allowed another MP to engage with his Taser. Chazz collapsed to the floor as the shock coursed through her and her muscles spasmed, then another MP tased her again. Two of them held her down as she struggled weakly while the third applied the chains that bound her wrists, waist, and feet. Then they lifted her under her armpits and dragged her out of the cell.

The six men carried her down the hall and outside to an SUV. She had recovered enough from the tasing to struggle ineffectually as they carried her. The SUV was a generic civilian model, nothing special. She knew that she really didn't want to be in that vehicle.

Chazz resisted being put into the SUV with everything she had. Her muscles had loosened enough to move her limbs. She grabbed the door frame with both bound hands. She kicked at the seat with her feet. Breathing hard, the MPs got all of her appendages under enough control to get her onto the seat. She bit one of them and received a hard slap in return. So they tased her again to settle her down. The MPs slammed the door, and Brickhouse locked the doors from the console, glancing back at her over the tall driver's seat.

"Tony?" The voice seemed distant, as if the caller were whispering into his phone.

Tony Ridger held his cell phone to his ear, wondering who the anonymous caller could be. Spam? After only a few hours of house arrest, he'd welcome talking with somebody selling him a timeshare in a Jamaican slum. Funny how restriction to doing nothing makes you want to do something. With the radio and streaming playing nothing but the coup anthem, anything appealed at this point.

"Yeah? Who is this?"

"Can't you tell by my voice?" The voice grew louder, and Tony recognized it. Mark. It was Mark. Mark whispered, "No names, buddy. Look, man, you got some serious problems."

"Well, no shit, my man. I'm restricted—"

"Shut up for a minute, Tony, and listen. A couple of freaking Guardsmen just took your girlfriend out of the brig. Transferring her to a Guard facility. Literally kicking and screaming. They tased her down."

Mark was an MP Tony met over a speeding incident with the Mustang. The guy admired the car so much he decided not to give Tony a ticket. He'd know about this. Kicking and screaming.

"What were those guys' names?" he asked with urgency.

"Brickhouse and, let's see, um, Calvo." Reading from a document.

"Oh, *Christ*."

"Yeah, that's what she thought. So I figured I'd better call—"

Tony hung up and stuffed the phone into a pocket.

The nice thing about restriction status: no guards, just the honor system. You checked in every two hours. There was a time for honor and a time to move your ass, and this, brother, was it. He called the MP on duty to check in, fifteen minutes early but what the hell. Two hours. Find Chazz, then...whatever. After that, he'd worry about a court martial. Yeah, right. Tony smiled with no genuine humor.

He ran to his closet, pulled out his camo combat uniform and gear, and suited up. He brought out the gun safe from under his bed and took out his personal Glock and his AR-15 from the drawer. They'd head up Basilone, the only road north from the brig.

Move, move, move!

After half an hour of driving, Calvo said, "Take that side road, sir."

"I'd rather wait until we get off the base, Calvo. Wouldn't it—"

"I don't want to wait. I want her dead," Calvo said. Chazz raised her manacled hands and gave him two middle fingers, then kicked Calvo's seat with her shackled feet. He ignored her. "And it's better, here. If they find her body, they won't be able to do anything about it. We're a separate country now."

A separate country. No wonder the MPs had smiled. They already knew about the coup. And accepted it. Her world shifted.

Brickhouse grunted and veered onto the gravel road, leading up a valley to a hill. Chazz realized she was at the end of the line. She'd never found prayer very useful. Instead, she seethed. General Simmonds knew about the coup and didn't care. It was all for nothing.

"Pull in there," Calvo said. A cleared area off the road held a few metal shacks scattered about. No people. "This is good," he said.

Calvo opened the back door. Chazz kicked with her chained feet, but Calvo was strong enough to grab her feet and drag her out of the SUV. She clutched at the door frame, but he pulled her to the ground. A brief struggle had her face down, his knee on her back.

"Get it done, Calvo," Brickhouse said.

Calvo wasn't ready to carry out that order, it turned out.

He tugged at her pants, and pulled them down part way.

"Calvo!"

"You can take a turn, sir. After me. Damn this chain. Give me the key. The chain's in the way."

Out of the corner of one eye, Chazz saw Brickhouse shake his head, his jaw set, but he reached into a pocket and handed Calvo a key. She felt him unhook the padlock on her waist chain. She jerked, but Calvo pressed an arm down on her neck.

"Hold still, damn it!" he growled. "Enjoy the ride, it'll be your last."

He pulled the waist chain away and tugged at her pants again. She felt him fumbling with one hand, the other still holding her neck. The trees closed in as the dark forest took over her body. Not again. No rational thought passed through her mind, just fear and hatred and disgust and weakness.

Whatever happened then, Chazz could never remember afterwards, but when she came out of her dark woods, she was free of Calvo, who was groaning on the ground next to her. This time, she wasn't drunk and incapacitated, but strong and angry. Not weak. She pushed herself up to her knees.

"God damn it!" Brickhouse yelled. She scrabbled away on the dry dirt, but the ankle restraints slowed her. The two men grabbed her. She punched and bit and did everything she could, but they soon had her pinned face down again. Calvo had his gun in his hand.

She heard a car approaching. It slewed across the dirt in front of her, raising a cloud of dust. She heard a car door open.

"Drop the guns!" It was Tony's voice.

Calvo rolled to the side and fired, but the obscure figure in the dust fired back with an automatic rifle, hitting him in several places. He jerked and was still. Brickhouse let go of her legs and ran to the SUV. But it wasn't to escape. He pulled out an M4 carbine and fired a burst into the settling dust.

Chazz scrambled to Calvo's body. His pistol had fallen from his hand into the dirt. She picked it up and aimed carefully, holding the gun with both hands, and fired three shots. All hits. Brickhouse collapsed to the ground.

"Tony?"

"Here," said a weak voice. "I'm..."

Chazz stood and moved toward the voice, pulling up her pants. Tony was lying next to his car. The blood spurting from his neck and groin told her his body armor hadn't protected him from the M4. She knelt beside to him and applied pressure.

"Tony, hold on, we'll get you help, we'll—"

"This is it, Chazz. Fucking amazing. We make it through two wars and get shot up at home. Fucking weird world...." He closed his eyes.

"Stay with me, Tony," she said. He opened his eyes. "I don't have a phone, Tony. I can't—"

"Phone...right pocket, under the vest." He shifted and groaned. "Saw the dust from the SUV, jammed it...." His voice trailed off.

Chazz pulled the quick-release lanyard, and the heavy vest came apart. She took the phone from his shirt pocket and clicked, but the phone prompted for a passcode. She pressed the emergency call button.

"911, what's your emergency?"

"Soldier down, shot twice with an M4, bleeding out. I need immediate medical help and chopper evac. I don't know where we are, somewhere near Basilone Road towards the Pendleton San Onofre Gate, on a side road." She ran her hand over Tony's cheek. Cold. Shock?

911 said, "Checking, hold the line." A pause. "Unable to pinpoint your location, ma'am, the cell service can't give it to us. I'll send a search chopper."

"OK. Please hurry."

"Stay on the line, ma'am."

"I'll try." She looked at Tony. His chest wasn't moving. "I'm going to perform CPR on him." She started CPR, the wrist-to-waist chains making it that much harder. He began to breathe again.

"Search and rescue chopper dispatched, ma'am. Who am I speaking with?"

"He's fading...." she said in despair.

"Stay on the line, ma'am. Can you identify yourself?"

She had to decide. Tony had only minutes to live. Too much blood gone. She'd seen this before, in Iraq. She hung up and leaned him against the tire.

"Tony. Open your eyes."

His eyes opened slowly, staring at something far away. She held up the phone.

"Tony. Look at the phone. Tony. Do it. Look at the phone."

His eyes sharpened. She checked; the facial recognition had worked, and the phone was open. As quickly as she could, she reset face recognition and set it up to recognize her face, then entered a new passcode.

Tony had stopped breathing again. She laid him back down and performed chest compressions and breathing for several minutes. His chest never moved. His eyes were half open, looking at nothing. She tried for a pulse. Nothing. The bleeding had stopped. She closed his eyelids and stood up.

The phone rang; 911 calling back. She ignored it. She picked up Calvo's gun and found the restraints key in the dirt. She unlocked the restraints and dropped them on Calvo's body. She crossed to the SUV. Brickhouse lay beside the open driver's door. He wasn't dead yet, just badly wounded and unconscious. Chazz took a moment, closing her eyes, but she had no choice. She put a bullet in his head to finish him.

Another decision. SUV or car? Tony's car was a late model Mustang Mach-E GT with nothing military about it. The SUV was an old-model gas guzzler. Speedy, no doubt. The Mustang had enough acceleration to escape pursuit, but it stood out. Chazz chose the Mustang. She went through Tony's pockets and found the Ford key fob. She also found Tony's Iraq challenge coin, which she'd returned to him when they'd broken up in San Diego. Chazz smoothed a finger over the coin and looked down at her friend. Her lover. She was cried out. She put the coin in her pocket.

Chazz thought about the journey ahead. One more thing. She searched each of the three bodies, found their wallets, and extracted their credit cards and cash. She left the IDs; if she needed to show an ID, she might as well use the Sig instead. She left the bodies where they were and gathered all the sidearms, Brickhouse's M4, and Tony's AR-15 and piled them in the trunk of the Mustang. She took a pistol and put it in the compartment next to the driver's seat after checking the magazine. Ten rounds left. Enough for now. She turned off the phone and ejected the SIM card.

Chazz familiarized herself with the Mustang's control systems, then navigated back down the gravel track to the main road. She waited for a passing car, turned right, and headed north toward the San Onofre gate.

She kept a low profile as she slowed for the kiosk and waved at the Marine manning it, who waved back.

Chazz turned on the radio to calm her nerves with some news. The Mamas and the Papas played on an endless loop. She tried to scan, but all the stations were playing the same song. She turned off the radio as she drove east through the new California Republic.

CHAPTER TWENTY-SEVEN
Myron's Choice

THE UH-1Y VENOM MEDEVAC chopper set down in an open area across from the black SUV, kicking up a cloud of dust. The pilot had spotted the SUV on his second pass over the North Pendleton ridge area in response to a 911 call. He made a circling pass to make sure the area was secure before landing. Nothing stirred.

The Marine medics jumped off the chopper and rushed through the settling dust to the casualties. They quickly assessed the situation, then calmly walked back to the chopper. A medic leaned in and yelled, "Three dead, sir. Two National Guard, one Marine, ID says Lieutenant Colonel Anthony Ridger. Looks like a firefight. Ridger's in full combat gear. No sign of anyone who might have called 911. No obvious weapons."

"Roger," said the pilot. He radioed in the toll to dispatch, which relayed it to the commanding general's office. The pilot recommended calling in a CID criminalist unit, as the situation was clearly a crime scene. No weapons and three dead bodies? They'd start a manhunt right away. He shut down the rotors and removed his helmet. A dead Marine lieutenant colonel? Simmonds wouldn't like that.

When Myron got back to his command center, he called his wife. After calming her down, he suggested she take the kids to the Tahoe condo until things cooled off. She complained about the kids' missing school and a party at a friend's house. He sternly told her to get going.

Myron had been at work for almost two hours when his cell phone rang: Marty Simmonds. He looked at the time, 1503 hours. "Hey, Marty," he answered. "Hope you got some good news for me."

"I wish I did, Myron." Simmonds's voice was cold. Marine-style cold, which is exceedingly frigid. "Your Colonel Silver will be a big pain in the ass for you."

"How so?"

"She fled the base after murdering your men and one of mine."

"Murdering—murder? My men? What are you talking about?" Myron crushed the phone against his ear.

"Brickhouse and Calvo. I assumed they were here on your orders, Myron. They said so. Their orders said so."

"They weren't." It must have been Chip. Damn the man. Him and Brickhouse. Chip had to stay in his lane. "Tell me what happened."

"Silver walked right into my office, all primed and ready to tell me about your coup. I stopped her with a bunch of MPs and put her in the brig. Then these two guardsmen show up this morning saying they're ordered to transfer the prisoner to a secure Guard facility. I countersigned their orders and sent them off to the brig. Next thing I know, they're both dead and Silver is gone."

"You said one of yours."

"Yeah. A lieutenant colonel named Ridger, Anthony Ridger. He was Silver's boyfriend. He showed up in my office with her. I put him on preliminary restriction to keep him quiet, but he took a hand anyway. Someone from the brig tipped him off that Silver was headed for a shallow grave."

"I don't appreciate the humor, Marty. This is serious."

"You have no idea, Myron. No idea. How the hell am I supposed to ignore a dead Marine? I can ignore dead guardsmen, but not one of my own. Troops won't stand for it. Hell, *I* won't stand for it. You don't go around killing Marines."

"Did she kill him?"

"Doubt it. He was her boyfriend. She called 911 for medical help, then took off." A moment of icy silence. "The alternative, Myron, is that your guardsmen killed a Marine. Not good, Myron. Just how much control do you have over this thing?"

"I'm in control, Marty," Myron said, wishing that this were so.

God damn Chip.

"We'll see, Myron, we'll see. In the meantime, I'm gonna have to make some noise. So get ready, Myron. Put on a good show, right? At Los Alamitos, the joint training base. We'll take it over and put out a press release. Unless your people screw up again, Myron. I would advise you not to let that happen."

Myron swallowed. Marty had promised not to intervene. Chip wouldn't like a show of force. And Myron needed the Los Alamitos Joint Base Training Facility. Roberts didn't have the capabilities for long-term strategic action. The joint forces' staging capabilities at Los Alamitos were exactly what he'd need if Marty did what Marines do: take over. He'd need those combined forces to fight back.

He tried to bring Marty back to the table. "I'm asking you not to do this, Marty. Stand down, like we planned. We'll handle the murder."

"Not good enough, Myron."

Myron considered several alternatives. What he needed was a scapegoat. It came to him. Give them Ortiz. She was a loose end and a liability.

"Marty. Here's my offer. Colonel Calvo was stationed at the Channel Islands Air Guard Station. The garrison commander there is Colonel Delfina Ortiz. She's in on the coup. Why don't you send a company of MPs up there and arrest her for treason, publicize it, then turn her over to us for internment?"

"A hostage, Myron?"

"A sacrifice, Marty. An offering."

"Accepted, Myron. But one more dead Marine, and you and your tiny little country will cease to exist."

* * *

"I'm begging you, Del. Do this for me." Myron rolled his eyes up to the ceiling as he held his cell phone to his ear. The things he had to do for this operation were driving him crazy.

"Myron, I'm not giving up my command to appease your ego."

Delfina was not thinking clearly. Myron heard the anger and determination in her voice. Delfina Ortiz was a strong woman. He'd encouraged the Air Guard commander to promote her and made sure she got the job at Channel Islands because of her strength. Not just the affair.

"It's not ego, Del. It's Calvo."

"What?"

"Good old Colonel Calvo, your ex."

"What about him?"

"He's dead."

She had no answer to that. Myron went on, "Silver killed him and Brickhouse. Did you know he went to Pendleton to kill Silver?"

Del's tone softened, and a note of fear entered. "No, Myron, no. I wasn't aware. He must have wanted revenge. That *bitch*. I swear, Myron —"

"It's OK, Del. Just cooperate with the jarheads, all right? Don't be a hero. We'll get you back and reinstated. I'll see to it personally."

"That's not what you promised me, Myron. In bed. That night."

"I know, I know."

"Where's your wifey, Myron? All safe and tucked in like a good little girl?" Del's mood had changed again.

"I don't like your tone, Del."

Angry, Ortiz switched to the barrio lingo of her youth. "You don't gotta like it, Myron. You better damn well deliver on your promises. I ain't gonna be sitting in no jail cell for the rest of my life for treason. I'll deal. The coup, the affair, the bullshit you filled me with. It all goes to the feds. Got it?"

"Sure thing, Del. We'll get you out."

"Do you still care about me, Myron?" Del's voice was sweet. Forgiving. Cajoling.

"You know I do, Del. I love you." Words meant nothing except what they made others do. Myron's words fluttered out on the airwaves and dissipated like a Pacific fog on a hot day. Myron grimaced. Chances were good that Del would resist. She was that kind of soldier. The Marines would handle that problem.

He had given her a choice. That's all he needed to do.

He had to get back to work.

Tech Sergeant Oliver Jones hadn't run far when he left the unconscious Calvo on Sunday after calling 911. He understood that his time in the Guard was over the moment he choked Lieutenant Colonel Calvo unconscious. He'd take his punishment. But first, he needed his family to be safe.

Ollie drove home to Oxnard and packed his family into the car. He drove them to Phoenix and settled Shirelle and their small son at the house of one of Shirelle's cousins. They spent most of Tuesday streaming developments on the TV as martial law overtook California. Despite Shirelle's protests, Ollie decided he had to return to California to fight back.

Ollie took a roundabout route from Phoenix to Oxnard. He arrived at his apartment Wednesday afternoon, checked carefully for surveillance, and gathered a few belongings. He checked into a small motel in Ventura and parked his car on a side street. Then he walked to a car rental agency to pick up a subcompact gas-powered car, rare these days.

The next day, he drove back to Channel Islands. He parked his car on a side road about a mile from the base and called a trusted friend. All was quiet. Calvo was AWOL and Ortiz was stomping around like a frustrated dragon. Everybody was keeping their heads down.

Jones sat in his car wondering what to do next. Had to do something; couldn't let this stand. He'd taken an oath, and he meant it. This was his country, and he would defend it.

As these thoughts bounced around in his head, he heard a loud noise approaching. Six Chinooks with Marine markings appeared overhead, heading for the air base. His tiny car shook as the huge choppers passed. Jones smiled. The calvary had arrived! The U. S. military was taking a hand.

He started up his car and drove to the base. The choppers had landed at the airfield near the headquarters. There were Marines everywhere. Jones sat in his car and waited for events to unfold.

He had a good view of the headquarters building. Several Marine squads in full combat gear converged on the building, taking fire from the windows. The squads formed an urban assault tactical pattern and entered the building, losing only one man that Ollie could see. Explosions from grenades cleared the door area, and the Marines stormed in.

A squad emerged, holding onto a struggling Colonel Ortiz. Jones grinned again. The cavalry had won the day and had captured the flag. He unbuckled his seatbelt and prepared to step out of his car to announce himself.

The Marine squad stopped in the parking lot. They forced Ortiz to her knees. Other Marine squads brought several men out of the building, hands behind their heads. The Marines lined them up in front of the little group holding Ortiz. Ollie thought they were going to restrain everyone for transport.

But no. A Marine officer put his sidearm to the back of Ortiz's head and fired. He then fired another shot into her crumpled body. He holstered the gun, then gestured and said something to the assembled prisoners. A demonstration.

Oliver Jones buckled his seatbelt and drove away as quietly as he could.

He made it a mile from the base on Highway 1 before the Marines caught up with him.

CHAPTER TWENTY-EIGHT
The Road Trip

TOM HAD QUESTIONS. MANY OF them. He wanted answers from Myron, without Chip's being in the room. So he drove over to the Mather command center. He found Myron monitoring events around the state. Myron reluctantly agreed to meet with Tom, and they walked to a small conference room. Myron described the arrests and killings at Pendleton, but Tom was only half listening. He really listened to what Myron *didn't* tell him.

He said, "Myron. You said the Marines arrested Chazz. She would have told them everything about what we're doing. Why no reaction?"

Myron replied, "It's like I told you and Chip, Tom. They won't move a muscle because the DoD won't let them."

"Not good enough, Myron. You're holding out on me, aren't you?"

"All right, all right. Marty Simmonds and I go way back. I let him in on the coup. He said he would stand down and let things take their course."

Tom frowned. "How long have you known this, Myron?"

"From the beginning. I wouldn't have gone ahead otherwise."

"I wish you'd told me. And what about Simmonds? After?"

"He's bringing 36,000 Marines into our new armed forces. Simmonds will be the new commandant of the California Marine Corps. He's pretending to be doing something. He'll take over the Channel Islands Air Station. The feds will think he's dealing with the coup. Then, when things settle down, he'll show his support for us. I'm sorry, Tom. I'm used to compartmentalizing things like this. We don't spread things around in the service."

Tom's sunny vision of the California Republic was crumbling in the face of a vast military he'd never dreamed of. How long would martial law last? His strategies all assumed a civil society based on the best of American political culture. But he didn't want to upset Myron right now. Change the subject.

"This Colonel Ridger. You say he was a friend of Chazz's?"

"I asked around. They were together in Iraq in 2005. And again, in San Diego, a few years back."

"So she ran to him after...."

"After she drowned you, yes." Myron half smiled.

"And he's dead?"

"I guarantee you Brickhouse or Calvo killed him. There are no details yet. Just that Colonel Silver fled the scene and everyone else there was dead."

Chip wanted Chazz dead. He'd told Brickhouse to kill her. Tom saved that for later. Right now, he needed everything Myron had done.

Tom asked, "Any more surprises for me, Myron?"

Myron smiled, unmoved by Tom's asperity. "Admiral Collett," he said.

"Third Fleet? He's in on this too?"

"Yes. Simmonds brought him in with the promise of full command of the California Navy."

San Diego. At least some of the major ships in California waters. Nuclear submarines? And what about the nuclear missiles stationed in California?

"We'll negotiate on the subs, Myron. They'll want them back because —"

"Collett won't let them go. Or the *Carl Vinson*." The largest nuclear aircraft carrier in the U.S. Navy.

"We can't keep them. The feds won't stand for it. Not nukes."

"We'll deal with the feds when we have to. Right now, we're more concerned with mutinies of loyalist sailors."

"Myron. You are a military governor under martial law. Take charge of all this." Tom cleared his throat. "I know I'm one step down the ladder. But you need to bring together the relevant parties, lock the doors, and get agreement to return the nukes to the feds."

"Can I be honest, Tom?"

"I don't know, Myron. Can you?" Tom stared into the general's eyes.

"Yes. And here it is. Chip will never allow those nukes to leave the country. And neither will I. They're the only thing standing between us and oblivion. Think of them as hostages. We have nuclear hostages to make sure that the feds won't shut us down. We're already moving them to secure locations and revising the command and launch protocols. Got it?"

"Yes, sir."

"Now stand down and do your job."

Tom walked out of the command center thinking about the shambles of his political strategy. And obsessing on Chazz and her whereabouts. And wondering about Tony Ridger, the Marine who had died saving her.

The curves and cliffs of the Santa Ana mountains on SR-74 wore an already tired Chazz out. A little roadside motel appeared as she descended into the Valley. She checked in and paid for one night with some of Brickhouse's cash. She parked her car in the back, grabbed a gun, and found her room. Opening the window to cool the hot room, she found the highway noise unbearable and closed it again. The old mattress, the thin pillow, and the hard outline of the Glock underneath it added to the discomfort. She woke several times, reaching for the gun, then fell back asleep.

The Dream woke her near dawn, sweating. The room was still hot. There were signs of minimal daylight through the curtained window. The Dream fragmented and went in different directions than her usual version. Current events had given her subconscious other things to worry about. She lay in bed for half an hour, recovering.

The digital clock on the nightstand said 10:45 p.m., which was unlikely. Her watch said 0637, which seemed closer to reality. Chazz stumbled into the small bathroom and tried the shower, but it just dribbled with no water pressure. She ran the sink faucet for ten minutes until the water warmed up to body temperature and washed what she could. She had no toilet kit. Chazz let her hair down, poked it, and put it back in the bun. Hopeless. She'd have to get a real shower to do anything with it.

Chazz checked the digital map app on Tony's phone for the route to Barstow on I-15. She'd stop there and decide: Fort Irwin or out of California to Arizona or Nevada. She'd be living in the car, and she'd need supplies.

At 0800, the Mustang's power display found the nearest charging station: a Costco on the other side of Lake Elsinore right off I-15. Chazz drove around the lake, found the fast chargers, and paid with Tony's phone. She used the thirty minutes of charging time to stock up on basic groceries, civvy clothes, and a slice of pizza. She raised the pizza to Tony's memory, then devoured it.

With a full 475-mile charge, she buckled up and drove north, windows open to let out the baked air that had accumulated in the car while it charged. The heat reminded her of Iraq, which reminded her of IEDs. Unlikely on this road, fortunately. She sped the car up to 80 m.p.h. to match the flow of traffic.

The Mustang was on AI-Assist, and Chazz was thinking about Barstow and Fort Irwin. The car announced an incoming call with a number she recognized. She hesitated, then told the car to answer.

"Tom. How did you get this number?" She'd left the phone on after the charge-up at Costco. Damn.

"A process of induction. Ex-lover. Firefight. Dead bodies. A smart woman without a smartphone. And I checked. They didn't find Ridger's phone on his body or in his quarters."

"How did you find out—"

"Simmonds is in on the coup. And Rear Admiral Collett."

Chazz relaxed the tense muscles in her body, tense from the long drives and the horrors of near execution. Even more tense from this dire news from Tom. She gripped the steering wheel without thinking, and the assist turned itself off, forcing her to concentrate on the road until she turned it back on.

"Chazz?"

"Yeah, Tom, I'm here. Just…shocked." Tom must think he's overwhelming her with the forces against her, to make her surrender.

Tom replied, "These guys are all in it together, Chazz. Shock is no longer possible."

"You're there too, Tom. You're *running* this thing."

"I wish that were true."

"Why did you attack me? On the pier?"

"I didn't."

"You did. You threw—"

"Dupont was tracking you through your phone, Chazz. You didn't seem to realize how far things had gone. I threw it away to help you."

"Ah." Chazz ran this explanation through her truth meter. Somewhere in the middle between obviousness and a damned lie. And after Tony's death, she wasn't ready for the soft emotions. She couldn't afford to be soft. She stopped herself from grabbing the Mustang's steering wheel again.

"Where are you?" Tom asked.

"No."

"I can have them track you. Where are you?"

"Tom, I'm going to Arizona. I'll contact the Army there, and I'll do everything I can to stop this thing." Her destination jelled: Fort Irwin. She needed to get to an Army facility as soon as she could. Simmonds and Collett, traitors? There was no way the U.S. Army would go along with this coup.

Tom kept trying. "We're already in control, Chazz. We've declared martial law. Dupont is military governor. Chip is president."

"And you're what—chief of staff?"

"Strategy, special assistant to the president for strategy."

"Such an important job, Tom. I hope the war crimes trials go well for you."

"Yeah. Look, none of this was my idea. Chazz, I love you, I want you to be safe. Go to Arizona before we close all the borders. Dupont will move Guard units to the Mexican border before turning to the U. S. ones. He's afraid the cartels will take over the south of the country while we're still weak."

"Fine. I'll go to Arizona."

"And ditch that phone."

"I will."

"And let's meet next month in Las Vegas. October 15, our anniversary. We can get married."

"Go fuck yourself, Tom. But thanks for the advice."

She hung up, clicked off the phone, and ejected the SIM card while the car drove itself for a while.

But she wasn't going to Arizona.

Tom, on his way to the office after the call to Chazz, called Myron to inform him of Chazz's intentions.

"Chazz is heading for Arizona, Myron. She's about to cross the border. And she's intending to work with the military there to stop us."

"Gee, that's too bad, Tom. Unfortunately, it's also incorrect."

"What?"

"Colonel Silver, a model of honor and duty, is going to Fort Irwin."

Tom swore to himself. Had he been too late to warn Chazz? "How—"

"Ridger's car. It's got the latest telematics system installed, with GPS and cellular networking. We've been able to track cars through those systems for several months, a secret program. She's halfway to Barstow on I-15."

"Barstow is one way to get to Arizona, Myron," said Tom.

The general cleared his throat. "It's the direct route to Irwin, and she could have gone to Arizona more directly on I-10. I've worked with Colonel Silver long enough to know she won't quit, and Irwin is the closest federal military base to her location. I can't let her get there."

Tom protested, "But if she goes to Arizona—"

Myron interrupted, "Or to Arizona. She knows too much about how we work. We need to contain her. The CHP is on the way. She doesn't stand a chance. If she resists, they have shoot-to-kill orders. But she's not stupid. She'll surrender and go to Manzanar."

Tom banged his hand on his steering wheel. "Myron—"

"Tom, stand down. Right now. Or do you want to join Colonel Silver on her desert vacation? You're a valuable member of the team. Don't blow everything over a woman."

CHAPTER TWENTY-NINE
The County Jail

CHAZZ TRIED THE RADIO AS the Mustang sped through San Bernardino. The endless loop of the Mamas & Papas song had mercifully stopped. She found some nice, soothing heavy metal from a Victorville station. The California Republic might crack down on dissent, but radio music was sacrosanct. She had a long drive up I-15 to Fort Irwin ahead of her.

SR-18 and Roy Rogers Drive flew by. Flashing lights in the rearview mirror caught her attention. CHP. Time to put the Mustang to work. She disabled AI-Assist and floored the accelerator and the car burst forward with enough G-force to thrust her back into the seat. 90, 105, 120, 135, and she passed other cars as if they were standing still.

The flashing lights fell far behind, and the faint wail of a siren faded.

Acceleration aside, CHP cars were more than capable of 150 m.p.h, and they'd catch her if she couldn't lose them. But I-15 through Victorville was a long, straight road. GPS showed the exits ahead, but she didn't know the area, and the CHP did. She pulled Calvo's Sig from the compartment next to her seat and set it on her lap. The fault wasn't hers or the CHP's, but now the pursuit was life or death.

Simple physics kicked in. The power gauge jumped way up from its usual level, and the range indicator had gone from 425 to 123 and was dropping fast.

Then a chopper appeared above her, whooshing past and coming around. She heard the crackle of a loudspeaker over the road noise.

"Colonel Silver, you are under arrest. Pull your car over NOW."

She looked in the rear-view mirror. Flashing lights came closer.

A sign flashed by, D Street, CA-18 East. Cars pulling over in response to the CHP warning sirens.

She rocketed along at 140 m.p.h., swerving around a slowing car. Horns. Sirens. Flashing lights still behind her but falling back. The chopper made another pass right over her roof.

Her GPS showed only small desert roads for the next twenty-five miles. Without knowing where a road ended, it would be a trap. And then her options ran out. The CHP had set up three flashing warning poles in the middle of the interstate behind huge spike strips.

The chopper's loudspeaker repeated the command to stop, warning her about the spikes.

Chazz slowed and looked for alternatives. If she crossed the shoulder of the freeway into the desert, she could evade capture.

She yanked the wheel and spun the Mustang off the road. At the crazy speed, she lost control on the loose sand and spun around, tires churning up desert sand and plants. She slowed, blew through a wire fence, slowed again, regained control, then stopped as her rear wheels spun in a loose sand pit.

The chopper descended toward the roof of the car, kicking up dust, and the flashing lights of the pursuit vehicle caught up.

Chazz picked up the gun and hefted it. Heavier than usual. Moral weight. As tough as she was, shooting up a bunch of cops doing their duty wouldn't get her into heaven. It was an unbearable moral failure coupled with instant death by cop. The radio segued into a gentle cover of Metallica's "Screaming Suicide." She shut off the car and hid the gun in the center compartment. She unbuckled her seatbelt, put her hands on top of the steering wheel, and waited for the inevitable.

It was over.

* * *

Tom forced himself to stop thinking about Chazz and the CHP. He occupied his mind by reviewing the reports from the political strategists he'd installed in the major cities around California. He'd insisted on daily email reports from all of them. The situation's unpredictability meant he had to know, not assume. Tom needed factual information from people on the ground. He'd fallen behind because of his adventures in Port Hueneme, and by Thursday in his office, he'd finally caught up. He reread the report from San Diego again, parsing the words carefully; something was wrong. The team there wasn't telling him the whole story.

His phone rang. Chip.

"Hey, Chip. What's up?"

"I can't get Myron on the phone, Tom. He won't take my calls. He says he's too busy. I want to know what's going on, and he's not telling me."

"Huh. How often did you call him?"

"Oh, seven or eight times. Since the declaration."

Christ. No wonder. "Well, he *is* busy, Chip. I'll check in with him, see what I can find out. OK?"

"If things are going south, I need to know, Tom. I don't like what I'm hearing. I don't want Marines crawling all over my office. Just call him, Tom." The president hung up.

Tom put aside his worries about San Diego and called Myron.

"Hey, Myron. Chip wants an update on the military stuff. Everything going OK?"

"You need to focus on your job, Tom," said Myron. He sounded irritated. Something was going wrong. Myron, the great stone face, did not show irritation.

Tom replied, "Sure, but we need to keep the President informed so he doesn't fly solo. Come on, Myron, give."

"He's already flown solo, Tom. I'm just ignoring him now. He needs to stay in his lane. He needs to keep making speeches to get the people and the power brokers on board. Chip shouldn't meddle in military affairs."

"He's the president, Myron. We can't ignore him."

"Oh, all right."

"First, what about Chazz?"

Myron reported in a flat voice. "The CHP caught up with Colonel Silver in Victorville, chased her down, and ran her off the road. Transported to Pitchess, the LA County Jail in Castaic. The internees there will soon be en route to Manzanar. My MPs have set up a tent city there until we can build permanent barracks."

"Any trouble with the park rangers?" Change the subject. Don't ask Myron if he's going to have Chazz shot by a firing squad or something. Don't put ideas in his head. But he's sounding as though he has bigger fish in his frying pan.

"The law enforcement ranger pulled a gun. He didn't make it. The interpretive ranger was a woman from Monterey there on temporary assignment. She got hysterical. We sent her home. The place is ours now."

"I'll tell Chip. What about the lockdowns?"

"I'm busy, Tom." The irritation resurfaced.

"Myron, Chip wants updates. A dribble is all I need to keep him happy. What problems are you having?"

"A tank in Sacramento blew up Interstate 5 and a news crew in a helicopter, and somebody in San Francisco blew up a tank on 101. I sent in a couple of companies of MPs to lock down SF. The tank crew took out the terrorist just before the tank blew."

"Suicide bombing?"

"They shot the man as he tried to escape. Pure carelessness, letting somebody get that close with explosives. We've arrested some suspects and put them in the county jail."

"How many?"

"Arrested? Three or four hundred, just a few. Activists and such."

"Christ. Here we go."

"Tom, I'm busy," Myron repeated, the irritation very clear now.

"What else is wrong, Myron?" None of this should perturb Myron. So why was he this upset?

After a pause, Myron said, "I'm worried about Simmonds and the Marines, Tom. Old friends are old friends. But I didn't like the way he was talking. Simmonds has always been a take-charge kind of guy."

"As in take charge of us?"

"Yes."

"Should I make contingency plans to, um, thwart him? Politically, I mean."

"Thwart. Sure, you do that. Yeah. Thwart him. Politically."

"What are you going to do?"

"Call up and arm about ten thousand Army and Air Guard troops and form a combat-ready, combined force division to deploy as needed. If the Marines decide to take charge, we'll have to finish them quickly."

"Christ. Here we go."

"I'm *busy*. Goodbye, Tom."

According to Chazz's CHP chopper pilot, Pitchess South Detention Center in Castaic was the largest facility in the Los Angeles County jail system. The high-security facility was now the staging area for political prisoners en route to Manzanar from Southern California. The military governor had chosen it for both its capacity and its security. Chazz looked down from the CHP chopper at the extensive array of fences, gates, and buildings scattered over a large area just east of Interstate 5.

The chopper overflew the facility and set down at a heliport near I-5. A van was waiting, and LA County Sheriff's deputies took charge of Chazz as soon as the Chippies unloaded her from the back of the CHP chopper. The CHP had placed her in transport restraints after arresting her. She admired their professionalism, even though she considered them traitors.

The Chippies told the Sheriff's deputies she was an internee. They'd heard.

"I want a lawyer," she said. She knew what the response would be. Poke the bear.

But there was no response at all. They ignored her. The Chippies returned to their helicopter.

She repeated her request. The deputies were anything but professional getting her into their van. They just laughed at her. One deputy took every opportunity to grab and push, and the grabs were in inappropriate places. Chazz calmly stated she would only cooperate if he stopped. She forcefully slapped his hands away. More pushing, but less grabbing. She tried her most ferocious expression, dredged up from her past. Men who overreached hated that face. Reflexively, she tried to cross her arms and failed, so instead she held herself very straight and upright, glaring at the man. How could she let this happen? Should she have gone out in a hail of bullets instead of surrendering? It would have been better than this. The shame of it. Like before.

She ended up in the back of the van behind a metal grille. That solved the grabbing problem, at least temporarily. The van drove along a narrow road, passing several buildings and taking her to the far eastern side of the facility. The deputies said nothing in response to her questions and taunts. An imposing building with the letters NCCF on the wall appeared, and the van turned into its garage entrance.

"What's NCCF?" she asked.

The grabby deputy smiled a wolfish grin. "North County Correctional Facility. You'll love it. I can tell you need a lot of correction."

When they arrived at a maximum-security cellblock, a deputy said to the female guard, "Internee. Check her in?"

"No names, no prisoner number," the guard replied. "We're not keeping records here. Take her. Just leave the restraints on. Not gonna be around that long. Manzanar awaits." The guard smiled disdainfully at Chazz.

Subconsciously, she'd been expecting the restraints to come off. She felt the urge to beat the hell out of that deputy, to tear up the NCCF, to escape or die. But in the Mustang, she'd made a choice. Stop the killing, stop the running. She'd put down her gun. But she'd never stop fighting. She'd taken an oath, and she'd keep it. She'd find a way.

They put her in a cell by herself. It was a still, silent place. Exhausted, she slept.

CHAPTER THIRTY
Abandon All Hope

THE PITCHESS DEPUTIES PUT CHAZZ on a bus with nineteen other NCCF women. The three-hour bus ride through the wilds of California took Chazz from lows of despair to highs of admiration for the desert landscape. Awe turned to depression after another hour of desert. Despair deepened as the bus arrived at Manzanar.

Chazz remembered visiting the place in her youth. It had been barren except for the Japanese internment memorial and the breathtaking view of the east side of the Sierra Nevada. Both were still there. But now there was also enough triple-strand concertina wire to seal the U.S. border, enclosing a sea of brown tents. Chazz recognized the tents. They were the ones the Guard used for exercise deployments. Dupont had efficiently used materials on hand. There were four stacked Conex container watchtowers, two wooden barracks, and a larger wooden building.

The twenty women filed off the bus and trudged along a path toward the larger building. Blue sky, gorgeous mountains, and 90 degrees. Dry heat. They entered the building that had been the national monument's visitor center, now a processing command post for the new internees of the California Republic. A giant bear flag festooned one wall, and Chazz picked out a photo portrait of the new president, José "Chip" Sanchez, on the opposite wall.

The guards removed the women's restraints. Chazz reconnoitered and saw ten MPs with rifles stationed around the center. Two tables had Guard officers behind them, and the prisoners advanced in pairs.

Chazz recognized one officer as a man she'd shared a table with in a training session in Sacramento a year ago. She approached his desk. Recognition dawned in the man's eyes. He looked down at his laptop, scrolled the mouse, and clicked. Checking off a name. Hers.

"Colonel," he greeted her smoothly, though his smile didn't reach his lips. "Terrible situation, I'm afraid."

"Captain Nolan, isn't it?" He wore an MP brigade patch on one arm of his OCPs. She read his name off his name patch to show empathy. Wasted.

"Yes, ma'am."

He handed her a piece of paper. Camp rules. Right up there at the top. "Attempting to exit the camp unlawfully will result in your being shot. No exceptions." And another one: "Attempting to escape will result in your being shot. No exceptions." And further down: "Disobeying the orders of work detail guards will result…" Work detail. Chazz hated the sound of that. Her National Guard did not impose work details in detention facilities.

She said, "Nice concentration camp you got here. I don't suppose there's any hope of ordering you to stand down and help me end this thing?" She waved the paper at him.

The captain's mouth opened and closed. Then his face hardened. "No, ma'am, sorry. Orders. And this is a detention facility."

"Those orders are treasonous. This whole place is treasonous."

"Not any more, ma'am. Welcome to the California Republic. Now, please, follow the tape on the floor to get your supplies. Wait a minute." He fiddled with his laptop, then wrote out some numbers on a form. "Here's your billet tent and cot numbers. I gave you one with a good view of Mount Williamson. VIPs. Best I can do, ma'am."

The captain was done with her. She stood, unsure whether to express her inner wolf or just move on.

Captain Nolan told her, his voice hard, "Move along, ma'am. A lot more folks behind you."

"Treason, treason, treason," Chazz said, just to light him up. She shook her head, gave him the finger, and followed the tape across the floor to a desk. An enlisted man handed her a blanket, a towel, and a water bottle. Empty. Chazz overcame a wave of despair to shake the bottle at the man.

"Fill 'er up outside, faucet." Smile. "Enjoy your stay with us."

"Fuck you."

No smile. "Move along, ma'am. Or I'll move you along."

"You're committing treason, soldier."

The man half rose from his seat. The MP behind him advised, "Don't do it, Jeff. Ma'am, please move along now." He put one hand on the baton hanging from his belt.

With a forceful gesture, she left the old visitors' center in search of water.

After taking a long drink and filling her water bottle, Chazz walked west along the line of brown tents. Beyond the concertina wire was a world-class view of the tall, snow-capped mountains.

She'd gone about halfway down the line of tents when a hand fell on her shoulder. It was the enlisted man from the visitors' center.

"Get your hand off me," she said.

He said nothing in return, but punched her hard in the stomach, then grabbed her arm and dragged her behind a tent out of sight of the path. He pulled a baton from his belt and laid into her. She thought, deep into her dark forest, "Not again." But the soldier wasn't a rapist, just a sadist. She tried to resist but had to endure. He avoided her head, concentrating on the softer tissues. The whole thing proceeded with only the thwack of the baton against her body sounding in the dry desert air. She ended up on her hands and knees, gasping, the dark forest receding into pain.

"OK, bitch," the private said. "Now you know. Fuck with us, we'll fuck you up. Fuck with us more, and we'll fuck you up more. Keep it up, and you'll go on a work detail in the desert. You won't come back. Get it?"

She said nothing as she staggered to her feet, and he swung the baton into her stomach. She doubled over.

"Get it?" he repeated.

"I get it, you treasonous pig." She coughed.

The man laughed. "Always wanted to beat the shit out of an officer." He swung again, hitting her above the kidneys, and she gasped in pain. "Oink, oink. *Ma'am.*" He left her gasping and sucking air into her lungs. After she recovered, she picked up her supplies from where they'd fallen and continued her quest for a place to rest, to the last row of tents.

She found the right tent, pulled the cloth door aside, and ducked inside. Several cloth windows were open, lighting up the interior. There were ten women scattered around the tent, all looking pretty damned down. She glanced at her slip of paper: cot thirteen. That was auspicious. She marched down the rows of cots and found number thirteen. She deposited her blanket and towel on the cot and put her water bottle on the ground.

"What're you, some kinda guard?" The woman lying on cot twelve gave her the eye. She was a beautiful Latina dressed in a tank top and a short skirt. Chazz looked around. The other women in the tent were dressed professionally. Chazz was still wearing her OCPs. The Latina on the cot raised herself up on one elbow, expecting an answer.

"No, not a guard. The powers that be didn't seem to like my attitude towards their coup. Colonel Silver. Chazz." She reached a hand down. The woman shook it.

"A colonel, huh? Wadj'ya do, sleep with the wrong general?"

"Are you being deliberately offensive? Or is that just the way your mouth works?" shot back Chazz.

The woman grinned and sat up on her cot. "More like it, bitch. Angélica, Angélica Arguello. Call me Angel, all my gringo friends do." She patted the cot. "Sit and tell me who the fuck you are and why you're here."

"I will if you will," Chazz smiled.

Angel used both hands to push up her breasts. "These beauties got me here. I slept with the wrong guy."

"And who would that be, Angel?" Chazz sat down on her cot. She needed to take a break after her beating. This woman was a delightful distraction.

"Guy named Sanchez." Angel's eyes slid to Chazz, expecting a response. Sanchez. Lots of those in California. VIPs? Oh. My God.

"The governor," she said.

"There ya go! Smart one for a uniform." She snickered. "El Presidente."

"Hey, Angel. I don't think it was them, it was that." Chazz pointed to the woman's mouth.

Angel nodded. "Got that one right, too. What about the nose? Bad boyfriend?"

Chazz touched her bandage. "No, a lieutenant colonel who tried hard to kill me."

"What happened to him?"

"We fought it out, a friend choked him unconscious, and I ran. The boyfriend showed up later, and I pushed him off a pier into the ocean. I shot up another colonel who tried to execute me and ran again. All because Sanchez and his gang didn't like what I was doing about their coup. The CHP caught up with me. That's why I'm here."

"OK, no chin check for *joo*." Angel pronounced the pronoun with an exaggerated Latina accent.

"Chin check?"

"Never been in la pinta, huh?" Angel laughed raucously. "Punch in the jaw just to see what you'd do." She looked Chazz up and down. "You're moving kind of careful, too. Something up with that?"

"A guard. He didn't like it when I called him a traitor."

Angel shook her head. "You got balls, sister."

Chazz grinned. A different take on her misadventures. "So the governor sent you here because...."

"I talked rings, he talked bed, I stopped talking, he took it bad." She grinned. "OK, there was a little threat in there, too. Drove him wacko. CHP got me, too."

Close enough to her own experience. Chazz just nodded. She wondered whether Angel knew anything she should know. Did Sanchez talk in his sleep? Did he brag about his power fantasies?

"He's moved on to bigger things," she said.

"So have I, bitch," said Angel. She got up from the cot and launched into a Beyoncé rap about prison.

"Oh shit" and "Shut the hell up" issued from the other women in the tent.

"Bitches don't like a little spontaneity," Angel said, sitting back down.

Chazz noticed the woman lying on cot fourteen was not responding to the impromptu concert.

"Who's that?" she asked.

"Fucking mayor of LA. She don't talk much. Gone psycho or something. She stares out the window at the mountains or sleeps. I been here a few days, and she ain't said one word." Angel shook her head in dismay. "Tried to cheer her up, but she just rolled over and ignored me."

"At least we're in good company."

"If you say so, Colonel. If you say so."

CHAPTER THIRTY-ONE
Mobilization

Tom hunched over the president's coffee table, sitting forward in his chair to study the huge map of California. He wasn't paying attention to Chip, who was rattling on. Fiddling with his pen, Tom bleakly reflected on Chazz. He located Manzanar on the map. Was she there yet? Would she be docile enough to escape a beating, or worse? He shook his head. Chazz, docile. On her best day, she was as badass as a bear with a sore butt. Christ.

"Tom. You're not paying attention." Chip broke into his stream of consciousness as he came over to the table and glared at him.

"Sorry, boss." He had to let go. He had to stop obsessing over her. Chazz. He'd tried. He'd tried to help her, but she wouldn't let him. Could he have done more? Could he do more now? "A lot on my mind."

"Glad to hear you have one. What are we going to do about him?"

"Who?" asked Tom.

"Oh for God's sake," Chip said. He strode over to the office door, opened it, and called out, "Sally. Coffee, two grandes. Now."

As he returned, he said, "Tom, we gotta do something. Myron's out of control."

Myron was out of control. Tom's anger crested at this misplaced criticism from the most out-of-control guy in the country. The guy who'd ordered Chazz killed. He got hot and started, "If you expect me—"

Sally came in carrying a tray of coffee and fixings. Tom had to swallow his rebuke. He cleared a spot on the coffee table, and Sally set the tray down. Tom thanked her.

"Anything else, sir?" she asked.

"Nah, we're good," the president said. Sally walked out.

Tom, having gotten the better of his anger, said, "Myron's in charge of military stuff, Chip. We know nothing about how it works. We've never served in the military."

"How hard can it be? Anyway, it's out of control. The Marines, Tom. What about the Marines?"

"They're on our side, Chip." Which, while technically true, was optimistic to a fault. But Tom hadn't mentioned Myron's concerns to Chip. The president wasn't ready to deal with marauding Marines.

But Chip had already caught up on his own. "Bullshit, Tom. I talked to Myron, and he's shitting his pants about Simmonds. Myron's calling up a division of combined forces, whatever that is. That's 10,000 soldiers, Tom. Ten. The plan involved only a few hundred troops. We put the opposition in Manzanar to get rid of our problems. And guess what? We got more problems. Marines running around the country shooting people. Our own army mobilizing to fight them. That colonel down at Channel Islands, Tom. She was on our side. They shot her in the head. No trial or anything. And what about those nuclear subs?"

Tom snapped back, "Is there a specific problem in there that you want me to address, Chip? Because I can't do anything about the Marines or Myron's army. Or nuclear subs! What the hell?" Seeing Chip's clenched jaw, he added a placating "Sir."

Chip ranted, "You think Myron is gonna sit there like a fat spider and let events wash over him? He's gonna take over, Tom, sure as hell. If Simmonds doesn't whup his ass and do it first." He looked out his office window. "We oughta post some guards here, just in case."

"In case of what? If those tanks decide to wake up everybody near the Capitol by blowing the shit out of it, a few guards won't stop them, Chip. And they won't stop a battalion of Marines, either."

Tom burned his tongue on a sip of coffee, cursed, and glanced at the office door. Oh, fuck. The door was open. He put down his coffee, stood up, and walked over. He looked out into the outer office and saw Sally, motionless at her desk, her expression pale, looking at nothing. How much of their war of words had she overheard? How much had she understood? He smiled at her and shut the door.

Chip continued his chatter as Tom sat back down on the couch. But he wasn't obsessing over Chazz anymore. He was speculating about Sally. Chip thought Sally was fantastic at her job but not the brightest crayon in the box. Sure, she was naïve, even after all her years working with the legislature. But she knew a lot of people, and they knew her. And she'd be right in the thick of things now. No presidential assistant could avoid being a repository of secrets a president desperately wanted to keep. Secrets like sending his girlfriend to a concentration camp. If Sally got wind of the terrible things going on and told her friends, there might be significant blowback. And if that blowback upset Chip enough, Sally might end up in Manzanar, too. Tom's gut told him he would hate it if that happened.

He'd better take Sally to lunch and explain things.

"They have a great Mexican chef here, Sally. One of my favorite places," said Tom as Sally worked her way through the menu. She sat across from him at a window seat at the Blind Pig. They'd walked over from the Capitol after Tom had invited her out to lunch. To talk. She'd mumbled thanks, but she was still less than her usual loquacious self.

"Ted doesn't like Mexican food, so we don't eat it much," said Sally. "How about this soup? Menudo? What's that?"

"No, that one's not for you. Try the fish tacos or the fresh corn and chipotle quesadilla." Or maybe not the quesadilla? Sally wasn't the kind of person who liked heat. "Try the tacos."

They ordered. Sally sipped her martini, and Tom ordered another sunrise, having used the first one to prepare himself for the explanations. Sally looked out the window, avoiding his gaze.

"We should talk about what you overheard, Sally," Tom said. "It's important stuff, strategic stuff. I'm sorry you heard it, but we need to talk about it."

"Ted says Chip is the best thing to happen to California in 100 years. He's got a Bear Republic flag out in front of the house. Ted says—"

"What's important right now is what *you* say, Sally," said Tom. "You're Sally-on-the-spot. You're a critical part of our operation now. Special assistant to the president. I don't want you to worry about anything."

Sally moved her eyes from the windows to study him. She wasn't smiling. "How can I not worry, Tom? Ted—well, let it go. Marines? Guard divisions? Battles? Executions? Tanks blowing up the Capitol? How bad *is* it?"

"Right now, it's all in Chip's head," Tom replied.

"Not the execution. That was real. Or the tanks."

Tom sighed. "A Marine unit got out of control, Sally. It was an isolated incident. And the tanks. That was me being snarky. I'm sure Myron won't—"

"Tom." She stopped him and put a hand on his arm. "Tell me the truth."

"It's messier than we expected, that's all. We're dealing with it. Chip was just talking. You know how he gets."

"Chip is a Hollywood actor, Tom." Sally closed her eyes. Her mouth trembled. She opened her eyes and stared at Tom. "He's not up to it, is he? Being president? Ted thinks he's great, a forceful leader. But I can see he's not." She picked up her fork and put it back down. "He's not, Tom. He drinks and says mean things to people."

A great time for Sally to get smart and speak truth. He could see the desperation in her face. He'd have to jolly her out of it.

He said, "He's just in over his head a bit. Look at Reagan. A cowboy turned into the greatest president in U.S. history."

"That was before I married Ted. I voted for Carter. Right out of high school. My first election." She sighed. "He almost didn't marry me when I told him. But things worked out."

"Things do, Sally, they do. It will all work out."

"Ted tells me that all the time. He's one of Chip's biggest fans. But, sometimes, I get—"

The server brought their lunch plates and arranged them, interrupting her thought, and they ate. He had to change the subject away from politics. He'd cheer Sally up and get her back on the team. She sounded down on her husband Ted. A little flirting would lift her spirits.

"You're a beautiful woman, Sally. Ted doesn't know what he's got in you."

"Thanks, Tom. I've been feeling pretty old lately."

"You're not old, Sally. If I weren't so busy saving Chip's ass, I'd talk about your eyes and steal a kiss."

"Now stop it, Tom. That's…you're just cheering me up."

"No, no, Sally. You're gorgeous, especially when you smile. Check out this crowd. You're the sweetest lady here."

Sally picked up her martini and drank it down. She looked right at him and said, "Tom, stop. I mean it. I…I don't. Like it. You're making me uncomfortable. Just stop."

"OK, sorry, Sally. I won't take it back, 'cause it's true, but I let myself say too much. Stress. Put it down to that."

Sally stared at him, then gave him a tiny smile and ate a taco. She tried to keep the conversation light. "This is good. I don't like fish, but this is tasty."

Tom, chewing his pork loin Adobo, nodded and smiled, unsure what to say next.

Sally tried again with a defensive move. "How is your girlfriend? Chazz? I saw her name on that VIP list the gov—the president had me type up. I hope she had an exciting time with all those important people."

Tom felt the punch like a boxer who'd taken one too many. He managed a smile and said, "She sure did. She's…traveling right now. In the desert." She'd sat right there, where Sally sat now, loving him. Now he was flirting with Sally. While Chazz baked in the sun at Manzanar.

Sally, oblivious, replied, "How exciting! I'll bet you miss her, don't you? I wanted to go to Joshua Tree, but Ted hates camping. Too many bugs, he says." She looked down. "But that's a federal park, isn't it? What about all the parks? What about Yosemite? I'd never thought about all the parks the U.S. government runs in the state. How are we—"

"We'll figure it out, don't worry. Look, Sally, everything will be fine. I'm sure Ted will take you there soon." He mentally handed Sally over to Ted. Bugs and all. But Chazz…he had to do something. Anything. To make things right. To get her free.

CHAPTER THIRTY-TWO
A Way Out?

CHAZZ ABRUPTLY AWOKE FROM THE Dream, her heart pounding. This time, it wasn't the haunting nightmare of the rape that woke her. It was her neighbor, Angel, who jolted her awake. She sat up on her narrow cot, trembling, with Angel's hand on her cheek. Light seeped in through the mesh windows of the tent. The air was cool and smelled of the desert, sandy and dry. Manzanar. The aches from the previous day's beating coalesced in a ball of pain. She wrapped her arms around herself. Angel sat on the cot beside her.

"Some nasty shit, Chazz. You were moaning and thrashing around like the cot was on fire." Concern etched lines in Angel's face in the early morning light.

"Yeah. Terrible memories. Iraq." She breathed and worked to control the pain. How would she endure Manzanar with all this turmoil? While her brain still worked on the problem, her lips said, "I don't want to talk about it."

Angel's expression twisted into a grimace. "OK, girl. Whatever. You just keep it bottled up, let it brew, and see what happens. I've seen a lot of that in people. Makes them ornery. Real ornery."

"Doesn't happen much, now. A lot of stress here." She put it back on Angel. "What makes you so God damn optimistic, anyway? Singing those trashy songs and all?"

"Hey! My songs ain't trashy, bitch! Whatever. Optimistic?" Angel sat on her cot and looked at Chazz, not smiling. "Let's go outside for a minute, OK? Get some air." She looked around at the slumbering VIPs. "Stuffy in here."

Chazz gingerly swung her legs off the cot, her body throbbing. The dull pain pulsed through her muscles. And her nose throbbed as well. She was in no shape for a full-blown fight with Angel. But her aching nastiness fueled an intense desire to throw a few punches anyway.

The two women ducked through the tent door. Curfew ended at six, according to the rules she'd read, so the guards paid no attention to them. The massif to the west glowed with the early morning light. Angel led Chazz to the wire fence, its metallic strands glinting in the sunlight. But it turned out Angel wasn't interested in fighting. She had something else in mind.

"I'm busting out of here in a few days," Angel whispered. "You got a lot of experience with these sons of bitches, right?" She nodded her head at the visible watchtower with its MP guards.

"Uh. Right."

"So you can help me, right? Find a way out."

"Optimistic is one thing, stupid is another." She stifled the laugh that bubbled up in her throat.

"You got a mouth on you too, babe." Angel slapped her on the shoulder, right on a bruise. It hurt.

Chazz suppressed her urge to lash out at her tormenter. Fighting wouldn't help. "Be realistic. What makes you think you can escape?"

"Six Latinos with M-16s and terrible attitudes. *Los chavos de mi hermano Juan. De Tijuana.*"

Chazz smiled in disbelief. "Sure. Just exactly who is your brother?"

Angel grinned. "Big deal in Tijuana. Took over the business there from *mi padre.*"

"Ah. And why would he send this crew to break you out?"

"We're tight. Papa told Juan to take care of me, so he hates my being here. I got word to him from Pitchess. Guards there know what's what.

And my brother has weight in LA. A lot of weight. But shit happened too fast to get me out of Pitchess."

Chazz's eyes locked on Angel's face, searching for any sign of deception or uncertainty. She needed more to understand the full scope of the plan. If Angel's brother truly had that kind of influence and resources, he could be their ticket out. But Chazz would be the gunner, the one who took a bullet every God damn time things went nonlinear. Her mind flashed back to that terrible day in Iraq when she lost her gunner, Ripley, in the chopper crash. The memories of past losses weighed on her, creating a knot of tension in her stomach. She forced herself to focus on the here and now.

"So…what's the plan?"

"They're coming in three days at two in the morning. I got the message before they trucked me up here to this shithole." Angel smiled. "Nice view and all, but it ain't no vacation wonderland. I'm ready to check out. You think you got problems with whatever's giving you dreams? Try this shitty place's guards hitting on you every time you pass by. Sweet Latina, great ass, big tits, guy with a gun? Might as well be in Ciudad Juarez with *los cholos*. You can come if you can figure out how to get to the road when the fellas light things up." She reached out and touched Chazz's bandaged nose. "And, Chazz, you'd be pretty good in a fight."

Since Chazz had already found four or five weak points about the MP deployment, this was not an unreasonable ask. Especially if it got her out. The biggest problem was Angel. Chazz could handle herself, but handling Angel was a different matter. If she had to be gunner, Chazz needed someone else, someone who'd have her back. Basic field tactics. Someone who knew what they were doing. Three days. She could find someone in three days.

"OK," she said. "Deal."

Angel wrapped her in a hug, reawakening the aches, and danced her way back to the VIP tent. Chazz followed more cautiously, conserving her energy as her body healed. Hope, a small dose, the ultimate medicine.

* * *

Two days later, wilting under the scorching desert sun, Angel told Chazz she had business elsewhere and would meet her for lunch at the mess tent. Chazz translated Angel's "business" into her desperate search for a cigarette and a match.

The mess tent smelled more like dry sand than food. At dinner the first night of her captivity, she understood why. The food was limited and served in small portions. The meals so far had been light in calories and taste. They hadn't had time to organize enough food for the internees. She'd heard her tent mates complaining about the hunger. Of course, these VIPs had never missed a meal in their lives. Chazz added hunger to the tension already tightening her stomach, but she presented a stoic, military face to the world.

She trudged through the lunch line with her tray. As she scanned the tent for a seat, her eyes landed on a surprising yet reassuring sight—Technical Sergeant Oliver Jones. The tension in her stomach dissipated as she approached him. Noticing her gaze, Jones waved her over with a broad smile. Tray in hand, she sank into one of the three empty chairs.

"Good to see you, Sergeant."

"You too, ma'am," he replied.

"I should thank you for saving my ass back at Channel Islands."

This was all she could say. It seemed inadequate. He had risked and lost so much. And now, here he was, in Manzanar.

"My pleasure, ma'am. Glad you made it."

"How is your family?"

"Safe in Phoenix, ma'am."

Chazz's mouth dropped open. "Why the hell aren't you with them?" she demanded.

"Unfinished business. At home, then at Channel Islands. I was there when the Marines invaded."

That was new. Chazz blinked and blurted out, "Uh, what?"

Jones's mouth twisted at Chazz's surprise. "You been out of circulation for a while, ma'am?"

"Yes, Sergeant, I have." Since fleeing Channel Islands, she'd heard nothing about events in the state. She only knew about the coup through her jailers and the radio, which had no news anymore.

Jones leaned forward to look her in the eyes and spoke in a low, serious tone. "I watched a hundred Marines storm the base and take everyone prisoner. Except Colonel Ortiz."

Chazz nodded. "Yeah, she was on their side."

The twisted mouth reappeared. "No, they shot her. In the head. I left then. Nothing I could do."

Chazz stared at her friend. Her mouth was dry. Shot her in the head; U.S. Marines? Simmonds. Now we know where we are. The new reality. She'd wanted retribution for Ortiz, but she'd had in mind a court martial, not a summary execution. She drank water and said nothing.

Jones leaned back in his chair and resumed his story. "I made it a mile down the highway. Then a squad of Marines caught up with me. And here I am. Been here for a week. You?" His expression was that of a friend catching her up on the trivial drift of life, a normal lunch date. Chazz shook her head in wonder. Then she mirrored his ease with a succinct summary of her own story.

"The CHP stopped my car in Victorville on the way to Fort Irwin after I escaped from Pendleton's brig and killed two guys. I've been here three days."

Jones's eyes widened at this revelation, and he opened his mouth to reply. Then he stopped. His eyes grew even wider as he looked up over her head. A voice from behind her said, "Hi, Chazz. Who's your good-looking friend?"

Angel had arrived, her plate containing a pitiful piece of unidentifiable meat and a small portion of mashed potatoes. Chazz looked down at her own tray. The meat looked gray and smelled off, while the mashed potatoes had lumps. No greens made the plate even less appetizing.

Chazz introduced them. "Angel, this is Tech Sergeant Oliver Jones. Sergeant, this is my friend Angel Arguello, from LA. She's the ex-girlfriend of Governor Sanchez."

"El Presidente," Angel sniped. "Always a pleasure to meet a guy with a body like yours." She sat down next to Jones. "Sergeant is stupid. I'll call you Oli." She gave the nickname a Spanish twist.

Jones looked at Chazz and raised his eyebrows. "Is she always like this?"

"So far," Chazz smiled.

"Say, either of you got a smoke? I'm dying, here."

Jones and Chazz shook their heads, and Angel sighed with frustration. "Nobody in the damn camp has any. What the hell are we supposed to trade if we don't have smokes?"

"Sex?" suggested Chazz, only half joking. Jones, not finding this amusing, didn't laugh along with Angel.

Angel put her hand on Jones's knee. "We can find somewhere private, Oli, anytime you want," she said coyly.

Jones, his composure unchanged, demurred. "I'm married, Angel, and not looking."

"Worth a try. I wouldn't let most of the guys here into my apartment, let alone my pants." She grimaced. "Not that they ain't tried. A lot. Got to tell you, I'm done with politicians right now."

Chazz shook her head in dismay. "Guard regulations call for separate detention facilities for men and women. They haven't got it right yet. The food, too."

Jones pushed away his unfinished lunch and exhaled. "They don't care what happens to us, ma'am. No point in wasting energy or food on us. Just dump us in the desert and lose the keys."

Chazz chuckled at the mixed metaphor. But Jones's comment reminded her of the upcoming escape plans. She'd found the ideal person to have her back. He'd already saved her life once. She said, "Angel. Sergeant Jones would be a wonderful addition to our exercise."

"Exercise? Oh. Yeah. Sure—I can see it. I can. Oh boy, oh boy, now we got a real *pandilla*!" At Jones's raised eyebrows, she translated. "Badass crew, Oli. Real badass, by the looks of you two."

Keeping her voice low, Chazz filled Jones in on the escape plans. Ollie nodded. "It's doable, ma'am. Especially with three of us. A little wire fence and a bunch of no-account, part-time MPs? Tomorrow at two?"

Angel complained, "Can we stop with the sergeant bullshit? It makes me itch."

Chazz looked at Jones. "Good idea, under the circumstances. OK, no ranks, I'm Chazz, and you're Ollie. You good with that?"

Ollie grinned. "Understood, Colonel Silver."

"Oh, for God's sake." Angel shook her head. "Fucking Army." She ate her meat in two bites, made a face, then said, "All this camping and fucking open air makes me hungry. Shitty food and not enough of it. How do you put up with this?"

Ollie said, "Years of training. And the cooks have guns."

When they'd processed her into the camp, Chazz had noticed a towering pile of trash behind the visitor's center. The Guard had brought in materials on trucks, unloaded them with a forklift, and left the pallets and packaging waste here instead of removing it. As she pointed out the pile to Angel on the way back to their quarters, the pungent smell of the pallets' freshly cut pine planks filled her nostrils.

"So what?" asked Angel. "It's just garbage, not weapons or anything."

"They haven't had time or materials yet to build a proper fence. They haven't deployed any construction engineers, and the troops aren't even cleaning up their shipping garbage. The MP guard patrols aren't well trained or deployed. That creates our opportunity. The site managers rely on prisoners not knowing anything and on weak patrols. First, we distract the guards. We each take a pallet and stick it on top of the concertina wire. The wire pushes down under the wood. We climb over and move the pallets to the second fence, and we're out." As they walked, her mind raced with thoughts of the action ahead, visualizing each step in intricate detail. It helped that there was no moon.

"Oh, ah. Wow!" Angel stopped short and slapped her forehead. "You're a lifesaver, Chazz! Don't worry, my brother's crew will distract the hell out of those idiots tomorrow. And we'll be ready." She looked at the pallets. "How heavy are these things?"

"Thirty-five pounds. What, you don't work out?"

Angel punched her arm and said, "I got better things to do. Don't worry, Chazz, I'll carry my load. Or I'll get Oli to do it," she grinned. To Chazz, Angel looked plenty strong enough to handle either the pallet or Ollie.

Chazz's mind worked out the logistics of the plan. She knew that distraction would be crucial. The plan depended on a bunch of thugs she had no control over. But if they delivered, the guards wouldn't see three invisible escapees using pallets to scale the fences. The weight of responsibility settled on her shoulders, but she accepted it with gratitude as a great alternative to the burdens of her past.

CHAPTER THIRTY-THREE
A Dark Night

IT WAS 2:05 A.M., and Chazz cursed the silence that enveloped the camp. In the pitch black, Angel and Ollie crouched beside her by the concertina wire fence at the front of the camp. Angel had brushed against a razor edge and had to stifle her reaction. Each of the three had their pallet. The minutes dragged by with nothing happening.

Then it did.

With a deafening explosion that shattered the silence, the watchtower at the southeast corner of the camp collapsed, sending the lookout guards plummeting to the desert floor. Flashlights danced through the night as foot patrols converged on the shattered tower. A symphony of automatic rifle fire erupted, playing in violent harmony with the shouts of the guards. More guards boiled out of the MP quarters outside the camp. Prisoners ran in all directions. Chaos ensued as the MPs rushed to contain everything. Explosions to the west captured everyone's attention, shifting it from the east side of the camp.

"Go!" said Chazz. The familiar rush of adrenaline propelled her forward. This must be what soldiers in World War I felt when they went over the top. Her mind filled with memories of clearing the Iraqi insurgents and the adrenaline that had fueled her as she moved from trench to trench. Staying alive was a victory, a triumph over death. The escapees picked up the pallets and pressed them on the unforgiving concertina wire. They stepped up onto the pallets and over the wire. Chazz pulled her pallet loose, looked up, and there was a guard pointing a rifle.

The MP said, "Stop! Drop the pallets and raise your hands! Now!"

Chazz straightened up, as did Ollie and Angel. The MP was young, a teenager, and his grip on his rifle was shaky. The muzzle bobbed with his trembling. "Now!" he repeated loudly, though Chazz could barely hear him over the explosions, automatic rifle fire, and chaos at the other end of the camp. Cursing internally, she thought about rushing the guard, but he was on the opposite side of the fence. The MP advanced on them, covering them with the wavering rifle.

A gunshot from behind her startled Chazz, and the guard collapsed. The bullet hit precisely between his eyes. She turned to see a man dressed in black with a black balaclava lowering a Five-Seven pistol.

"¡Ay, vamanos!" the man said in a hoarse, whispered command, waving the gun in the highway's direction. The escapees grabbed their pallets and carried them to the outer fence. A skip and a hop had them out in the eastern desert, heading for the highway. They followed the man in black to three SUVs that blended seamlessly into the darkness. The middle doors of the front SUV were open, and the man waved them inside with the gun.

They piled into the SUV, and the door slammed shut behind them. Acceleration pressed them into their seats, the force matching the intensity of the adrenaline rush. The sudden silence in the EV SUV contrasted with the chaos left behind. Another SUV followed closely, filled with gunmen. After firing grenades or rockets to distract the guards, Angel's crew was withdrawing. Chazz looked back and saw watchtower searchlights sweeping the western desert. Fortunately, they were to the east. Unnoticed, they slipped away, cloaked by the night. The electric SUVs sped silently south, taking them to freedom.

They were out.

The man in black in the passenger seat of the SUV pulled off his balaclava, revealing a black beard and sharp features drawn into a deep frown. He barked, "Who the hell are these guys, Angélica?" His voice, sharp and loud, echoed through the closed, intense silence of the SUV.

"Friends, Paco. They helped me get out," Angel reassured the man.

"They're army," Paco said, his voice heavy with suspicion. He pulled out his Five-Seven pistol and brandished it.

"No, Paco! They're on our side. Against California. They're friends," Angel insisted. "Put that away."

"Angél, you know nothing!" Paco pointed the gun at Ollie and Chazz, who looked at it warily and didn't move. He stared back at them with unblinking eyes. Tension built up in Chazz's body, and she fought hard to stay in control. Ollie, sitting next to her, put a restraining hand on her arm.

Angel said in a firm voice, "I know Juan, Paco. That's enough. Do what I say." Angel patted Chazz's arm. "They helped me. They want to stop the coup."

"Fucking coup ain't nothing to do with us, Angél. We get you out, get you to Tijuana, that's all Juan wants. He don't want hangers-on. Why the fuck are we talking gringo?"

Paco and Angel argued in rapid-fire Spanish. Paco lost the argument. He put the gun away and stared out the front window, his jaw set, his face bitter. The threatening atmosphere in the SUV eased. The convoy of SUVs had turned on their headlights and were approaching 100 m.p.h. as they headed south.

"Does he have a phone?" asked Chazz. "I need to search for something."

Angel gave a command in Spanish, and without a word, Paco handed her his phone.

"Here you go, babe." Angel handed the phone to Chazz, who searched for a car rental agency. Bishop. That was…north. Damn. The nearest one to the south was 100 miles.

"Where are we going?" she asked.

At Angel's repeated prompting, Paco said, "Lone Pine. Chopper waiting for us there. Then Tijuana."

"I need to go to Bishop," Chazz said in a firm voice.

Paco turned to glare at her in frustration. "You got no need to go anywhere but six feet under, lady. Now shut up."

Chazz spent the next five miles telling Angel in a low voice what she needed and why Lone Pine or Tijuana wouldn't do. As the gateway to Mount Whitney, Lone Pine was stellar. As anything else, it was a bump in the road with nothing they needed. And Tijuana was out. Chazz had to stop Sanchez and Dupont. Staying safe in Tijuana wouldn't help with that. Ollie, eavesdropping, told Chazz he'd stick with her. She had her own ideas about that, but she put them aside for later.

Angel rolled her eyes, but she went after Paco. The atmosphere grew tense again. Another five miles and they saw the Lone Pine town sign, population 1,941. Which was about the year anything important happened there: Bogart made *High Sierra*. Time stood still in this town.

Paco got the worst of it again. "All right, all right. Fuck." The set of his shoulders emphatically declared his frustration.

The SUVs veered off the road and pulled up to a chopper, blades spinning lazily.

"Everybody out. Except you, girlie, and your boyfriend."

Angel kissed Chazz goodbye and gave her a big hug. She said, "I owe you one, Chazz. Come and collect sometime, OK? And Oli too." She hugged and kissed Ollie like she meant it. She and the driver got out. Paco came around to the driver's seat. He yelled out the window, "*¡Regreso en diez minutos! ¡Mantenlo calientito para mí!*" Chazz had enough Spanish to get the gist: Paco wanted the chopper to wait ten minutes while he got rid of Chazz and Ollie somewhere.

Paco floored the SUV and headed into Lone Pine. He pulled the SUV into a 24-hour gas station and parked off to the side. There was one pickup truck at the pumps, dark blue, empty, with a gas hose attached.

Paco reached into his jacket pocket and pulled out a wallet. He handed it to Chazz.

"What's this?" she asked, holding it up in one hand.

"Got it off a guard whose throat we cut right before we blew up the tower. Couple of credit cards and a nice little wad of cash." He looked at Chazz and Ollie with his trademark frown. "ID won't do you much good. The guy doesn't look like either of you enough to fool a Chippie." He shook his head. "Hate to give it up to you *pendejos,* but Angél insisted."

Chazz couldn't decide whether to pocket the wallet or throw it in Paco's face. The MPs in the camp were the enemy, but they were also soldiers under her command. Once upon a time. She kept the wallet and planned to return it to the MP's family after everything settled down.

Paco scowled as he pointed to the back of the SUV. "You *pendejos* stand over there. I'll be right back."

Chazz and Ollie stood next to the SUV, their eyes glued on Paco as he stomped over to the convenience store attached to the gas station. The pickup was the only car in sight. The highway was eerily quiet in the early morning.

"Is he gettin' us an early breakfast or what?" asked Ollie.

Paco pulled out his Five-Seven, gleaming in the bright lights of the station, and pushed his way into the store. Moments later, a young man with a blond crew cut emerged with his hands raised and shaking, holding a bag above his head. With his gun pressed against the man's back, Paco forced him to unhook the hose and to surrender the key fob and bag. Paco got into the pickup and drove over to where Chazz and Ollie waited. He got out, leaving the truck's door open. He tossed the key fob at Ollie, who grabbed it and stared at him.

Paco threw the bag to Chazz, who caught it reflexively. Then he pulled out his gun. Chazz instinctively took a step back, but Paco just handed her the gun and scowled. "Angél insisted," he repeated in a growl. "OK, *pendejos,* this is it. Your ride. Now get the hell out of here. If I ever see you again, I'll cut your gringo army heads off." Paco got back in the SUV and took off, tires screeching, as he turned north onto the highway, heading for his chopper ride. The SUV soon disappeared into the night.

Chazz looked at Ollie. The young man with the crew cut and now with a bright red face advanced toward them, shouting something unintelligibly angry.

"Come on, Bonnie," Ollie said, grinning as he climbed into the driver's seat.

Chazz realized that accepting the unacceptable was easy in a dire situation. "OK, Clyde," she replied. She tucked the gun into her belt behind her. With more adrenaline coursing through her veins, she ran around to the passenger's side and jumped in. She held the bag in her lap and put the gun in the glove compartment. "And breakfast, too."

Ollie stepped on the gas, and they headed north after the now vanished SUV. Next stop, Bishop.

CHAPTER THIRTY-FOUR
Bishop

CHAZZ AND OLLIE PASSED MANZANAR in their pickup with no headlights, blending into the darkness of the moonless night. The highway was empty at 3:30 in the morning. The Owens Valley was not a hotbed of nightlife.

Manzanar was. Illuminated by six large searchlights that played over the camp, it was like a late-night party in a trailer park. In their glare, Chazz watched several patrols come in from the desert. One patrol was herding several prisoners, internees who'd taken advantage of the chaos to escape into the desert. Without Angel's support team, they didn't get far.

But her earlier assessment that the MP leadership hadn't organized things still held true. Even with their escape, no one had set up a checkpoint on the highway. There were no signs of pursuit. No one was interested in their pickup, if anyone noticed it at all. A failure of imagination. She'd arrange some advanced training for the MPs once she was back in charge. After some housecleaning, of course.

Ollie was more pessimistic. "Ma'am, we got about a fifteen minute lead on these folks. Ain't gonna be easy to lose them, 'cause this highway is the only road goin' anywhere. And that dude has reported his pickup stolen by now."

Chazz considered the odds of survival if the Republican Guard caught up with them. Given the shoot-to-kill approach of the CHP, she imagined the Guard—her Guard—would show little restraint. Her experience with the beating at Manzanar told her they would not survive recapture by the Guard, and Simmonds and his Marines would kill them on sight. Dupont had little reason to want Chazz alive, and they'd kill Ollie just for being her ally. And if Sanchez had sent Brickhouse and Calvo for her, then he wanted her dead, too. There was no going back, no way to negotiate her way out. She could at least get Ollie to safety with his family in Arizona. But she had to finish what she'd started.

So, on to the practical details. She said, "We're going to switch vehicles, Ollie. Bishop has a car rental place in the middle of town. We have to hide until business hours, then switch cars."

"Ma'am, we got no money to pay for a car."

She brought out the wallet. Ollie looked, then looked again. "Where did that come from?"

"He...it's from a guard. Killed. Paco gave it to me."

"Shit." Ollie stared forward into the blackness before him. "Well, damn. Gotta do it."

"Should you or I rent the car?"

"Huh. Male license, right?"

"Right."

"White guy, too?"

"Right."

Ollie took off his OCP cap and handed it to Chazz, who had long since lost hers.

"You got a better chance, Chazz. Squeeze your bun into the cap and talk deep. Inyo County? They'd be calling 911 the minute I walked in the door."

A poor imitation of a male soldier would not cut it. At least she could do something instead of letting things happen to her. A one in five chance of success. But Ollie was right. His odds would be much worse.

"Let's stop outside of town and walk in at 10 a.m. You can wait someplace quiet, and I'll get the car and pick you up, all right?"

"I don't like sittin' there like a duck, Colonel. What if—"

"Chazz. Please. It's smarter than sitting in a stolen pickup truck in a county where there's nothing else to distract the CHP."

"OK. You're the boss, Chazz." She heard a distinct note of doubt in his agreement.

They left the pickup in a quiet cul-de-sac on the east side of Bishop. They walked a mile into Bishop's business district. The empty US-395 turned into Main Street there with little change in traffic, and the car rental agency was half a block away. As they prepared to cross the street, Chazz spotted a cell phone store half a block up Main.

"Serendipity," she said. "OK, Ollie. See that store? Get us a cheap prepaid phone. Here's $100." She handed him the money. This guy Lawrence had been pretty flush for a Guardsman. There was $360 in twenties in the wallet. She sighed at the dead man's money. "I'll rent the car, and we can meet up across the street, there." She pointed north up past the phone store. "Good luck."

"You too, Chazz."

Like most small California highway towns, the downtown comprised rows of one-story buildings advertising everything from tacos to knitting supplies to real estate. It was an unchanging landscape under stress. The strip mall that housed the rental car agency had a weathered for-sale sign and four other businesses. Chazz saw no customers. She took out the wallet and pulled out the driver's license and credit card and wrapped them in five $20 bills. U.S. money, but she was sure it was still legal tender. Tom couldn't have stopped all use of the old currency yet. She put the small package in a pocket and entered the car rental office.

The rental car agent behind the counter was a young man with a pencil mustache and a nametag that read Bill Whitman. His expectant smile faltered as he took in Chazz's OCPs and nose bandage. But she hadn't taken him completely aback.

"How can I help you, ma'am?" he asked, as Chazz stepped up to the counter.

"I'd like to rent a car and drop it off in Vegas, Bill," Chazz said. "Small, good gas mileage."

He smiled and asked, "EV OK?"

"Yeah, that's fine."

"Good, 'cause we only have one car right now. A BYD M10. The others are reserved."

She smiled back. "Well, then." The little Chinese import was a big step down from Tony's Mustang, but she'd make do.

"I'll need a driver's license and a credit card."

"Here you go." She handed him the $100 package with a smile. This was the first time she'd ever even dreamed of committing outright fraud. She relaxed her tensed shoulders.

The rental agent unwrapped the license, his eyebrows doing a little startled dance.

He looked from the license to Chazz and back. Chazz involuntarily held her breath.

"Ah. Oh." He was silent. He said quietly, "Manzanar?"

"Only if it gets me the car, Bill," she said. And if it didn't, she'd take it anyway. How much worse would she be today? She felt the renewed tension in her stomach and shoulders as her pulse quickened and she braced herself for action.

But Bill didn't seem too worried. He smiled, eyes crinkling.

"No problem. Sir." He read from the card. "Mr. Lawrence. Absolutely."

Bill typed into the computer, ran the card, printed out the agreement, and rustled in a drawer. She tensed again, expecting a gun, but he handed her a key fob along with the license and credit card.

"Here you go. Make sure you charge it before you return it." He grinned. "Or not. Space 5, around the corner. Don't forget to unplug it first."

He glanced at the five bills he held. He pocketed one and thrust the others back to her. "Take this, you'll need it."

"Always ready, always there," she replied, taking the bills. She signed the agreement with an illegible scrawl. Bill's support, minor though it was, liberated her from doubt. The California resistance was forming, and she was ready, and she was there. She hadn't appreciated the depth of meaning in the Guard's motto before.

Chazz drove the M10 across Main and stopped for Ollie.

He jumped into the car and said hastily, "Cop car spotted me hanging out. He'll be back, for sure."

"We won't be here." She drove a few blocks and parked. "Let's switch places. You drive. I told the rental agent we're heading for Vegas—north, away from Manzanar."

As they traded places outside the car, Ollie handed her a plastic bag and said, "Here's the phone, and the doughnuts are under the seat."

Ollie started the car and drove to Main Street. As he pulled up to a stop sign to turn north, five CHP cars screamed by, lights flashing and sirens blaring. They turned down the street that led to the abandoned pickup. Ollie pursed his lips and waited until the last one disappeared, then turned right and headed north.

Chazz rolled down her window, the cool breeze bathing her face. It was a hot day, and the M10's air conditioning wasn't up to it. Their sweating was as much from the heat as it was from the close call they'd narrowly avoided. Her common sense made her think about the other risks they'd taken. When would someone report the wallet and its contents stolen from the Guard soldier? That made her feel bad for Bill Whitman, who would surely have to answer some tough questions about renting a car to someone who presented a stolen credit card. It was crucial for them to get to where she wanted to go, and fast.

"Ollie," she advised him, "The speed limit doesn't matter anymore."

"Yeah," was his terse agreement.

Twenty miles north of Bishop, with no sign of CHP pursuit, Ollie advanced his pawn. "We really going to Vegas, Chazz? Givin' up?"

"You are. After you drop me off."

"And *why* would I do *that,* ma'am?"

"I want you back with Shirelle and the kids, Ollie. This isn't your fight." She put a colonel's tone of command into her voice. It didn't have the desired effect.

Ollie just shook his head as he drove. "Hell it's not, Chazz. I took an oath." His voice was intense.

"Me too. I have to do this myself, Ollie. It's my responsibility." It had all happened on her watch: the tanks and everything. She hadn't stopped the coup, and she had made mistakes. Tom. Simmonds. And she didn't want Ollie's death on her conscience. It wasn't much of a conscience anymore. Too much killing already. But she wanted to preserve some of her remaining conscience. And if anything happened to Ollie, Shirelle would find her and kill her, if nothing else. "I order you to stop. Pull over, and I'll drive from here." A direct order should do it. She looked over to gauge Ollie's reaction.

He smiled. "No way, lady. It's my responsibility too. Why I came back. Why I signed up with you and Angel to get outta the camp. I want this done, Chazz—finished. Shirelle knows that. If I got to die, so be it." He glanced at her. "And you ain't Captain Marvel, Chazz."

She picked out the important part of his criticism of her command style. "Nobody's going to die, Ollie."

"You say. Now, where we goin'?"

Chazz surrendered, accepting this minor mutiny as a done deal. At that moment, she reconsidered her chain of command. Ollie, a friend and ally, didn't need a soldier's discipline. Shocked, she realized she had let go of her own chain of command: she herself was no longer subordinate. To anyone.

Forty miles north of Bishop, Chazz asked, "Ever been to the Sonora Pass?"

Ollie's eyes questioned her. "Never," he said.

"Mountain Warfare Training Center?"

"Tell me more."

"U.S. Marines. Like Camp Roberts, only with skis and tents. In the winter." Winter seemed a long way off. Since the M10's air conditioning had proven worthless, they had the windows wide open. A cooling breeze came through as they drove.

"Where is this place?" asked Ollie, suspicion in his voice.

"Near a town called Bridgeport, about 50 miles north. After that, west up into the mountains. Toward the pass."

Ollie examined the Sierra massif to the west. "Huh. Considering my run-in with the Marines, why would I go there?"

"I have a friend who'll hide us. We can regroup and form a resistance. If the Marines there are loyal, they can help us."

"He's expecting us?" Ollie sounded skeptical.

"She. From Iraq. I haven't talked to Kat in years. Colonel Kat Taylor." She pictured Kat in her mind. Why had they lost touch? The years passing. Their jobs keeping them both busy. Kat was an active-duty Marine. Chazz's gut told her there was more to it, but Ollie interrupted her introspection.

"All due respect, you gotta make that phone call, Chazz. Now." He took his eyes off the road to stare her down. But she realized he was right.

She took the phone out of its bag and turned it on. She rolled up her window to reduce the road noise and dialed Kat's number from memory. Miraculously, her friend answered.

"Yes?"

"Kat, Chazz Silver."

"Fucking Chazz! All right!" There was a brief silence as the two women processed their feelings. In a more cautious tone, Kat said, "Unless you're calling from JFHQ in Sacramento."

Kat knew about the coup. "Nope. 395. Heading north. CHP and God knows who else is on our tail."

"Right. How long till you get here?"

"Is it safe? Simmonds—"

"I know all about fucking Simmonds. Just get here, Chazz. We'll take it from there." Kat sounded as positive and determined as ever.

"There's two of us. Me and a tech sergeant, Oliver Jones. We're heading north out of Bishop. CHP and the Republican Guard are looking for us."

"The more the merrier. Two hours if you don't stop to eat. Don't. And Chazz, don't drive onto the base. Things are…confused, here."

"All right, thanks. I'll call you when we get near the sentry gate, OK?"

"You do that." She disconnected.

"We're set," Chazz told Ollie.

"Yeah. Can we trust this Marine?"

Chazz heard generations of inter-service distrust in Ollie's voice. Not to mention his recent run-in with the Marines. She understood his reservations. What he didn't understand was the bond she shared with Kat. Time to fix that.

She said, "We were women pilots in Iraq. Kat flew fighter jets, I piloted choppers, both of us out of the Al-Asad Air Base. We spent most of our downtime together. And she.…" Chazz's voice trailed off as the memories flooded back. After the rape, Kat had gone out of her way to support her. Kat had seen she was in pain. Chazz didn't tell her about the attack, but she was there. Solid as a rock. The rape. Her throat tightened. That's why she hadn't reached out all these years. Embarrassed by her weakness and not yet ready to explain everything to Kat. The rape.

Ollie glanced sideways. "You got a pretty good stone face on, Chazz. You sure about this?"

Chazz pulled herself together. "Let's just say I know Kat, Ollie. She's a rock. You can trust her with your life."

"OK, I get it. But you'll forgive me if I trust and verify, right?"

"Of course. She'll do the same with you, I'm sure."

She looked into the bag of doughnuts. Chocolate icing with sprinkles. Not her favorite, but starving beggars can't be choosers.

"Gimme," Ollie said, holding out his hand. She gave him a doughnut and took one herself. Sprinkles escaped onto her lap as they sped north.

CHAPTER THIRTY-FIVE
Keeping the Lid On

Myron was up to his ass in alligators, with a few heavier predators thrown in for good measure. And they were snapping. Word came in that Simmonds had mobilized a task force to head south to San Diego to help secure the military installations there. In theory, Myron should welcome the help. He was absolutely certain that Simmonds, that treacherous bastard, was up to no good. And what about Admiral Collett? Those guys considered themselves the "real" military. They considered Myron's people to be amateurs, Sunday morning soldiers. All of which distracted him from his other duties administering martial law in the fledgling country. The weight of duty pressed down relentlessly.

Colonel Silver would have lifted some of that burden. Myron was a fine organizer, but Silver got things done, done right, and done fast. A great right hand. Putting together a division of 10,000 soldiers was a daunting task at the best of times. These times weren't the best. If he didn't have that division ready to go to contain the Marines, or at least slow them down, the government in Sacramento wouldn't last past next week.

"Sir, you'd better take a look at this," said a lieutenant from the floor of the command center. He was looking at his monitor. Myron walked over and read the screen.

What he saw made him shake his head in frustration and disbelief. "God damn it! What are we paying these people for?" he asked rhetorically. The lieutenant swallowed unhappily.

The screen told Myron that the Manzanar brigade commander had reported an early morning riot and escape from the camp. He'd waited to report it until the MPs investigated and figured out what had happened. And who was missing. Report received at 1400 hours. Thus delaying the search for ten hours, goddamn it!

Ten hours. Myron seethed as he read the report. An outside group blew up a guard tower as a diversion, allowing at least three internees to escape by car and fourteen others by running into the desert. Subject vehicles drove south to Lone Pine, where they transferred the escapees to a chopper that flew to Mexico. Tijuana, according to radar traces. No Air Guard interceptors were dispatched because none were operational yet. Myron gritted his teeth. Three escapees were still unaccounted for.

Missing: Colonel Chastity Silver, Technical Sergeant Oliver Jones, and a civilian named Angélica Arguello. He'd put Chazz there himself. Jones—from Channel Islands. Something to do with Del's execution. Silver's ally now? He read on. The MPs interned Arguello at the explicit request of the president. Background checks revealed that she was the sister of the head of a mid-level Tijuana cartel.

Well, wasn't that just fine? More alligators. Mexican ones with sharp teeth.

To chase down the gators, Myron picked up his phone to start the search. Chazz sure as hell hadn't gone to Tijuana. Fort Irwin? One of those federal bases near Vegas? That would be a royal pain.

Then there was the Mexican. What was Chip thinking, interning a cartel member? The stupid bastard was risking a war with the cartels. Myron was already swamped. He'd call Chip to find out who this Mexican woman was to him. As if he couldn't guess.

"President Sanchez's office. How may I help you?" asked Sally, touching the answer button on her headset.

"Sally, I need to speak to him," demanded the familiar voice of General Dupont.

"Oh, yes, General Dupont, of course. But he's not here right now."

"Not...where is he?" the general barked.

Sally winced at the volume in her headset but kept her composure and replied calmly, "Sir, he never tells me where he's going when he leaves."

"Well, he needs to do a hell of a lot better than that," the general snapped.

Sally sensed the general was having a bad day. "Yes, sir," she said, struggling to find words of reassurance.

Dupont softened his tone as he realized he was venting to the wrong person. "Give him a message, will you? Tell him that Colonel Silver has escaped, along with Arguello. They're fugitives."

Sally's eyes opened wide at this. Shocked, she asked a question before thinking. "Fugitives? Colonel...Is that Tom's girlfriend, sir?"

"Uh...ex-girlfriend, yes. Never mind. Just tell Chip as soon as you can. Have him call me."

Tom. Tom had to know about this. Oh, he'll be.... She asked, "Should I call Tom and—"

General Dupont cut her off with a military order. "No. Keep him out of the loop." Clearly a bad day for the general.

"Yes, sir. Who is Arguello, sir?" she ventured. That pushed some boundaries, but Chip would want more information.

"What I'd like to know. Just tell him, Sally. Thanks." And the general abruptly hung up.

Ex-girlfriend? Fugitive? Sally felt any trust she'd had in these people evaporate. What was happening?

Chip savored the taste of the chili cheeseburger he'd eaten for lunch as he slipped back into the Capitol through a side door. In the elevator, he removed the baseball cap and sunglasses he'd used to disguise himself at the fast-food joint. Getting out of the office had become more difficult as his responsibilities grew. He'd tipped the military guards well, but their sneering expressions rubbed him the wrong way. Chip knew what was behind their smiles; he'd dealt with it all his life.

Even Sally pushed him relentlessly. Calls, papers, appointments, Jesus Christ. Enough was enough. He needed a break, some junk food, and some personal time to recharge. He had three meetings and a bill signing ceremony this afternoon. A little downtime was all he needed. At least he could have a tequila in his office without anyone criticizing his leadership. Sometimes he felt like an actor playing a role, not the president of a fledgling nation. He rubbed his mouth in exasperation as he opened the outer office door and marched past Sally, but she stopped him in his tracks.

"Oh, sir, there's an urgent message from General Dupont." She gave him the news.

"Silver? And Angélica? Oh, shit." His worst nightmare had just come true.

Sally asked, biting her lip, "Sir, um, where was Colonel Silver when she, uh, escaped?"

"Manzanar." And how did she do that? Myron's people screwed up, that's how. Chip's jaw clenched.

"Where? And who's Angélica?" Sally's fingers rose to cover her mouth. The woman didn't have a clue.

Chip snarled, "Never mind, Sally! Get me Dupont. Put him through to the office. Now!"

"Yes, sir," Sally said, her face a little flushed as she reached for her phone. Chip sensed a hint of disapproval. Even Sally wasn't reliable these days. Well, screw her, screw Dupont, screw Colonel Silver, and especially screw that damned Angélica. Screw them all.

He stomped into his office, forcefully slammed the door behind him, and went to his desk. He poured himself a shot of tequila and picked up the ringing phone.

After putting General Dupont through to Chip, Sally searched the Web. Manzanar. Angélica Arguello.

Manzanar was a relocation center for Japanese-Americans during the last century, World War II. Now just a barren memorial in the desert. Or is it? Escaped?

Sally called a friend in the budget office. She asked about the status of the Manzanar camp budget. Her friend's off-the-cuff summary made her squeeze her eyes shut in shock. The Guard had not yet spent $54 million of the $94 million budget, but they would soon exceed it. The budget office had fifteen supplemental budget requests for projects requiring building materials, food supplies, and prison equipment for the camp.

Sally hung up in dismay. Prison camp? Colonel Silver? Tom said she was "traveling in the desert." Her stomach hurt. He'd put his girlfriend in that camp.

Her Internet search turned up nothing about Angélica Arguello. Sally dialed and got a friend in the DMV.

"The president needs a last known address for an Angélica Arguello. Can you get her information and email it to me? Thanks."

The picture was as bad as most driver's license pictures, but Angélica Arguello was a stunning woman. The address was in LA. Wait. She'd seen that address before. She scrolled back through her outgoing mail and found it: a check every month, signed by Chip. For consulting services. Addressed to Agnes Jones. Agnes Jones!

She looked up the CHP organizational chart and scanned the divisions. Yes, Special Services Southern Division, they could help. She jotted down the commander's name and phone number on her notepad. Sally looked at it for a full two minutes. She'd done nothing like this before, not even for that rotten, corrupt senator she'd worked for before Chip. Sally's mouth was dry as she dialed the commander's number.

"May I speak to Captain Kane, please? President Sanchez's office calling."

"Kane here."

Sally closed her eyes, then dove into the deep end. "Captain Kane, the president needs some information about a woman named Angélica Arguello."

"Who am I speaking to?"

"Sally Reed, special assistant to the president."

"I'll call you back." Sally guessed that he wanted to check that it was her by calling her published number.

She waited, her fingers tapping nervously on her desk. The phone buzzed, and she touched her headset. "President Sanchez's office. How may I help you?"

"Ms. Reed?"

"Yes, Captain."

"What else does the President need?"

"Excuse me?"

"After the dossier I sent, I mean."

"Is there any more information available about her background? The president asked."

"No, we have little information on her brother's cartel in Tijuana, except that he's very close to the Mexican president. Corrupt as hell down there. Please remind the president that an affair with a woman like that has terrible optics. Considering he interned her at Manzanar, she might even blackmail him."

Sally summoned all her resources to end the call without screaming. "All right, well, thank you, Captain, for all your help. And for your good advice."

Sally's mouth tightened as she pressed the line button to hang up. My God. Chip had thrown *his* girlfriend into the prison camp, too. Tom and Chip. Gangsters and prison camps and girlfriends and Marines and tanks and who knew what else. Her heart pounded as her face flushed with anger. What had she gotten herself into? What could she do about it? And who could help her?

CHAPTER THIRTY-SIX
The Resistance

Chazz saw bars on the phone. "Signal's back," she said. "We must be close. The MWTC has the only cell tower in this area. Pull in there so I can call Kat and tell her we're here." Ollie did as he was told, easing the car onto the gravel shoulder turnout, tires crunching.

Chazz made the call.

Kat's voice echoed from the phone's speaker. "Chazz. Where are you?"

"Nearby. Down the road. Three miles up from Sonora Junction on CA-108."

"OK. Here's the plan. Ditch the car and wait by the road. I'll be along in an official SUV. I'll have the emergency blinkers on so you know it's me, all right? Wave and I'll pick you up."

"So, I can't just drive onto the base?"

"Pbfft," Kat snorted to confirm her earlier advice.

"She's on her way," Chazz told Ollie. She put the phone in her pocket. "Ollie, this is your last chance. Drop me here and go to Vegas. To Shirelle and the kids in Arizona. You owe it to them to survive."

Ollie smiled and shook his head. He started the car and slowly made his way up the road until he spotted an opening in the valley's scrub.

"There's a clump of junipers up that slope," he said. "Rough going, but it oughta hide the car."

He powered up the slope through the rocks and scrub, jolting and bouncing, the scrubby bushes scraping loudly against the side of the car. Chazz grabbed the handhold above the door. Ollie rounded the juniper copse and stopped with the driver's side door against the trees. The car tilted upward at about fifteen degrees. He switched off the car.

"Get out, then I'll climb over," he said.

Chazz had trouble opening the door up the hill. She pulled herself out onto the hillside and held the door open for Ollie. The door slammed shut. They stood in the scorching sun without a breath of a breeze.

Chazz said, "OK, let's find a bush close to the road and wait for Kat." They climbed down the hill through the scrub, loose rocks sliding away from under their boots. They found a large bush near the road and sat down behind it, their green OCPs blending with the scrubby green of the plants. The silence was absolute. No bird calls or chipmunks rustling in the underbrush. She took in the vastness of the landscape, with the high, brown mountains surrounding them. They were in a river valley with sides that hid the snowy mountain peaks of the Sierra they'd driven past to get here. Chazz listened but heard no water running. The ten minutes they waited seemed like an hour.

The black SUV finally approached with its blinking emergency lights. Chazz scrambled onto the shoulder of the highway and waved as it went by. The SUV did an abrupt U-turn and pulled up beside her, tires screeching as the brakes took hold. Ollie emerged from behind the bush, sweeping dead leaves from his OCPs.

Chazz opened the passenger door. There was Kat in her Marine OCPs, grinning conspiratorially. She had the same wide face, same buzz cut, same open expression. She was the same ebullient Kat.

Kat bellowed in her deep voice, "Chazz! Christ, it's great to see you. It's been five or six years, right?"

"Yeah, that bar in San Diego at the inter-service contingency conference."

Kat shook her head, grinning wider. "I'm a little hazy on that evening. I remember you were in fine form." She looked her friend over and asked, "What's with the nose?"

"Long story. I've been better than now." She stepped aside so Kat could see Ollie.

Ollie saluted. "Colonel. Tech Sergeant Oliver Jones, California Air National Guard." He paused. "Re-tired."

"Nice to meet you, Sergeant."

The normalcy of the interaction hit Chazz like a hammer. Anxiety set in. What was she thinking, involving her friend in this madness? She said, "Kat, like I told you, we're fugitives from the new authorities in California, escapees from their prison camp. You're a working Marine officer. You should realize that helping us could bring you a world of hurt."

"Semper Fi, right? Marine loyal. My read is that you're the living embodiment of loyalty in this crazy-shit situation, Chazz. Whether my outfit is heading in the right direction is not clear to me. We can explore that mess later. We need to get you off the public highway. I'll take care of Semper Fi. You get yourselves in the back, under the tarp." She opened the rear hatch of the SUV and motioned for them to hurry.

Despite the order coming from a Marine, the soldier and airman promptly obeyed. The hatch closed over them.

The SUV stopped, and the sound of an automatic garage door closing reached Chazz's ears. Moments later, the hatch opened, and the tarp peeled away. Kat led them to a door in the wall. The house was small, with windows overlooking the sparsely vegetated hillside of the Mountain Warfare Training Center. The room was dark and uninviting.

"Not much, is it?" grinned Kat.

"Let me tell you, the colonels at Pendleton have it better," Chazz said.

Kat grinned even wider. "Tony. You were, ah, together with Tony again. How's he doing?"

Chazz's face fell and her back stiffened. "He's dead." She swallowed, then told Kat the basic story. Despite herself, tears streaked down her cheeks as she remembered Tony's lovemaking and his death.

"Oh my God, I'm so sorry, Chazz." Kat gave her friend a bear hug. "It must be terrible for you."

"I'll just go in the kitchen and check the fridge," said Ollie.

"No, wait," said Chazz, pulling away from her friend and wiping her cheeks. Her muscles tensed as grief gave way to anger. "We have to be a team. We have to trust each other implicitly. No ranks, no chain of command. One team. Otherwise, we're dead, and so is California. Kat, decide. Right now. Can we read you in?"

"No chain of command doesn't sound very Army to me." Kat ignored the tension in the air. "But OK."

Chazz shrugged to relieve her tight shoulders. Kat's humor and Ollie's stolidity cooled her anger into determination. She explained Ollie's background to Kat. "Ollie was a chopper mechanic at Channel Islands. The Marines took control of the base and fatally shot the commanding officer." Why complicate things?

"I heard about *that* one," Kat said, frowning.

"We both ended up in Manzanar." Chazz gave a condensed version of her ordeals in Sacramento, Channel Islands, Pendleton, and Victorville. She held back the tears as she related more details about the firefight that cost Tony his life.

Kat sighed. "I am sorry about Tony. He was a great guy, for a married man."

"They got divorced." The words slipped out of her mouth unconsciously. Oh, Tony.

"Better, but still a man. And you two, uh…"

Chazz closed her eyes. "Yeah. I slept with him. I shouldn't have…." Shouldn't have what? Let him think he had to rescue me? How deep was her responsibility for his death? And could she handle responsibility for more deaths? Ollie's? Kat's?

Kat threw a curveball, hearing only the passion, not the doubt. "Still not interested in women?" she asked with mischievous eyes.

"Sorry, Kat. Not built that way." She gave Kat a half smile and some relaxed body language. God knew where she got that from. She wasn't relaxed.

"I'll go check the fridge—" said Ollie, growing increasingly uncomfortable.

"Nope. Stay put, Ollie. Off limits to enlisted." Kat patted him on the shoulder and went to get three cans of beer. Chazz and Ollie sat on the couch, which sank alarmingly under their combined weight. The room had a coffee table and an armchair. Spartan. Kat took the chair.

"OK, I'm in," she said. "We're a team. Chazz, Ollie, and Kat. What's the situation here at the base? It's pretty confused right now because of Simmons and the Pendleton command. My boss, Colonel Bingham, doesn't yet feel the wind blowing on his puffy pink cheeks, so he's still on the fence. But I can tell you that he won't help you. If you waltz into his office, you'll wind up in the brig."

Chazz bit her lip. "There goes my plan. We'll need to figure something out. Can we stay and do that?"

"Damn right you can. But you'll need to keep a low profile." Kat shook her head. "I'm in, whatever we come up with. I've never liked that bastard Simmonds. He's a strong leader and a great Marine. But he's also a traitor and a murderer now. I want to do something about that."

"You got a deal, Kat," Ollie said. "Cheers."

Chazz slept on the sagging, worn-out couch with an old wool blanket. Ollie preferred the subordinate position on the carpet in an ancient and musty sleeping bag Kat had pulled out of her garage. Between the relative safety of Kat's house and the beer, Chazz fell asleep as soon as her head hit the beat-up cushion she used as a pillow.

She awoke at sunrise and lay on the couch staring up at the ceiling, barely visible in the dim morning light. Shadows played across the cracks and creases above her. The heat of the day had dissipated overnight, leaving the small house pleasantly cool. Her mind wandered over her immediate past and what the future might hold. The terrible traumas of the past few days tried their best to overwhelm her, but she needed to think about the future, not the past. To plan the future, she needed information.

She'd lost track of events since pushing Tom off the pier in Port Hueneme. Her priorities had been staying alive and escaping the myrmidons of the California Republic. Then dealing with her failure at the latter. But she was still alive.

Feeling eyes on her, she looked over at Ollie. His eyes were as bright as dimes in the dim light.

"Hey, Ollie. Where's the phone?" she whispered.

The sleeping bag rustled, and his hand appeared holding the burner they'd picked up in Bishop. Sitting up, she caught the tossed phone and dialed Captain Serrano's cell phone number. She trusted him. He would know what was going on.

"Yeah?" The man sounded disgruntled, and his voice was sleepy. It was early, 5:30 in the morning. Tough.

"Carlos, it's Colonel Silver."

"Um." Silence. "Yeah. OK. Sure. Sure it is," Serrano said, skepticism filling his awakening voice.

"It's me, Carlos. I'm on the run, and I need help. I need information."

"Who is this?" Skepticism turned to caution.

"Carlos, it's me." She took a moment to choose her words carefully. "Do you remember the conversation we had after the change of command ceremony? You gave me that paperweight. Do you remember what it said on the bottom? 'When in doubt, throw me.'"

Serrano laughed. "Yeah, I remember."

"So, Captain Serrano—"

"Not anymore, ma'am. Not a captain anymore. They kicked me out."

"From your job?"

"From the Guard. I'm sitting here at home doing nothing."

"It could be worse. You could be in Manzanar, like me. Either way, you're still a captain, and you still report to me. Never think otherwise. You're just unpaid right now. You want to do something about all this?"

Serrano's voice returned to caution. "What kind of something?"

Instead of jumping straight into plans or pleas, Chazz opted for a more roundabout approach. "You heard about Lieutenant Sellars?"

"Just that he's still missing. I figure—"

She interrupted with the brutal reality. "I found his body, Carlos. Brickhouse or Flattery killed him. They're both dead now." She hesitated, then chose trust. "They tried to kill me, Carlos. First Flattery at Camp Roberts, then Brickhouse at Camp Pendleton. I took care of them, Carlos. Self defense."

Alarmed at her confession and disturbed by the death of his friend, Serrano said in an unsteady voice, "Uh, ma'am—"

She interrupted again. Now that he's warmed up, shift his thoughts to the future. "Yeah. Tough stuff. It's a tough time, Captain. But those killings were just the beginning. Now we've got a civil war on our hands. I'll ask you again. Will you join us? Can I count on you?"

Serrano said unreservedly, "Yes, ma'am. You bet. These bastards, we have to stop them. What can I do?"

"First, intelligence. I'm holed up with a small group. We need to know what's happening in the state."

"You mean the country?" Serrano had never shown sarcasm before. But it was a difficult time. "Martial law, General Dupont's in charge. The new president dominates the news. There's a war in San Diego. Marines versus Guard. That's all over the news, too."

"Huh. Things have moved on. Carlos, these people are powerful and committed to their treasonous path. I need some names, people I can trust, to form a resistance. Can you help with that?"

"I can try, ma'am. I want to. Let me talk to some people. Carefully. Will that do?"

"That will do just fine, Carlos. I'll be in touch." She disconnected. Now things were moving.

Ollie said, "Was that wise, Chazz?" His eyes were still on her. "And who're Serrano and Sellars?"

"A long story. The short version is that Sellars told Serrano about tanks moving out of Roberts, and they killed him when they found out he'd leaked. Then they tried to kill me. Serrano and Sellars were friends, and Serrano told me about Sellars's information. And Serrano can help. We can't do this alone, Ollie. He's a good man. An honorable man."

"So are we all, Chazz. So are we all." Ollie tucked his head back into his sleeping bag and fell silent.

CHAPTER THIRTY-SEVEN
The Battle of San Diego

CHIP SANCHEZ PACED AROUND HIS office. Tom and Myron were there for a breakfast meeting, but Chip wasn't interested in listening to a bunch of talky-talk. That damn Marine was taking over his country.

He stopped and glared at Myron. "Damn it, Myron, you got to do something."

"We have the advantage, Chip," Myron said, tapping a pencil on the notepad in front of him. "The Marines don't have tanks. They ditched them around the time of the COVID pandemic."

Chip sat down in his chair. It creaked. Why couldn't he get a damn office chair that didn't creak? No tanks? "Well, hell, Myron. What were they thinking?"

"China, Chip. They wouldn't need tanks hopping from island to island in the South China Sea and storming the beaches of Guangdong. They need ships and planes for that. But until Simmonds fights his way to the beaches of Coronado, he won't have those ships and planes. He's vulnerable as he rolls down the freeway toward San Diego. We'll stop him there."

"How's your combined force coming, Myron?" asked Tom, leaning back in his chair and rubbing his chin. Chip could never remember all the ridiculous military jargon. That's what he paid Tom for. Strategy.

Myron smiled. "Mobilization is well underway, and six battalions are already on their way to reinforce the Guard forces mobilized in San

Diego. They're setting up defensive positions all around the city and the suburbs. All those winding canyons! We're already on the high ground with artillery and troops."

Myron walked over to the giant map of Southern California on the wall. Chip had helped Sally put it up before the meeting. Ever since Tom had told him of his concerns about Sally's dismay at events, Chip had fretted about her keeping quiet and staying loyal. He figured he'd just include her in the command meetings as secretary to take notes and to help with administrative tasks. That way, he'd keep her close and involved. Make her feel important. He had called her in and told her she was part of the team. She gave him a funny look, but Chip trusted Sally more than anyone, even Tom. She was solid, her husband was a major financial backer of the new government, and she could keep her mouth shut. Unlike Tom, who criticized at every opportunity. Or Myron, who made opportunities to criticize. Chip reached for the tequila and poured himself a shot. Myron was starting another lecture.

Myron pointed out the main defensive routes and fighting positions around San Diego, then ran them through some scenarios involving the Navy. After some tense negotiations, Admiral Collett had joined the Republican forces and pledged to patrol the coast. Myron had talked to the admiral through the new secure satellite setup the Navy had installed at the Guard command center at Mather. The admiral didn't like the idea of reporting to Simmonds. Not at all. He made no bones about it. And now he had concentrated his battle fleet right off Carlsbad. Now *that* would surprise Simmonds.

"When do we attack?" Chip asked. "I want to see everything. I want drones transmitting video. Do we have drones?"

"Six million Californians have drones, Chip," Tom said impatiently. "Along with all the streaming news sites. Just watch one of the damn news streams. You'll see everything."

"I thought we shut down the media," Chip said, frowning.

Tom replied in a calm tone, "No, Chip, we didn't. We got them on board, gave them access, and subtly threatened to shut down the Internet in California if there was too much disinformation."

Chip smiled. "Disinformation" was any statement that barely hinted at anything wrong in the new republic. So far, so good, anyway. The media loved interviews with the war heroes who supported the coup. Embedding them in the tank units deployed around the state sent them into a frenzy. Kept them out of trouble. Except for that one guy in Eureka. But there was nothing Chip could do about him except console his widow. Which he did with a phone call, expressing regret for the miscommunication that had led to such deplorable collateral damage. Tom's media people outdid themselves with collateral damage.

That son of a bitch Simmonds. He'd pay if he tried to take San Diego. Myron and Tom made things happen. They were slow, but they were sure. They'd win this battle. The California Republic was secure. Chip could get on with nation building. He leaned back in his chair. It creaked.

Captain Jonas T. Packer, skipper of the littoral combat ship CRS Lompoc, LCS-23, steadied his binoculars as he hove to off the coast near Carlsbad. A nice little town, nothing special except for the fabulous Legoland theme park. It brought back memories of the day he and two other officers painstakingly built a model of the ship out of little gray bricks and got roaring drunk in the Hilton bar. A great day. LCS, Little Crappy Ship my ass.

And here they came. The first of the line of transport vehicles coming down I-5. He'd take care of them before they got too far into town. It would be a shame if a mis-guided missile took out the Pirate Reef. His orders were to slow the column to give the defenders time to prepare for further action down the freeway. Killing Marines was secondary to the mission. But if they kept coming, he knew what he had to do.

Packer picked up the captain's command phone and gave the order to signal the LCS-15, the CRS Key West, to begin the coordinated attack. He then ordered general quarters and the coordinated missile barrage, followed by the attack chopper sortie.

"That'll slow 'em down," he muttered to no one in particular on the bridge, eagerly anticipating his first real battle in years. In the resulting silence, he saw the watch officers staring hard at the shore with grim expressions. But they were all doing their jobs. This Little Crappy Ship was about to prove its worth in a real war.

He stifled a shrug, squared his shoulders to show stoic calm, and raised his binoculars to observe the devastation he was about to unleash. Oh well, another wardroom disagreement tonight. After completing the mission. A pang of sympathy for the troops he was about to massacre threatened his stoic posture, but he easily stifled that, too.

The Marines had to learn their place. And Legoland wasn't it.

Specialist Stanley McTeague of the California Republican Guard placed the wireless detonator transmitter on the bulldozed berm that would shield him from the blast. Once in position, he radioed the lieutenant in charge of the mission that he was ready. The reply crackled with static and told him to stand by.

Waiting for a demolition was always a challenge. After all, the fun was in the fireworks.

Ten long minutes later, the order to go came over his radio. He carefully punched in the command code that activated the detonation switch, then pressed it.

The I-5 bridge over the canyon instantly crumbled to dust, great clouds of concrete powder rising into the La Jolla sky, the simultaneous booms punctuating the action. The other sappers had done their duty and done it well. A traditional Guard soldier who took part in monthly drills, Stan hadn't enjoyed his favorite pastime of blowing things up in a long time. Even during the annual exercise out in the desert. The Guard considered real explosives too expensive. Satisfaction washed over him as he watched the dust clouds billow and slowly dissipate in the mild breeze of the warm day. Beautiful.

Fighting positions and artillery would take care of any Marines that tried to cross the canyon. Stan stood up and gathered his equipment together for transport to his next defensive position.

Stan grinned. CalTrans would not be pleased. No, they would not. Your tax dollars at work.

Chip sat in his squeaky office chair absorbing the firehose of news and flipping quickly between streams with his remote on the smart TV Sally had arranged for him. The San Diego news crews were out in full force with their helicopters and drones. Videos of the Carlsbad shelling, the I-5 collapse, arroyo diversions, and the artillery salvos near La Jolla played on loops in the news feeds. The press emphasized the California Republic's commitment to protect its citizens from the chaos caused by the madmen of the United States. Only three news helicopters and twenty-seven drones had disappeared in balls of flame. So far. All by Marine rockets.

Because of this carnage, editorials and opinion shows heaped scorn on the Marine Corps attempts to "stifle freedom by killing clearly identified journalists." The news organizations bought a few hundred more drones and expanded aerial coverage over the various battlefields, just out of spite. Why did the media outshine the Army at procurement and field operations? He marveled at their efficiency. They could assemble a media special ops team faster than the fucking Seals. With better equipment, too. Myron and Tom needed to see this.

Tom stopped by the office around 2 p.m. with a stack of papers, just as Chip saw a flaming helicopter crash on the TV. Tom said, "Hey, Chip. Here are some EOs for you to sign." He placed the papers on Chip's desk in front of him.

Chip ignored the odious papers and gestured to the screen on the wall, a sight to behold. "Look at this one, Tom! K-Whatever in San Diego lost their best reporter, shot down over La Jolla. Another team captured the video from a drone. Now it's all over the feeds." A talking head pontificated as the crash played over and over in an inset video.

Tom smiled at the TV. "I'm going to put out another press release blaming the Marines. I've already put out three. They all say the Marines are attacking in the name of the United States. It's working, too. The latest poll shows that public support for us is now at 63%."

Chip's face lit up at the poll results. He slapped his desk, scattering the papers. "Atta boy!" he exclaimed. Tom bent down and picked up the papers from the floor and replaced them. He explained that the Marines had disappeared from the news because they either denied everything or just ignored the relentless press. The videos of civilian casualties in Vietnam, Iraq, Afghanistan, Ukraine, Gaza, and Iran had once been a twisted form of entertainment for the masses. But the Marines storming through La Jolla blasting everything in their path served as a wake-up call. Tom took a pen from its holder and handed it to Chip, who groaned but signed all the papers, shuffled them together, and handed them back to Tom.

Leaning back in his chair, Chip turned his attention back to the TV. He said, "We got ourselves a country here, Tom."

CHAPTER THIRTY-EIGHT
Ollie's Idea

Monday's lunch at Kat's had turned into a group therapy session as Chazz, fortified by two beers, tried to explain why she'd tossed and turned on the couch again Sunday night. The Dream and three days in the small house doing nothing.

"Come on, honey, tell Mama," urged Kat.

"You a shrink now, Kat? You used to be a friend." But Kat was a friend. Still, Chazz stuck with the denial treatment. She didn't want to rip the works off and bleed to death.

"I get it. You don't want to deal. Tough. What's going on, Chazz?"

Relentless. Fucking Marines. First Tony, then Simmonds, now Kat. Refusing to talk was not an option for her.

Chazz said impatiently, "PTSD, OK? PTSD. Too much killing, too much blood. So I dream."

Kat leaned toward Chazz and said, "You think I don't know? Tony knew, too, Chazz."

"What?"

"The rape."

"I...." Chazz's throat closed up on her. She shook her head. They knew? Tony? Now Ollie, too. Her gaze shifted to him, seeing his eyes dart between her and Kat. His lips were tight. His fingers wrapped around a can of beer as though it might bite him.

"You need to talk this out, Chazz. There's no time. If you want to lead the resistance, move on."

"It's too much, Kat." She ate some pizza, mostly as an excuse to say as little as possible. But excuses didn't work with Kat.

Kat replied forcefully. "The rape happened a long time ago. You need to let it go."

"How did you find out?"

"When I found you, you were drunk, but there was this look in your eye…I knew. Rumors around the base. Tony. He wanted to kill the guy. But you'd already shown Tony the door. He didn't think you'd appreciate it. He'd completed his tour and was en route back home to his wife. Before he flew out, he suggested I kill the guy, but I told him that wasn't the answer. So I did my best, but it looks like you didn't get over it. I don't know how much good I did. Then I redeployed to the carrier group in the Med. I hated having to leave you on your own, but you were a big girl. I figured you'd bounce back."

Chazz shook her head. "Why didn't you confront me at the time?"

"I thought that confronting you would make it worse. Heavy stuff, rape. There *was* no solution. I knew that. Tony did too, in his heart, but he didn't want to admit it. Semper Fi."

"The Army wouldn't have done anything," Chazz mumbled through a piece of pizza. "What you did, after—that's why I'm here, talking to you, Kat. You helped. But this doesn't go away."

"Of course not. I was a lot younger and imagined everyone was tough and would just fix it or move on. Even today, it would be hard to take it up the chain of command. And you Army folks don't do hard." She laughed again. "Unless it's with an M4. That works for insurgents, not for rapist colonels. Or their commanders."

Tears began to fall. Chazz let them drop. Why not? Friendly territory.

Kat insisted, "Go ahead, Chazz." She held out a hand, and Chazz took it. "Just feel the pain and let go."

"I hope…I won't embarrass you." Chazz swallowed. "I got broke, Kat. Like an egg. And when Calvo and Brickhouse were going to kill me, they…had other plans, too. I fought them off, then Tony showed up."

"Marines don't get embarrassed, they get even. And we have work to do. You are not Humpty Dumpty. You're a fucking war hero." Kat looked at Ollie. "Well, Ollie? Any thoughts?"

Ollie cleared his throat. "No." He raised the beer to his lips and drank.

Chazz said, "It's OK, Ollie. No secrets. All for one and one for all. Tell me." She valued Ollie's opinions, which so far had proven to be sound and effective. She could use insights from anywhere to help her deal with her inner terrors. But she was overly optimistic.

"Nope. Not going there, Chazz," Ollie said. "Unqualified and uncertified for this one. I fix choppers, not colonels."

Kat said, "Ollie, can you handle all of this emotional crap from our friend here? Do we need to work on you?" She leaned forward slightly, fixing Ollie with her direct gaze.

Ollie's eyes went to the ceiling as he took another swig of beer. He said, "I sure do wish Shirelle was here, 'cause she'd know what to tell you. But I seen Chazz in action, and I got no problem with that whatsoever."

"Who's Shirelle?" asked Kat.

Chazz said, "Ollie's wife. Lives in Phoenix now with their kids. Ollie should be with them, but he's thrown his lot in with us instead." Even though Ollie had refused to get involved in her darker psychological issues, he was a friend and a powerful ally. He and Kat were people she could count on.

The emotional pressure made Ollie shift in his chair. "You got something to share, Kat? Just to make my day even worse?" Ollie's normally bland expression had hardened into a frown as he processed all the emotional baggage in the room.

"Naw. Just outrage at the current shitshow in this country."

Ollie put his bottle on the coffee table and stood up, his patience clearly at an end. Chazz smiled. Three days holed up plus her issues? Ollie liked straightforward, bold progress, not deep emotional conflict. He confirmed that assessment by saying, "I need some air."

Chazz said, "Whoa there. It's not advisable to wander around the base annoying Marines. Why don't we go for a ride, Kat? You can show us around the base from inside your car. A change of scenery, new ideas? And get some air."

"Not under a tarp again," Ollie said. His lips twitched. "Tarps screw up my thinking."

Kat laughed out loud. "You can even sit in the front seat. Though if you see anybody with a fat face and a colonel's insignia, don't call attention to yourself."

The SUV roared up a sharp slope filled with scrub and not much else. Kat pointed out the mountains that the trainers used. "This road leads to a tangle of roads. It's clear in the summer and fall, but when the snows come, it's a challenge. We're heading up to that ridge. Back down on another road. Fabulous views."

Chazz looked out the sunroof at the blue sky. There was something fundamental about the Sierra Nevada sky. Once you got above the tree line, the blue became infinite. She'd like to fly into that blue. Instead, she had to stop a civil war by honoring her oath to the Constitution. Now she hid and admired the scenery. She realized she'd clenched both hands into fists and relaxed them.

The road gave them enough jolts and curves to satisfy any need for exercise. They descended through more scrub and worked their way back to the base.

"This is the airstrip. I do my training sessions in that building on the left. Air operations training," Kat said.

"Hey!" Ollie exclaimed. "That's an F-35B. One of the STOVLs, right?" The short takeoff and landing bird had settled in the middle of the runway, all alone. Chazz imagined lifting off, the lift fan and vertical engine shaking everything around it. Zooming into the blue sky, the only limit being the fuel in the stealth fighter.

"Right," Kat said. "F-35B Lightning, the Joint Strike Fighter. The base has several of them. This one is U/S, waiting for a mechanic to look at it."

Ollie enthused, "Can we check it out? I took a course in F-35 maintenance, I'd love to see a real bird. I can figure out what's wrong with it."

"Sure thing," Kat said. The SUV turned onto the road leading to the airstrip and parked.

While Ollie checked out the plane, Chazz and Kat stood near the front admiring the sleek lines of the stealth fighter.

"How many times have you flown this?" asked Chazz.

Kat grimaced. "Exactly once. I'm a trainer now because the chain of command disqualified me. Can't fly. Eye problems."

"I'm so sorry, Kat!" Chazz hugged her friend with one arm as she looked up at the cockpit above them.

"Can't be helped. I had fun while it lasted."

Ollie walked around the jet and grinned. "Got an idea," he said. "Don't know if it'll work."

"Let's hear your idea," Chazz said.

"Why not fly this bird to Sacramento and disrupt the coup?" Ollie asked. "Kat could do that in fifteen minutes. All we need is a target. Tanks? The Guard command center? Something central to the coup leadership. It would be a start. It would surely have an impact."

Kat's eyes narrowed. "I just told Chazz I can't fly anymore, eye problems."

"Well, that's too bad," Ollie said, shaking his head.

"I can do it," Chazz said. "With Kat showing me around. I've had jet training and flight time. I just loved flying choppers instead." The beast of a fighter filled her with warmth as she imagined flying it into action against the coup. Her mind sharpened as it filled with tactical ideas for confronting Myron Dupont with a situation he couldn't wiggle out of. She worked up a mental list of targets in the Sacramento area. Targets that would literally show up on Dupont's radar and make him think twice. Something that would break the momentum of the coup and give her resistance movement the spark it needed. "How much time will it take me to get up to speed?" she asked.

"Three days," Kat said. "My job is to train the pilots here on these things. The JSF flies itself, fly-by-wire. I'll teach you how to tell it what to do."

Chazz looked up at the fighter and imagined what those three days would be like. It certainly wouldn't be a leisurely flight school lesson, not with Kat training her. She shivered.

Kat continued enthusiastically, "We get this bird repaired and armed. We create a stealth strategy to get you close to the target, and boom!"

Ollie grinned. "Let's get the manuals and go."

"My God, Ollie," said Kat. "You are without a doubt the man of action among us. I'll make up a story so no one questions what we're doing until the deal is sealed, OK? The lieutenant colonel in charge of the air operations is a friend. He'll go along with it. I'll have to reserve the flight simulator for three days, a little unusual but I'll fake it. And I'll get access to a JSOW, the Joint Standoff Weapon. A smart missile. Program in the target's GPS coordinates, fire, and forget. But we have to keep it quiet. So, first thing tomorrow morning, I'll get you the tech manuals on a secure laptop and the report on what grounded the plane. You've got three days to fix the bird. Think you can do it?"

"If I can't, I've wasted the best years of my life," Ollie declared, grinning and patting the fuselage of the fighter. "And I haven't."

CHAPTER THIRTY-NINE
Sally's Resistance

SALLY REED DID NOT SEE herself as a resistance fighter.

Under normal circumstances, she saw herself as a professional executive assistant with a normal home life, a perfect marriage, and no particular interest in politics other than whether her current boss was likely to be reelected.

That had all changed. Circumstances were far from normal now.

Sally sat at her desk at 9 a.m. Monday morning seething as she dealt with the barrage of calls and administrative tasks in the president's office. Learning about Colonel Silver and Angélica Arguello had made her more and more angry about her own situation. Now Chip had drawn her into the conspiracy by pretending she was important. She'd lost her fantasies about Hollywood and Chip's future, and it had become obvious to her that he just wanted to make sure she didn't talk. Sally rarely drank coffee at the office, but today she was on her second cup. Last night's fight with Ted had upset her so much that she had trouble sleeping. And it hadn't even been a fight, just straight-up abuse from her so-called wonderful, supportive husband.

She'd gone home Friday night, cooked dinner in her well-equipped kitchen, carefully set the table, opened a bottle of Ted's favorite Zinfandel, and changed into sexy casual clothes. At dinner, she'd tried to talk to Ted about her concerns. He waved his hands dismissively.

"Everything's fine, Sally. Enemies of the state. Tools of the United States. Damn it, this is important! Why in the hell are you even thinking about this? You do your job. Help Chip do what he needs to do. Or quit and come home and clean this house. It's filthy."

It wasn't, but the remark reflected Ted's habit of distracting her from the real issue. Sally took this abuse in silence and had another glass of wine. She'd never disagreed with Ted before. Now that she had, she saw him for the bully he truly was. One who knew nothing about anything. For the first time, she admitted to herself that she even hated his cologne. And the Zinfandel sucked, too. And were Chip, Tom, and General Dupont any different from Ted? Or just more polite in their bullying.

Thank God we didn't have kids, she told herself. I'd be back in the stone age.

After an exhausting weekend, she closed the door to her suburban home behind her with heartfelt relief, eager to get back to work. But when she arrived, the lack of sleep, her fears over Ted's bullshit, and her anger at her predicament caught up with her.

Sally sipped some of the excellent coffee, rubbed her aching forehead, and seethed even more.

Ted's suggestion to quit took hold, as did the idea of calling a divorce lawyer, but she reconsidered. Or at least reconsidered Ted's suggestion to quit. She should stay in the job and find someone who could use her knowledge. Then she'd go to the feds.

Sally's five years working for the senator taught her the art of gathering clandestine information in pursuit of things no one wanted to talk about. The bills that lay hidden under a table in the Capitol until they emerged as done deals. The hushed conversations between senators that led to the passage of obscure, money-laden bills to benefit developers or business people or criminals. Late-night meetings that involved a lot of secret phone calls to very shady people. Assignations for the senator with a dozen different escort services. And the occasional dinner reservation for the senator and his wife.

They had stretched interminably, those five years. Too long. After the more than justified gubernatorial recall, she quit to work for Chip Sanchez. The previous governor was so obviously corrupt, he might as well have had $100 bills hanging out of his pockets.

Now, she used her skills to locate people who might oppose the current regime in Sacramento. The euphemisms, the subtly worded questions, the anonymous tips—she used all the old tools she'd become so good at. But this time, for a good cause.

When Chip sneaked out again for a fast-food lunch, she called a lawyer she knew to talk through the divorce. No kids, a good job, excellent career skills, and no punitive impulse—the lawyer called it a slam dunk, even if Ted went ballistic and contested spousal support. Irreconcilable differences would shut him up. After the lawyer explained the options, she mused a bit about "incurable insanity," but decided Ted wasn't insane, he was just an asshole. She'd go with irreconcilable differences. With that task done, she turned to her network. The phone traffic through her headset doubled to an insane workload, but she could finally do something.

After just two days of phone calls and meetings while juggling Chip's schedule, she found ten trustworthy people who were hiding in plain sight. Everyone warned her against going to the feds. Each had a different reason. Some thought the feds wouldn't help, that they'd be happy to see the backside of California. But the rest of the arguments boiled down to a reluctance to risk anything. They were worried about their jobs, for God's sake. "Let the situation play out," they said. "Wait for the opportunity," they urged.

While these people seemed reliable, they lacked her deep understanding of the situation. Opportunity would pass them by. Sally wanted *action*. Right now.

The feds were out. Sally now understood that they were the problem, not the solution. Action? Someone in the military? They were more action oriented. Too bad Colonel Silver was on the run. Sally had met her once, when Tom had brought her by to meet the governor. A straight arrow, sure of herself, and friendly in an undemonstrative way. But she was gone. What about someone who had worked for her?

Sally spent every free moment calling people who might know people who might know other people in the military. But she came up empty. General Dupont was more feared than Chip Sanchez. Twice she'd come close to touching a live wire when she realized the person she was talking to was on board with the coup. With each call, she became more cautious. She wasn't getting results this way.

A conversation she'd overheard in a meeting came back to her. General Dupont informed Tom that he had dismissed several members of the Guard who refused to accept the new regime. Cleaning house, he'd called it. The dismissed Guard members would surely want to help her in her quest to fight the coup. But how would she find them? Wouldn't there be records of dismissals? These people were in the state civil service, not the U.S. military. State bureaucracy never rests. All she needed was the right bureaucrat.

A rush of people wanting to talk to Chip kept her busy for an hour. Then she got someone at CalHR who had the answers. Sally explained that the president had some concerns about terminated Republican Guard members and their pensions. She said she needed a list of everyone the Guard had let go after the change in government, with contact information. Ten minutes later, she received an email with twenty-seven names, titles, and phone numbers. Only one was in the old Joint Forces Headquarters unit of the National Guard, a captain named Carlos Serrano.

So on Wednesday at 4 p.m., Sally called Serrano, but her heart sank when the phone kept ringing. She left a message, but her near-disasters with other military types had made her cautious. Still a risk, but a contained one.

"Captain Serrano, this is Sally Reed, special assistant to President Sanchez. Please call me back. I'd like to discuss some issues arising from your termination last week. We want to distribute your CalPERS pension, but there is an issue with your record that requires some information. President Sanchez wants to make sure the Guard is taking care of everyone, including terminated members." She left her cell phone number and hoped for the best.

Sally Reed did not see herself as a resistance fighter. But she was.

CHAPTER FORTY
The Recruit

CHAZZ, EXHAUSTED FROM HER INTENSE first day in the flight simulator, lay on the couch in Kat's house with her eyes closed. Kat had put her through hours of relentless scenarios, stopping only for a fifteen-minute lunch and a thirty-minute dinner, both of which she brought into the simulator. "No time for frills. Just don't touch anything I haven't shown you, and you'll be fine," Kat had advised after the second crash in the simulator had left Chazz cursing her own stupidity.

The phone in Chazz's pocket buzzed, jolting her back to reality. She sat up on the couch and dug it out. The caller ID showed Captain Serrano.

"Carlos! What's up?" she asked.

"I have a list for you, ma'am. Eight names."

"Carlos, that's fabulous. Wait, let me get something to write on," she exclaimed, motioning to Kat with an anxious wave. Kat hurried to the kitchen and returned with a crumpled paper bag and a pen.

"All I could find," Kat hissed.

Chazz grabbed the bag and pen, then ripped open the bag and smoothed it out on the coffee table.

"Carlos? Read them off."

Serrano recited the names and phone numbers one by one, commenting on each person's reliability and expertise. Chazz wrote furiously on the crumpled paper.

When Serrano read off the seventh name, Chazz gasped in disbelief.

"Sally Reed!" she exclaimed.

"Yes, Ms. Reed called me about my pension, and as we talked, she warmed up and dropped your name, ma'am. She seemed OK, sympathetic, so I gave her the pitch. She told me she could offer insights into the office of the president."

Chazz frowned as caution washed over her. She asked, "Could she be a plant? For the new government?" Was Tom lurking in the background, deceiving her again? How well did Sally know Tom? He was in her office every day. Chazz groaned in frustration.

Serrano said, "She didn't act like a plant, ma'am. She seemed very open, a little naïve. But I wouldn't tell her anything you didn't want Sanchez to hear. Sorry."

"That's OK, Carlos. She's a valuable addition to the team. Give me her number and get on with the list."

After Serrano hung up, Chazz sat, staring at the list. She'd been obsessing over the short-term actions she needed to take. Now she had the beginnings of a long-term resistance movement. Several Army Guard officers, two bureaucrats, a media person. And Sally Reed.

"Ms. Reed?" Chazz kept her voice calm and professional, a skill she'd had to learn when dealing with all the people a Chief of Staff had to appease. She sat on Kat's sagging couch and clutched the phone. She'd slept on the knowledge that Reed wanted to help and called her before resuming flight training in the morning.

"Yes. Who is this, please?"

"I'm calling on behalf of Carlos Serrano. Can you speak freely?"

"Oh. Um. Just a minute. Can you hold on?"

"Yes."

Chazz waited, hearing rustling and a door closing.

"All right," Reed said. "I can talk now. But I can't leave my husband alone for too long. He's…he'll be suspicious. And he's on their side." Sally did not have to say who "they" were.

"This shouldn't take long. This is Colonel Silver."

"Oh, my! You're...oh, I'm so sorry for everything that's happened to you!" Reed's voice broke.

"What do you know?"

"Manzanar. I can't even imagine what you went through. Was it, did they, were you...." The unspoken questions conveyed Reed's dismay at Chazz's plight.

"Tortured?" Chazz laughed, a little ruefully. She could understand why Carlos thought Reed was naïve. She needed Reed calm and receptive. Chazz explained, "I escaped before anyone could do much more than give me a beating. But some people want me dead, so...keep it quiet?"

"Oh, yes, of course."

"Thank you, Ms. Reed, and thank you for your help."

"Sally, please."

"We should talk about how you can help, Sally. I shouldn't keep you away from your breakfast."

"Oh, sorry, yeah, I wasn't thinking," Sally apologized. "I'm not usually this flustered, Colonel Silver. But this. This is too much. My...President Sanchez. And...Tom."

"Yeah, I get it. My boss, too."

"General Dupont. And I liked him." Sally's voice filled with a regret that quickly turned to determination. "What can I do to help?"

"Sally, we aren't terrorists. I'll tell you that up front. But sometimes military action is necessary. We're staging an operation that we hope will stop this thing in its tracks. We need your help to tell us when Sanchez and Dupont are meeting."

A gasp. "Not...terrorists? You're going to...oh. You want me to tell you where they are? At a certain time." Chazz heard the woman's breath quicken. Would she panic?

"Can you do that? Or is it too much, too hard?" asked Chazz, her voice steady.

A longer silence. Then Sally's voice firmed as she said, "Yes. I can do this. What they did—it's wrong. Wicked." She swallowed, then squeezed out the word. "Treason."

"I agree, Sally. I took an oath to protect the U.S. Constitution. I have to act."

"Yes. Yes."

"All right. Are Sanchez and Dupont meeting in the next few days?"

"Yes, they've scheduled a meeting tomorrow, Tuesday, at 2 p.m."

"At the National Guard Command Center at Mather?"

"Why, no. They always meet in the gov—the president's office, in the Capitol."

"And you're in the outer office, right? But you're at home right now?"

"Yes. I'll go to work soon. What do you want me to do?"

"Go to your Maps app and text me the GPS coordinates once you're in the office. How long are the meetings?"

"Oh, anywhere from a half hour to two hours."

"All right, Sally. You're going to get a call from an associate of mine tomorrow at 1405 hours—that's 2:05 p.m. She's going to use the code word 'Gold Rush' to identify herself. I won't be there, but my associate will relay the information to me. Tell her if the meeting is on. All right?"

"Yes. All right."

"Then leave, fast. Away from the Capitol building. Can you do that?"

Sally replied in a shaky voice, "Uh, yes. But—"

Chazz kept her voice firm and calm. "No buts, Sally. This is the real thing. You're in, or you're out. And I want you safe."

"Ohhhh," Sally groaned. "Yes, all right. I'm in."

An hour later, Sally sent the coordinates, and Chazz verified them. The Capitol. The president's office. An excellent target.

CHAPTER FORTY-ONE
The Capitol

CHAZZ AND OLLIE MADE THE final checks on the fighter's readiness as Kat supervised. Chazz walked around the fighter and joined Kat. Ollie climbed down from the fuselage with a big smile on his face.

He said, "Good to go, Colonel. Everything checks out. Fuel's topped off. Flight data programmed into the avionics. GPS coordinates programmed into the JSOW."

Chazz held Kat's flight helmet by her side. Kat had devoted three training hours to that helmet, which was a technological marvel that gave the pilot everything from a 360-degree heads-up display to night vision. Kat said, "I've taught you everything you need to know, girl."

She embraced Chazz, who hugged her tightly. She released her friend and turned to Ollie. He held out a hand.

"The hell with that," Chazz said and hugged him, too.

Kat said, "OK, we got all the touchy-feely stuff out of the way. Let's see if you're ready. What's your flight plan, Colonel?"

Chazz grinned and said, "Just turn the thing on and let it do everything. Just like you taught me, Kat."

"Nice try, Colonel. Nice, but cocky. Let's see what you got before your feet leave the ground. Seriously, now. What's your flight plan?"

Chazz came down from her preflight high. "Lift fan on, nozzles down, lift off, and transition to horizontal flight. Cruise at low altitude over the

Sonora Pass, increasing speed to 1,300 kph. Increase to 1,600 once I'm over the foothills and maintain low altitude all the way to Sacramento, about five minutes. Arm the JSOW C-1 missile at 2 km from the target. Then let the avionics do the work."

"Right. What do you do if someone's stupid enough to intercept you?"

"Arm the Sidewinders and direct the helmet's targeting system to eliminate the attacker."

"What do you do if you're compromised and in an emergency?"

"Activate the ejection handle." And hope to hell the built-in parachute worked. Ollie had assured her it was in perfect condition, only used by a little old lady on Sundays.

The final exam took some time. Kat pounced on every little wrong thing that leaked from Chazz's overstuffed brain. It was merciless. It was necessary. She glanced at Ollie, who was out of the line of fire. She returned his grin with one of her own. With each question and answer, she gained confidence and fanned her inner fire for the mission. When they'd gone through the return-to-base plan, Kat slapped her on the back. "You're good, Colonel. Make it count."

Chazz climbed into the cockpit and activated the canopy lock. She heard the latches click into place and began the preflight checks.

Every time her phone rang on Friday morning, Sally jumped. She had skipped lunch. She knew she wouldn't be able to keep it down. Chip had said nothing about her jitters when he and the general went into their meeting. Both men seemed preoccupied and ignored her.

The time on her phone, 2:04, ticked over to 2:05.

The phone rang. She tore off her office phone headset and grabbed her cell phone from the desk, nearly dropping it.

"Hello?" she said.

"Gold rush," a voice said. "Go?"

"Yes, the meeting is on. They're both there, the gov—president, and the general. An hour," said Sally, stumbling over the words. "It's going to be an hour."

"OK, now leave the Capitol. Fast. We'll be in touch." The call ended.

Sally picked up the box she'd filled with her belongings and stashed behind her desk. She tossed her phone into the box, then quickly left the office, but without running. It wouldn't be appropriate to run. Not in the Capitol.

The F-35B Lightning JSF was all green at 1,600 kph. Chazz flew at a higher altitude than she usually flew in a chopper, but not nearly as high as usual for a fighter. She imagined the scene below her. Stealth was relative. At this altitude, the people below must be wondering what the hell was going on. Or running for cover. This beast would only fool the radar. No sign of interceptors or incoming SAMs. Approaching the 2-click distance, she prepared to arm the JSOW.

"Goldrush, this is Silverlode, over."

"Silverlode, this is Goldrush, over."

"Goldrush, this is Silverlode. Ready to arm. Query go? Over."

"Silverlode, this is Goldrush, good to go, over."

"Goldrush, this is Silverlode. WILCO. Out."

Chazz armed the JSOW and watched the ground pass beneath her as she approached Sacramento at 1,600 kph.

Sally shifted from foot to foot, waiting for the damn elevator. She'd just decided to run for the stairwell door when the elevator opened. Tom stepped out.

"Hi, Sally. Hey, I need to talk to Chip. They're in the meeting?"

"Yes, but—"

"OK, I'll stop by and tell them the good news. San Diego is ours!"

"But, Tom—" She stopped, unable to think of a way to warn him without betraying herself. Her treachery.

Tom held the elevator door for her. "Heading out? Delivering something?" He tapped the box.

Sally gave up and entered the elevator. "Yeah, delivering," she muttered with a defeated sigh.

"See you later!" He stepped back and the elevator doors began to close. He extended his hand to hold the door and asked, "Do you remember Colonel Silver, Chazz? I'm going out later to bring her back here. I'll bring her by to see you when we get back to town!"

His hand retreated as the elevator doors shut, leaving Sally speechless. The elevator dropped like a stone, and Sally's stomach went with it.

Kat sat in the chair in the comms room, waiting for Chazz's final go signal. Her cell phone rang. She answered and lifted the phone to her ear.

"Gold rush?" Sally Reed's voice, shaky.

"Yes."

"Uh, there's, uh, it's, a problem."

"Tell me."

"Tom Peña just went into the meeting."

"Are you outside?"

"Yes, walking away from the building. Oh, please, let her know that—"

Kat tossed the phone down and turned to the comm panel. She hesitated for only a second. There was no time. It had to be Chazz's decision.

"Silverlode, this is Goldrush, over."

"Goldrush, this is Silverlode, over." Something was wrong. Chazz was too close to the target for Kat to call with anything but disaster.

"Silverlode, this is Goldrush. Advise Tom Peña is in the room. Over."

Chazz's mind locked.

"Silverlode, this is Goldrush. Please acknowledge. Over."

"Goldrush, this is Silverlode. Acknowledged. Over."

"Silverlode, this is Goldrush. Query abort mission? Over."

She had somewhere between twenty and twenty-five seconds to decide.

But there was nothing to decide. Was there?

"Goldrush, this is Silverlode. Negative. Out."

Sacramento passed beneath her, but Chazz couldn't see it anymore. She'd closed her eyes and let the fighter take control.

* * *

Sally ran awkwardly along the path through the trees behind the Capitol. She wished she'd worn sneakers or something. Her stomach was in knots. Tears had wet her cheeks after leaving the elevator.

The explosion behind her threw her forward onto her face, and she covered her head with her hands. Chunks of concrete fell all around her. Staggering to her feet, all she saw was dust settling over the remains of the Capitol building. The orange of the flames glowed faintly through the cloud. The dome remained intact. As the dust clouds rose, Sally surveyed the veiled, jagged remains of the rear of the building. The president's office. Her own office. Now fire and dust.

She heard sirens starting up and a bell ringing somewhere, and car alarms screaming from every direction.

Time to go home. Ted would be worried.

CHAPTER FORTY-TWO
The Aftermath

CHAZZ RODE SHOTGUN IN THE Army JLTV while Ollie drove. They'd outfitted themselves in new combat uniforms at Fort Irwin before the task force headed up CA-395 to do something about Manzanar. It had been a while since Chazz had suited up with all the tactical bells and whistles, but she decided it would give her more credibility. Some of the Army officers on the task force had expressed strong opinions about a lady colonel going rogue with a Marine aircraft. She reminded them that according to the Army brass, nothing of the sort had happened, and if they didn't like it, they knew where they could put it. Ollie's glare over her shoulder helped. But full combat gear was even better.

The Republican Guard had upgraded the concertina-wire fence around the camp since she'd last been a guest. Now there were three rows of the stuff, interspersed with concertina-wrapped dragon's teeth. That would stop escapees, but also a frontal assault, even with tanks.

She saw that Colonel Healy had already deployed his forces around the entire perimeter of the camp. The flat desert offered no cover. Healy had deployed the assault force in Bradleys stationed around the perimeter. All was quiet, even though the scene bristled with military tension.

Chazz saw Healy and his XO over behind a Bradley parked on the highway. "Pull up next to that Bradley, Sergeant. I want to talk to Healy."

"Yes, ma'am." They'd reverted to rank-appropriate behavior once they'd rejoined the U.S. military, but Chazz smiled at her friend, acknowledging the genuine relationship. She'd borrowed him from the Air Force for this operation, and he was going to retire and move to Phoenix after it. Shirelle had issued a standing invitation to visit anytime. She might consider going in January, when it wasn't 120 degrees in the shade.

She stepped out of the Jolt and approached Healy. His face was pugnacious.

Chazz said, "What can I do for you, Colonel?"

The man's face said, "Go away." But his training kicked in before the words were out of his mouth.

"How familiar are you with the layout and deployment inside the camp, Colonel Silver?"

"Too familiar. Standard Guard setup, light weapons only, and from what I observed while I was in the camp, weak leadership."

"Bunch of sorry assholes," commented the XO, a weary Lieutenant Colonel. Healy gave him a withering stare.

"The Guard makes do with what they have, Colonel," said Chazz.

"So if we just roll in there, we'll wipe them out," Healy said.

No more killing. Chazz was tired of death. She stayed calm. "Yeah, and kill the prisoners, too. They're politicians and bureaucrats, so no loss. You sure you want that, though?"

The colonel grunted. "What would you suggest?"

"A couple of forays against the fence to show we mean business, then negotiate a surrender."

"I don't want to risk my men for no good reason."

Chazz smiled. "Commendable, Colonel, but I'm sure you have your mission orders in mind."

"That will be all, Colonel," Healy said. He raised his binoculars in a sign of dismissal.

Chazz rejoined Ollie in the Jolt.

"What's the situation, ma'am?"

"Normal, Sergeant. Situation normal. With any luck, no one will die, and they'll free the prisoners without firing a shot." But Healy did not look like a lucky Army officer to her.

From their front-row view of the operation, Chazz and Ollie watched as the brigade made several probing attacks on the fence. The Republican Guard fired a few rounds, the Army returned fire. No casualties. The Bradleys provided cover as the Army retreated, and silence fell. The scene stood still for fifteen minutes.

Chazz got out of the Jolt again and approached Colonel Healy. He continued to examine the situation through his binoculars. Nothing moved.

Chazz said, "I'd be happy to visit the camp to discover what's what, Colonel."

Healy lowered his binocs and stared at her, lips tight.

"Can't hurt, might help," she said. "I know most of these guys."

Healy grunted, then said, "OK, Colonel Silver. Get a flag of truce from the command vehicle and go ahead." He smiled. "We'll back you up in case they start shooting. And we'll go in if you fail." He left unsaid what that failure might look like.

"Great. Glad to hear it," she replied with a smile.

Six hours later, twelve Army-requisitioned school buses loaded most of the freed prisoners for the long journey home. The Republican Guard soldiers had already left for various destinations and their courts martial. The Army separated out a few prisoners and led them to the headquarters building. Chazz stood next to Healy as he gave a little speech to the separated group. He might be an idiot, but he could organize his thoughts and say what he meant.

"Listen up, folks. The front line of the war runs from San Simeon through Fresno and down through Barstow and Baker. The Army controls everything north of that except for a few pockets of resistance in urban areas like San Francisco. You are all from the rebel area, so we can't bus you home. You have a choice of camps in Redding or Lake Tahoe until we end the rebellion."

Shouting broke out. "I've got family in San Diego, damn it! Get me down there. I'm the mayor, for chrissakes!"

"Yeah, I hear you, man. Can't do it. It's a war zone, and San Diego is all shot up. And the Republican Guard is strong there, a whole division."

"But—"

Healy spoke over the objections. "There's four buses, signs in the windows. Redding or Tahoe, take your choice. First come, first served."

A few people in the back rushed out of the room, eager to get to their preferred bus. This became a general stampede. By popular demand, and after a near riot, all four buses went to Tahoe. Go figure.

The last stand of the Republican Guard in Northern California was at the San Francisco Presidio. Local partisans had taken a heavy toll, pushing the remnants of the Guard all the way into a corner of the City. With their leadership gone, the Guard officers were rudderless. Technically, the USNORTHCOM command fully supported the efforts of the loyal Americans of the resistance to take back California from the coup plotters and their Republican Guard. In reality, not so much, Chazz found.

"Yeah, yeah," grumbled the major general, who was also the commander of NORAD. "I got my ass in a sling over the Russians and Chinese waving nukes at us, Silver. They're taking undue advantage of the chaos, the bastards. I really didn't need this California headache. And the last thing we need is a bunch of gun-toting citizens running wild through the streets of San Francisco. Why I want you there. You take charge. I'm giving you a brigade from Fort, what's-it, Fort Liberty." The general shook his head, disconsolate over the renaming of the old Fort Bragg, his earlier command. "I'm promoting you to brevet brigadier general. Don't screw up."

Chazz checked into the Beacon Grand, the renamed Union Square hotel that had been named after Sir Francis Drake, a famous privateer and slaver. She'd held a quick change of command ceremony in the ballroom, then invited the partisan leadership group to the restaurant for a thank-you lunch. Instead of confronting them, she was going to stand them down diplomatically. No point in causing more trouble.

A vain hope. The trouble came from the doorman and the hotel staff. Major Serrano, her XO, got the high sign from the restaurant manager and went to check out the problem. He came back grinning, leading five apparently homeless people. Carrying assault rifles.

Chazz, in fresh OCPs, rose to her feet at the large, round table she'd reserved.

Serrano, still grinning, introduced the partisan leader. "Ma'am, this is Sergeant Roy Pearce, ex-U.S. Army. Served in Iraq, at Mosul."

Pearce held up a filthy hand. "Sorry about our appearance, ma'am. No time for shaving, let alone rehab. It'll be good to give it another chance," he apologized, then yawned uncontrollably. Chazz noticed a few missing teeth as he yawned. A walking case of PTSD, and a hero. It made her troubles seem insignificant. She scanned the disheveled guerrillas accompanying Sergeant Pearce. None of them looked any better than he did. They were all heroes. She would pay much more attention to homeless vets in the future. As the world burned, these partisans stoked the fire within her.

Chazz noticed the restaurant host and a couple of servers looking anxious. It wasn't hard to diagnose their problem. The solution was against their rules, but it was an emergency.

"Carlos, please escort our guests to the restrooms. They can wash up before joining us for lunch."

Pearce grinned broadly and looked around the restaurant at the other diners. "Wouldn't miss it, ma'am. Thank you. And I apologize again for our appearance."

As she considered her future in this new world, Chazz had a sudden idea. "No apologies necessary, sergeant. Well done, you and your team." She searched her pockets, then scribbled her personal phone number on a page torn from her small copy of the Constitution and handed it to him. "Call me when you're clean. I might have a job for you. After this is over."

"Yes, ma'am, thank you!" Roy ambled off to the restrooms with his team of homeless heroes. Chazz watched them go, true patriots. The host grimly returned to his station.

At lunch, Roy and his men proved more than happy to stand down. Roy explained that he'd started by blowing up a tank with an IED. The United States had ignored their ask for weapons, so they improvised. The merchant community helped with supplies, and the gangs helped with the assault rifles and explosives. Now the remnants of the Republican Guard occupied only part of the Presidio, the closed Army base in the northern corner of the City. Roy described a few of the partisan actions they'd undertaken, and the others chimed in with their parts as they consumed the best of the hotel chef's cuisine.

Chazz put Major Serrano in charge of coordinating with the City's government to get the partisans permanent housing, medical treatment, and jobs.

"And, Carlos. Make sure the mayor understands that this is not optional. It gets immediate action or else." She pursed her lips. "Might as well extend it to the entire homeless population while you're at it. Tell the City they've got plenty of room at City Hall if nowhere else. Right?"

"Yes, ma'am," Major Serrano said.

After seeing off the partisans, Chazz stood at the sidewalk on Powell Street as a cable car rattled by carrying a crowd of her off-duty troops. It was time for the City and state to return to normal. Long past time.

Brevet Brigadier General Silver moved out of the fancy Union Square hotel to create a command center closer to the action. The old Travelodge motel, near the Presidio at Lombard and I-101, had no cable cars, but you could walk down the block and see the Golden Gate Bridge. She commandeered the beat-up couch in the old office, but sleep eluded her. So she sat at her desk, going over the negotiation report and planning her attack at 0400 on a fog-damp October Tuesday.

The remnants of the Republican Guard had taken control of the Presidio Main Post down the street. According to intel, 746 soldiers of various ranks were enjoying the Disney Museum and the other delights of the old Army base. Closed by the U.S. Army, the Presidio had long since become a national park. The Republican Guard had taken three hostages, the park rangers, and held them incommunicado in the Officer's Club.

Chazz commanded a full brigade of 3,500 men and women, U.S. Army soldiers ready and willing to take back the federal lands occupied by the rebels. She'd deployed squads and fireteams around the perimeter of the Main Post to keep things contained. The hostages complicated matters. Word filtered down the chain of command for her to take her time. "Keep the casualties as low as possible. On both sides. There's no point in massacring Americans."

Unless she had to, of course. The commanding general giving her the orders said that twice. She guessed he wanted to make sure she knew he wasn't tying her hands. But he'd also said there was no air support or artillery available. And the Army had committed all its tanks to the Bakersfield campaign, because Southern California was taking longer to subdue than the north. The situation had evolved as the Marines, Navy, and Republican Guard carved up the area with enough arms and armor to make it stick. USNORTHCOM dithered over which bunch of renegades to attack first. So would she, pretty please, keep the casualties down? She said, "Yes, sir," as the Army had trained her to do.

After the Capitol, Chazz was eager to avoid more bloodshed. She still considered the Presidio renegades as *her* soldiers, even now. So they'd invited a negotiating team from the Presidio under a flag of truce. They'd arrived in a weathered, rusty old Humvee left over from the Gulf War. They'd also arrived with chips on their shoulders. Negotiations were "continuing," but the rebels insisted they'd hold out until the feds recognized the San Francisco Autonomous Region as a formal enclave. They'd negotiated a treaty with the Chinese consulate that gave the entity formal recognition by the PRC. They claimed Chinese protectorate status.

A shrewd captain orchestrated a visit to the men's room with his counterpart. He suggested it might be possible to negotiate a solution if they changed the protectorate to the United States instead of China. He'd reported the positive response to Chazz. The City's sizable Asian population might or might not support the PRC, but the bulk of the Republican Guard was Latino or White, not Asian. The U.S. would naturally reclaim everything after establishing the "protectorate." Treaty or no treaty. Chazz could live with this deception. It might not be necessary if the Army Rangers lived up to their reputation.

In the deserted San Francisco Presidio Main Base, the silence of the early morning hours was absolute. Only one picket stood watch. Sloppy. The U.S. Army Rangers split into three squads, one for each tank. Intel claimed the tank crews slept in tents next to their tanks, leaving a picket to sound the alarm if the shooting started. The Republican Guard remnants in San Francisco were not the highest quality troops.

Blue squad dealt with the picket first, taking him down silently and leaving him trussed like a turkey with a guard to keep him company. The commander shook her head. Easier to just cut the guy's throat. But the general insisted on minimal killing, which only made her job harder. They'd get the job done anyway.

The squads surrounded the tents and waited. The commander signaled "go" to their wireless earbuds, and the squads simultaneously silenced the sleeping tank crews. She stayed on edge, waiting for an alarm, but nothing happened. The guys must have been exhausted to sleep so soundly. Poor babies.

The commander detailed one squad to transfer the prisoners to the transport vehicle hidden behind the old bowling alley, while the other squads disabled the tanks. Then she turned her attention to the Officer's Club. The Republican Guard had locked the prisoners in a pantry off the main lounge. One sentry—no, two—silenced, and they were inside.

The three park rangers were still in uniform, though they'd lost their Smokey Bear hats. The commander ordered their ties cut and got them off to the transports.

Mission accomplished, no casualties. The general would be pleased.

The Travelodge command center light flickered with fluorescent inadequacy as Chazz wrestled with the complexities of her mission. US-NORTHCOM command had given her until today to retake the Presidio. But after a heated argument with her team, the rebel negotiators had walked out.

The Army would rescind her brevet-general status. That would doom the Guard soldiers in the Presidio. If she couldn't end this today, the Army would replace her and show no mercy. That sword over her head and the lingering pain of Tom's death kept her awake at 0430. Her missile attack had exhausted her willingness to kill to save California.

Flicker. Flicker. The damned light marked the seconds of her procrastination on the decision to attack. She climbed onto the desk and pushed at the fluorescent bulb to settle it, but the thing kept flickering. But no flicker of hope remained. The cost of war was high, and this one would be extremely expensive. In lives.

Major Serrano walked into Chazz's Travelodge office, just like old times—two months ago. It was still dark out, though, and his entrance startled Chazz at this early hour. Something must be wrong.

"I saw your light on, ma'am. The Rangers—"

Chazz shut her eyes and voiced her worst fear. "The hostages are dead."

Serrano grinned. "Nope. Alive, well, and drinking coffee. Rangers got 'em out without a shot fired and no one else killed." He looked up at her. "Um. Ma'am. Why are you standing on your desk?"

Chazz's heart stopped beating wildly as relief flooded through her. She climbed down and slapped her XO on the back. "Don't worry about it. Let's go check them out. What about the tanks?"

Serrano cheerfully said, "All disabled, ma'am. Crews are prisoners over in the garage."

"Let's see them first, Carlos." She followed Serrano into the motel garage. The Rangers had corralled twelve hangdog soldiers in tattered combat uniforms against a wall. They sat with their hands cuffed behind them, their legs stretched out, all in a row. What a beautiful tableau! Chazz stood and admired it for a few seconds before turning to the Ranger commander and asking for details.

The commander, a tall Black woman, grinned at Chazz as she reported the capture of the crews, the spiking of the tank cannons, and the confiscation of the 50-caliber ammunition.

"Very well done, Captain," Chazz said. The Rangers had made her job much easier. Without armored cavalry, the Presidio renegades would be meat. She turned to the prisoners. "Which one of you sorry tankers is in charge?"

The soldiers looked at one another. One spoke up. "That would be me, ma'am."

"Name and rank?"

"Staff Sergeant Leroy Briscoe, ma'am, California Republican Guard. That's B-R-I—"

Asshole. Chazz interrupted in a harsh voice. "I'll get those details later, Sergeant. What the hell were you thinking?"

Despite having his arms cuffed behind him and looking up at a tall, angry general, Briscoe was truculent. He struggled to his feet to look Chazz in the eye. "All due respect, ma'am, I was thinking what every other real Californian is thinking, that the U.S. has abandoned us and is doing everything it can to fuck us over. And, again with all due respect, ma'am, that's all the hell I'm gonna say to you. You're a traitor to the Republic. Soldiers are aware, ma'am. In the Army, not just the Guard. They're all around you. Just you wait. OK, that's it. I'm zipped." He turned his head away and stared off into space, defiant.

A Ranger slammed Briscoe against the garage wall with a thud. "This asshole was bragging about being responsible for the carnage in Sacramento, ma'am." He prodded Briscoe's chest with the tip of his rifle.

Chazz inspected Briscoe and recognized him as the soldier she'd confronted in the tank in Sacramento. Full circle. Could she learn things from the rebels? Things that would keep her soldiers safe? Briscoe's belligerent face refused without words. She smiled contemptuously and gave orders to the Ranger commander. "Captain, form up this flock of turkeys and take them over to the County Jail Intake Center on 7th Street for a nice, long rest."

"Yes, ma'am. Gladly." The Ranger saluted. The Rangers pushed and prodded the tankers to their feet into a ragged line, then marched them out of the garage.

Chazz stepped out into the dimly lit parking lot and looked up at the dank marine layer hanging overhead. The sun rises in two hours. Plenty of time to end this travesty. She turned to her XO and gave the order to take the Presidio.

"Carlos, execute the plan we discussed yesterday, which was contingent on the tanks being inoperable. I want prisoners, not corpses. Shock and awe, Carlos, but no killing. Hurry, before they discover the tanks are kaput."

"Yes, ma'am." Serrano saluted and hurried off to get the Battle of San Francisco underway.

In the dead of night, two pilots traded their familiar cockpits for the alien shadows behind enemy lines in San Diego. Unusual mission, extraordinary soldiers; but pilots rarely infiltrate, especially at night. Unless they must.

Chazz had consulted with her Ranger commander on tactics a week after the fall of the San Francisco Presidio. The commander gave them black combat hoodies and balaclavas and a few special-purpose items. After going over the basics, she wished them luck.

"Do you have the intel?" whispered Chazz, taking a quick look at her watch. 0300 hours, right on time.

Kat held up the phone so that Chazz could see the report. "COL-2 ROW D 435-A. Should be easy to find."

The plan: arrive at 0300, leave by 0330, then back to San Francisco for lunch.

Chazz adjusted her AI VR night vision goggles while Kat grabbed the tool kit from the back seat of their black civilian sedan. They found COL-2 without encountering another soul. Chazz located Row D and scanned the plaques.

"There it is, up at the top. Can you reach it?"

"We should have brought the ladder, damn it," Kat replied.

Chazz scanned the area through her VR goggles. "Over there, a large shrub pot," she said. The two tried to lift the pot and failed.

"Dump it," Kat hissed.

The two women stood behind the pot and leaned into it, toppling the shrub. Chazz pulled on the trunk, and the shrub and soil came free. They picked up the pot between them, carried it back to the wall, and placed it upside down under plaque 435-A.

Kat opened the tool kit and took out the drill. She fitted it with a screwdriver bit and climbed up onto the pot. Chazz heard the low whir of the drill, and a minute later, Kat jumped down.

"It's all yours," Kat said, running her hand over the engraved plaque she'd unscrewed.

Chazz climbed onto the pot and peered into the niche at the sealed box destined for eternity, or at least until Miramar National Cemetery vanished into the mists of time. She brought her hand to her lips, kissed it, and touched the box. She reached into her pocket and pulled out two coins: Tony's Iraq challenge coin and her own. Chazz lined up the coins in the niche. She said a silent prayer for the man she'd loved, whose ashes rested in peace.

"Hurry up, we're late," Kat hissed.

Chazz whispered, "Safe journey, Tony," and jumped off the pot. "Seal him up," she ordered.

Kat obeyed and screwed the plaque back over the niche. Chazz could just barely make out the engraved name through the VR goggles: LT COL Anthony R. Ridger, United States Marine Corps. She couldn't read the dates, but that was OK: she knew them by heart. She saw the faint letters of the end line: "No greater love than for country." Have to think that one over when she had time.

Kat helped her roll the pot back to the dumped shrub, where they left it for the groundskeeper to find. Another death on her conscience, but the shrub died for a good cause: mourning Tony. He was gone, but in that moment of grief, Chazz found a new strength. Who knew what lay ahead for her? Tony's sacrifice had given her a future. She wasn't going to waste it. Kat's hand on her shoulder silently reminded her of the risks they had taken and the lines they had crossed.

"Let's go home," she whispered. They had come to grieve, but they were leaving with a mighty weapon: the enduring power of honor and the will to fight for it. No matter the cost.

CHAPTER FORTY-THREE
Baja California

Until the day of Tom's wake, Chazz had not decided whether to attend. That morning, she sat on her couch and stared at the invitation. "We cordially invite you to celebrate the life of our son, Tomás Peña." Did they understand who she was? Did she understand her overwhelming desire to be there? Tom was a traitor, she was a general in charge of rooting out people like him, and the big one: firing the missile that killed him. They surely didn't know that. No one knew except a few top Army and Marine brass, who wanted the fact buried deep.

And yet. Tom had been her lover. She'd told him she loved him, and she'd meant it. Time and events had worsened their relationship, but there was still love there. She had to grieve for him. She had to embrace guilt and release it. That's what a wake was for. Why not?

Chazz walked into her walk-in closet. She found the crossroads of her past and present: her soldier's dress uniform and the black silk dress that whispered the grief of her father's funeral. She pulled out the plastic bag and let the silk run over her hand. Soft, conservative, and respectful. Wearing an Army general's dress uniform with all the fruit salad to a wake for a leader of an anti-government coup was not respectful. Nor would it help her grieve for her ex-lover. She laid the silk on her bed and dug out the necessary underwear.

Two hours later, she entered the grand foyer of the Sacramento mansion, its opulence a stark contrast to the somber occasion. The curving wooden staircase with its ornate balustrades rose and disappeared into the upstairs realm. A large dining table through an archway held an intricate array of food and wine. The guests stood around in small, whispering groups to bid Tom farewell.

Tom's parents had flown in from LA on a special dispensation from the military government in Monterey. Chazz would pay her respects and leave as soon as possible. She moved through the small crowd of mourners, not recognizing anyone. Was she really a part of Tom's life or just a well-kept secret? Chazz took a glass of Paso Robles Cabernet from a server at the table to serve as camouflage while she waited for her opportunity. She looked out a large window onto the patio and garden of the mansion. She came for herself and Tom, not his friends and relatives. What they didn't know wouldn't hurt them, but it wouldn't do her any good either. Except for his parents.

After the crowd had thinned, she walked over to Tom's mother and silently handed her the glass of wine as a bridge across the abyss of loss. She'd never get another chance to make things right.

"Thank you, I was dying for a drink," the grieving parent said. "I'm Noelia Peña."

"Chastity Silver. Nice to meet you, Noelia. I'm so sorry for your loss."

"Oh," said Noelia. "You're that Army general. We found your name in our son's address book. Even though, well, you were against, uh, we thought…an invitation." Noelia's embarrassment made it difficult for her to express herself.

"Did Tom ever mention me?" Chazz asked.

A worried look crossed Mrs. Peña's face. "Why, no, I don't think so." A hint of Spanish accent colored her voice. Chazz had looked her up—third generation Californian from a Mexican family.

"Tom and I—" Her throat closed down. She hadn't lost the pain of Tom's death, especially since it was at her hands. But his mother didn't need to know. No one needed to know. But she had to tell his parents something to ease her own pain. At that moment, looking into his mother's sad eyes, she couldn't confess that she had killed him. Too many questions about state secrets, too much pain for his mother, and too much guilt. Instead, she said, "Yes, we were on different sides, but…Tom proposed to me before he died."

"Oh!" Mrs. Peña's eyebrows rose. "No, he didn't mention anything. That boy. Always the secrets." His mother shook her head. "But oh, I should be sorry for your loss, too." She held out a hand, and Chazz took it in hers. Enough. It hurt too much. Let the healing begin. Time to go. She'd paid her respects. She turned to the door only to find Tom's father holding a Modelo Especial. Noelia introduced Chazz to him and told him about the proposal. Then she said, "I should make the rounds, talk to other people. Rafael, why don't you think of something we can do for Chastity to help her grieve?" She left them. No chance for the door now.

Rafael Peña raised his eyebrows and smiled. "Just tell me, Chastity. What can I do for you?"

"Oh, no, Mr. Peña, no, I couldn't accept—"

"Rafael, please. And what Noelia says, goes. Wait, I have just the thing!"

He switched the beer bottle to his left hand and reached into his suit pocket. He pulled out a key on a small tagged ring.

"Here you go," he said, handing her the key.

"What is this?" Chazz looked at the tag. "Tam? What's that?"

"It's our cabaña in Tamarindo, near the ecological reserve down in the Costalegre."

Chazz's hand involuntarily closed over the key. Guilt and grief washed over her, leaving her speechless. The Costalegre. Tom's beach. Images from what seemed like a very long time ago filled her mind. Fantasies she'd had while considering Tom's offer. She struggled to find a semblance of her normal voice. "Um. Tom mentioned.…"

"He loved the place. I can't think of a better way to help you grieve. Take all the time you want there. Send the key back, or give it to our family down there. Here's my card with the address." Peña handed her a business card for his construction company and wrote a Mexican name, address, and phone number on the back. "With our best wishes, Chastity. I know Tom would have wanted this."

Chazz knew no such thing. But getting out of the United States for a few weeks seemed like a good idea. The brass hinted that her presence in the Army was no longer needed. And it would help her grieve. To work through what might have been. And what would be. On the beach Tom had loved.

Chazz called Kat Taylor the day after Tom's wake. The strength she'd found in Miramar returned in full force, enhanced by the easing of her sense of loss over Tom's death. The key to the cabaña lay on her kitchen counter, a symbol of transitioning from a fraught past to an ambiguous future. At the very least, a new beginning. Time, sun, and sand might clarify things. And people. The right people.

Would Kat like to spend a few weeks on a secluded Mexican beach? Kat accepted the invitation without hesitation. She'd resigned from the Marines as an alternative to facing a court martial. The Marines' problem with it all was the cost of the JSOW missile, Kat half-jokingly told her. They let Kat keep her government pension on the condition that she never say a word about what happened at the Mountain Warfare Training Center. She took the pension and moved to Oakland, the city where she'd grown up. Their brief mission to Miramar had only brought the two women closer together.

Chazz and Kat flew directly from the Oakland airport to Tijuana. AeroMéxico had rerouted flights that used to stop in LA to go direct because Mexico had not recognized the provisional republican government in Southern California that now controlled LAX. An SUV waited for them outside the Tijuana airport with a visibly angry Paco at the wheel and Angélica Arguello riding shotgun, vaping a smoke.

"I hope—" Chazz said, but Paco cut her off.

"Shut up. If Angél weren't here, I would not be so nice to you." Paco glared over his shoulder at them.

"But I *am* here, you fool," Angélica said, blowing a cloud of smoke at Paco.

Kat looked at Chazz with a raised eyebrow. "Should we do something about him?"

Chazz grinned. "No, Paco's fine. He's just upset because he had to give me some of his hard-earned money and his gun." Chazz took out her wallet. "Here, Paco. This is what's left." She handed him some twenties. Then she pulled out a Five-Seven pistol and handed it to Paco, handle first. "And here's your gun. Unused." She'd brought the thing, unloaded, in her checked luggage, just for this opportunity.

He wadded the money into a ball and flipped it back in her face. He smiled a lupine smile at the two women and waved the gun at them. "I so wish I could make use of this present to fix past mistakes." He slipped the gun into a pocket and turned back to his driving. The SUV roared out of the airport and headed south for the Costalegre through the busy streets of Tijuana, tires screeching, engine roaring, Angélica laughing raucously and Kat and Chazz joining in.

The *tres amigas* returned to the cabaña after watching the sun set over the Pacific. Glorious oranges, reds, and purples had dissipated with the sun's disappearance. The early evening sounds of the jungle provided a musical backdrop as they sat on the couch and chairs in the large living room. The "cabin" turned out to be a four-bedroom beach villa with a private beach next to one of the big resorts. But the tourist noise never bothered them, as it was far away.

Kat shared glasses of tequila and said, "Are you ready, Chazz? For my idea?"

Chazz sipped the tequila and checked her internal grief meter, which resided somewhere behind her aorta. Days at the beach relieved much of the pain of the past few months. And the missile shock therapy had helped while simultaneously traumatizing her even more.

Missile shock therapy. She still dreamed from time to time. That pain would never leave her. She'd mourned Tony with the coins at Miramar.

The pain of Tom was persistent but manageable. Kat told her she was healing, so it must be true. Angélica, when Chazz brought her up to speed on all her traumas, just laughed. She suggested Chazz try being *mexicana* for a while. Then she swore on her mother's grave to help Chazz in any way she could.

Angélica also helped with her stories about Chip Sanchez, which put Tom in perspective. Tom had been a traitor, but Sanchez had been a complete asshole. As for General Myron Dupont, Chazz harbored about as much sympathy and sorrow for him as she did for John Wilkes Booth. His death freed her from the complexities of dealing with a chain of command.

There was only one way to deal with her trauma. She'd do it the same way she always had. Keep busy. Was she ready for Kat's proposal? Her Army career was nearing its final chapter after the final dissolution of the Northern California rebellion. The Army and the National Guard no longer needed her services. Despite her success, her methods did not enthrall the brass. The future was wide open. "Yeah, I'm ready," she said.

"We should set up as military consultants, Chazz," Kat said. "Charge big bucks to help countries prevent coups. Or maybe help them happen, when circumstances suggest it's a good thing. Which is almost never the case."

"I don't know, Kat. I was looking forward to a nice retirement and reading a lot of romance novels," Chazz joked. But she liked the idea of working for herself instead of for the chain of command. And romance novels—no. She preferred reality to fantasy. So, her reality was pretty dark so far. Maybe she could improve that.

"Fuck romance," Angélica said firmly. "I've had enough of that. You need capital? 'Cause I got plenty of it."

"We could afford our own tanks," Kat said. "Or some choppers. And we should get new passports. Somewhere that doesn't care about what advisors like us do. No more oaths. All for one and one for all, right?"

"Oh, yeah. What about Ollie? Let's bring him down here with Shirelle and the kids. They'll love the beach and the ocean, and we can coax Ollie out of retirement. We need someone who can fix things. Shirelle, too. She's even more useful than Ollie." Chazz grinned at her two partners. "I also have someone in mind from San Francisco, too, a homeless vet up there named Roy. A change of scenery will do him good."

"I know some people in Ciudad de México who need advice," Angélica said. "About taking back some land in Alta California. They'd pay. *Mucho dinero.*"

Chazz looked at her friend the Latina dynamo and thought about the woman's connections. She had capital, but the strings stretched out of sight into very dark places. Places where honor was thin on the ground. Men, and no doubt women, with motives she could only guess at. Chazz smiled slowly. This new world would challenge her and help her overcome her naïve and simple perspective. The image of Sally Reed formed in her mind. And Kat and Ollie would have her back.

Kat raised her glass. Chazz and Angélica clinked theirs with it.

"Always ready, always there," Chazz said, and emptied her glass with the others, the warmth of the strong liquor and the stronger friends spreading through her.

Acknowledgements

Death of a Golden State is fiction unadulterated by any known fact. In particular, I wanted to show how a real coup might happen in the United States of America in the 21st century. That requires great stretches of imagination. The Army and Air National Guards in California comprise some of the best and most professional men and women soldiers in the country. We are fortunate to have them. No way anything in this novel would happen on their watch.

I had to decide, early in plot development, whether to make the villains extremists from the left or right. I punted and made the villains apolitical in that sense, just out for power. Though it is a bright blue state, there are as many extremists in California on both sides as anywhere else. But it would be a stretch for the right to take over in a coup at the governor's level in California. The State of Jefferson may someday come to reality, but it would remain an isolated state from the rest of California. That said, for Latino extremists to take over would be as difficult, though not as unimaginable. So I punted.

I'd like to acknowledge taking much of Chazz's silver star story from the 2005 real-life example of Sergeant Leigh Ann Hester of the 617th Military Police Company, Army National Guard out of Richmond, Kentucky. No chopper involved, but that just makes Sergeant Hester's valor more remarkable. Thank you for your service.

I'd like to thank my writing group at the Mechanics' Institute of San Francisco for their invaluable and unflagging critiques; it's a much better book for their hard work. I also would like to thank Lila C for her insightful beta read.

I want to thank my sister, Colonel Grace Edinboro (California Army National Guard retired) for her support and advice on military and administrative details. I could not have written the novel without that advice. I remain responsible for any errors or exaggerations.

Thank You

Thanks for reading *Death of a Golden State*. If you liked the book, please leave a review on the web site through which you bought it.
Sign up to our mailing list for notifications and get a free ebook!

https://www.poesys.com

Milton Keynes UK
Ingram Content Group UK Ltd.
UKHW042103241124
3056UKWH00001B/51